"Situated at the intersection of film studies and settler colonial studies, Cinematic Settlers is an extremely valuable volume that reflects on settler colonialism as a multifaceted process that is, in fundamental ways, still ongoing and in which cinema has been, since its invention, centrally involved. With sixteen carefully considered and clearly written essays, the collection produces an understanding of settler colonialism, and the film cultures it has produced, that is grounded in historical and textual specificity on the one hand and expansive, indeed global, on the other. The result is a volume of remarkable depth and breadth that throws into fresh relief the politics – of place, of representation, of identity – that structure settler societies."

– *Corinn Columpar, University of Toronto, Canada*

"*Cinematic Settlers* challenges the field of settler–colonial studies with its ambitious geographical breadth and redefines conceptions of world cinema by interrogating the settler structures that underpin the medium. It is an essential text that spans multiple genres and historical periods to address urgent questions about the state of cinema and its role in cultivating a path beyond settlement."

– *Jerod Ra'Del Hollyfield, Carson-Newman University, USA*

"Settler colonialism is at the very core of modern global history. This wide-ranging collection reveals its huge impact on transnational film and popular culture."

– *Angela Woollacott, The Australian National University, Australia*

"This collection of essays on cinema from across the globe offers rich new insights on the distinct cultures settler colonialism produced by mirroring and affirming settler interests, perspectives and fantasies. The collection also tackles difficult questions of how contemporary filmmakers grapple with Indigenous critiques and post-settlement politics in diverse ways, from adopting multivocal perspectives to re-staging settler narratives in new imaginary frontiers. When representing diversity in film is such a pressing issue, this timely collection explores the deep histories and ambivalences of settler cinema."

– *Shino Konishi, University of Western Australia, Australia*

I0592995

CINEMATIC SETTLERS

This anthology adds to the burgeoning field of settler colonial studies by examining settler colonial narratives in the under-analyzed medium of film.

Cinematic Settlers discusses different cinematic genres, national traditions, and specific movies in order to expose related threads, shared circulations of knowledge, and paralleled representations. Organized into thematic groupings—conquest, settlers, natives, and space—the contributors explore the question of how film compares to written genres and other visual media in representing and effecting settler colonialism on a global scale. Striving for inclusiveness, the volume covers different eras and settler colonial situations in Australia, New Zealand, Taiwan, Hawaii, the American West, Canada, Latin America, Russia, France, Algeria, German Africa, South Africa, and even the next frontier: outer space. By showing how films offer layered, contested, and dynamic settler colonial narratives that advance and challenge settler hegemonic readings, the essays enable students to better analyze and understand the complex history of diversity and colonialism in film.

This book is important reading for undergraduate classes on the history of empire, colonialism, and film.

Dr Janne Lahti is an Academy of Finland Research Fellow in History at the University of Helsinki, Finland. He specializes in global and transnational histories of settler colonialism, borderlands, American West, and Nordic colonialism. His books include *German and United States Colonialism in a Connected World: Entangled Empires* (2020), *The American West and the World: Transnational and Comparative Perspectives* (2019), and *Wars for Empire: Apaches, the United States, and the Southwest Borderlands* (2017).

Professor Rebecca Weaver-Hightower is Chair of English at North Dakota State University. Her publications include *Frontier Fictions: Settler Sagas and Postcolonial Guilt* (2018), *Empire Islands: Castaways, Cannibals, and Fantasies of Conquest* (2007), *Postcolonial Film: History, Empire, Resistance* (2014, co-edited with Peter Hulme), and another collection on settler literatures *Archiving Settler Colonialism: Culture, Space and Race* (2018, co-edited with Yuting Huang).

CINEMATIC SETTLERS

The Settler Colonial World in Film

Edited by Janne Lahti and Rebecca Weaver-Hightower

Routledge
Taylor & Francis Group

NEW YORK AND LONDON

First published 2020
by Routledge
52 Vanderbilt Avenue, New York, NY 10017

and by Routledge
2 Park Square, Milton Park, Abingdon, Oxon OX14 4RN

Routledge is an imprint of the Taylor & Francis Group, an informa business

© 2020 Taylor & Francis

Library of Congress Cataloging-in-Publication Data
A catalog record for this title has been requested

ISBN: 978-0-367-22998-6 (hbk)
ISBN: 978-0-367-50383-3 (pbk)
ISBN: 978-1-003-05727-7 (ebk)

Typeset in Bembo
by Taylor & Francis Books

CONTENTS

FIGURES

PROLOGUE

Mike Bruised Head

A common belief of settlers around the world was that the places they were "settling" did not have names. Of course, settlers could see that people were already there, but the settlers chose to think of them as barbaric and savage, lacking proper religion, and without ownership. The settlers imported their laws and religion to these areas, whether in North America, Australasia, Africa, or elsewhere; and the settlers convinced themselves that as the "first" persons to see a mountain or a river or a new landscape, they had the right to attach their names to those places.

Movies—especially the historical settler films known as "Westerns"—had a role in perpetuating this perception for later generations. Films created the illusion that there were no Indigenous people as real, complicated, and rooted communities and peoples with emotions, agendas, and agency, and this illusion enhanced the settler mentality that the lands continued to be free to be taken. This cinema fostered and displayed the attitudes of settler supremacy over Indigenous peoples, feeding the formation of laws for religion and land occupancy. In films, settlers used the premise that the Indigenous people had no structured religion and did not demonstrate the white mentality of farming to indicate that it was the settlers who had the right to occupy the land. As the Western would have, there was usually a church built at the end of town, demonstrating that Christianity prevailed.

There was no consultation with the Indigenous peoples as the settlers tried to make sense of landscapes and territories that were "foreign" to their eyes, places that they had no relationship with, by giving those places names that made sense to themselves and thereby pretending that they "owned" them. Unlike Indigenous place names, which are deeply rooted in place and tell a story about the reality and characteristics of a place, those new colonial names had no real association to the place itself and were often just the names of white men who had never been to that place.

These new names were settler colonial fantasies because they tell stories about white men, property, and ownership, instead of the older true stories told by Indigenous mothers and grandmothers about land and spirit. The stories of the geographical names eroded by early map makers and surveyors not only removed the history, but created language genocide and silenced the cultural relationship with Indigenous lands and spiritual places. For a culture to survive it must have the ability to maintain its own cultural and geographical knowledge. The new names tell stories about the European nations to come, not the ancient Indigenous territories that are already there. Settler cinemas created the illusion that it was okay to give names and steal the land by showing stories of settlers defending their homesteads and cabins, often from invading indigenes, though in fact, it was the setters who were the invaders. Renaming the landscape and erasing the original names meant stealing the voices of the peoples who lived there, the places they valued, and damaging the sacred relationships between Indigenous peoples and their territories. It's as if someone kicked you out of your house just by saying that it was now their house. The settler cinemas of the world assisted in kicking Indigenous people out of their houses and making it look natural and inevitable.

Films naturalized and normalized settler colonial dispossession and continued oppression for a hundred years of viewers. But these same films could provide—and still might provide—a more complicated view of that history, one where viewers savvy to the multiple perspectives of historical events could see the man behind the curtain, or one where Indigenous people took possession of the camera themselves and used cinema to tell an alternate version of their own history, taking back their ownership by capturing space on film and through creating their own narration, naming their own space. The essays to follow examine film as such a medium of settler invasion and resistance—fascinating, flawed, and yet filled with potential as a tool of free expression.

CONTRIBUTORS

Dominique Brégent-Heald is an associate professor in the Department of History at Memorial University of Newfoundland. Her articles have appeared in such journals as *Western Historical Quarterly, American Review of Canadian Studies, Journal of Canadian Studies*, and *Canadian Journal of Film Studies*. She is the author of *Borderland Films: American Cinema, Mexico and Canada during the Progressive Era* (University of Nebraska Press, 2015). Her current SSHRC-funded research project *Northern Getaway: The Tourism Film and Selling Canada* explores the complex interplay between film and tourism in Canada during the first half of the twentieth century.

Mike Bruised Head is of Blackfoot heritage from Southern Alberta, Canada. He is presently a PhD candidate in Cultural, Social, and Political Thought at the University of Lethbridge, Lethbridge, Alberta, Canada. His thesis is titled "The Colonial Impact on the Eradication of the Historic Blackfoot Names of the Mountains Located in the Waterton Lake National Park." He is involved in Blackfoot ceremonies as ceremonialist elder and speaks his Blackfoot Language. He has also been part of various documentaries, and quoted in several publications.

M. Bianet Castellanos is an associate professor of American Studies and an affiliated faculty member in the departments of American Indian Studies and Chicano Latino Studies at the University of Minnesota. Trained as an anthropologist, she works with Yucatec Maya communities in Mexico and Los Angeles. Her publications include *A Return to Servitude: Maya Migration and the Tourist Trade in Cancún* (University of Minnesota Press, 2010) and the anthology *Detours: Travel and the Ethics of Research in the Global South* (University of Arizona Press, 2019). She also edited a forum on settler colonialism in Latin America for *American Quarterly*. She is currently working on a book on Indigenous home ownership in Cancún, Mexico.

Maria Flood is a senior lecturer in Film Studies at Keele University. She has published widely on Francophone and world cinema and political violence, most recently in *JCMS* and *Studies in French Cinema*. Her monograph entitled *France, Algeria and the Moving Image: Screening Histories of Violence* was published with Legenda, Oxford, in 2017. She is currently working on a project on the representation of political extremism and affect in post-9/11 world cinema.

Travis Franks is a post-doctoral fellow in the Kilachand Honors College at Boston University. Trained as a literary scholar, he specializes in contemporary multi-ethnic literatures of the US and Australia. His book project, *Settler Nativism: Indigeneity and Diaspora in Contemporary Narratives of Belonging*, details narrative strategies of belonging at work in settler-authored texts, as well as works by Indigenous and non-Indigenous writers of color that problematize these strategies. His work appears in *Western American Literature, American Indian Quarterly*, and *MELUS*.

Wolfgang Fuhrmann has a PhD in Film Studies and is an associate researcher in the Department of Film Studies, University of Zurich. His research interests include transnational film history, Latin American cinema, and German colonial cinema. He is the author of *Imperial Projections: Screening the German Colonies* (Berghahn, 2015) and "Cinema Nacional, para quem? Associações, Recepção e Transnacionalismo," in *História: Debates e Tendências* 16.2 (2016), 328–341. He has held teaching positions in Germany, Switzerland, and the Americas. He is currently living in Bogotá, Colombia.

Barry Judd is professor and director, Indigenous Studies, The University of Melbourne. He is a descendent of the Pitjantjatjara people of north-west South Australia, British immigrants, and Afghan cameleers. He is a leading Australian scholar on the Aboriginal participation in Australian sports. His recent publications include "Kapi Wiya: Water Insecurity and Aqua-Nullius in Remote Inland Aboriginal Australia," *Thesis Eleven* 150.1, 102–118, and, with Katherine Ellinghaus, "Writing as Kin: Producing Ethical Histories Through Collaboration in Unexpected Places. Researching F.W. Albrecht, Assimilation Policy, and Lutheran Experiments in Aboriginal Education," in Sarah Maddison & Sana Nakata, eds., *Questioning Indigenous-Settler Relations: Interdisciplinary Perspectives* (Springer, 2019), 55–68.

Misha Kavka is a professor of Cross-Media Culture at the University of Amsterdam. She has published widely on gender, celebrity, and affect in relation to factual television, New Zealand film and online media. She is the author of *Reality Television, Affect and Intimacy* (Palgrave Macmillan, 2008) and *Reality TV* (Edinburgh UP, 2012), and the co-editor of volumes on transnational reality television, New Zealand gothic culture, and feminist theory.

Lawrence H. Kessler is a postdoctoral fellow at the Consortium for History of Science, Technology and Medicine, in Philadelphia. His work focuses on the intersection of environmental history, agricultural history, and history of science and technology, with particular attention to the history of sugarcane plantation systems. His forthcoming book, *Planter's Paradise: Sugar and the Conquest of Hawai'i*, examines how sugarcane influenced Hawai'i's history throughout the nineteenth and twentieth centuries. Kessler's other publications include "A Plantation upon a Hill; Or, Sugar without Rum: Hawai'i's Missionaries and the Founding of the Hawaiian Sugarcane Plantation System," *Pacific Historical Review* 84.2 (Spring 2015), 129–162.

Delia Malia Konzett is a professor of English, Cinema Studies, and Women's and Gender Studies at the University of New Hampshire. Her publications include the monographs *Ethnic Modernisms* (Palgrave, 2002) and *Hollywood's Hawaii: Race, Nation, and War* (Rutgers University Press, 2017) as well as the edited anthology *Hollywood at the Intersection of Race and Identity* (Rutgers University Press, 2019). Her recent work focuses on the representation and performance of race in Hollywood cinema.

Janne Lahti currently researches and teaches at the University of Helsinki, Finland, as an Academy of Finland Research Fellow. His research focuses on global and transnational histories of settler colonialism, borderlands, the American West, and Nordic colonialism. He has published four books, including *The American West and the World: Transnational and Comparative Perspectives* (Routledge, 2019) and *Wars for Empire: Apaches, the United States, and the Southwest Borderlands* (University of Oklahoma Press, 2017). His articles have appeared in academic journals such as the *Western Historical Quarterly, Journal of Colonialism and Colonial History*, and *Journal of the West*.

Sheila McManus is a professor of History at the University of Lethbridge. Her research focuses on the borderlands of the North American West. Her publications include *The Line Which Separates: Race, Gender, and the Making of the Alberta-Montana Borderlands* (University of Nebraska Press, 2005); *One Step Over the Line: Toward an Inclusive History of Women in the North American West*, co-edited with Elizabeth Jameson (University of Alberta Press and Athabasca University Press, 2008); and *Choices and Chances: A History of Women in the U.S. West* (Wiley Blackwell, 2011).

Alexander Morrison is fellow and tutor in History at New College Oxford. He was previously professor of History at Nazarbayev University, lecturer in Imperial History at the University of Liverpool, and a prize fellow of All Souls College, Oxford. He is the author of *Russian Rule in Samarkand, 1868–1910: A Comparison with British India* (Oxford University Press, 2008) and the editor (with Aminat Chokobaeva and Cloe Drieu) of *The Central Asian Revolt of 1916: A Collapsing Empire in the Age of War and Revolution* (Manchester University Press, 2020). He is currently completing a history of the Russian conquest of Central Asia.

Ian-Malcolm Rijsdijk is a senior lecturer in the Centre for Film and Media Studies and a member of the Environmental Humanities South research program at the University of Cape Town. He has published widely in the field of contemporary South African film. His recent publications include "The Flexible City: Cinematic (re)Constructions of Cape Town," *Journal of African Cinemas* 10 (1–2), 81–94, as well as "Framing Democracy: Film in Post-Democracy South Africa," in *Routledge Companion to World Cinema*, edited by Rob Stone, Paul Cooke, Stephanie Dennison, and Alex Marlow-Mann (Routledge, 2017).

Lin-chin Tsai is currently assistant adjunct professor in the Department of Asian Languages and Cultures at the University of California, Los Angeles (UCLA). He received his PhD at UCLA, with a focus on Taiwan as a settler colony and its cultural productions. His articles on Taiwan literature and cinema have been published in academic journals in English and Mandarin, including *Concentric, Tamkang Review, Chung-Wai Literary Quarterly*, and an edited volume, *Keywords of Taiwan Theory* (Linking Publishing, 2019). He also co-authored a book with scholars specializing in Taiwan literature, entitled *100 Years of Taiwan Literature* (Linking Publishing, 2018).

Stephen Turner works as a senior lecturer in Media and Communication at University of Auckland. His research interests include geo-media, decolonization, and public pedagogy through media technologies. He is currently writing books on the challenge of Indigenous law to western constitutionalism in Aotearoa New Zealand, and, with Sean Sturm, on the university and dissent. He has produced collaborative artwork concerned with photography and settler colonial historiography, a co-edited book on governance by land and water, and numerous publications concerned with the overlap of nature, technology, and environment.

Lorenzo Veracini is associate professor of History at Swinburne University of Technology, Melbourne. His research focuses on the comparative history of colonial systems and settler colonialism as a mode of domination. He has authored *Israel and Settler Society* (Pluto Press, 2006), *Settler Colonialism: A Theoretical Overview* (Palgrave, 2010), and *The Settler Colonial Present* (Palgrave, 2015). He also co-edited *The Routledge Handbook of the History of Settler Colonialism* (Routledge, 2016), manages the settler colonial studies blog, and is Founding Editor of *Settler Colonial Studies*. His *Displacement as Politics: A Global History* is forthcoming in early 2020.

Rebecca Weaver-Hightower is a professor of English specializing in post-colonial studies and Chair of English at North Dakota State University. Her monograph (*Frontier Fictions: Settler Sagas and Postcolonial Guilt*, Palgrave 2018) focuses on settler colonial literatures of South Africa, Canada, the US, and Australia. She has published a monograph on island castaway narratives (*Empire Islands:*

Castaways, Cannibals and Fantasies of Conquest, Minnesota 2007), co-edited with Peter Hulme the collection *Postcolonial Film: History, Empire, Resistance* (Routledge 2014), and co-edited with Yuting Huang another collection on settler literatures (*Archiving Settler Colonialism: Culture, Space and Race*, Routledge 2018).

Natale Zappia is associate professor of History and Director of the Institute for Sustainability at California State University, Northridge. He is the author of *Traders and Raiders: The Indigenous World of the Colorado Basin* (University of North Carolina Press, 2014); *The Many Faces of Edward Sherriff Curtis: A Collection of Portraits and Stories from Native North America* (with Steadman Upham; University of Washington Press, 2006); and *Rez Metal: Inside the Navajo Heavy Metal Scene* (with Ashkan Soltani; University of Nebraska Press, forthcoming, 2020).

INTRODUCTION

Reel Settler Colonialism: Gazing, Reception, and Production of Global Settler Cinemas

Rebecca Weaver-Hightower and Janne Lahti

The 1916 South African silent film *The Voortrekkers: Winning a Continent* tells the story of "the Great Trek," where hundreds of Dutch settlers in the 1830s moved northward from the Cape Colony to seek independence from British rule by settling a space inhabited by the Zulu.[1] After its title screen, the film gives its first intertitle (the caption screen typical of silent films). Using the two settler colonial languages of South Africa—English and Afrikaans—it reads: "Piet Retief, a farmer in the Cape Colony, has planned a great emigration to the unknown north for the purpose of buying territory from the natives upon which to establish a free Dutch republic." This statement sets up the 53-minute film with several interesting ideological claims. It declares the journey as "great," indicating not only the distance traveled from the "civilized sphere," but the size of the task the early settlers had to master. It makes the settler a farmer, revealing his intentions on the land. It also depicts the journey as "emigration," not conquest or war, thus masking violence by representing that settlers came with peaceful intentions. Then it claims the land "unknown" while at the same time acknowledging native ownership (since they could sell the land). And, by declaring that the land will be bought, the statement disavows the land theft inherent in settlement.

This notion of the land being fairly purchased is continued in the third intertitle screen, which explains that this "fair trade" is meant to "thereby gain [the natives'] assistance in establishing a model republic for our posterity." The intertitle presents settlement resulting from the "Great Trek" of 1836–1838 as not an invasion, but the beginning of a republic. Moreover, the "our" in the statement leaves open that the republic might involve collaboration with natives or even equal rights for Africans and Dutch. This notion of fairness is contained in the film's subtitle— "winning a continent"—where settlement is made to appear as a fair contest that could be "won," and where the stakes are all of Africa.

As it progresses, the film shows this plan for a purportedly fair republic despoiled by the actions of two bad colonizers, Portuguese traders, who get labeled as "unwelcome visitors" by the intertitle.[2] These traders plan to thwart the Dutch plan of peaceful negotiation and purchase because, as they explain, "if these cursed Dutchmen get into Zululand they will teach the natives trade valuations, and ruin our business." So, these men plan to travel ahead of the Voortrekkers to "poison the mind of the Zulu king against the Boers." And, thus the film proffers an explanation for the real-world hostilities that met the real Voortrekkers, including the killing of Piet Retief's party by the Zulu and the battle between the Zulu and trekkers on the Ncome River on 16 December 1838. This fight, "the Battle of Blood River," derived its name from the superior number of spear wielding Zulu forces that were killed by the smaller number of Voortrekkers with firearms, their blood dying the river red. But in the film, this fight was not an Indigenous force trying and failing to repel an invasion but the result of two bad colonizers trying to despoil the peaceful efforts of benevolent colonizers.

The Great Trek remains famous in South Africa as a founding myth of Afrikaner nationalism, and *The Voortrekkers: Winning a Continent* holds a crucial role. This early popular film acted as a propaganda tool, legitimizing settler colonialism and explaining settler righteousness. It was shown for years as part of "Day of the Vow," the annual celebration of the battle that for many Afrikaners was seen as God's sanction of their settlement by granting their victory over the most powerful of the native peoples, the Zulu.[3] This film also related a more global story of righteous conquest, which settler audiences around the world could recognize and relate to. It spoke a settler "language" of expansion, native threat, settler victory, and promise of settler futures, a discourse that resonated far beyond the ethnic, national, and imperial boundaries of South Africa.

We begin by referencing *The Voortrekkers: Winning a Continent* because it serves as an apt example for the kind of work depicted and scrutinized in *Cinematic Settlers* overall, which intersects film studies and settler colonial studies to better understand how cinema connected the local with the global and captured and furthered a global settlement project. Because the medium came into its own in the twentieth century, films about settlement succeed most of the events they chronicle.[4] *The Voortrekkers: Winning a Continent*, for instance, follows the events it narrates by eighty years. So, for its viewers, who probably weren't alive to witness the Great Trek, the film brought the experience of the Voortrekkers into reality in a way not available through text, tale, or static image (painting, tapestry, drawing, or photograph). Viewers could experience the perilous crossing of a swift-flowing river with horses, oxen, and wagons submerged above their axels. They could marvel over the intimate view of the Zulu village and its dome shaped dwellings surrounded by hundreds of be-skirted and shield carrying Zulu. They could relive the danger of the massive battle between the Zulu and Afrikaners and celebrate the tactics and technologies that allowed the Boers to fight off the larger Zulu force. The magic of film provides a verisimilitude necessary to the settler myth, creating through its successive frames a version of reality that replaces (or attempts to) other versions of events and that allows the descendants of settlers to relive the experiences of first-generation settler ancestors to better appreciate their "sacrifice" and legacy. By its nature, film offers viewers a recreation of the historic events of settlement and also, through its continual replaying of settlement stories, reminds contemporary critics and viewers that settlement is far from accomplished.

That is, *The Voortrekkers: Winning a Continent* is important in 1916 (against the backdrop of the First World War, into which South Africa had been drawn as a member of the British Empire, despite protest from much of its Afrikaner population) not just because it replays an important act of settlement from the prior generation, but because it does so in such a way as to justify the continued presence of the white minority as a ruling power. As anthropologist Patrick Wolfe has argued, settler colonialism is a structure and not an event, so it needs to be continually reasserted and legitimized, as the settler's position on the land is constantly challenged. The settler story must be recreated and retold because settlement is never fully accomplished. It is in this context that film as a genre and industry developed, ascended, and morphed into the digital medium of the twenty-first century.

Investigation of the making of *The Voortrekkers: Winning a Continent* says more about this fascinating intersection between cinema and the settler.[5] The film's maker, Herold M. Shaw, an American apprentice of Thomas Edison, had a long career making films in the U.S., England, Russia, and for a brief period, South Africa. Shaw's background as an American, as well as the film's apologetic stance for white supremacy, led to comparisons in its own time and since with D. W. Griffiths' three-and-a-half-hour American epic, *Birth of a Nation*, an infamous defense of white supremacy in the United States. *Birth of a Nation* chronicled white settler conflicts with formerly enslaved Africans instead of conflicts between American settlers and the country's indigenes, collectively known as "Native Americans," but the U.S. settler–indigene conflict would be played over and over in the genre that became known as "the Western," which several of the essays in this volume, including ones by Sheila McManus and Janne Lahti, work to unpack.

Like film, settler colonialism is a global phenomenon.[6] Settler colonialism stands for both a historical process and a particular way of looking at the past, a field of enquiry. Settler colonialism is typically defined as something that involves conquest and capture of land, long-range migration, permanent settlement (or at least intent of such), the elimination of Natives and/or native sovereignty, and the reproduction of one's own society on what used to be other people's lands. According to Wolfe, settler colonialism is not primarily an effort to build a master–servant relationship interested in exploitation of Native labor or the extraction of natural resources, but instead is more concerned about replacement and access to territory, the land itself. Wolfe underlines that as "settlers come to stay: invasion is a structure not an event" or a series of isolated events. It "destroys to replace," introduces "a zero-sum contest over land," and is characterized by a "logic of elimination," a sustained institutional tendency to eliminate the Natives who stand in the way of settlers' ambitions of making the land their own.[7] As settler colonialism spread in North America, Australia, New Zealand, Africa, and Asia it relied on transnational circulations, networks, and connections of peoples, ideas, knowledge, and commodities. It was built on exchanges, shared methods, and common mentalities between and within empires.[8]

Settler colonialism also created global settler colonial cinemas with interlinked themes and joint narratives. Films provide a window to the settler, speak to a common, international, audience, and use a shared "language" of settler colonialism in doing so: the stories of empty lands, settler civilizations and righteousness, and of othering and elimination. Yet, a careful reading of settler cinemas can also reveal stories of ambiguity, settler vulnerability, and native resistance and agency. How this all has been represented in a range of films across the globe is the purview of this collection, which contains analyses of films about settled spaces around the world: from the South Sea islands to the former USSR, from stories of settler ideology in Australia to settler ambivalence in Taiwan, in filmed spaces with settings real and constructed.

Existing at this nexus of the two dynamic fields of film and settler colonial studies, *Cinematic Settlers* builds on prior work, like Peter Limbrick's landmark *Making Settler Cinemas* and Corinn Columpar's *Unsettling Sights: The Fourth World on Film,* to bring insights to both fields that wouldn't otherwise exist.[9] In its focus on form, representation reception, and production, *Cinematic Settlers* brings valuable insights to settler colonial studies and to films about settlers. Film studies tends to focus on the medium as well as the narrative and how the visual narrative and production process create a unique experience for viewers across time and space. Essays in this book perform that type of analysis, like Dominique Bregent-Heald's and Lawrence Kessler's, which both analyze how film employs the scopophilic pleasure of gazing at the landscape as part of the viewer imaginatively settling the cinematic setting. Likewise, Maria Flood, Ian-Malcolm Rijsdijk, and Natale Zappia examine how settings were created, staged, and choreographed as part of the visual appeal of the settler story.

Film also brings into conversation the discussion of representation and reception, working to unpack the experience of a text, as part of understanding its distribution and existence as a commodity. Film is the lingua franca of the twentieth century, the medium to which most of the settled globe had access. In spaces where literacy rates were low, books hard to come by, and television the purview of the privileged, films could still be found. Film could thus be dangerous, since the power of image could incite resistance, as in South Africa, where American films showing black actors on screen were banned. This volume, thus, also addresses reception. Travis Franks' essay, for instance, reads film as an intervention at a particularly volatile moment in Australian culture when settler–indigene relations threatened to be explosive. Similarly, essays that focus on genre inherently address audience reception, as does Sheila McManus' and Janne Lahti's. Alexander Morrison's analysis of how the USSR adapted the Western genre under communism would equally bring attention to viewer reception.

Moreover, because film is a global phenomenon, as industries across the globe capture and in some cases preserve a range of experiences, its recording of the settler experience brings into comparison different kinds of settlers in different spaces, which is also the aim of settler colonial studies and *Cinematic Settlers*. For instance, this book juxtaposes Wolfgang Fuhrmann' s essay on German settlers in Africa, Delia Malia Konzett's analysis of American settlers in the South Seas, Lin-Chin Tsai's examination of Chinese settlement of Taiwan, and Lorenzo Veracini's study of the fantasy settlement of outer space. Other essays cover different eras and settler colonial situations in Australia, New Zealand, Hawaiʻi, the American West, Canada, Latin America, Russia, France, Algeria, and South Africa.

It is also important to remember that film as an interdisciplinary medium is inherently collaborative—as writers and directors, cinematographers, editors, actors, and a range of other technicians and support staff collaborate to produce the feature film. Smaller budget, home-grown films, as well, would require multiple hands to complete; only with the technology of the end of the twentieth and early twenty-first centuries could filmmakers with a computer or smart phone be writer, actor, director, and cinematographer (though none of the films under analysis in this volume are of that sort). The disciplines drawn upon in this collaborative collection mirror this interdisciplinary orientation of film. *Cinematic Settlers* blends history, literature, anthropology, and area and film studies, with authors representing different national backgrounds, originating from America, Europe, Asia, Africa, and Australasia.

Settler colonial studies also has insights to bring to film studies, which make this collection equally useful to scholars and students of film. Postcolonial film has been well examined, but the focus on the settler and settled experience is relatively new.[10] Settler colonial studies brings new topics and conceptualizations to film studies, including a new approach to Indigenous studies and to resistance. Film is a structure of settlement but also a means for resistance, as film industries in newly independent countries have been mobilized in the service of creating a post-settler national identity. Essays in this volume—including those by Misha Kavka and Stephen Turner, as well as by Bianet Castellanos and Barry Judd—touch on this issue of film as a complicated and convoluted tool of resistance.

Finally, it is worth considering how film is itself a settler technology—an invention of settlers, with early films primarily existing in the US and France to document everyday settler life for other settlers—the gate of a horse, a drive down a settlement street, the working of a snowplow, the routine of workers leaving a factory.[11] Settler colonialism was and is a global historical phenomenon that has a shared history filled with connections, circulations of ideas that are visible in films.

The book is organized into four thematic groupings, representing the major facets and questions of settler colonialism: conquest, settlers, Natives, and space. Each section offers a specific window into the settler cinematic experience, yet, the essays overlap in myriad ways, showing the layered and multidirectional narrative strands of settler cinemas. "Conquest" in this case isn't simply the historical events that first led to settlement but the conquest of reel landscapes and cinematic space. For instance, the first essay in the section, Delia Malia Konzett's "The South Pacific as the Final Frontier: Hollywood's South Seas Fantasies, the Beachcomber, and Militarization" discusses Hollywood's South Seas genre and its conversion into the Pacific combat genre as contributions to US settler colonialism that validated US expansionism as entertainment. The "conquest" in this essay is of the filmed Pacific space as part of the settler colonial imaginary. Lawrence H. Kessler's "Environments of Settler Colonialism in Statehood-Era U. S. Cinematic Depictions of the Hawaiian Islands" also focuses on the American Pacific in its examination of three U.S. films set in Hawai'i produced shortly after statehood: *Blue Hawaii, Diamond Head*, and *Hawaii*. Kessler spotlights descriptions of the natural environment and ways that non-human nature exerts agency in determining settler colonial narratives of conquest, how nature both bolsters and challenges settler colonialism, provoking ambivalence in settler approaches and outlooks in regards to Hawai'i.

In "Settler-Aboriginal Alliance and the Threat of Foreign Invasion in Baz Luhrmann's *Australia*," Travis Franks scrutinizes how traditional conquest narratives get reimaged in present-day Australia through a retelling of the past as a struggle where the settler and indigene together faced an Asian threat. As has been the case with Prime Minister Kevin Rudd's apology to Aboriginal Australians, critics of Luhrmann's film tend to argue that it ultimately serves to alleviate culpability and shame amongst the settler population by promoting a fantasy of triumphant national unity. This chapter adds to this scholarly discourse by discussing the film's reliance on the invasion narrative and its attendant Asian stereotype to forge a bond between settler and Aboriginal characters.

The section on conquest ends with Alexander Morrison's "Settler Bolsheviks in the Soviet 'Eastern'," which analyzes how the Revolutionary and Civil War period in Central Asia became a popular subject for novels and films in the USSR portraying Russians as the main agents of progress in Central Asia against the villainous Basmachi, bandits who resisted the new Soviet order. Morrison explores how the film *Alye Maki Issyk-Kulya (The Scarlet Poppies of Issyk-Kul*, Bolotbek Shamshiev, 1972) and the novel on which it was based, Alexander Sytin's *Kontrabandisty Tian'-Shanya (The Smugglers of the Tian-Shan*, 1930), both follow and challenge the notions of "Easterns" as settler colonial narratives.

The second section of the collection, "Settlers," includes four essays that each examine different settler groups as portrayed in film in the North American West, German Africa, and Taiwan. Each essay, in its way, explores how cinematic depictions of settler lives betray the cracks in settler ideology in the midst of perpetuating that ideology. The section begins with Sheila McManus's "*Gunless* as Settler Colonial Borderlands Fantasy," which uses the highly portable tropes, themes, and settings of the American "Western" film genre to discuss a "Canadian Western," the 2010 film *Gunless*, which takes many of those classic tropes and themes and puts them to use to tell a nationalist tale about Canadian settler colonialism. Just like settler colonial projects around the world, McManus argues, Canada began by rendering Indigenous peoples and places invisible; it then created its own nationalist tales about multiculturalism and Mounties to create the image of a kinder, gentler West. Next Janne Lahti's "The Unbearable Settler West in *The Ballad of Buster Scruggs*" examines this Western anthology for its typical Western scenarios, which coexist with challenges to classic settler colonial narrative outcomes, but without managing to overcome them. The film, Lahti argues, depicts a settler West that is a twisted and aimless, filled with dread, fear, and violence, making the settler West unbearable. Yet, the settler West is also unbearably white, hiding the ethnic diversity of the historic West and thus, once again, reaffirming the settler colonial West as a white space.

Wolfgang Fuhrmann's "*Unser Haus in Kamerun*: The Restauration of Settler Colonial Memory in German Post-World War II Cinema," examines one of the few German films of the 1950s and 1960s that explicitly deals with Germany's colonial past—*Unser Haus in Kamerun* (Our House in Cameroon) from 1961— against the background of post-colonial discourses in Germany, especially in regard to Ralph Giordano's provoking two-part TV report *Heia Safari* from 1966. The essay teases the tensions embedded in narratives of settler families and benevolence at a time of decolonization, showing how settler colonial narratives responded, or failed to do so, to changing historical circumstances.

The final essay, Lin-chin Tsai's "Negotiating Between Homelands: Settler Colonial Situation and Settler Ambivalence in Taiwan Cinema," moves the conversation to yet another controversial settled space, Taiwan, in order to analyze two Taiwan films by two Han settler directors, Bai Jingrui's *Home Sweet Home* (*Jia zai Taibei*, 1970) and Lee Hsing's *The Land of the Brave* (*Long de chuanren*, 1981). Tsai argues that the two films manifest a specific form of settler ambivalent mentality where Taiwan's settler colonial situation should be comprehended through both the tensions sustaining the metropole (China), the settler colony (Taiwan), and the Indigenous population, and through the circulations linking the exogenous neocolonial power (the U.S.), the Han settlers, and the Indigenous peoples.

The essays in the collection's third section, "Natives" examine films about Indigenous peoples in settled spaces, some that seek to recuperate a sense of Indigenous agency and others that depict Indigenous lives, often in contrast to settlers and with the participation of settler-owned film companies. Barry Judd's "Hero or Dupe: Jay Swan and the Ambivalences of Aboriginal Masculinity in the Films of Ivan Sen" tackles depictions of Aboriginal masculinity—as "lazy," "immoral," and "stupid"—in Australian settler cinema through the films of an Aboriginal filmmaker. By discussing the key protagonist, Jay Swan, of the films *Mystery Road* and *Goldstone*, Judd argues that the construction of Swan as both Aboriginal man and detective, functions to undermine and question core settler colonial understanding of Aboriginal masculinities in ways that few others have chosen to do.

Natale Zappia's "*In the Land of the Head Hunters*: Kwakwaka'wakw Archives and the Settler Colonial Lens" takes the collection back to an early documentary of an Indigenous group, the 1914 motion picture by Edward Curtis of the Kwakwak'wakw in the Pacific Northwest. Like all of Curtis' work, the film was anything but "documentary," as Zappia notes that, while designed to cater to white American expectations of pristine wilderness and the "other," the choreographed scenes, sets, props, and actions were also Indigenous. This delicate and complex relationship between the film reel and Native culture played out in remarkable ways during this process and has taken on new meaning in the twenty-first century as Native communities respond to settler colonialism by utilizing technology, film, and narrative.

M. Bianet Castellanos' "Disrupting Settler Innocence in Latin American Films" analyzes Roland Joffé's *The Mission* (1986) and Icíar Bollaín's *Even the Rain* (2010), showing how settler colonial narratives of discovery and Indigenous elimination are fundamental in advancing settler identities as socially progressive, even innocent. Indigenous identities, in turn, Castellanos argues, are rendered sympathetic and at times revolutionary, but these portrayals remain one-dimensional because they are reliant on settler colonial narratives of discovery and elimination. Encounters between the settler and Indian become the focal point through which to understand Indigenous lives. Yet, as Castellanos shows, these encounters cannot account for the complexity of Indigenous lives under settler colonialism.

The final essay in the "natives" section, Misha Kavka and Stephen Turner's "Having the 'Knack': Post-Settlement Cinema in Aotearoa New Zealand," also inspects Indigenous people as portrayed in films largely created by and for white settler audiences. Kavka and Turner focus on Taika Waititi's *Hunt for the Wilderpeople* (2016), which, they argue, is infused with nostalgia for a shared media culture while, at the same time, being interrupted by the oblique assertion of Māori claims. What they call "settler colonial jouissance," rooted in a double structure of colonial wound and Indigenous history, pervades post-settlement cinema and calls for a director with a particular "knack."

The book ends with the grouping entitled "Space" that includes essays that, in different ways, interrogate the appropriation and portrayal of cinematic spaces within and by films. Dominique Brégent-Heald's "Landscapes, Wildlife, and Grey Owl: Settler Colonial Imaginaries and Tourist Spaces in William J. Oliver's Parks Branch Films, 1920s-1930s" examines a selection of short films by William J. Oliver promoting the scenic, recreational, and wildlife features of Canada's National Parks to the American tourist market. It also discusses Oliver's films featuring Grey Owl, the ersatz Indigenous identity of Englishman Archie Belaney, whom the Parks Branch hired to promote beaver conservation and tourism. Although replete with clichéd tropes of the travelogue genre, upon further examination these short subjects reveal the complex and ongoing legacy of Indigenous expulsion consistent with settler colonial spaces.

Maria Flood's "From Colonial Casbah to Casbah-Banlieue: Settlement and Space in *Pépé le Moko* (1937) and *La Haine* (1996)," also focuses on examining space as portrayed in twentieth-century cinema, but instead of the park landscape, here the space is urban. Flood studies the geographic and symbolic space of the Casbah as an indicator of the unstable narratives of space, settlement, and identity in the two French films. If the Algerian Casbah was a site of French fantasies about the colony, the Casbah-banlieue offers similar projections in the metropolitan space of Paris, even if these projections are mitigated by consideration for the colonized struggle.

Ian-Malcolm Rijsdijk's "Between Sherwood Forest and the Red Sea: Settler Colonial South Africa in early Hollywood" brings to the discussion of cinematic space a literal map, Paramount Studios' location map from 1927 indicating areas in California that could double for different parts of the world. In the south-east of the state, sandwiched between the "Red Sea" and "Sherwood Forest" was "South Africa." Rijsdijk investigates South Africa's appeal through its frontier tales of gold and diamond prospecting, bold colonial adventure, and mythologized Zulus as narrative and aesthetic "place" in Hollywood, principally in the settler cinematic discourses.

The volume ends with an examination of settler space in outer space. In "Settler Evasions in *Interstellar* and *Cowboys and Aliens*: Thinking the End of the World is Still Easier than Thinking the End of Settler Colonialism," Lorenzo Veracini shows how science fiction films tell typically settler colonial stories, with equally typical settler colonial solutions. *Interstellar* faces environmental crisis and proposes a settler colonial way out: colonize somewhere else, thus welcoming displacement. *Cowboys and Aliens* also faces a settler colonial quandary. Settlers need to become indigenous, meaning they want the Indigenous land and an Indigenous way to enjoy the land in order to legitimate possession, as Veracini argues. The solution: settler indigenization via nativist struggle. Both films envision the desolation of worlds and a return—a return to settling in *Interstellar*, and a return to the historical moment of colonizing in *Cowboys and Aliens*.

In all, these essays show how films offer layered, diffused, contested, and dynamic settler colonial narratives that advance not merely settler hegemonic readings, but also nuanced representations, resistances, multiple voices, and continuous reinterpretations of historical processes and present-day realities. They show us a world made of settler colonial narrative strands, tensions, and imagery that shares common mindsets, visual language, colonial knowledge, and views of historical processes, but that also contains openings for multivocal discourses.

Notes

1 This film has been widely analyzed, cf. Hannes van Zyl, "'De Voortrekkers' (1916): Some Stereotypes and Narrative Conventions," *Critical Arts: A Journal of South-North Cultural Studies* 1.1 (1980), 24–31; Edwin Hees, "The Voortrekkers on Film: From Preller to Pornography," *Critical Arts: A Journal for Cultural Studies* 10.1 (1996), 1–22; and Neil Parsons, "Nation-Building Movies Made in South Africa (1916–18): I.W.

Schlesinger, Harold Shaw, and the Lingering Ambiguities of South African Union," *Journal of Southern African Studies* 39.3 (2013), 641–659. Parsons's bibliography includes further analyses.

2 Van Zyl and Hees both speculate that these characters were written as Portuguese instead of British (the colonial competition for the Dutch) because the film production company was British.

3 Van Zyl reports that the film was shown for at least three decades to "packed audiences" (24).

4 Early technologies for moving pictures go back to the 1880s with several inventions linking still cells of film into a fluid connection, but the standard feature film with a unified narrative and editing is thought to have begun in 1906, with Australian Charles Tait's *The Story of the Kelly Gang* about the notorious Australian bushranger Ned Kelly, which is a settler narrative in its own right. *The Great Grain Robbery* of 1903 also contained a unified narrative but in a short film (12 minutes).

5 Parsons, in "Nation Building Movies," examines the production history of *The Voortrekkers: Winning a Continent* in greater detail.

6 Beginning as an offshoot of postcolonialism, settler colonialism has become a field in its own right. Leaders like Patrick Wolfe and Lorenzo Veracini have written foundation studies, like Veracini's *Settler Colonialism: A Theoretical Overview* (New York: Palgrave, 2010), and an independent journal (*Settler Colonial Studies*) has been established.

7 Patrick Wolfe, "Land, Labor, and Difference: Elementary Structures of Race," *American Historical Review* 106.3 (2001), esp. 868; Patrick Wolfe, "Settler Colonialism and the Elimination of the Native," *Journal of Genocide Research* 8.4 (2006), esp. 388.

8 James Belich, *Replenishing the Earth: The Settler Revolution and the Rise of the Angloworld* (Oxford: Oxford University Press, 2011).

9 Peter Limbrick, *Making Settler Cinemas: Film and Colonial Encounters in the United States, Australia, and New Zealand* (New York: Palgave, 2010); Corinn Columpar, *Unsettling Sights: The Fourth World on Film* (Carbondale, Il: Southern Illinois University Press, 2010).

10 For more on this postcolonial background, see Sandra Ponzanesi, Marguerite R Waller, eds., *Postcolonial Cinema Studies* (New York: Routledge, 2002); Rebecca Weaver-Hightower and Peter Hulme, eds., *Postcolonial Film: History, Empire, Resistance* (New York: Routledge, 2018).

11 One can find some of these early films of everyday settler life, mostly by Thomas Edison in the 1880s and 1890s, here: https://www.youtube.com/watch?v=dvIrfJnicBk. The 1911 "A Trip Through New York" can be found here: https://www.youtube.com/watch?v=aohXOpKtns0. YouTube contains many other examples of everyday life in early silent films.

PART I

Conquest

1

THE SOUTH PACIFIC AS THE FINAL FRONTIER: HOLLYWOOD'S SOUTH SEAS FANTASIES, THE BEACHCOMBER, AND MILITARIZATION

Delia Malia Konzett

The West and the Push into the Pacific

The American West has figured prominently in Hollywood's imagination as a reflection of the United States' nation building, continental expansionism, and Manifest Destiny. It led to the formation of the timeless Western film genre and the cinematic myth of the American frontier in the silent era of the 1910s and 1920s, a timeline paralleled by Hollywood's South Seas genre dramatizing the conquest of the Pacific. Thus, two distinctly different moments of American settler colonialism emerged on Hollywood's screens simultaneously, contributing to the national narrative of the US empire. With the illegal military coup and annexation of Hawai'i in 1893 and 1898 respectively, sponsored by New England colonizers (descendants of missionaries), the United States began to assert itself as a global power, viewing Hawai'i as a crucial gateway to Asia. Whereas the settler colonization of Hawai'i in the nineteenth century led to the dominance of a white New England ruling class represented by its industrial agricultural barons, Hollywood's representational colonization of this new territory of Hawai'i and the South Pacific proceeded with more caution so as not to unsettle the symbolic order of race on the mainland built around Jim Crow segregation. Nevertheless, Hollywood's institutional complicity with settler colonialism is undeniable in its release of numerous films representing the agenda of US colonialism in Hawai'i from the very beginning of the islands' annexation, which roughly coincides with the birth of cinema in the mid-1890s.

US cinema begins to explore Hawai'i as early as 1898 in the form of the widely disseminated documentary Edison shorts, focusing on the island's resources such as its maritime ports and harbors and its fertile lands, especially agrarian crops such as sugar cane.[1] These shorts also stress that the New England settlers are rightfully in charge of the islands based on their superior technology and ability to cultivate and develop the land in modern industrial style, following the Protestant ethic of capitalism and "its providential interpretation of profit-making."[2] Historian Emily Rosenberg refers to the colonizing triad of "Capitalists, Christians, [and] Cowboys" as instrumental in implementing American Manifest Destiny in the conquest of overseas lands.[3] "Traders, investors, missionaries, philanthropists, and entertainers," Rosenberg notes, "contributed both to expansion and the liberal developmental paradigm that accompanied it."[4] Significant feature films depicting a romanticized South Pacific emerge around 1915, leading to the creation of the South Seas fantasy genre rife with contradictions concerning settlement and colonization. As mass cultural products of repetitive formula, these films, not unlike the Buffalo Bill shows discussed by Rosenberg, "build [their] appeal on a mixture of nostalgia and promotional hype."[5] And, in spite of their fantasy driven plots, they envision and already anticipate a more systematic conquest of the South Pacific with permanently stationed military as the ultimate settler group, producing what philosopher Paul Virilio calls the paradigmatic "vision machine" of cinema in which war, technology, and representation are intertwined.[6] For the purpose of this essay, I will focus specifically on the military adaptation of the South Seas genre, thereby creating a historical continuity of imperial territorial claims that often began with settler colonialism in the guise of benign missionary work.[7]

I will explore here the South Seas genre and its corpus of films as an expression of US expansionism and its subsequent militarization in the South Pacific combat genre during World War II. Unlike the Western genre, where narratives of mythical gunslingers and unstoppable white settler conquest prevail, the Hollywood narrative of westward expansion into the Pacific enters the treacherous ground of non-western cultural contexts reframing its white hegemony. Its white settler protagonists find themselves in a racial limbo from which they either emerge in a return to mainstream norms, signaled by a return to the US mainland, or succumb to a dissolution of their white identity via interracial marriage. Even after the significant industrialization and modernization of Hawaiʻi at the turn of the twentieth century, Hollywood South Seas film narratives routinely depict Hawaiʻi and the South Pacific in first contact scenarios, showing its populations stuck in inferior pre-modern and "primitive" lifestyles. In fact, the South Seas genre, informed by prohibitive Jim Crow segregationist racial laws, produces inherently contradictory narratives of simultaneous compromised settlement or necessary departure from the conquered lands. Not until the military fully enters the picture in the leadup to World War II, is permanent settlement in the Pacific seriously entertained in Hollywood narratives. Contrary to these fictionalized narratives, permanent settlement had already started in the early nineteenth century with white elites consolidating land possessions with the active help of the military, eventually ruling majority-non-white populations in Pacific territories such as Hawaiʻi and deriving large scale economic benefit from their colonized lands with their industrialized agriculture. In addition, the military actively joined in the colonization, establishing a naval base at Pearl Harbor in 1899 that was to be expanded over the coming decades to become the home of the Pacific Fleet.

Hollywood's Beachcomber

The initial uncertainty about the extent and limits of settler colonial conquest of the South Pacific is expressed in Hollywood's trope of the white male beachcomber. As viewed by various anthropological studies, the historical figure of the beachcomber functions initially as a vanguard of Pacific explorers.[8] Often drawn from ex-whalers or ex-convicts, beachcombers managed to settle on various Pacific islands in the early years of large-scale Pacific discoveries and conquests (e.g. in Hawai'i from 1790s–1820s) and were useful to local chiefs as intermediaries with white traders, securing tools and weapons. In return, they secured some form of social integration into the tribal cultures of the Pacific. With the spread of illnesses such as smallpox, however, the newly arriving missionaries eventually gained the upper hand and marginalized the beachcomber, as they were able to provide vaccines in return for religious conversion.[9] Additionally, naval officers increasingly usurped the mediating position of beachcombers concerning military affairs. The late stages of the beachcomber are characterized by moral dissolution, alcoholism, and their obsolescence. Sociologists Martin Zelinietz and David Kravitz note that this period "correlates with the rapid increase of the beachcombing population, and the bad character manifested by some of the beachcombers."[10] Hollywood's fascination with the beachcomber mostly focuses on this later phase as his immoral lifestyle offers a more adequate representation of transgressive cultural fantasies popular during the roaring 1920s and the pre-Code Hollywood era (1930–1934).[11]

This pre-Code era is frequently associated with a non-regulated Hollywood cinema permitting a wider range of freedom concerning sexuality and controversial topics. However, as film scholar Ellen C. Scott has argued in *Cinema Civil Rights* (2014), unofficial racial codes were already in place during the late 1920s with its soft regulation by the Studio Relationship Committee (SRC, 1926–1934). As Scott points out, SRC regulator Jason Joy, known for his permissiveness on sexuality sought "to establish a firm color line and called for the elimination of racial integration."[12] Indeed, as political scientist and cultural scholar Cedric Robinson comments on the origins of early cinema, it appears that an unwritten racial code is operative from the very beginning of cinema, reflecting the agenda of US imperialism and white nationalism: "The commercial exploitation of motion pictures, beginning in the last decade of the nineteenth century, coincided exactly with the onset of Jim Crow ... there is also compelling evidence that cohesion and control of American motion pictures was spurred by the powerful interests implicated in the formulation of a new racial regime."[13] Its voluntary implementation can be found in the early shorts of American cinema's founder, Thomas Edison. For example, shorts such as "Kanakas Diving for Money" (1898) and "Harvesting Sugar Cane" (1902) document the colonization of Hawai'i as a legitimate enterprise of US territorial expansion led by a superior culture and race much like his short "Watermelon Contest" (1896) denigrates African Americans from within its scopic perspective of whiteness.

In contrast to the Western genre known for its open panoramic landscapes, South Seas fantasy films could not immediately use the Pacific setting as the backdrop for their promotional narratives due to distance and technical challenges. Instead, backlot recreations on the mainland were augmented with various black and brownface performances similar to early B Westerns that relied on stereotypical screen Indians and Mexicans. *McVeagh of the South Seas* (1914, dir. Harry Carey) offers an early example of Pacific settler colonialism not yet refined in its promotional filmic and narrative rhetoric. McVeagh (Harry Carey), described as a New England Harvard graduate and "self-exiled to the South Seas," transforms in the film into a brutal colonizer known for torturing his native subjects. He acquires Liana (Fern Foster), the daughter of the native chief, through trade with liquor but is double-crossed by his shipmate Gates (Herbert Russell) who equally succumbs to her spell and instigates a local rebellion against his rule. The film ends with McVeagh eventually escaping to San Francisco "toward civilization – and happiness," dismissing his and Gates' behavior as episodes caused by the corrupting climate or tropical fever of the Pacific, a common assumption in the rhetoric of Euro-American colonialism.[14] *Aloha Oe* (1915, dir. Richard Stanton), a film that is no longer extant, offers instead a more romantic fascination of the beachcomber David Harmon (Willard Mack) marooned on a tropical island. He saves the chief's daughter, Kalaniweo (Enid Markey), from impending sacrifice to appease the spirit of an erupting volcano, fathers a child with her, and after a short stay on the US continent returns to her upon hearing the alluring song "Aloha 'Oe."[15] Both films agree about the civilizational superiority of the white American settler but disagree on whether the new territories should be abandoned or cultivated and assimilated.

D.W. Griffith's South Seas fantasy *The Idol Dancer* (1920), unfettered by any studio regulation, deepened the discourse of racism via extensive use of blackface performances and non-disguised racist content conflating stereotypical exotic and savage depictions of Asians and Africans to capture the fluid racial spectrum of Micronesia, Melanesia, and Polynesia that anticipates the cultural setting of Skull Island in *King Kong* (1933). Like Griffith's *Birth of a Nation* (1915), *The Idol Dancer* embraces Manifest Destiny and aligns it with US overseas expansionism and the nation's newly emerging global role. As French philosopher and film scholar Gilles Deleuze observes, "The American cinema constantly shoots and reshoots a single fundamental film, which is the birth of a nation–civilization, whose first version was provided by Griffith."[16]

The film initially contrasts the bland and ethical behavior of white New England missionaries with the more exciting loose morals and vibrant lives of Dan (Richard Barthelmess), the white gin-drinking beachcomber, and the native islanders marked by their aversion to western clothes and their passion for dancing. In a significant shot showing the beachcomber across from his rival in love for the native Mary, we can see the film anticipating the coming role reversal of the beachcomber (See Figure 1.1). Due to the tragic sacrificial death of the young white missionary and rival suitor Walter Kincaid (Creighton Hale), Dan is eventually reformed and his Polynesian girlfriend Mary (Clarine Seymour) converts to Christianity, abandoning her Tiki idols. Of mixed Javanese, Samoan, and white descent, Mary dresses in Polynesian costume but appears

D.W. GRIFFITH ~~~ "The Idol Dancer"

A FIRST NATIONAL ATTRACTION

The derelict felt for his knife when his love threw the garland over the head of his rival.

FIGURE 1.1 The island girl in between her two rivals, the ethical missionary and the hedonist beachcomber (right).

clearly as white on screen, and hence does not endanger the racial code. In promotional posters, Mary was in fact falsely described as "a beautiful white girl cast away," living "among the cannibals, head-hunters and black birders of the South Sea Isles."[17]

The happy ending in matrimony of the interracial couple Dan and Mary sanctioned by the Christian missionary Reverend Blythe (George MacQuarrie) does not redeem the many overt racist depictions of the film (all performed by white actors in blackface). These include the missionaries' foolish native servants, the maid Pansy (Florence Short) and aspiring convert Reverend Peter (Porter Strong), and the native skull carrying Chief Wando (Walter James), a cannibal with a bone piercing his nose. The film's goal is to conquer the fantasy space of the South Seas, offer it up as suspenseful entertainment with scenarios of distress and rescue, while stressing the superiority of white American culture and its legitimate claim to overseas Pacific territories. Griffith's style of parallel editing enhances suspense and spectacle elements of the film, as the audience roots nervously for the women in distress. Under attack by Chief Wando and the white pirate Blackbirder, the rescue headed by the beachcomber arrives ever so slowly. The film's manipulative editing technique and its play with time and space ensure a stronger audience identification with the struggle of civilization to prevail against perceived threats of savagery.

The use of blackface in Griffith's films display an early complicity with Jim Crow segregation, as its use is systemic and informs the dominant industry practices that follow his lead. As film scholar Drake Stutesman notes "A black cast could consist of whites and blacks in blackface as well as African American actors not in blackface ... Griffith insist[ed] that black characters appearing in intimate scenes with white actors be white actors in blackface."[18] This practice leads to *Idol Dancer*'s contradiction of an interracial romance cast with white characters, one that culminates in Hollywood's traditional happy ending of marriage, implying family and settlement. The film's psychotic desire plots contact with Polynesian cultures – shown also in the casting of Hawaiian Walter Kolomoku in the role of a native musician – while actually desiring no contact whatsoever, as indicated by the many white blackface performances. As screen fantasy, *Idol Dancer* sends a mixed and ambivalent message to its audiences, dismissing its interracial reality as that of a transgressive race fascination while, however, promoting the conquest and development of new territories based on national ideology and racism.

Hollywood's Ethnography of the South Seas

In contrast to Griffith's overt racism on screen, W. S. Van Dyke resorts to ethnography with its pseudo-scientific judgments on race, hence sanitizing its messages while preserving them in substance. Van Dyke began as an assistant director under his mentor Griffith and was known for his highly popular *Thin Man* detective series (1930s) that nostalgically evokes the freewheeling roaring twenties with plenty of booze and parties. A skilled commercial Hollywood director, he provided popular escapist screen fantasies with a keen sense for both entertainment and contemporaneity of the film's subject matter. In his South Seas fantasies of the 1920s (1928, *White Shadows in the South Seas*; 1929, *The Pagan*), Van Dyke accommodated both the US imperialist and settler expansionist push into the Pacific in the wake of World War I and the transgressive Jazz Age with its slightly loosening codes on race that permitted a problematic fascination with the racial Other. The South Seas genre with its embedded interracial romance similarly accommodates a race fascination within the safe frame of fantasy.

Van Dyke's (and co-director Robert Flaherty's) *White Shadows in the South Seas* (1928) offers a significant departure from Griffith's blackface South Seas films such as *The Idol Dancer* (1920) or *The Love Flower* (1920). Shot entirely in Tahiti, it gives the appearance of documentary authenticity informed by Flaherty's celebrated ethnographic style depicted in *Nanook of the North* (1922). Focusing on a less idealized Pacific, *White Shadows* initially suspends the cliché-ridden first contact scenarios prevalent in this genre and does away with blackface performance, using instead a large segment of Tahiti's native population. It opens with an indictment of white colonialism in its intertitles, one that is shown nostalgically and mournfully to be inevitable by the film's end: "But the white man, in his greedy trek across the planet, cast his withering shadow over these islands ... And the business of 'civilizing' them to his interests began." Following an initial idyllic tracking shot, a reverse tracking shot suggests regression rather than progress, and focuses with greater close-up detail on disease, chaos, industriousness, and fragmented modern life, "the results of 'civilization.'"

The spectacular and extended tracking sequence also accomplishes a new form of spectator immersion and refers to what film scholar Miriam Hansen calls "a system that assumed the very notion of the spectator as an implicit reference point, functionally comparable to the vanishing point in Renaissance perspective."[19] As such, while critiquing colonialism, the film also erects a more elaborate scopic regime of the colonial gaze and its visual imperialism, one enabling mainland audiences to own these foreign possessions and bearing analogy to the popular 1899 illustrated travelogue volume set, *Our Islands and Their People.*[20] This volume, documenting new territories and cultures in the Pacific, suggests that ownership and settlement of the land is preferable to that of the cultural integration of "their people," a notion that the film reduplicates by presenting native life in a state of decline. Van Dyke's recently discovered journals similarly reveal the director's visceral tropophobia while working in Tahiti, deriding natives as primitive and inferior. As film scholar Jeffrey Geiger notes, "Van Dyke's journal can be seen to unravel the presumption that MGM's *White Shadows* is fundamentally a diatribe against colonial exploitation."[21]

Van Dyke's film highlights this ambivalence of attraction and repulsion, as the Pacific territory is shown to be in disarray and disrupted in its Edenic state. The hero, Matthew Lloyd (Monte Blue), a derelict beachcomber and former medical doctor, is called by the white pearl trader Sebastian "a disgrace to the white race." As he challenges Sebastian's exploitative practices, he is eventually forced off the island and marooned on a yet "untouched island." This change to a new location, shown in the film's warm sepia-toned footage, allows for South Seas fantasies to take up the center of the film, reverting to the formulaic first contact scenario in which the land, its riches, and women are presented as theirs for the taking. Spying on young bathing native beauties, the beachcomber faints and must be revived by them via an administered coconut oil massage *lomilomi,* fulfilling sexual screen fantasies akin to Margaret Mead's influential and controversial anthropological study *Coming of Age in Samoa* (1928) and its presentation of the Pacific as a pornotopia of promiscuous premarital sex.[22]

Viewed as a white god after saving the life a young boy, the protagonist goes native and takes on the name Matta Loa and a native wife, Fayaway, the chief's daughter, played by the light skinned actress Raquel Torres in ethnic cross-dressing. In one scene, the beachcomber gone native is visibly embedded in a local luau ceremony highlighting both his cultural integration and his exceptional position (see Figure 1.2).

Predictably, Matta Loa, who cannot resist his American capitalist fascination with pearls, betrays his Polynesian mistress, and is eventually killed by Sebastian's men. The island idyll is destroyed irreversibly, and the potential interracial marriage is safely aborted before a mixed-race family is formed. Whereas the film may have opened on a critique of colonialism, it ends on divorcing the people from their land

FIGURE 1.2 The beachcomber celebrated at a special feast and receiving the chief's daughter in marriage. Screenshot from *White Shadows*.

and prohibitively puts an end to any serious intimate contact with natives. Told in melodramatic terms, the old Edenic paradise must give way to the new Edenic vision of capitalism, however ruthless it may appear in its practices on the outer borders of the empire. The film's ending repeats the opening tracking shots, showing the so-called untouched island transformed into a colonized and commercially developed space. Subsequent South Seas films by Van Dyke similarly advance this ambivalent critique of colonialism such as in *The Pagan* (1929), where naïve islanders are commercially incompetent and are forced to sell their land for minimal profit, showing the inevitable expansion of superior western capitalism. Retracting the interracial South Seas fantasy altogether in *Never the Twain Shall Meet* (1931), Van Dyke openly mocks the interracial romance and attributes its motivation to the loose morals of the exotic islands, involving promiscuity and drinking.

Beyond the South Seas Genre and the Militarization of the Pacific

During the Depression era when white poverty takes center stage, South Seas fantasies and their transgressive miscegenation plots lose a good deal of their cultural appeal and appear disconnected from the new harsh social realities. Van Dyke's films become more prohibitive on race, following the racial guidelines of the production code articulated in 1930 though not yet fully enforced. His popular *Trader Horn* (1931), an African racial adventure narrative, resembles his earlier *White Shadows* but now places strong emphasis on the dark continent as the antithesis to white civilization. Yet the white perception of the African body also gave reason for concern, as the black body displayed a type of raw masculinity that a sophisticated white civilization had seemingly lost. The history of film is often disconnected from the history of cultural imperialism, making it appear as if only technological innovations are at stake. However, as film scholar Fatimah Tobing Rony points out, Edward Muybridge's nineteenth-century technological breakthrough of chrono-photography, a precursor to cinema, was instantly put to ideological use by French anthropologist Felix Regnault who recorded the gait of African tribe members on display at the Paris World Exhibition in 1895 to study its difference from the western body: "Regnault made his films of West Africans, who were seen as hardier and more agile, not only to confirm notions of western superiority, but in an effort to improve the French military march."[23] The West African body was in this sense idealized as possessing original qualities of health and nobility that had eroded in bodies of western civilization. Western cinema in turn incorporates and ideologically manipulates those images that contradict its Eurocentric storylines.

Van Dyke's *Tarzan The Ape Man* (1932) follows this trajectory, transferring the idealized version of the African body back onto the white body. With an additional modification to Edgar Rice Burroughs's popular novels, the film's narrative further makes its story match the ambitions of American imperialism. The British colonial body is now depicted as decadent and Tarzan's white indigenous African body serves as the model of the healthy and normative body. In casting Olympic US gold medalist swimmer Johnny Weissmuller as king of the jungle, this superior body is coded as American and annexes the colonial power from the declining British empire. Compared with the beachcomber protagonist of 1920s South Seas fantasies, an example of an unhealthy and alcoholic western dropout, the *Tarzan* series strikes a new assertive and confident tone of US imperialism in the 1930s.

The South Seas genre would continue throughout the 1930s with films such as King Vidor's *Bird of Paradise* (1932) with its racy nude underwater photography of Dolores del Rio provided by celebrated cinematographer Clyde de Vinna. Having worked with Van Dyke on *White Shadows,* de Vinna understood that spectacular underwater cinematography was the South Seas' equivalent to the panoramic and monumental Western landscape. Nevertheless, with the aggressive imperialist expansion of Japan in the Pacific, the genre's romantic focus appeared increasingly out of touch with the tougher 1930s Depression era and the looming military threat in the Asia-Pacific. The popular Hawaiian Chinese detective Charlie Chan (played by Warner Oland in yellowface) emerges prominently in 1931 in *Charlie Chan Carries On* (lost) and *The Black Camel*. The latter film, featuring the spectacular Royal Hawaiian Hotel in an on-location Honolulu production, shows the beachcomber as obsolete – he is murdered in a subplot that is only tangentially relevant to the overall story – and presents a thoroughly modern and contemporary Hawai'i ruled by a segregated white elite, anticipating the end of the South Seas fantasy. The Chan series, though seriously tainted by racist stereotypes, was intended to promote a more progressive image of Asians and Asian Americans, particularly appealing to the Chinese with whom the US sought alliance against Japan.[24]

Lewis Milestone's *Rain* (1932) in turn foregrounds the military as the new guardian of South Pacific native life and devalues the outdated missionary presence in conflict with its hypocritical attitude towards sexuality. The musical *Flirtation Walk* (1934) militarizes the South Seas genre further by focusing on a West Point military cadet stationed in Honolulu and finding romance with a white mainland girl against the backdrop of Hawaiian entertainment, now fully implementing the PCA code prohibiting interracial romance which could still be shown as a family subplot in *Rain*. The self-aware romantic comedy *Waikiki Wedding* (1937) presents the South Seas genre as a staged tourist hoax and focuses instead on the conversion of Hawai'i's pineapple industry to the newly emerging industry of mass tourism and advertising, starring Hawai'i as a tropical backdrop for white heterosexual love stories that usually end in marriage. John Ford's dark and ominous *Hurricane* (1937) predicts the genre's demise in a tale of destruction, systemic racial violence, and the melodramatic attempt of a Polynesian family seeking to survive a typhoon.

The Pearl Harbor bombing finally suspends this form of fantasy engagement with the Pacific and instead transforms it into another fantasy, the spectacle of war, with Hollywood producing what film scholar Jeanine Basinger calls an entirely new form of the war genre, the combat film. This genre, inaugurated by the multiracial/ethnic Pacific combat film *Bataan* (1943), breaks with traditional war film and, according to Basinger, does away with the distinction between war and the home front. In doing so, the genre evokes incessant combat as the new reality and attempts to do away with non-democratic representation via its fantasy creation and utopian vision of a multiracial/ethnic combat team.[25] The depiction of the South Pacific would subsequently never fully depart from this World War II context, reframing settlement in military rather than civilian terms. To be sure, Hawai'i would become representative of the military industrial complex, intertwining war, tourism, R&R, business, and the military entertainment complex. Films such as *Blue Hawaii* (1961) or the popular TV series *Hawaii Five-O* (1968–1980) made certain that the perception of Hawai'i and the Pacific never strays too far from its military reality as a geopolitical outpost of the US empire.

Cinema's Camouflage of the Militarization of the Pacific

South Pacific (1958, dir. Joshua Logan; music Richard Rodgers and Oscar Hammerstein), filmed in glorious technicolor and super widescreen format shot on Todd-AO camera, represents a high production value synthesis of the many variations of the South Seas genre that eventually found itself revived in the Pacific combat film. Various color filters were used for special effects, giving the film a hallucinatory quality, highlighting its mystical island Bali Ha'i, which deceptively mirrors the fantasies of US military personnel serving in the Pacific theater. As a musical, this postwar film seeks to decommission the harsher military elements of the Pacific combat genre, returning the nation to peacetime normality, one sustained by a strong US military presence at the periphery of its empire. The film revisits the question of race that, since the 1930s, had been contained in the South Seas genre, and that curiously emerged again in the multicultural combat genre designed to rally support for the war from all racial and ethnic groups in the US. The question of intermarriage is once again at stake and now sanctioned in the new spirit of the civil rights era. This concession, however, is not made without also apologetically letting the former European colonizers off the hook, as they now become the progressive vanguard of racial intermarriage. In practical terms, the film addresses the military reality of overseas war brides and interracial relationships that compromise mainland racial codes.

In the post-World War II era, the US drastically increases its military presence in the Pacific, incorporating multiple island archipelagos in addition to the already owned territories of Hawai'i , Guam, and Samoa. Military bases in the Philippines and wars in Korea and eventually Vietnam show an aggressive expansion explained as necessary outposts in the Cold War constellation. Hawai'i has since become the headquarters of the US Pacific Command, comprising the Army, Navy, Marine Corps, and Air Force. A large military population residing on Oahu and numerous military installations have significantly changed the appearance of this former tropical paradise. As political scientists Kathy Ferguson and Phyllis Turnbull note, the military in Hawai'i "hides in plain sight": "Everywhere you look in Hawai'i, you see the military. Yet in daily life relatively few people in Hawai'i see the military at all."[26] *South Pacific*, a militarized South Seas musical, points to the widespread presence of the military industrial complex as a new social reality. In similar fashion, Pacific combat films seamlessly transition to postwar military comedies (e.g. John Ford's *Mister Roberts*, 1955; or *Donovan's Reef*, 1963), normalizing the military and its ubiquitous presence as an everyday reality of American life. The image of John Wayne captures this fluid spectrum that ranges from South Seas fantasy (*Wake of the Red Witch*, 1948), Western (*Stagecoach*, 1939), and Pacific combat film (*Back to Bataan*, 1945) to postwar military comedies (*Donovan's Reef*), with Wayne starring prominently in all these genres and making settler colonialism a national norm.

Conclusion

Working in tandem with other film genres, the South Seas genre contributes to a propaganda effect of advocated US exceptionalism, Manifest Destiny, and settler colonialism. As a genre, it also quickly adapted to the condition of war, morphing into the Pacific combat genre and eventually downplaying its militarism in postwar military comedies. Notable other genres in this joint effort are the domestic Southern plantation genre promoting historical amnesia that ignored, in particular, the violence of slavery; the Western genre and its distorted national history of conquest; the racial adventure genre highlighting eugenics and the superior white body; and the combat film, in which a temporary war engagement is turned into the national spectacle of permanent war fought by a fictionalized multicultural combat team. Hollywood systemically participated in the colonization of the South Pacific and in nation building from the moment of its birth as the major mass medium of national articulation, providing a visual vocabulary of conquest as entertainment and legitimating the nation's history of settler colonialism as its pre-ordained purpose.

Notes

1 See my discussion of these shorts in *Hollywood's Hawaii: Race, Nation, and War* (New Brunswick, NJ: Rutgers University Press, 2017), 11–16.
2 Max Weber, *The Protestant Ethic and the Spirit of Capitalism*, trans. Talcott Parsons (New York: Dover, 2003; 1958), 163.
3 Emily S. Rosenberg, *Spreading the American Dream: Economic and Cultural Expansionism 1890–1945* (New York: Hill & Wang, 1982), chap. 2 "Capitalists, Christians, Cowboys," 14–38.
4 Rosenberg, *Spreading the American Dream*, 15.
5 Rosenberg, *Spreading the American Dream*, 35.
6 Paul Virilio, *The Vision Machine*, trans. Julie Rose (London, Bloomington, IN: BFI Publishing and Indiana University Press, 1994). It is important to recall here that the eventual overthrow of Hawai'i's kingdom was paved with the help of the United States Marines, leading to its Bayonet Constitution in 1887, forcing King Kalakaua to transfer much of the kingdom's authority to the American settler elites.
7 As I have shown in the first comprehensive book-length study on Hollywood's Hawai'i , this cinematic colonization of the periphery of the American empire is systematic and deliberate rather than sporadic or accidental in nature. See *Hollywood's Hawaii*.
8 See H. E. Maude, "Beachcombers and Castaways," *The Journal of the Polynesian Society*, 73, no. 3 (1964), 254–293; Martin Zelenietz and David Kravitz, "Absorption, Trade and Warfare: Beachcombers on Ponape, 1830–1854," *Ethnohistory*, 21, no. 3 (1974), 223–249; Thomas Bargatzky, "Beachcombers and Castaways as Innovators," *Journal of Pacific History*, 15, no. 2 (1980), 93–102.
9 Zelenietz and Kravitz, "Absorption, Trade and Warfare," 236.
10 Zelenietz and Kravitz, "Absorption, Trade and Warfare," 241.
11 See Thomas Doherty, *Pre-Code Hollywood: Sex, Immorality, and Insurrection in American Cinema, 1930–1934* (New York: Columbia University Press, 1999).
12 Ellen C. Scott, *Cinema Civil Rights: Regulation, Repression, and Race in the Classical Hollywood Era* (New Brunswick, NJ; Rutgers University Press, 2015), 13.
13 Cedric J. Robinson, *Forgeries of Memory and Meaning: Blacks and the Regime of Race in American Theater and Film before World War II* (Chapel Hill, NC: University of North Carolina Press, 2007), 180–181.
14 See Gary Y. Okihiro, *Pineapple Culture: A History of Tropical and Temperate Zones* (Berkeley: University of California Press, 2009) 18.
15 "Aloha 'Oe" is a composition by Hawai'i's last Queen Lili'uokalani and has become the island's unofficial anthem.
16 Gilles Deleuze, *Cinema I: The Movement-Image*, trans. Hugh Tomlinson and Barbara Habberjam (Minneapolis: University of Minnesota Press, 1986), 148.
17 Konzett, *Hollywood's Hawaii*, 21–22.
18 Drake Stutesman, "The Silent Screen, 1895–1927," in *Costume, Makeup, and Hair*, Adrienne L. McLean, ed. (New Brunswick, NJ: Rutgers University Press, 2016), 34.
19 Miriam Hansen, *Babel & Babylon: Spectatorship in American Silent Film* (Cambridge, MA: Harvard University Press, 1991), 81.
20 *Our Islands and Their People as Seen with Camera and Pencil*, William S. Bryan, ed. (New York: N.D. Thompson Publishing Co., 1899). For a discussion of this volume set that sold over 400 000 copies upon its release, see Jane C. Desmond's *Staging Tourism: Bodies on Display from Waikiki to Sea World* (Chicago: University of Chicago Press, 1999), 49.

21 Jeffrey Geiger, *Facing the Pacific: Polynesia and the US Imperial Imagination* (Honolulu: University of Hawai'i Press, 2007), 161. Concerning Van Dyke's journals, see Geiger's section "Troppophobia," 168–173.

22 See Derek Freeman, *Margaret Mead and Samoa: The Making and Unmaking of an Anthropological Myth* (Cambridge: Harvard University Press, 1983). Freeman refutes Mead's classic work on adolescent sexuality in Samoa with its seemingly simple sexual freedom, arguing instead that Mead's work upheld Western anthropological theory and misrepresented reality. Freeman's work sparked intense debate about Mead's study and the discipline of anthropology that continues today.

23 Fatimah Tobing Rony, *The Third Eye: Race, Cinema, and Ethnographic Spectacle* (Durham, NC: Duke University Press, 1996), 42.

24 Delia Malia Konzett, "Yellowface, Minstrelsy, and Hollywood Happy Endings: *The Black Camel* (1931), *Charlie Chan in Egypt* (1935), and *Charlie Chan at the Olympics* (1937)," in *Hollywood at the Intersection of Race and Identity*, Delia Malia Konzett, ed. (New Brunswick, NJ: Rutgers University Press, 2019), 84–102.

25 See Jeanine Basinger, *The World War II Combat Film: Anatomy of a Genre* (New York: Columbia University Press, 1986).

26 Kathy E. Ferguson and Phyllis Turnbull, *Oh, Say Can you See? The Semiotics of the Military in Hawai'i* (Minneapolis: University of Minnesota Press, 1999), xiii.

2

ENVIRONMENTS OF SETTLER COLONIALISM IN STATEHOOD-ERA U.S. CINEMATIC DEPICTIONS OF THE HAWAIIAN ISLANDS

Lawrence H. Kessler

The natural environment looms large in settler colonial narratives of the American West, as an object fraught with danger but also laden with potential for pleasure and profit. Nature acts as an obstacle to settlement in stories of pioneers who had to subdue and conquer the frontier. But nature is also the object of settlers' desire: the promised land of Manifest Destiny flowing with riches and offering settlers an easier life. If this may seem paradoxical, it is because environmental conditions and non-human nature—plants, animals, and microbes, especially—operate beyond human control. Elements of the natural environment have acted in ways that sometimes helped and sometimes hindered settler colonialism in the West.[1]

Much like the continental American West, the environment of the Hawaiian Islands has captivated many white Americans since the late eighteenth century, when the first published reports regarding the islands reached the United States.[2]

Over the course of the nineteenth century, as "haole" (literally "foreigners;" by the mid-nineteenth century, "white people") from the United States became increasingly entrenched in the islands and their affairs, American interest in the islands' environment grew as well. Shortly after the overthrow of the Hawaiian monarchy by haole sugarcane planters and businessmen in 1893, and the subsequent U.S. annexation of Hawai'i five years later, Americans on the mainland could turn to the medium of film to glimpse the natural splendor of this latest U.S. possession. As film scholar Delia Malia Konzett notes, filmmakers were infatuated with Hawai'i's natural environment from the earliest days of the medium.[3] At the turn of the twentieth century, film shorts typically depicted Kānaka Maoli (Indigenous Hawaiians) diving for coins and paddling wa'a (boats similar to canoes). They also showed workers cutting sugarcane and loading it onto carts. In all, the marine and agricultural environments were crucial not only to cinematic representations of the islands, but to U.S. plans for Hawai'i as a port for naval and commercial vessels, as well as a draw for leisure activities, and for the production of agricultural commodities unable to thrive on mainland U.S. soil.

Scholars including Konzett, Gary Okihiro, and Robert Schmitt have examined the depictions and uses of Hawai'i in American cinema, with specific attention to the ways that Hollywood constructed particular visions of the islands that supported the U.S. occupation.[4] This essay builds on previous work by foregrounding the active role that environmental factors play in cinematic narratives about Hawai'i, with particular attention to films produced in the aftermath of Hawai'i's 1959 statehood. As Hawai'i became a state in the American Union, cinema afforded American mainlanders the opportunity to glimpse a land that, despite its geographic distance, cultural difference, and history of conquest and occupation, was now part of the union. In the eyes of mainlanders, films such as *Blue Hawaii* (dir. Norman Taurog, 1961), *Diamond Head* (dir. Guy Green, 1962), and *Hawaii* (dir. George Roy Hill, 1966), helped transform Hawai'i's nature from an alluring but sometimes dangerous and exotic environment to something tamed for settlement, agricultural production, and leisure. By focusing on cinematic depictions of non-human natural actors and conditions, this essay explores how the above-mentioned three films present a settler colonial narrative of white Americans replacing Kānaka Maoli, dominating a foreign environment, and creating a contrived island paradise for white land barons and tourists.

The settler colonial narrative, however, is hardly monolithic in these films. Although they reify U.S. conquest of Hawai'i, they also challenge settler colonialism as an interpretive model for understanding the history of Hawai'i. From the unpredictability of disease agents to the persistence of Kānaka Maoli who maintained agency in the face of haole dominance, to pockets of nature that remain stubbornly unconquered, these films point to ways that settler colonialism as a project remained contested. These examples suggest anxiety and ambivalence within these films over the consequences, for both Hawaiians and haole, of settler colonization and conquest.

After a brief synopsis of the films, this essay discusses non-human agency in the case of disease introductions, and ways in which the films display attempts to overcome and control the natural environment. It also examines the production of idealized landscapes for leisure consumption, and finally ways in which the films depict a natural environment resistant to settler impositions. I argue that these films show an ambiguous narrative of settler triumph, uncertainty, and fear. Control over nature and indigenous peoples empowers the settler state, but also seems fleeting, leading to vulnerabilities. This ambiguity suggests that the settler notion of environmental control and replacement remained more an aspiration—a fantasy—than reality. By portraying an environment that remained resistant to settlers' attempts at control, these films reveal the limits of the settler colonial project.

The Films

Hawai'i's transition from U.S. territory to statehood in 1959 might suggest a kind of fulfillment of the American settler colonial project in the islands. However, in some important ways, statehood created greater need for a settler colonial narrative that Americans could accept. Mainland whites needed to get to know Hawai'i as a place that fitted their conception of the Union. U.S. territories such as Guam and Puerto Rico could remain outside the bounds of this understanding as geographically remote, populated with people of color, and, most importantly for this essay, composed of exotic flora and fauna. They remained outside the settler colonial nationhood and unity, but Hawai'i did not. Its inclusion as a state required rhetorical differentiation from these other exotic island territories. It demanded a discussion of the ways that haole settlers had rendered Hawai'i more similar to the mainland, both culturally and ecologically.

Films of the 1960s helped introduce Hawai'i to mainlanders who often had no idea of what Hawai'i was like. Although more and more Americans could visit Hawai'i in person as travel became increasingly accessible, film presented another means of getting to know the islands for those masses who could not travel.

Hawaii, an adaptation of part of James Michener's epic 1959 novel, follows the life of Abner Hale (Max von Sydow), a devout member of an early-nineteenth-century Protestant mission to Hawai'i based on the American Board of Commissioners for Foreign Missions (ABCFM). Fictionalized though the story may be, Abner's character and the events that transpire in the film borrow heavily from actual events. After working to convince Jerusha (Julie Andrews), a religiously like-minded New England woman to marry him (the ABCFM sent married couples on missions to model its ideals of family behavior and to prevent sex between missionaries and Kānaka Maoli), Abner, Jerusha, and several other missionaries make the arduous ocean voyage to the Hawaiian Islands. Stationed in Lāhainā, Maui, Abner demonstrates unbending religious absolutism bordering on zealotry. While Jerusha and several other missionaries stationed at different locations around the islands attempt to show Kānaka Maoli a loving God, Abner's message is one of damnation for anyone who strays slightly from the path of piety. Abner's career is met with tragedy, including the untimely deaths of Jerusha and many others. Ultimately, the successful church Abner has managed to build after decades of work is taken away from him, as the mission leaders find his dogmatism and irascibility to be bothersome and incongruent with the more comfortable and acquisitive position they have taken in Hawaiian society.

Blue Hawaii and *Diamond Head* are both set in the years immediately following statehood. In the comedy *Blue Hawaii*, Chad Gates (Elvis Presley) returns to Honolulu after two years in Europe with the U.S. Army. The film plays to Elvis's embodiment of a new generation rejecting the conservative mores of its predecessor: Chad's parents want him to take a job in his father's plantation business, the Southern Hawaiian Fruit Company, but Chad insists on making his own way. He rejects his parents' efforts to have him join Hawai'i's white planter class, and instead maintains relations with his disreputable but good-natured brown-skinned friends and French–Hawaiian girlfriend, Maile Duval (Joan Blackman). Chad finds alternative employment as a tour guide with Maile's employer, and is hired by a mainland schoolteacher with four teenage schoolgirls in tow. After a series of comic misadventures through Oahu and Kaua'i, Chad redeems himself and satisfies his parents by founding his own tourism business catering particularly to corporate tourism, including the mainland employees of the Southern Hawaiian Fruit Company.

Diamond Head takes a more dramatic and tragic view of the planter class in Hawai'i. Loosely based on a 1960 novel by Peter Gilman, *Diamond Head* tells the story of Big Island planter Richard "King" Howland (Charleton Heston) and his younger sister, Sloane (Yvette Mimieux). King and Sloane are the last of a hundred-year planter family dynasty looking to the future. Sloane wants to marry Paul Kahana (James Darren), a Kanaka Maoli, but King is adamantly opposed to miscegenation, even though he hypocritically has a Chinese mistress, Mai Chen (France Nuyen). King, however, is forced to confront his beliefs about race when Mai Chen becomes pregnant, and he eventually accepts his mixed-race son and his sister's mixed-race relationship.

None of these films are directly or overtly concerned with the natural environment; human interactions and relations are at the center of each plot. Yet issues involving nature are hiding in plain sight throughout the films, and ecological factors play a crucial role in their stories. Collectively, these films display settler colonial attitudes toward Hawai'i's natural environment in the aftermath of statehood: infatuation with, but also anxiety over exotic (to the mainlander) tropical environments; questions regarding the influence of tropical nature for the transplantation white settler society; and an underlying interest in acquisition and exploitation of natural resources through integration in the colonial economy. Each of these films also touches on Hawai'i's pervasive plantation system: *Hawaii* addresses its founding through missionary family land acquisitions, while *Blue Hawaii* and *Diamond Head* focus on the plantation system of the early 1960s and a white planter class entrenched at the top of Hawai'i's social hierarchy but integrated into mainland white society as well. Calling forth the history of haole appropriation and disciplining of nature for export commodity production, the films point to the centrality of Hawai'i's ecology to Hawai'i-U.S. relations.

Disease Agents or Agents of Colonialism?

One of the most important changes foreign visitors and settlers alike brought on Hawai'i was the introduction of new diseases. The outcome proved devastating to the Kānaka Maoli population. Foreigners introduced smallpox, sexually transmitted infections, measles, and many other afflictions. These pathogens were part of what historian Alfred Crosby called the "portmanteau biota" of European colonists and imperialists: biological agents that had opportunities to expand their biotic ranges along with human travel.[5] The late eighteenth and early nineteenth centuries saw waves of epidemics course through Indigenous Hawaiian communities as foreign visitors inaugurated a new era of ecological exchange to an archipelago protected from such pathogens by the vastness of the surrounding Pacific Ocean. Estimates of population decline vary widely but suggest a drop from approximately 500,000 persons in 1778, at the time of first contact with Europeans, to 130,000 in 1831 and 47,000 in 1878. Disease-borne social disruption was a factor as great or greater than any organized settler colonial policy in the colonization of the Hawaiian Islands.[6]

There is no evidence that the devastation of Hawai'i through microbes was in any way deliberate, and some visitors even attempted to limit the introduction of foreign pathogens. As historian Andrew Isenberg and I have argued elsewhere, settlers were often the beneficiaries of biological exchange over which they had little control.[7] Disease, however, became part of the settler colonial narrative. Missionaries under the auspices of the Boston-based ABCFM, who began settling in Hawai'i in the 1820s, wrote with concern over the decline of the Kanaka Maoli population, but occasionally wondered if it was part of a divine plan to aid white settlement.[8] Later, popular U.S. writers romanticized the seemingly futile struggle of Kanaka Maoli against disease. In early-twentieth-century stories such as "Koolau the Leper" (1912), Jack London valorized the title character who struggled not only with Hansen's Disease, but with the draconian, often racist, public health policies that exiled afflicted Hawaiians to the leper colony of Moloka'i.[9]

Similar notions of hopelessness and inevitability regarding the demise of the Hawaiian population appear in Hill's *Hawaii*. Yet the film also claims that Hawai'i was a pristine, Edenic environment before the arrival of foreigners. After an outbreak of measles in Lāhainā, missionary physician John Whipple (Gene Hackman) laments, "When Captain Cook discovered these islands 50 years ago, they were a true paradise. Infectious disease was unknown. They didn't even catch cold! And there were 400,000 of them—now there are less than 150,000. You and I may well live to see the last Hawaiian lowered into his grave—with proper Christian services, of course." Whipple at once acknowledges the deadly consequences of the introduction of disease, essentializes the Hawaiian environment as a static Paradise, and highlights the irony of religious missions that had greater interest in the spiritual rather than physical wellbeing of the people they professed to want to save.

For some white settlers in the nineteenth century, Hawaiian depopulation was often a tragic inevitability, but one that gave them license to inherit the land as they saw weaker peoples receding in the face of white expansion.[10] Indeed, the Judeo-Christian value of making land agriculturally productive, expressed in the Protestant tenet of "improvement" as a way of putting land to its intended use and thereby demonstrating the right to ownership, was common in British and Anglo-American appropriation of Indigenous lands throughout the New World.[11] This reflects a tortured, brutal conceit of the place of nature in the settler colonial narrative: environmental change that settlers benefitted from provides the rationale for conquest and expropriation of land from Indigenous People. *Hawaii* lays this bare in its tragic conclusion. By the end of the film, Abner Hale, now old, frail, and alone among his missionary brethren in his enduring commitment to pious asceticism, finds he cannot come to grips with a missionary cohort that is looking to capitalize on its position in Hawaiian society and start acquiring land. He complains to Rev. Immanuel Quigley (John Cullum), the mission's leader, "We are taking the land of the people whose souls we came to save, while they are dying ... The whole race is dying before our eyes!" Quigley responds, "I'm afraid that is true. But the Lord's ways are not our ways. And the only answer that I can find is that perhaps, the Lord intends for these islands gradually to pass into other hands." Absolving himself of responsibility, Quigley finds in disease a sort of divine sanction for the conquest of the islands.

The dichotomy between the notion of a pristine Eden before the arrival of whites and that of a place despoiled by whites' incursion fails to acknowledge the contingency of the movement of pathogens, which did not operate according to the whims of settlers. Yet it also supports the settler narrative that Indigenous Hawaiians were not strong enough to resist or withstand haole colonialism. The consequences of this are suggested through important absences in *Blue Hawaii* and *Diamond Head*. Although both films feature Hawaiian and part-Hawaiian characters, neither has an intact Hawaiian nuclear family. Indeed, only one non-white adult male, Dean Kahana (George Chakiris) has a significant role, and he is explicitly regarded as hapa haole (half white and half Hawaiian). Maile Duvall has a Kānaka Maoli mother and a French father; Paul Kahana's father is absent from the film. Both films feature a strong Hawaiian matriarch who laments the disappearance of her people. The implication that adult Kānaka Maoli men had disappeared from Hawai'i fits with similar notions of feminized foreign populations waiting for white American men to fill the void.[12]

Overcoming Nature

With the settler narrative transforming the agency of microbes into providential license to occupy Native land, haole settlers could set to work dominating nature to construct a replica of mainland society. Statehood-era films like the three examined in this essay depict the triumph of haole over nature to be held in contrast with Indigenous closeness to nature. Calling forth persistent tropes of claiming land by putting it to use and "improving" it, films show natural environments being remade to suit haole purposes.

Hawaii, for instance, depicts the gradual convergence of Lāhainā with built environments from New England. The film's early scenes create a counterpoint of idyllic, verdant landscapes in Hawai'i contrasted with gray winter scenes in the missionaries' homeland. The contrast is made starker by the inclusion in the New England scenes of horses, cows, sheep, and dogs, all quadrupeds that were absent from Hawai'i until Euro-Americans brought them to the islands in the late eighteenth century. The distance between Hawai'i and New England, figurative as well as geographic, is also emphasized by the film's depiction of the missionaries' harrowing, six-month ocean voyage from Boston to Hawai'i via Cape Horn. Similar to wagon train voyages featured in movie Westerns, the perils of the natural world test the mettle of settlers and serve to emphasize the risks inherent in settlers' move away from the colonial homeland.[13]

As Abner Hale and his fellow missionaries settle Lahaina, they transform it from a village of "hale" (thatched grass single-room structures) to a western-style town with wood and stone buildings. Hale's church occupies many buildings over the course of the film, first a grass house like those of the Hawaiians, but as Abner builds his congregation and power, and his settlement takes root, he builds an imposing stone house of worship, with walls, he boasts, two feet thick. In an ambivalent suggestion of the tragedy of replacing the Kānaka Maoli, Abner tells a fellow missionary that he leaves the windows of the building open, to catch the breezes that his Hawaiian congregants say hold the spirits of deceased ali'i. But, Abner notes wistfully, there are no ali'i left. The stone church presents an enduring reminder of foreign impositions onto Hawaiian land.

By the statehood era depicted in *Blue Hawaii* and *Diamond Head*, white Hawai'i is thoroughly modern, with Western technology available to help haole overcome nature. Flashy cars and airplanes are prominently featured in both *Blue Hawaii* and *Diamond Head*, where they serve to compress the distances and dangers of travel that were symbolically and materially crucial to the divide between perceived civilization and frontier in the eighteenth and nineteenth centuries. *Blue Hawaii's* Chad and Maile drive around downtown Honolulu and Waikiki in a bright red 1960 MG roadster; later they and the "malihini" (newcomer) tourists they are guiding drive and fly easily to different tourist destinations. Similarly, King and Sloane Howland fly back and forth between Oahu and Hawai'i Island, and Sloane races around in a Jaguar coupe. Settler haole have compressed the distances and dangers of travel that were part of missionary settlers' real and symbolic movement from perceived civilization to frontier.

The compression of distances and development of a built environment in the mold of the United States were significant, but the most drastic way that haole settlement transformed Hawai'i's environment was through the establishment of a plantation system that pervaded Hawai'i's land and economy. By the turn of the twentieth century, sugarcane plantations covered over 250,000 acres across the islands and accounted for over ninety percent of the Hawaiian economy.[14] *Hawaii* notes the portentous decision of the missionaries to adopt sugarcane planting. As the mission leader notes, "It is felt that the time has come for our missions to become self-supporting, to that end we voted to authorize our members to invest in plantation lands and sugar mills and to operate them also if they have the skill." This was based on actual events in the late 1830s, when ABCFM missionaries, struggling to support themselves, turned to commercial agriculture.[15]

While *Hawaii* only references the adoption of plantation agriculture, it is central to the plots of *Blue Hawaii* and *Diamond Head*. Both the Gates family of *Blue Hawaii* and the Howland family of *Diamond Head* are in the plantation business, though the Gateses are relative newcomers and the Howlands' plantation has been in the family for a century. Both films also provide imagery of the plantations that evoke a domination of nature for orderly production. In *Blue Hawaii*, one of the first destinations Chad Gates takes his tourist charges to is a pineapple plantation, where anonymous female workers feed an industrial combine, and the tourists enjoy fresh-picked pineapple in the field, the literal fruits of settler's appropriation of Hawaiian land for agricultural production.

The plantation is even more crucial to the plot of *Diamond Head*. Richard Howland is the last man in a hundred-year dynasty of haole land barons. His nickname is "King," and he acts like one on his Big Island plantation. When he and his sister, Sloane, fly in their private plane from Oahu to the Big Island, she asks who owns the ocean; King responds, "the fish, but we're gaining on them." The Howlands' plantation is orderly and industrialized: a large manor house boasts carefully tended gardens and two stately rows of imposing palm trees. Industrial plantation equipment dots scenes of cane fields, and King rides on an imposing white horse as he surveys his estate. Nature on the Howland plantation is disciplined to Howland's requirements for production.

Paradise Contrived

While plantations drove Hawai'i's economy and the U.S. conquest of the islands in the nineteenth century, as statehood dawned, leisure travel was a quickly growing economic power and a significant factor in introducing Hawai'i to mainland Americans. By the 1960s, Hawai'i's natural environments were sites for leisure, escape, and enactment of South Seas fantasies. As the narrator of *Blue Hawaii*'s film trailer intones, Elvis "is your guide to America's exotic Eden, our Polynesian Paradise." The image in Figure 2.1 shows Chad and Maile at the iconic Tantalus Lookout (Puʻu Ualakaʻa

FIGURE 2.1 Screenshot of Chad Gates (Elvis Presley) and Maile Duval (Joan Blackman) in *Blue Hawaii* (1961).

State Park). Perched above Honolulu, with a view of the Manoa Valley and the Pacific Ocean, Chad and Maile can enjoy the view while escape the city below. Chad also has a beach shack on a secluded strip of sand, a place where he goes to avoid his parents and their demand for him to get a job. Instead, at the shack he can enjoy time with Maile and his Hawaiian beach bum friends, of whom his mother disapproves. The beach shack provides an opportunity, as Delia Konzett notes, for Chad to go native, swimming, surfing, boating, and singing.[16] It is also remote from the bustle of Honolulu; the frenetic pace of the roadster speeding through the built-up city gives way to an idyllic setting of sand, sea, and palm trees.

Like Chad, Sloane Howland also flees to a beach, although in this case it is to escape the tragedy and conflict that have marred her previously happy existence. Sloane runs away to the beaches of Waikīkī, where she drinks and tries to forget her troubles. Mingling with tourists, Sloane attempts to buy into the tourist fantasy sold to so many vacationers: that they can leave the real world behind as they enjoy a tropical paradise. This belies the fact that Waikīkī itself is actually artifice. The Ala Wai Canal, built in 1928, dredged wetlands and rice paddies to create the modern resort district of Waikīkī.

In fact, both *Blue Hawaii* and *Diamond Head* demonstrate disdain for tourists and the malihini conception of Hawaiian nature. Sloane cannot find peace at the hotel bar, and drinks herself sick. Similar excess is evident in *Blue Hawaii*. At a hotel hula show, performers in obviously plastic grass skirts entertain guests, while drunk and obnoxious tourists from Oklahoma cause disruptions. The negative image of tourists and the contrived version of nature that they consume in Hawai'i is echoed by Chad's mother, who exclaims, "tourists aren't people! They're … they're tourists!" These tourists are offered in distinction to the Gateses and Howlands, who have, through their colonization internalized native identities.

The artificial, superficial idea of nature sold to most mainland tourists is contrasted with Chad Gates's tours, which take his charges to a working plantation and an evening hukilau (seine-fishing party), in which they join Chad's Hawaiian friends in some seemingly authentic Hawaiian fun and entertainment, where they can act the part of what historian Philip Deloria called "Playing Indian."[17] Chad also takes his tourist clients to the more secluded island of Kaua'i, where they can ride horses and find isolated beaches. By the end of the film, Chad establishes his own tourist agency, arguing that no one knows the islands better than he does, so he is the person most qualified to provide mainland tourists with genuine experiences of Hawai'i. The film offers a message that haole settlers can replace Kānaka Maoli, or at least join them to become kama'āina (literally people of the land; established residents), and thus have access to a more authentic Hawai'i.

Hawaiian Nature Untamed

The conceit of the haole settler becoming naturalized within the Hawaiian environment, however, does not withstand scrutiny. Even established settlers such as Chad Gates and King Howland are not at home in Hawaiʻi's natural environment. Even with the establishment of Protestant congregations, plantations, and luxury hotels, Hawaiʻi's natural environment still presented a daunting challenge to settler control. White settlers saw tropical environments in ambivalent terms, as places that were rich in potential but also in risk. The tropics were over-abundant, in contrast to the perceived balanced environments of temperate climates. What historian Karen Ordhal Kuperman characterized as the "fear of hot climates," as well as a broader fear that tropical nature would cause settlers to revert from civilized to savage, introduced an element of risk to the settler colonial narrative.[18] Being colonists meant becoming subject to a more potent nature.

For the missionaries of *Hawaii*, their commitment meant subjecting themselves to unhealthy, menacing nature. When Rafer Hoxworth (Richard Harris), the captain of a whaler who was once romantically entangled with Jerusha Hale, sees Jerusha and Abner's grass hale, he is aghast, and worries that living so close to nature will destroy his former lover. After years pass, Hoxworth returns to the Hales with a gift for Jerusha: a house constructed and then disassembled in New England, with instructions for rebuilding the house in Lāhainā. Hoxworth presents the gift to Abner Hale, only to learn that Jerusha has already died. Exposure to nature and missionary labor without the comforts of civilization were too destructive for her white female constitution.

Jerusha is not the only settler haole to be exposed to mortal danger in these films. In a story recounted but not depicted in *Diamond Head*, a tsunami kills King Howland's wife and three-year-old son, extinguishing the Howland dynasty and, as with Jerusha, demonstrating the dangers of colonialism to those who lack the proper masculinity. This episode of potent environmental agency serves as a reminder that, though settlers may subdue nature to a large extent with orderly plantations and tourist attractions, they cannot completely neutralize the threat of untamed nature.

Hawaiian nature holds another risk for white settlers: the danger of being overwhelmed and losing one's sense of civilization, whiteness, and propriety. In contrast with King's ordered garden and his walled-off study, the home of his Chinese mistress, Mai Chen, features a "lānai" (veranda) teeming with tropical plants that hang so far over the railing that they appear as though they might invade the house. This is the place where King loses restraint and gives in to his passion, with tropical nature defying the order of the rest of his life. Similarly, Sloane Howland's formative encounter with one of her Hawaiian love interests is in a forest pool, untamed by haole settlement. Sloane's scandalous relationships with both Kānaka Maoli and hapa haole men, as well as Chad's relationship with hapa haole Maile despite his mother's disapproval, also serve as reminders that Kānaka Maoli were never fully eliminated and replaced on the land, as the settler colonial framework suggests, but rather endure, and threaten to transform the settlers who become entangled with them.

Finally, *Diamond Head's* denouement comes when King, overwhelmed by the familial drama that has consumed his life, frantically rides his horse into the untamed forest bordering his plantation. He rides recklessly and aimlessly, nearly overwhelmed by the forest that surrounds him, and only stops when he comes to a clearing and sees the Big Island stretched out below him. The view brings him back to his senses. At last he seems to clearly see Hawai'i in its variegated entirety, with plantation fields and forests bounded by the same ocean, and accepts his mixed-race son and perhaps a more enlightened place in multiracial Hawai'i.

Conclusion

In these films, nature is not only scenery but also an actor in itself; it is something that characters both act in and interact with. The environment is very much a contested one. These films highlight how settler power remains incomplete in the face of environmental factors such as disease, and how, despite the success of haole in transforming Hawai'i's environments into sites of agricultural production and leisure, untamed nature persisted as a threatening Indigenous space. They capture a broader interest in a narrative of domesticating exotic environments, as well as anxiety over such a project.

With statehood completed, these films point to the fact that differences endured between Hawai'i and the continental United States. The difference of Hawai'i's environment from that of the mainland, and its importance to both the history of Hawai'i-U.S. relations and the themes of cinematic infatuation with the islands serves as a reminder that scholars of settler colonialism would do well to consider the role of the nature and account for environmental agency in their analyses.

Notes

1 On the interaction of human societies and non-human agency, especially as it pertains to the North American West and Pacific region, see Timothy J. LeCain, *The Matter of History: How Things Create the Past* (Cambridge: Cambridge University Press, 2017); Richard White, *The Organic Machine: The Remaking of the Columbia River* (New York: Hill and Wang, 1995).
2 On the question of locating Hawai'i as part of the U.S. West, see John Whitehead, "Hawai'i: The First and Last Far West?" *Western Historical Quarterly* 23, no. 2 (1992), 153–77. On the similarities of ecological imperialism in Hawai'i and the North American West, see John Ryan Fischer, *Cattle Colonialism: An Environmental History of the Conquest of California and Hawai'i* (Chapel Hill: University of North Carolina Press, 2015).
3 Delia Malia Caparoso Konzett, *Hollywood's Hawaii: Race, Nation, and War* (New Brunswick, NJ: Rutgers University Press, 2017).
4 Gary Y. Okihiro, *Island World: A History of Hawai'i and the United States* (Berkeley: University of California Press, 2008); Robert C. Schmitt, *Hawaii in the Movies, 1898–1959* (Honolulu: University of Hawai'i Press, 1990).
5 Alfred W. Crosby, *Ecological Imperialism: The Biological Expansion of Europe, 900–1900* (Cambridge: Cambridge University Press, 1986).

6 Patrick Vinton Kirch, *A Shark Going Inland Is My Chief: The Island Civilization of Ancient Hawai'i* (Berkeley, CA: University of California Press, 2012), 152–170. Robert C. Schmitt, *Historical Statistics of Hawaii* (Honolulu: University Press of Hawaii, 1977), 7, 25, 58.

7 Andrew C. Isenberg and Lawrence H. Kessler, "Settler Colonialism and the Environmental History of the North American West," *Journal of the West* 56, no. 4 (2017), 57–66.

8 See, for example, Robert Crichton Wyllie, *Answers to Questions Posed by His Excellency, R.C. Wyllie, His Hawaiian Majesty's Minister of Foreign Relations, and Addressed to All the Missionaries in the Hawaiian Islands, May 1846* (Honolulu, 1848), 11.

9 Jack London, "Koolau the Leper," in *House of Pride, and Other Tales of Hawaii* (New York: Macmillan, 1912).

10 For an application of ideas about replacement of natives taken from the North American Continent to Hawai'i, see Amy S. Greenberg, *Manifest Manhood and the Antebellum American Empire* (Cambridge: Cambridge University Press, 2005), 251.

11 William Cronon, *Changes in the Land: Indians, Colonists, and the Ecology of New England* (New York: Hill and Wang, 1983).

12 Greenberg, *Manifest Manhood and the Antebellum American Empire*.

13 Janne Lahti, "Settler Passages: Mobility and Settler Colonial Narratives in Westerns," *Journal of the West* 56, no. 4 (2017), 67–77.

14 Schmidt, *Historical Statistics of Hawaii*.

15 Lawrence H. Kessler, "A Plantation upon a Hill; Or, Sugar without Rum: Hawai'i's Missionaries and the Founding of the Hawaiian Sugarcane Plantation System," *Pacific Historical Review* 84, no. 2 (2015), 129–162

16 Konzett, *Hollywood's Hawaii*, 188.

17 Philip J. Deloria, *Playing Indian* (New Haven: Yale University Press, 1998).

18 Karen Ordahl Kupperman, "Fear of Hot Climates in the Anglo-American Colonial Experience," *The William and Mary Quarterly* 41, no. 2 (1984), 213–240. See also David Arnold, *The Tropics and the Traveling Gaze: India, Landscape, and Science, 1800–1856* (Seattle: University of Washington Press, 2005).

3

SETTLER-ABORIGINAL ALLIANCE AND THE THREAT OF FOREIGN INVASION IN BAZ LUHRMANN'S *AUSTRALIA**

Travis Franks

When anthropologist Patrick Wolfe wrote that "invasion is a structure, not an event," he provided in shorthand a suggestion for how to analyze settler colonial projects and their cultural productions.[1] Wolfe's application of "invasion" in this instance refers specifically to settlers' continuing intrusion into Indigenous spaces, and given his insistence that "[t]erritoriality is settler colonialism's specific, irreducible element," analyses of settler cultural productions have largely focused on works depicting frontiers, where colonizing land grabs are perhaps most evident.[2] While immensely valuable, this kind of critique risks focusing solely on contact between settler and Indigenous populations at the expense of other exogenous populations who, for reasons relating to race, ethnicity, gender, sexuality, and/or class do not fit neatly into the classification "settler." Indigenous studies scholar Jodi A. Byrd's distinction between Indigenous, settler, and "arrivant" populations—groups of exogenous peoples who, while excluded from the settler class, contribute to the colonizing project voluntarily (immigrants) or involuntarily (enslaved or indentured laborers)—expands the analytic potential for settler colonial studies. Accounting for arrivant populations within settler colonial paradigms should not lessen the centrality of Indigenous dispossession, however.[3]

Migrant peoples are too often caught within a dichotomy that distinguishes between "model immigrants and undesirable aliens."[4] Members of the former are praised for an ability to integrate into and contribute to the social and political orders of their new homes, whereas members of the latter are perceived as being unable or unwilling to do so. Seen as perpetually foreign Others, these individuals and their communities are routinely viewed as pariahs for offenses ranging from draining government resources to threatening national security. For instance, the so-called

---

* Please note: this chapter contains the name and image of an Aboriginal person now deceased.

Yellow Peril of the mid-nineteenth century linked anxieties about national and cultural erosion—as well as racial devolution—to an Asian invasion into countries with majority white populations. The United States *Chinese Exclusion Act* (1882) corresponded with a set of policies in Australia that have come to be collectively referred to as the White Australia policy.[5] Similar associations are regularly applied today to Arab, Asian, Muslim, and (at least in the US) Latina/o populations, stoking an insecurity that I have elsewhere referred to as "settler nativism."[6]

Triangulating settler, Indigenous, and arrivant populations in this way reveals that invasion is, on one hand, an ongoing process that settler populations tend to obscure as an act of their own indigenization, legitimizing their belonging while displacing Indigenous people. On the other hand, fear of invasion is a recurring insecurity aimed at certain arrivant populations labeled as "foreigners" who potentially threaten settler belonging.[7] In both instances, invasion works to unify the settler polity and strengthen bonds between nation and landscape. Moving beyond the settler–Indigenous binary in this particular direction asks us to think about ways in which non-Indigenous, non-settler populations are labeled and located in hierarchical orderings of settler societies. I contend that Baz Luhrmann's *Australia* (2008) is particularly apt for this sort of analysis because, while it primarily focuses on domestic relationships between settler and Aboriginal Australians, it also relies on the concept of Asian invasion to fortify the bonds between black and white characters as national subjects.

Literary, film, and media studies are particularly suited for making legible the narrative double movement that normalizes or obscures settler invasion while simultaneously heightening the threat of foreign invasion. Film is unique, of course, not only for its modes of production but also for the ways in which it renders narrative visible to audiences. Luhrmann's *Australia* yokes together two of the settler nation's formative literary storytelling traditions in one visual narrative: the bush romance and the invasion saga. From the celebrated works of Henry Lawson and Banjo Paterson to the perhaps lesser-known novels of William Lane, Kenneth Mackay, and C. H. Kirmess, bush and invasion narratives have played a formative role in the national imaginary, straddling the periods before and after Australia's national federation in 1901—the very moment when White Australia policies were first enacted.[8] The country's cinematic tradition has been influenced by these story modes as well, so much so that scholars contend that the very image of the archetypal Australian cultivated by the national film industry—an athletic white male not unlike *Australia*'s protagonist The Drover (Hugh Jackman)—depends on the simultaneous construction of two oppositional Others: the Aborigine and the Asian.[9]

Aborigines and Asians have served related functions as figures against which a unified white Australian identity could be constructed. Clearly, the notion of a singularly identifiable Australian persona is problematic in that it potentially normalizes biases on race, gender, sexuality, ability, and age. Aborigine and Asian figures are likewise problematic because they associate racial identities with negative qualities or behaviors and homogenize ethnic and cultural diversities into a coherent singularity. These stock types often lack depth as characters, and their primary purpose is to reveal or develop the qualities that distinguish their white set-tler counterparts, who are more central to the narrative. According to anthropologist Annette Hamilton and film scholar Belinda Small, stereotypical filmic Aboriginal and Asian characters are generally associated with regions thought to be unpopulated by or unknown to white settlers, imbuing the spaces inhabited by these dual Others with settlers' anxieties over belonging. Aborigines are thus understood to inhabit the fringes of settler society, either on reserves or missions or, alternatively, in the remote interior of the continent, somewhere beyond the frontier, and therefore "wild," but simultaneously more "authentically Australian." Hamilton and Small note that ste-reotypical Asians are peripheral in their own way, populating ethnic enclaves within cities or, more abstractly, occupying a somewhat nebulous space within the Aus-tralian settler imaginary that has been described at various points as "the Orient," "the Pacific," or simply "Asia."[10] To some extent, each of these descriptors high-lights Australia's geographical isolation from the British metropole and the related fear of defenselessness against a seemingly imminent invasion.

Australia has garnered a considerable amount of scholarly attention over the last decade. Critiques tend to focus on the film's clumsy engagement with the politics surrounding the Stolen Generations, the Aboriginal and Torres Strait Islander victims of official child removal policies that were in effect for much of the twentieth century. The monumental *Bringing Them Home Report* (1997), the culmination of a national inquiry into the removal practices and intergenerational traumas inflicted on Aboriginal families, made the experiences of members of the Stolen Generations, and the question of whether they were owed a formal apology by the Australian government, a key component of a broader reconci-liation platform begun in the late 1980s and early 1990s. Child removal was once again weighing on Australian's minds in 2008 after the newly installed Prime Minister Kevin Rudd offered a public formal apology to Indigenous Australians.

As has been the case with Rudd's apology, critics of *Australia* argue that the film's acknowledgement and framing of child removal ultimately serve to alleviate culpability and shame amongst the settler population by promoting a fantasy of tri-umphant national unity.[11] This chapter adds to this scholarly discourse by discussing the film's reliance on the invasion narrative and its attendant Asian stereotype to forge a bond between settler and Aboriginal characters. I demonstrate how the film's depiction of events surrounding Japan's bombing of Darwin in 1942 marries negative tropes of Asian invasion and Aboriginal sacrificial death in a way that mirrors decades of segregationist policies aimed at excluding Asian arrivants *to* and assimilating Aboriginal inhabitants *of* Australia's northern regions prior to World War II.

Becoming Indigenous in *Australia*

Luhrmann's nearly three-hour epic takes place in the country's Northern Territory between 1939 and 1942. The film is an unapologetic romance—part Western, part war story, and part homage to classic films, most noticeably *The Wizard of Oz* (1939).

Lady Sarah Ashley (Nicole Kidman) travels from her native England to the Faraway Downs cattle station to discover her husband recently murdered. She soon finds herself ensnared in cattle baron "King" Carney's (Bryan Brown) plan to secure a monopoly over Australia's grazing lands and sign a lucrative contract to supply beef to the Australian armed forces. Carney has secretly employed Faraway Downs's station manager Neil Fletcher (David Wenham) to sabotage the Ashley cattle business, though Carney is unaware of the man's deep depravity. Fletcher has not only consistently stolen Ashley-owned cattle for Carney, he has also killed his previous employer and framed Aboriginal elder King George (David Gulpilil), whose daughter he has habitually raped, for the murder. As a result of his sexual violence, Fletcher has fathered an Aboriginal son named Nullah (Brandon Walters), whom he repeatedly tries to have removed to a mission school. One such attempt ends in tragedy, as Nullah's mother Daisy (Ursula Yovich) drowns while trying to hide their son in a water tank.

Lady Ashley eventually learns of Fletcher's deceit and resolves to make Faraway Downs the successful cattle station her husband envisioned. She enlists the fiercely independent Drover to drive a herd of cattle north to Darwin. Against all odds, they successfully outmaneuver King Carney and secure the military supply contract. Lady Ashley, Drover, and Nullah live in momentary bliss together at the cattle station until King George's request to take Nullah on an initiation walkabout fractures the makeshift family. Drover defiantly heads north on another drive, while Lady Ashley relocates to Darwin in order to join the war effort and be close to Nullah, who has been kidnapped and removed to Mission Island. Fletcher has since married King Carney's daughter and murdered his new father-in-law to become the head of the Carney Cattle Company, which happens to be headquartered at Darwin.

The Japanese military, just having bombed the US Naval base at Pearl Harbor, attacks amidst all of this turmoil, devastating the town and exacerbating the personal drama that has developed between the film's primary characters. Drover arrives in town after receiving news of the bombing, only to find Lady Ashley reported among the confirmed dead. Worse, all the children at the mission school—including Nullah—are also presumed dead. Miraculously, both Lady Ashley and Nullah are unharmed and eventually reunited with Drover, sealing the familial bonds first formed on the cattle drive years ago. Fletcher, too, has survived the initial bombing, and determines to murder his ill-begotten son. Fittingly, King George prevents Fletcher from shooting the boy by spearing him. The film concludes back on Faraway Downs, with King George leading Nullah off into the bush for his ceremonial rites of passage while Lady Ashley and Drover—Nullah's new adoptive parents—look on with approval.

Australia is deeply concerned with the gendered and raced politics behind the removal of the Stolen Generations. However, several scholars make the compelling argument that the relationship between Lady Ashley and Nullah not only romanticizes the nation's colonial history but ultimately reiterates whites' possessive claim over Aboriginal children—even as the film clearly intends to condemn the historical practice of forced child removal.[12] Lady Ashley's character development depends on maternal and social reformist impulses, making her akin to the figure historian Margaret D. Jacobs calls "The Great White Mother."[13] Having decided to formally adopt Nullah following his mother's death, Lady Ashley appeals to a government official who declares removal and training at mission schools are the only means by which Aboriginal children might be successfully assimilated into settler society. This official further assures her of "the fact of science that the Aboriginal mother soon forgets her offspring," to which Lady Ashley responds "No mother forgets her child." Jacobs' research suggests that white women of Lady Ashley's social standing were highly unlikely to have held such beliefs at this time in Australia. Indeed, proponents of women's reformist movements of the period actively supported child removal, which they justified with misnomers depicting Aboriginal women as unfit caregivers and homemakers lacking motherly instincts. These attitudes fitted within a broader campaign for white women's increased public participation by supporting the establishment and preservation of racially-coded laws, including the White Australia policies.[14]

Less attention has been paid to the sexual politics of Drover's unlikely relationships with Aboriginal Australians. Early comments made by Lady Ashley regarding her husband's interest in Australia alert viewers to the historical truth that white men routinely sexually exploited black women. This is certainly the case regarding Nullah's parentage, as the villainous Fletcher is depicted as having routinely raped Daisy—what Nullah innocently refers to as "wrong-side business." Lady Ashley initially assumes the same of Drover, though he eventually reveals to her that he was *married* to a black woman and is, as a result, outcast from Darwin society: "I'm as good as black to that mob," he ruefully declares. Cultural studies scholar Fiona Probyn-Rapsey observes that "[t]he low rate of marriage between Europeans and Aboriginal women between 1901 and 1914 (but a high birth rate of 'half-castes') suggests unwillingness to form recognized unions."[15] In other words, it is not beyond possibility that Drover would have been "legitimately" married to an Aboriginal woman, but theirs would have been an unlikely alliance for the period.

The film depicts Drover's intimate relationships with Aborigines prior to meeting Lady Ashley as a type of indigenization that legitimizes him as an eventual co-owner of Faraway Downs cattle station and a father-figure in Nullah's life. His first marriage resulted in no children, though Lady Ashley responds to this information by stating "Well, that's a shame. I think you would have made a great father," foreshadowing his role in the film's conclusion. Drover's sense of independence prevents him from acting as a husband to Lady Ashley or father to Nullah for much of the movie, and the tenuous family bonds holding the three together quickly dissolve when Lady Ashley refuses to allow Nullah to participate in initiation rites with his grandfather, a cultural practice Drover respects and supports.

At this point, neither Lady Ashley nor Drover are yet capable of serving as Nullah's adoptive parents and must therefore experience still more transformative, indigenizing experiences before the film can conclude. Their character limitations in this regard are akin to what cultural studies scholars Adriana Estill and Lee Bebout term "white lack," a sense that whiteness "is exposed as incomplete and insufficient once it knows and 'feels' [Othered] affective fullness."[16] In the context of settler colonialism, white lack coincides with the persistent problem of settlers' lack of indigeneity, which translates to a deeply felt sense of belonging and connection to a native homeland. Back out on the isolated northern plains, Drover's closest confidant—an Aboriginal stockman named Magarri (David Ngoombujarra)—confronts Drover, asserting "You're just hiding behind that blackfella business so you don't get hurt. This isn't about walkabout, is it? You're running." When Drover denies the accusation, Magarri insists "Yes you are, brother. You're scared of getting your heart hurt like before, when my sister died ... You got no love in your heart, you got nothing. No Dreaming, no story. Nothing." Though Drover and Magarri have shared a number of scenes and are clearly fond of one another, this scene—two hours into the film—marks the first acknowledgment of their actual kinship. In fact, Magarri has only referred to Drover by that name or simply as "Boss" up until this point, though they consistently refer to one another as "Brother" after Magarri scolds his white brother-in-law. It is also noteworthy that Magarri suggests that, should Drover acknowledge his love for Lady Ashley and Nullah, he will also connect to the Dreamtime, the period described in Aboriginal origin stories during which ancestral beings established Laws that continue to govern physical and cultural connections on earth. This exchange effectively contrasts the earlier scene in which Drover was pejoratively deemed "as good as black" by Darwin townspeople, thereby removing the stigma associated with his indigenization and implying, perhaps, that he is *good enough* to be black.

The relationship formed between Nullah's maternal grandfather King George and his adoptive white parents represents the most unlikely of all fantasy alliances formed in *Australia*. Narrating the film's opening scene, Nullah explains that "King George angry at them whitefellas. King George say them whitefellas bad spirit, must be taken from this land." Contrast this with the film's final scene, in which King George speaks the following lines to Nullah and Lady Ashley: "You have been on a journey. Now we are heading home to my country ... to our country." Whites have essentially been transformed from invaders to indigenes. Including Lady Ashley in the collective claim on country not only legitimizes her ownership of Faraway Downs but suggests that King George approves of her taking Daisy's place as Nullah's mother and, by extension, as his own daughter. This scene is one of several in which the heroic deeds of "good" whites and the absence of Aborigines minimize or erase altogether Aboriginal grievances in order to justify settler presence and possession. King George's recognition of Lady Ashley's journey and his use of "our" suggests, as does Prime Minister Rudd's 2008 apology, that Aboriginal-settler reconciliation had been achieved through a single acknowledgement and that a future of mutual respect, cohabitation, and unification lay ahead. My analysis here thus agrees with related work by a number of critics who suggest that Lady Ashley, Drover, and *Australia* overtly appeal to the political sensibilities of a white contemporary Australian viewing public that embraces supposedly progressive policies such as multi-culturalism and reconciliation with Aboriginal Australians.[17]

Countering Invasion in *Australia*

Critique of Luhrmann's *Australia* has not yet adequately analyzed the Japanese military attack on Darwin as the impetus for key alliances between the film's Aboriginal and settler characters. Indeed, in the film's final act, the external forces of foreign invasion solidify bonds of intimacy and allow for the mediation of potential settler guilt through heroic actions. Drover arrives in Darwin looking for Lady Ashley after Magarri has chided him, and, overcome with grief and guilt when he is misinformed that she has died in the bombings, Drover turns to the pub for solace. Recalling the scene in which Magarri and Drover first appear onscreen, Magarri is refused entry on the basis of his being black—this despite the fact that the building is now in a shambles as a result of the bombing. "That's how it is" remarks the incredulous barman Ivan, whose heavy accent codes him as an eastern European immigrant who upholds the mores of white Australia's racial hierarchy. With tears in his eyes, Drover responds "Just because it is, doesn't ... doesn't mean it should be. Serve him a fuckin' drink." Ivan acquiesces, but not before stating "Ah, what does it matter? I'm a total bloody ruin. I'm evacuating south, like everybody else ... I leave this place for the looters and the Japs. Why not the boongs?" Despite the derogatory, racist language, Drover, Magarri, and Ivan share what seems to be a meaningful moment of camaraderie as they lift their glasses in unison.

Japanese characters do not appear in this scene, yet the effects of their invasion are profound. Not only has the pub been reduced to rubble but one of the most enforced social codes barring blacks from drinking in white-dominated spaces has been temporarily set aside. The shared drink places the white Australian archetype (Drover), the detribalized black stockman (Magarri), and the assimilated off-white immigrant (Ivan) physically side-by-side, a visual representation of the settler-centric ideals underpinning a supposedly multicultural Australia. In this moment, Drover embodies authentic Aboriginal kinship as he simultaneously commands the settler society that once excluded him, demonstrating his bravery and righteousness that move him a step further in filling the emptiness of his own particular white lack as an emotionally unattached outsider.

These traits are reinforced in the ensuing scene, in which Drover, Magarri, and Ivan undertake a daring voyage to Mission Island, where they attempt to rescue a number of Aboriginal children who had previously been removed by the state. Drover and Magarri are overjoyed to find Nullah unharmed, though their rescue mission is nearly thwarted when an armed Japanese patrol arrives to kill survivors of the initial bombing—a detail Belinda Small notes is a fabrication and not a reflection of actual events.[18] Magarri volunteers to distract the soldiers so that the others can escape. When Drover protests "You'll never make it," Magarri exclaims "Well, you gotta make it! You got family now! You gotta drove this mob home, Drover." Magarri's reference to family seems to imply that Drover is now responsible for raising Nullah as his own son, which conveniently overlooks the fact that Nullah's maternal grandfather is still alive and capable of raising the boy *and* that Drover already has a family if, indeed, Magarri is his brother.

Magarri's sacrifice serves as a crucial moment for the films' conclusion and the particular fantasy of settler–Indigenous alliance that *Australia* represents. His death is not *only* the reenactment of war narrative trope in which a minor(ity) character sacrifices his or her life so that the white protagonist can carry out his heroic quest in battle. Magarri also offers up his life so that Drover can redeem his previous short-comings as a father to a black child. The diversion of Japanese soldiers is successful in that it allows Drover, Ivan, and the rescued children to escape to the relative safety of Darwin. However, Magarri's rifle jams and he is shot in the back while attempting to flee the beach. Lying prostrate in the sand, a Japanese soldier standing above him with a pistol aimed at his head (Figure 3.1), Magarri turns to make eye contact with Drover, now safely aboard with all of the children. "Drove 'em home, Drover," Magarri says, just before a gunshot rings out. Critics note that Magarri's death scene not only imagines an essentialized Japanese invader but, even more problematically, also substitutes the non-white soldiers in place of white settlers as the perpetrators of colonial violence on black bodies.[19] And just as Daisy's accidental drowning does for Lady Ashley, Magarri's murder also presents an uncomplicated path for Drover to assume a paternal role in Nullah's life.

Film's unique narrative qualities are particularly legible in this scene. In the wide shot depicted below, the two pervasive stereotypical representations of Asian and Aborigine figures are especially noticeable in the positioning of the actors' bodies. The Japanese appear to "swarm" as a body made up of almost entirely indistinguishable soldiers, echoing nativist fears that Asians possessed a significant population advantage that would aide them if they ever decided to invade northern Australia. Magarri's positioning, on the other hand, can be read as confirmation of the vanishing Aborigine trope that associates Indigenous bodies with death and absence.

FIGURE 3.1 Magarri (David Ngoombujurra) lies wounded on the beach at Mission Island, moments before being executed by an unnamed Japanese soldier. Screenshot from *Australia* (2008) by the author.

Note, too, that the mission school is clearly visible in the background, conveniently framed between two soldiers' bodies and engulfed in flames. This is an interesting decision given the film's political investment in acknowledging the Stolen Generations, who suffered innumerable mental, physical, and spiritual abuses in schools just like this one. Indeed, Nullah's narrative for much of the film revolves on the ever-present threat that he will be abducted and sent to Mission Island. The school's destruction as a result of the Japanese air raid, however, links it with other depictions of the devastation wrought upon Darwin's built landscape—as with Ivan's pub, for example. Therefore, even as *Australia* openly embraces reconciliation politics and acknowledging the shameful history of child removal, it reimagines the mission not as a site of colonial genocide but as a proving ground for Australian "mateship," Aboriginal death, and Asian invasion.[20]

Drover eventually fulfills Magarri's dying wish, but not before the remaining family members' dramatic reunification. The scene following Magarri's execution sees Drover, Nullah, and Lady Ashley come together on the same Darwin wharf where, earlier in the film, Nullah was forcibly taken from Lady Ashley's arms and removed to Mission Island. The previous animosity between Drover and Lady Ashley regarding their being a family no longer exists, a revelation made possible precisely because the threat of foreign invasion has fortified their emotional bonds and cemented them as the traditional heteronormative settler family unit of husband, wife, and child. Indeed, upon seeing Lady Ashley on the wharf, Nullah cries out "Them Japs nearly got us!" The slur against Japanese soldiers is obvious, but so too should be Magarri's absence, whose sacrifice goes unmentioned. Nonetheless, these three central characters have now "got" one another and, in turn, contemporary audiences have had a look at the national reconciliation fantasy many of them would have deeply desired when the film premiered mere months after Rudd's apology. There is still the matter of Nullah's biological father to resolve before the narrative can conclude, however. In perhaps the film's most overt invocation of twenty-first-century Australian reconciliation politics, King George, having fatally speared Fletcher, admonishes him as he dies: "He's your son," he says, "and my grandson." The united family returns to Faraway Downs, seemingly leaving their hardships at Darwin and the coming war behind them.

Just as the film neatly sidesteps events surrounding the bombing, it also belies decades of intercultural exchange between Asian and Aboriginal peoples and the anxiety that such alliances inspired in settler governance prior to World War II. As early as 1897, Australian legislators enacted segregationist laws that policed interactions between Aboriginal and Chinese Australians. A Darwin ordinance first enacted in 1911 enforced social and economic prohibitions that simultaneously isolated Aborigines from what had become a polyethnic community and precipitated the decline of a Chinese population that had played a fundamental role in Darwin's development.[21] The official justification for such restrictions held that Asian groups preyed upon vulnerable Aborigines, though the general consensus today is that deterring Aboriginal-Asian alliances was intended to further settlers' economic and political dominance in a region where their authority seemed most tenuous.[22] The Darwin of Luhrmann's *Australia* evinces a black-white racial divide that makes outsiders of Drover and Magarri, but it does not similarly account for the spatialization of anti-Asian racism. Instead, the film amplifies the Japanese bombing in 1942, most noticeably in the fabricated scene in which Magarri is executed.

Further, Magarri's death at the hand of a Japanese invader obfuscates a widespread paranoia amongst settlers in northern Australia. Historians Regina Ganter and Peta Stephenson note the circulation of persistent rumors claiming Aborigines assisted the Japanese military in conquering Australia as retribution for their mistreatment by Anglo colonizers. In response to this unfounded fear, an estimated 98% of Japanese-origin people in Australia were immediately arrested and interred in prison camps, while many Aborigines were judiciously "evacuated" from their ancestral lands in the north.[23] To be sure, the Japanese aerial attacks on northern Australia had a number of tragic consequences, not least among them the deaths and destruction they caused. In the broader sense, they escalated the restrictive measures placed on Asian and Aboriginal people attempting to live, work, and, in some cases, build families together.

Conclusion

In the context of settler colonialism, Luhrmann's *Australia* is valuable for its positioning of well-known archetypes like Drover in relation to progressive twenty-first-century attitudes about settler-Aboriginal reconciliation. At the same time, the film substantiates a scholarly concern over the partitioning of issues relating to Aboriginal and Asian Australians. *Australia*'s treatment of the 1942 bombing of Darwin by the Japanese military strengthens intimate bonds between black and white protagonists by providing them with a common exogenous enemy. This historical fantasy is problematic, in part, because it invokes Australia's tradition of Asian invasion narratives without complicating it. The film transmutes colonial violence onto a one-dimensional Japanese perpetrator while simultaneously deepening Anglo Australians' sense of "native" belonging. This fantasy is also at odds with the more complex history of Aboriginal-Asian intercultural exchange and its attempted prohibition by settler governance at the turn of the twentieth century. *Australia* thus embraces contemporary optimism about the nation's future and expresses nostalgia for a romantic settler colonial past that simply does not exist—and, perhaps, a naïve hopefulness for a post-Apology Australia that has not yet materialized.

Notes

1 Patrick Wolfe, "Settler Colonialism and the Elimination of the Native," *Journal of Genocide Research* 8 (2006), 388.
2 Wolfe, "Settler Colonialism."
3 Jodi A. Byrd, *The Transit of Empire: Indigenous Critiques of Colonialism* (Minneapolis: University of Minnesota Press, 2011), xix; JoAnna Poblette-Cross, "Bridging Indigenous and

Immigrant Struggles: A Case Study of American Sāmoa," *American Quarterly* 62 (2010), 501–02.

4 Christina Gerken, *Model Immigrants and Undesirable Aliens: The Cost of Immigration Reform in the 1990s* (Minneapolis: University of Minnesota Press, 2013), 16.

5 James Jupp, *From White Australia to Woomera: The Story of Australian Immigration*, 2nd ed. (Cambridge: Cambridge University Press, 2007), 8–11.

6 Travis Franks, "'We Are Considered Undesirable Foreigners' in 'This Our Texas': Mexican American Settler Nativism in *Caballero*," *MELUS: Multi-Ethnic Literature of the U.S.* 43 (2018), 88.

7 I use "indigenization" after Terry Goldie, *Fear and Temptation: The Image of the Indigene in Canadian, Australian, and New Zealand Literatures* (Montreal: McGill-Queen's University Press, 1989), 3.

8 Robert Dixon, *Writing the Colonial Adventure: Race, Gender and Nation in Anglo-Australian Popular Fiction, 1875–1914* (Cambridge: Cambridge University Press, 1995), 72–99, 135–53; David Walker, *Anxious Nation: Australia and the Rise of Asia, 1850–1939* (Brisbane: University of Queensland Press, 1999), 98–104; Catriona Elder, *Being Australian: Narratives of National Identity* (Crows Nest, NSW: Allen and Unwin, 2007), 32–40; Linzi Murrie, "The Australian Legend: Writing Australian Masculinity/Writing 'Australian' Masculine," *Journal of Australian Studies* 22 (2009), 68–77.

9 Annette Hamilton, "Fear and Desire: Aborigines, Asians, and the National Imaginary," *Australian Cultural History* 9 (1990), 14–19; Anne Curthoys, "An Uneasy Conversation: The Multicultural and the Indigenous," in *Race, Colour, and Identity in Australia and New Zealand*, eds. John Docker and Gerhard Fischer (Sydney, University of New South Wales Press, 2000), 24; Belinda Small, "Asianness and Aboriginality in Australian Cinema," *Quarterly Review of Film and Video* 30 (2013), 89–90; Peta Stephenson, *The Outsiders Within: Telling Australia's Indigenous-Asian Story* (Sydney: University of New South Wales Press, 2007), 2–9; Regina Ganter, *Mixed Relations: Asian-Aboriginal Contact in North Australia* (Crawley: University of Western Australia Press, 2006), 118; Penny Edwards and Shen Yuanfang, "Something More: Towards Reconfiguring Australian History," in *Lost in the Whitewash: Aboriginal-Asian Encounters in Australia, 1901–200*, eds. Penny Edwards and Shen Yuanfang (Canberra: Humanities Research Centre, 2003), 6. The otherwise unnamed Drover is likely an homage to similarly unnamed characters in Henry Lawson's formative short story "The Drover's Wife."

10 Hamilton, "Fear and Desire," 18–27; Small, "Asianness and Aboriginality," 89–90.

11 Tony Barta, "Sorry, and Not Sorry, in Australia: How the Apology to the Stolen Generations Buried a History of Genocide," *Journal of Genocide Research* 10 (2008), 201–14; Odette Kelada, "Love is a Battlefield: 'Maternal' Emotions and White Catharsis in Luhrmann's Post-Apology Australia," *Studies in Australasian Cinema* 8 (2014), 83–84.

12 Liz Conor, "A 'Nation So Ill-Begotten': Racialized Childhood and Conceptions of National Belonging in Xavier Herbert's *Poor Fellow My Country* and Baz Luhrmann's *Australia*," *Studies in Australasian Cinema* 4 (2010), 109–10; Jerod Ra'Del Hollyfield, "Approximate Others: Peter Weir's *The Last Wave* (1977)," in *Postcolonial Film: History, Empire, Resistance*, eds. Rebecca Weaver-Hightower and Peter Hulme (London: Routledge, 2014), 3–4; Kelada, "Love is a Battlefield," 91–92; Small, "Asianness and Aboriginality," 95–98.

13 Margaret D. Jacobs, *White Mother to a Dark Race: Settler Colonialism, Maternalism, and the Removal of Indigenous Children in the American West and Australia, 1880–1940* (Lincoln: University of Nebraska Press, 2009), 87.

14 Jacobs, *White Mother*, 207–08; Jane Carey, "'Wanted! A Real White Australia': The Women's Movement, Whiteness, and the Settler Colonial Project, 1900–1940," in *Studies in Settler Colonialism: Politics, Identity, and Culture*, eds. Fiona Bateman and Lionel Pilkington (London: Palgrave, 2011), 122–23.

15 Fiona Probyn-Rapsey, *Made to Matter: White Fathers, Stolen Generations* (Sydney: Sydney University Press, 2013), 5.
16 Adriana Estill and Lee Bebout, "Yearning to Belong, Drawn to be Mexican: Hollywood Depictions of White Lack and Mexican Affective Fullness," *Aztlán: A Journal of Chicano Studies* 43 (2018), 105.
17 Jane Stadler and Peta Mitchell, "Never-Never Land: Affective Landscapes, the Touristic Gaze, and Heterotropic Space in *Australia*," *Studies in Australasian Cinema* 4 (2010), 182; Jackie Hogan, "Gendered and Racialised Discourses of National Identity in Baz Luhrmann's *Australia*," *Journal of Australian Studies* 34 (2010), 63; Conor, "A 'Nation So Ill-Begotten,'" 109–10; Kelada, "Love is a Battlefield," 91–92.
18 Small, "Asianness and Aboriginality," 98.
19 Hogan, "Gendered and Racialised Discourses," 70–71; Small, "Asianness and Aboriginality," 98–99; Kelada, "Love is a Battlefield," 89.
20 It is beyond the scope of this chapter, but the themes of "mateship" and sacrifice in this scene may be alluding to the national origin myth of the ANZAC soldiers' Gallipoli campaign in WWI.
21 Julia Martinez, "Ethnic Policy and Practice in Darwin," in *Mixed Relations: Asian-Aboriginal Contact in North Australia*, ed. Regina Ganter (Crawley: University of Western Australia Press, 2006), 123–27; Edwards and Yuanfang, "Something More," 6.
22 Edwards and Yuanfang, "Something More," 14; Ganter, *Mixed Relations*, 76–80, Stephenson, *The Outsiders Within*, 4.
23 Ganter, *Mixed Relations*, 215–17; Stephenson, *The Outsiders Within*, 104–05, 114.

4

SETTLER BOLSHEVIKS IN THE SOVIET "EASTERN"

Alexander Morrison

Russia and the Soviet Union are often excluded from histories of settler coloni-alism, partly because it is seen as an Anglophone phenomenon, and partly because the colonization of Siberia and parts of Central Asia by Russians and other peo-ples from European Russia did not involve either movement overseas or the creation of new settler colonial states. Nevertheless, a process which saw the indigenous peoples of Siberia reduced to small minorities, with Europeans also forming a majority of the population of Kazakhstan by 1989, clearly needs to be understood as part of the wider phenomenon of settler colonialism which demographically re-made entire continents between the eighteenth and the twentieth centuries. Russian settlers, just like their western European counter-parts, were not simply migrants in a strange country, but brought a form of sovereignty with them. By the late nineteenth century, this meant that the Russian state recognized settlers' pre-eminent claim to the land, even in Central Asia where a large indigenous population was present, and still more in Siberia where settlement was often explicitly compared to that of Eur-opeans in North America.[1]

As historian Lorenzo Veracini has argued, narratives are important to settler colonialism – whether ideas of "empty lands" and "manifest destiny," tales of frontier pioneering, the confrontation between barbarism and civilization, or the "inevitability" of the disappearance of indigenous peoples – because they serve to soften or blur a brutal reality.[2] In the twentieth century cinema has played an important role in creating and sustaining these narratives, and no form has been more potent than the classic American Western, in which all these themes feature prominently: from early films such as John Ford's *The Iron Horse* (1924), through to later classics such as the same director's "Cavalry Trilogy" (1948–50), Westerns seek to indigenize the settlers in the landscape, establish their claims to it in the face of any indigenous opposition, and show how they are remaking it. If the American Western is the *locus classicus* of settler colonial cinema, a convincing case can be made for parallels in Australian, New Zealand, and South African film.[3]

In the Russian-speaking world, the closest parallels to the American Western are found in Soviet films about the Revolution and Civil War in Central Asia, set in the years between 1917 and the mid-1920s, a genre often known as the Soviet "Eastern." These films depicted the struggles of the fledgling Soviet regime against an array of villainous and reactionary opponents: former Tsarist officials and officers, the pre-Revolutionary Central Asian commercial and religious elite (known generically as "Bais" and "Mullahs"), and above all the so-called *Basmachi* – much-mythologized groups of bandits and guerrillas mounting raids on the outposts of Bolshevik power or otherwise subverting the new Soviet order.[4] In terms of basic plot and aesthetics "Easterns" were strongly influenced by American Westerns, with the *Basmachi* playing the role of American Indians, and Bolshevik commissars, Red Army soldiers, and border guards the cowboys and cavalry.[5]

"Easterns" followed a narrative which, while paying lip-service to Soviet ideals of the friendship and equality of peoples, often presented Russians, or more broadly Europeans, as the main agents of progress in Central Asia. This was certainly true of the most famous of the "Easterns," Vladimir Motyl's *Beloe Solntse Pustiny* (*The White Sun of the Desert*, 1969), which has been the focus of much of the existing scholarship on the genre.[6] After a slow start it became one of the most popular of all Soviet films, whose catchphrase – *Vostok – delo tonkoe* (the East is a delicate matter) – has come to symbolize Russia's relations with its "own Orient."[7] Reflecting on his service in the Soviet Afghan War of the 1980s, one of Nobel laureate Svetlana Alexievich's interviewees recalled:

> Back then there was an image of the enemy, one familiar to us from books, from school, from films about the *Basmachis* after the Russian Revolution. I watched the movie *The White Sun of the Desert* about five times. And there he was, the enemy![8]

While *The White Sun of the Desert* continues to play an outsized role in forming Russian attitudes to Central Asia, it was in many ways uncharacteristic of the wider "Eastern" genre, which it sought to satirize. It was produced by the central studio Mosfilm, and had a European director and predominantly non-Central Asian actors. Although popular with Russian audiences, "Easterns" were usually made by Central Asian directors and film studios, whose output in the 1960s and 1970s was heavily focused on them – to the extent that the Tajik SSR's film studio, Tajikfilm, was sometimes known as *Basmach-kino.*[9] Some of the best-known "Easterns" include *Reshaiushchii Shag* (*The Decisive Step*, Arty Karliev/Turkmenfilm, 1965), *Krasnye Peski* (*Red Sands*, Ali Khamraev/Uzbekfilm, 1968) and *Konets Atamana* (*The End of the Ataman*, Shaken Aimanov/Kazakhfilm, 1970). All of these had Central Asian directors and an overwhelmingly Central Asian cast. *The White Sun of the Desert*, which both in Russia and beyond the former USSR became the most famous of the "Easterns", is thus a misleading archetype.

Soviet "Easterns" uneasily combined proletarian rhetoric with a portrayal of Central Asia as exotic, savage, and backward, and as such are usually analyzed through the lens of Orientalist discourse.[10] While the fact that they drew their plots and basic aesthetics from the Western genre is well-established, the extent to which they reflect similar settler colonial themes – the indigenization of settlers in a supposedly pristine or empty landscape, their pre-eminent right to this land, and the inevitable triumph of European civilization over barbarism – is much less clear. On the face of it, the Bolshevik claim to be bringing enlightenment and progress to a backward region does have clear commonalities with settler colonialism elsewhere – the theme of the railway opening up and civilizing "empty" landscapes, for instance, is common to both ideologies – but there are other factors that render comparison less straightforward. Most "Easterns" were set in the deserts and oases of Uzbekistan and Turkmenistan, where Russian settlers were very few, and many of them had few or no Russian characters. Hence, in this paper I will focus my analysis on the film *Alye Maki Issyk-Kulya* (*The Scarlet Poppies of Issyk-Kul*, Bolotbek Shamshiev, 1972),[11] which was filmed and set in northern Kyrgyzstan in the fertile region of Semirechie. This had been the main Russian settler colony in southern Central Asia before 1917, and would remain a major area of Russian settlement even after the Revolution, where colonial structures of power and land use seem to have been more durable than elsewhere in Soviet Central Asia.[12] The paper will give a brief outline of the origins of cinema in Central Asia, before narrowing the focus specifically to the Kyrgyz SSR. I will explore the literary source material of *Scarlet Poppies*, before comparing this with the plot and characterization of the film, and providing a visual analysis. Overall I would argue that while settler colonial themes and aesthetics borrowed from the "Western" are certainly present in the *Scarlet Poppies*, these are eclipsed by a much more powerful Kyrgyz national narrative, something which is quite characteristic of the cultural politics of Soviet Central Asia in the 1970s.

The Origins of Central Asian and Kyrgyz Cinema

The use of film as a propaganda tool was one of the hallmarks of the Soviet regime throughout its existence, and this was combined in its early years with some remarkable artistic innovations in the new medium. The first Soviet film shot in Central Asia to gain wide circulation was Viktor Turin's *Turksib* (1929), a highly stylized documentary about the construction of the Turkestan-Siberia railway from Tashkent to Semipalatinsk as part of the first five-year plan. As historian Matthew Payne has shown, the popularity of the film with Russian and international audiences was because it reproduced conventional colonial tropes: of a backward, sleeping Asia awakened by European science and civilization, of the conquering power of technology, and of the primitive naivety of the "natives." As such it failed

to reflect the political orthodoxy of the USSR's nationalities policy in the 1920s –
korenizatsiya ("striking roots," i.e. indigenization) which saw the local population
not as passive recipients of progress, but as the bearers of Soviet power and
enlightenment themselves.[13]

Most early Soviet fiction films shot in Central Asia conformed to the same
Orientalist pattern as *Turksib*. *The Minaret of Death* (Vyacheslav Viskovskii, 1925),
filmed in Uzbekistan and set in an imagined seventeenth-century Bukhara, was
"off the scale in its exoticism."[14] Such films were unpopular with Central Asian
intellectuals and party cadres who believed that they denigrated and patronized
the local population, and they were also criticized as escapism, which lacked
necessary Revolutionary spirit. The reconciliation of these imperatives – the need
to entertain audiences with tales of adventure in exotic landscapes, while
simultaneously presenting a correct Revolutionary and national spirit – would be
found in the Civil War heroism of the *Basmachi* genre.

The first of the *Basmachi* films was probably Mikhail Romm's *Trinadtsat'* (*The
Thirteen*, 1937), which was modelled on John Ford's *Lost Patrol* (1934) and bore
strong visual and thematic affinities with contemporary Westerns.[15] The elegiac
description of it in the otherwise turgid official history of Soviet Cinema gives a vivid
impression of the aesthetic that many later examples of the genre sought to reproduce: "uninhabited desert, the rippling dunes, thin streams of crumbling sand, and a
lone string of horsemen, shot as if in negative, moving as jerky black silhouettes on
the white sand."[16] Although the commander of the eponymous thirteen is Russian,
the group includes representatives of Central Asian nationalities, who are shown
fighting and dying for Soviet power. This reflects what historian Cloé Drieu calls the
"hybridization between Colonial-type discourse and a not yet fully-formulated
Soviet (Proletarian Russian) discourse" in which it was essential to show Central
Asians as having class-consciousness and agency of their own.[17] By the time the
Basmachi genre emerged fully in the 1960s and 1970s further ideological changes had
taken place, which Drieu argues saw "images symbolically decolonized" and the
"oriental" replaced by the "national."[18] Traces of the former certainly remained, as
we will see, but national narratives became steadily more important after Stalin's
death in 1953, and the Khrushchev "thaw" which followed.

Within Central Asian Cinema, Kyrgyzstan remained a backwater until well
after the Second World War. Production centered on Uzbekistan and Kazakhstan, and early Kyrgyz films were likely to be co-productions with Mosfilm or
Lenfilm, and to have Russian directors.[19] The latter was true of the breakthrough
film in Kyrgyz cinema, Andrei Mikhalkov-Konchalovskii's *Pervyi uchitel'* (*The
First Teacher*, 1965), based on a story by Chingiz Aitmatov, for which Natalya Arin-
basarova won the Volpi cup at the Venice Film Festival.[20] The only major Kyrgyz
director to venture into the *Basmachi* genre was Bolotbek Shamshiev (1941–2020).[21]
His first film, *Vystrel na perevale Karash* (*Gunshot at the Karash Pass*, 1968), a co-production with Kazakhfilm, included many of the recurring themes of the *Basmachi*
genre. There is the outlaw or brigand who gains class-consciousness – played by the

famous Kyrgyz actor Suimenkul Chokmorov (1939–1992) both here and in *Scarlet Poppies* – ravishing landscapes, high adventure and horses. Based on a short story by the great Kazakh writer Mukhtar Auezov, the film is set in a pre-Revolutionary Semirechie where poor Kyrgyz and Russian settlers alike suffer from the oppression of wealthy *bais*: the chief villain, Zharasbai, also serves the Russian colonial state as a "native" administrator. It includes a deeply implausible scene in which Zharasbai orders the whipping of a Russian peasant settler who had dared to complain about the damage done to his crops by Zharasbai's *Jigits* (mounted bodyguards), only to be protected by the hero, Baktygul, in an evocation of the Soviet friendship of peoples.

This insistence that the structures of oppression in pre-Revolutionary Central Asia were economic rather than ethnic, with "the native bourgeoisie dominating Russian military and colonial society" had already appeared in Soviet film in the 1920s, and are quite unlike anything one finds in the Western genre.[22] This, and the touching scene in which Baktygul says farewell to the children of his peasant settler friend, were also intended to convey the message that the 1916 revolt against Tsarist rule in Central Asia – when in Semirechie many Russian peasant settlers had been killed by Kyrgyz in its early stages – had been fueled by class, not ethnic conflict.[23] The 1916 revolt would also loom large in the background of *Scarlet Poppies*, which is in some ways an oblique cinematic response to a topic that was still considered highly sensitive even in the late Soviet period.[24] However while Shamshiev's film, in common with most *Basmachi* dramas, was as much national as it was Soviet, the text from which it derives was older and much more overtly settler colonial in its themes, language, and characterization.

The Literary Sources of *The Scarlet Poppies of Issyk-Kul*

Shamshiev's film is based on *Kontrabandisty Tian'-Shanya* (*The Smugglers of the Tian-Shan*), a novel by Alexander Pavlovich Sytin (1894–1974). This was first published as a short story under the more ominous title *Zheltyi Mrak* (*Yellow Darkness*) in 1927.[25] A much-expanded version sporting the new title appeared first in Kharkov the same year, and then under the prestigious *Molodaya Gvardiya* imprint in 1930.[26] It was republished again in Tbilisi (where Sytin had settled) in 1964, lacking the rather luridly orientalist illustrations of the original.[27] The long gap between these editions of the novel reflected the fortunes of its author. Sytin served in the Tsarist army during the First World War, and was evacuated to Central Asia after being wounded in 1916. In 1918 he joined the Red Army, and participated in the campaign to reconquer the Emirate of Bukhara under Mikhail Frunze's command, before becoming commandant of the fortress at Namangan in the Ferghana valley.[28] In 1925 he returned to Moscow and a full-time writing career. In 1930 he was arrested and sent to a camp near Murmansk. He was released in 1936, but only rehabilitated and re-elected to the Union of Writers in 1962.[29] Apart from *The Smugglers of the Tian-Shan*, Sytin was the author of numerous adventure stories, usually with a Turkestan setting, in popular magazines such as *Ogonёk* or *Vsemirnyi Sledopyt'*.[30] Two of these stories – *Vesy Zhazhdy* (*The Weight of Thirst*, 1927) and *v Peskakh Kara-Kuma* (*In the Sands of the Qara-Qum*, 1928) – deal with the Basmachi revolt among the Turkmen, a popular subject for later films.[31]

Sytin's text can be understood as part of the Civil War genre exemplified by Dmitrii Furmanov's *Chapaev* (1923),[32] but with its villainous Orientals and central captivity narrative it also shows clear influences from the broader genre of European colonial literature. His adventure stories read like something that could have been published in *The Boy's Own Paper* or *Chums* at the same time, with overtones of what Patrick Brantlinger refers to as "Imperial Gothic," and *Zheltyi Mrak/Kontrabandisty* is no exception.[33] Opening in a Kyrgyz *yurt* deep in the Tian-Shan mountains near the Chinese border, we are introduced to the main protagonists – the border guard Budai (a Ukrainian) and his nemesis, the "Father of Smugglers," Baizak – who has wormed his way into the structures of Soviet power as the chair of the local Consumers' cooperative (*potrebkooperatsii*).

Budai is on the brink of securing proof that Baizak is behind the smuggling of opium from China into Soviet Semirechie. However, the villainous and cunning Baizak (luridly depicted in the original 1928 publication, see Figure 4.1), has Budai arrested on a trumped-up charge of corruption. The task of clearing Budai's name and securing proof of Baizak's villainy then falls to his friend, the fierce, diminutive cavalry officer Kondratii and his loyal Kyrgyz guide Janmurchi, who had once been a smuggler before Budai rescued him in a mountain pass. Baizak manages to evade the authorities for so long partly because he has the support of a Kyrgyz elder, Jantai, who had become alienated from the Russians before the Revolution when a colonial police chief stole his wife and beat him. Jantai killed the official and retreated to the mountains, where he is still unaware that Tsarist colonial rule is no more, and that Soviet power has introduced equality. Baizak kidnaps Kondratii's wife Marianna, and while in captivity with Jantai's Kyrgyz, she is forced to roll felt until her hands bleed. Assisted by a Kyrgyz girl, Kalych, she escapes easily, slipping out of the yurt in the darkness. In the original story they rather fortuitously reach safety when they run into a Red Army patrol, in a passage worthy of Zane Grey:

> [T]hey smelt the scent of *makhorka* [coarse tobacco] and saw the red glint at the end of a cigar, while a rough voice said 'who goes there?'. After that it was as if she was asleep. Marianna knew only that she had returned to her own, and that a Red Army man, seizing her with tough hands like steel, swept her into the saddle.[34]

In the longer novel Marianna's captivity and escape are treated more fully. Both versions meanwhile contain an ethnographic aside, in which Sytin tells a story of the legendary origins of Lake Issyk-Kul – quite clearly derived from the same source as that of King Midas and his donkey's ears, which was also narrated by the Swiss traveler Ella Maillart, who visited Issyk-Kul in 1932.[35]

FIGURE 4.1 The "Father of Smugglers," Baizak, illustration from *Yellow Darkness*, the 1928 version of Sytin's tale. Screenshot by the author.

Sytin's novel certainly has sympathetic and heroic Kyrgyz protagonists – Janmurchi and Jantai, both of whom will serve the Soviets and play a key role in bringing Baizak to justice – but nevertheless it reserves greater agency for its European characters, Budai and Kondratii. It also makes great play of the plight of a European woman kidnapped by nomads, a familiar narrative in the Western and indeed other films featuring "Orientals" (famously *The Sheikh*, 1921). Throughout both versions of the novel the Kyrgyz characters address the Russian Bolsheviks as *Tura*, an honorific for Europeans in Central Asia which was the equivalent of the Anglo-Indian *Sahib*. The settler colonial flavoring of the literary source of *The Scarlet Poppies of Issyk-Kul* is thus clear. What then did a Kyrgyz – but also Soviet – director, Bolotbek Shamshiev, make of this?

Nationalizing the Colonial in *The Scarlet Poppies of Issyk-Kul*

Certain elements of the colonial narrative and power relations do survive in Sham-shiev's film, particularly in its early scenes. The film opens with a group of young European Red Army horsemen galloping through a field of opium poppies in order to destroy them, when one is felled by a bullet from a hidden assailant, his blood dripping across the scarlet blossoms. As in many Westerns, the Soviet cavalrymen appear overwhelmed by the vastness of the landscape, while the smugglers, like Native Americans in the Western, are elusive figures whose control of that space has to be broken in order for civilization (in this case Bolshevism) to triumph.[36] The treacherous Baizak, played by Sovetbek Dzhumadilov, seen in Soviet uniform (Figure 4.2), appears to be a model Soviet official assisting the commandant, Kon-dratii, in the operation. We then see the latter awakening before dawn to receive news of the smugglers from his scout, Qarabalta – a hybrid of the figures of Budai

FIGURE 4.2 Baizak (L) and Kondratii (R) inspect a field of opium poppies in the opening scene of *The Scarlet Poppies of Issyk-Kul*. Photograph © Alexander Fedorov, Kyrgyzfilm.

and Janmurchi in Sytin's novel – played by Suimenkul Chokmorov. He is described as strange and unwilling to submit to discipline, but loyal. Kondratii's wife, Olga, is enchanted both by the glorious mountain scenery (one of those overwhelming natural landscapes so characteristic of Westerns) and the yurt which has been erected in the fortress courtyard. In a later scene we see her being welcomed and shown inside by a Kyrgyz woman. With the cavalry riding forth from the stockade and the mountains in the background, we could easily be in the American West. Within the first ten minutes, Kondratii refers obliquely to the 1916 revolt, and the flight of the Kyrgyz to China which followed (the *Ürkün*); the yurt in the stockade belongs to a returning refugee. The pre-Revolutionary settler colonial past is also referred to when the son of Kalmat (Jantai), a Kyrgyz elder, is brought into the fort. In a defiant speech he says that his father is not a bandit, but an honorable man who killed a colonial official "[w]hen the White Tsar took our land," and then led his lineage away from Issyk-Kul into the mountains where they have dwelt ever since. In a conversation with Baizak we learn that Kondratii had served for two years in Bukhara, a clear reference to Mikhail Frunze's campaign of re-conquest of 1920–1921 in which Sytin had also participated. Kondratii is shown at ease with Central Asian customs of hospitality and tea-drinking, and in later scenes we hear him speaking in (dubbed) Kyrgyz: rather like Kirby York and Nathan Brittles in Ford's "Cavalry Trilogy," Kondratii (also a cavalry officer) has close and friendly relations with the indigenous population, which establishes both his indigeneity as a settler and his credentials as a Bolshevik commander.[37] However Baizak exploits these intimate social relations to sow distrust in Kondratii's mind, hinting that Qarabalta is politically suspect: he had been exiled for murder under "Nikolai" (Nicholas II), taken part in the 1916 uprising, and then spent a long period in China.

Although Kondratii and his men (all of whom are Russian) play an important role, and represent the monopoly of legitimate violence claimed by Soviet power, they are not the focus of *Scarlet Poppies*. Instead the hero is unquestionably Qarabalta (an intense, brooding performance from Chokmorov), and its two most dramatic moments have no Russian involvement at all. The first comes after Kondratii has rejected Qarabalta, convinced by circumstances and Baizak's lies that he cannot be trusted. In a local tavern Qarabalta then sings a dramatic lament in Qazaq, accompanying himself on the *dombyra* (two-stringed instrument); it is a song which he says he learnt when returning across the Qazaq steppe from Siberian exile. The other moment of emotional climax is the final struggle between Qarabalta and Baizak, in which they wrestle on horseback over a sheer drop, gripping their *kamcha*s (whips) in their teeth.

The film retains the kidnapping of Kondratii's wife during a raid on the Red Army stockade, but we see much less of her captivity than in the novel. Most significantly, the climax of the film is neither the downfall of Baizak nor the triumph of Soviet power, but the moment when Kalman leads his people down out of the mountains to the shores of Issyk-Kul. This is a clear evocation of the return of the Kyrgyz refugees who had fled the repression of the 1916 revolt. A longing for the waters and lands of Issyk-Kul is a powerful theme in much of the poetry and oral epic produced at that time.[38] Thus, although the aesthetics and imagery of *Scarlet Poppies* owe a good deal to the Western – its setting, Semirechie, was indeed a site of Russian settlement, and the source material on which it was based, Sytin's novel, undoubtedly did have colonial overtones – Shamshiev bends Sytin's narrative in new directions and reimagines the Russian author's characters. He patches these together with references to the 1916 revolt and its suppression in the forging of a Kyrgyz collective identity, and the role of Kyrgyz agency and heroism in defending Soviet power. The result is a film infused with Kyrgyz ethnic sensibilities, which in many ways subverts the colonial text on which it is based.

Conclusion

Despite some aesthetic and thematic similarities to the Western, the Soviet "Eastern" is a very distinctive genre in its own right. Even *The Scarlet Poppies of Issyk-Kul*, which unlike most of these films has many Russian characters and is set in a region of extensive Russian settlement, still affords much greater prominence to Kyrgyz national than to Russian settler colonial narratives. Central Asian *Basmachi* films, though to modern eyes they may seem riddled with Orientalist stereotyping and hackneyed Soviet propaganda, were often perceived at the time as a product of national culture – none more so than Ali Khamraev's masterpiece *Sed'maya Pulya* (*The Seventh Bullet*, 1972) also starring Chokmorov, which has no Russian characters at all. Although they certainly celebrated the victory of Soviet power over indigenous forces of resistance, in these films the agents of that power were usually Central Asians themselves: Soviet and national narratives were intertwined. This was at least partly a reflection of historical reality; the coming of Soviet Power to Central Asia during the Civil War was not simply the resurrection of Russian colonialism in another form, and early Soviet nationalities policy had a surprising amount in common with modernizing, nationalizing states such as Kemalist Turkey.[39] "National in form, Socialist in content" was the slogan for Soviet state-building in Central Asia, and as a wealth of recent scholarship has shown, Soviet nationalities policy was not simply window-dressing, neither in its origins in the 1920s, nor even at the height of the Stalin era.[40] By the time the "Eastern" genre came into its own in the 1960s and 1970s, there was increasing national autonomy in the cultural sphere in Soviet Central Asia, partly as a safety-valve given the very limited freedom in the political sphere.[41] While cultural Russianness was accorded pre-eminence in the USSR, this was not always true of Russians (or more broadly Europeans) as an ethnicity. The nationalizing component of Soviet rule remained crucially important and gained in strength in the 1970s, the period of supposed Brezhnevian *zastoi* (stagnation), while the independent states that emerged in the region after 1991 have built their new national identities on Soviet foundations.[42] Settler colonial themes are certainly present in much Russian literature and film with Central Asian settings, but the late Soviet *Basmachi* films or "Easterns" are better seen as a small but important facet of the Soviet nation-building project.

Acknowledgments

My thanks to Aminat Chokobaeva and Chris Baker for their comments on this paper, and to Alexander Fedorov for permission to re-use his photograph of Baizak and Kondratii.

Notes

1 Alexander Morrison, "Russian Settler Colonialism," in *The Routledge Handbook of the History of Settler Colonialism*, eds. Edward Cavanagh and Lorenzo Veracini. (Abingdon: Routledge, 2016), 313–326.
2 Lorenzo Veracini, *Settler Colonialism: A Theoretical Overview* (Basingstoke: Palgrave Macmillan, 2010), 3, 95–104.
3 Peter Limbrick, *Making Settler Cinemas: Film and Colonial Encounters in the United States, Australia, and New Zealand* (Basingstoke: Palgrave Macmillan, 2010); Janne Lahti "What is Settler Colonialism and What is Has to Do with the American West?," *Journal of the West* 56, no. 4 (2018), 8–12.
4 Marco Buttino, *La Rivoluzione Capovolta: L'Asia Centrale tra il crolle dell'impero zarista e la formazione dell'URSS* (Naples: l'Ancora del mediterraneo, 2003), 285–326; Beatrice Penati, "The reconquest of East Bukhara: the struggle against the Basmachi as a prelude to Sovietization," *Central Asian Survey* 26, no. 4 (2007), 521–538.
5 Alexander V. Prusin & Scott C. Zeman, "Taming Russia's Wild East: The Central Asian historical-Revolutionary film as Soviet Orientalism," *Historical Journal of Film, Radio and Television*, 23, no. 3 (2003), 259–270.
6 Birgit Beumers, "Soviet and Russian Blockbusters: A Question of Genre?' *Slavic Review* 62, no. 3 (2003), 441–454, here 452.
7 Devid Skhimmel'pennink van der Oie, "Orientalizm – delo tonkoe," *Ab Imperio* (2002) No.1: 249–264; Vincent Bohlinger "'The East is a Delicate Matter' *White Sun of the Desert* and the Soviet Western," in *International Westerns: Re-Locating the Frontier*, eds. Cynthia J. Miller & Riper A. Bowdoin. (Lanham: Scarecrow Press, 2013), 373–393; Elvira Kulieva, "The East is A Delicate Matter' or Soviet Orientalism in Films about Central Asia 1955–1970," (MA Thesis, Ibn Khaldun University, 2018), 71–78.
8 Svetlana Alexievich, *Boys in Zinc* trans. Andrew Bromfield (London: Penguin, 2016), 106; Svetlana Alexievich, *Tsinkovye mal'chiki* (Moscow: Vremya, 2015), 116.
9 Kirill Nourzhanov "Bandits, warlords, national heroes: interpretations of the Basmachi movement in Tajikistan," *Central Asian Survey*, 34, no. 2 (2015), 177–189, here 178–179.
10 Michael G. Smith, "Cinema for the 'Soviet East': National Fact and Revolutionary Fiction in Early Azerbaijani Film," *Slavic Review* 56, no. 4 (1997), 645–67, here 647–657.
11 The film is also discussed briefly in Prusin & Zeman "Taming Russia's Wild East," 266–267.
12 Aminat Chokobaeva, "Frontiers of Violence: State and Conflict in Semirechye, 1850–1938," (PhD Dissertation, Australian National University, 2017); Alexander Morrison, "Peasant Settlers and the Civilising Mission in Russian Turkestan," *Journal of Imperial & Commonwealth History* 43, no. 3 (2015), 387–417.
13 Matthew J. Payne, "Viktor Turin's Turksib (1929) and Soviet Orientalism," *Historical Journal of Film, Radio and Television*, 21, no. 1 (2001), 37–62; Gabrielle Chomentowski, "Vostokkino and the Foundation of Central Asian Cinema," in *Cinema in Central Asia. Rewriting Cultural Histories*, eds. Michael Rouland, Gulnara Abikeyeva and Birgit Beumers (London: I. B. Tauris, 2013), 39–40.
14 Cloe Drieu, *Cinema, Nation and Empire in Uzbekistan, 1919–1937* (Bloomington, IN: Indiana University Press, 2018), 29, 64–65.
15 Prusin & Zeman, "Taming Russia's Wild East," 262–263.

16 Kh. Abulkasymova *et al* eds., *Istoriya Sovetskogo Kino* vol. 2 *1931–1941* (Moscow: Izd. Iskusstvo, 1973), 200–201.

17 Drieu, *Cinema, Nation and Empire in Uzbekistan*, 70.

18 Drieu, *Cinema, Nation and Empire in Uzbekistan*, 82.

19 Abulkasymova *et al* eds., *Istoriya Sovetskogo Kino* vol.4 *1952–1967* (Moscow: Izd. Iskusstvo, 1978), 245–246; Lino Micciché, "The Cinema of the Transcaucasian and Central Asian Soviet Republics," in *The Red Screen: Politics, Society, Art in Soviet Cinema*, ed. Anna Lawton (London: Routledge, 1992), 298–9; Michael Rouland, "Historical Introduction," & Joel Chapron, "A Small History of Kyrgyz Cinema," both in *Cinema in Central Asia*, 14, 128.

20 Abulkasymova, *Istoriya Sovetskogo Kino*, 250–253; Kulieva "The East is a Delicate Matter," 63–71.

21 Chapron, "A Small History of Kyrgyz Cinema," in *Cinema in Central Asia*, 129.

22 Drieu, *Cinema, Nation and Empire*, 82.

23 Aminat Chokobaeva, "When the nomads went to war: the uprising of 1916 in Semirech'e'," in *The Central Asian Revolt of 1916: A Collapsing Empire in an Age of War and Revolution*, eds. Aminat Chokobaeva, Cloé Drieu, and Alexander Morrison (Manchester: Manchester University Press, 2020), 145–168.

24 "Editors Introduction," in *The Central Asian Revolt of 1916*, 7–8.

25 Aleksandr Sytin, 'Zheltyi mrak' *Al'manakh prikliuchenii – Zheltyi mrak* (Moscow: Moskovskoe tov. pisatelei, 1927), 3–28

26 Aleksandr Sytin, *Kontrabandisty Tian'-Shania* (Kharkov: Tip. "Proletarii", 1927); Aleksandr Sytin *Kontrabandisty Tian'-Shania* (Moscow: Molodaya Gvardiya, 1930).

27 Aleksandr Sytin, *Kontrabandisty Tian'-Shania. Povest'* (Tbilisi: Literatura da khelovneba, 1964).

28 Vladimir Genis, *"S Bukharoi nado konchat'"* K *istorii butaforskoi revoliutsii* (Moscow: TSPI, 2001); Alex Marshall, "Turkfront: Frunze and the development of Soviet counter-insurgency in Central Asia," in *Central Asia. Aspects of Transition*, ed. Tom Everett-Heath (London: Routledge, 2003), 5–29.

29 'Zakleimennye vlast'iu. Ankety, pis'ma, zayavleniya politzakliuchennykh v Moskovskii Krasnyi Krest' http://pkk.memo.ru/letters_pdf/002609.pdf

30 *Boi Paukov* ['Battle of Spiders'] – *Rasskazy* (Moscow: "Ogonëk", 1928); *Brat Idola* ['The Idol's Brother'] – *Rasskazy* (Moscow-Leningrad: Zemlya i Fabrika, 1928); *v Teni Mechetei* ['In the Shadow of the Mosques'] *Rasskazy* (Moscow-Leningrad: Zemlya i Fabrika, 1930).

31 Aleksandr Sytin, 'Vesy Zhazhdy. Rasskaz iz epokhy grazhdanskoi voiny v Turkestane' *Vsemirnyi Sledopyt'* (1927) No. 11, 822–843; A. P. Sytin *v peskakh Kara-Kuma. Epizod iz istorii bor'by s basmachestvom* (Moscow: Gosizdat, 1928).

32 On *Chapaev* (which was filmed in 1934) see Katerina Clark, *The Soviet Novel. History as Ritual* 3rd ed. (Bloomington, IN: Indiana University Press, 2000), 84–88; Evgeny Dobrenko 'Creation Myth and Myth Creation in Stalinist Cinema' *Studies in Russian and Soviet Cinema* 1/3 (2007): 239–264; Julian Graffy, *Chapaev* (London: I. B. Tauris, 2010), 8–11; Angela Brintlinger, *Chapaev and His Comrades: War and the Russian Literary Hero Across the Twentieth Century* (Academic Studies Press, 2012), 42–52.

33 Patrick Brantlinger, *Rule of Darkness: British Literature and Imperialism 1830–1914* (Ithaca, NY: Cornell University Press, 1988), 227–253.

34 Sytin, "Zheltyi mrak," 26.

35 Ella Maillart, *Turkestan Solo* (London: Unwin, 1934), 48–9.

36 Limbrick, *Making Settler Cinemas*, 74–5, 80.

37 Limbrick, *Making Settler Cinemas*, 72.

38 Jipar Duishembieva, "From rebels to refugees: memorialising the revolt of 1916 in oral poetry," in *The Central Asian Revolt of 1916*, 294–301.

39 Adeeb Khalid, "Backwardness and the Quest for Civilization: Early Soviet Central Asia in Comparative Perspective," *Slavic Review* 65.2 (2006), 231–251.

40 Terry Martin, *The Affirmative Action Empire: Nations and Nationalism in the Soviet Union, 1923–1939* (Ithaca, NY: Cornell University Press, 2001), 125–181; Jeremy Smith, *Red Nations. The Nationalities Experience in and after the USSR* (Cambridge: Cambridge University Press, 2013), 76–84; Adeeb Khalid, *Making Uzbekistan: Nation, Empire and Revolution in the Early USSR* (Ithaca, NY: Cornell University Press, 2015); Eren Tasar, *Soviet and Muslim: The Institutionalization of Islam in Central Asia* (Oxford: Oxford University Press, 2017).

41 Shoshana Keller, "Going to School in Uzbekistan," in *Everyday Life in Central Asia: Past and Present*, Jeff Sahadeo and Russell Zanca, eds. (Bloomington, IN: Indiana University Press, 2007), 254–260.

42 Nick Megoran, *Nationalism in Central Asia: A Biography of the Uzbekistan-Kyrgyzstan Boundary* (Pittsburgh, PA: Pittsburgh University Press, 2017), 32–40, 77–88.

PART II
Settlers

5

GUNLESS AS SETTLER COLONIAL BORDERLANDS FANTASY

Sheila McManus

Director William Phillips describes his 2010 film *Gunless* as a "Canadian Western" – a film that embraces many of the tropes of the classic (American) Western film genre but sets it in the Canadian West to tell a Canadian story. Anyone with a passing familiarity with Western Canadian geography and history would guess that the story is meant to be seen as taking place in southern Alberta, somewhere just north of the border with Montana, and sometime in the early 1880s.[1] After surviving a botched hanging, American gunfighter the Montana Kid (played by well-known Canadian actor Paul Gross) finds himself in a small town just north of the border where the residents' kind behavior and distinct lack of functioning pistols mystify him.[2] Determined to settle a grievance with the local blacksmith through a gun duel, the Montana Kid is forced to wait around for a few days while the same blacksmith helps him repair the only other handgun in town besides his own. That delay, interspersed with scenes of four American bounty hunters riding north to capture him, gives the town's residents, and their stereotypically "Canadian" values, time to convince him that he can be a better person. The final, inevitable shootout, an inescapable feature of the genre, is as much between two sets of cultural norms, two supposedly different settler colonial projects, as it is between men with guns.

All the classic elements of a Western film are here – a morality tale and crises over different masculinities wrapped in a story about respectable white people working hard to start a new life in a dusty little place far from anywhere else. The Western genre is also, at its heart, a fantasy genre because it creatively re-imagines Western spaces as blank slates on which white fantasies about those spaces can then be written.[3] *Gunless* is unquestionably a Canadian nationalist fantasy in its earnest efforts to showcase a variety of white settler ethnicities; the polite racism where visible minorities are marginalized but not attacked; and its effort to associate every negative characteristic with Americans. Those Canadian stereotypes, along with the evidence that this film is situated in the Alberta-Montana borderlands in the early 1880s, means that this is also a border-lands tale, an origin tale used to shore up the symbolic divide between "Canadians" and "Americans." In this chapter I explore four key features of the film to argue that it can be read not just as a Canadian Western but as a Canadian settler colonial border-lands fantasy: the erasure of Indigenous peoples and place-names; a celebration of the myth of Canadian multiculturalism; the veneration of white Canadian masculinity through the figure of the North West Mounted Police (NWMP) officer; and the way the explicitly anti-American narratives in the film justify the Canadian colonial project and its borderlines. Erasing Indigeneity is common to settler colonialism worldwide, but the last three features are uniquely Canadian twists on a global pattern.

Creating a Blank Slate

Gunless presents viewers with a classic Western scene – a small town is being con-structed apparently in the middle of nowhere. This generic place is called "Barclay's Brush," but none of the townspeople are named Barclay. In keeping with colonized spaces everywhere, Barclay's Brush seems to have been named after a white person who is not there and perhaps never was. At no point in the film does any character reference the Indigenous territory they are in, or name the original peoples who would have had to be defeated or moved aside to make way for the town. As scholars Paul Carter and Daniel Francis have argued, settler colonialism assumes the right to sprinkle names across the landscape that have little or no connection to the places they are naming, and needs Indigenous peoples to disappear so that those new names, and the land grabs they represent, seem legitimate.[4] Anthropologist Patrick Wolfe adds that settler society doesn't just require the "practical elimination of the natives in order to establish itself on their territory;" settler colonial nations then have a tendency to try and recuperate some semblance of "indigeneity in order to express its difference – and, accordingly, its independence – from the mother country."[5]

This tension is evident in *Gunless*, where Indigenous place names and commu-nities are gone but a single character remains. The only Indigenous person we see in the film (but never in the town itself) is "N'Kwala" or "Two Dogs," played by iconic Oneida actor Graham Greene. N'Kwala only appears in three scenes and is not given a specific national designation; the character has few lines but when he speaks it is in perfect, unaccented English; and his main purpose seems to be to guide and advise the hapless but well-meaning North West Mounted Police officer, Cor-poral Kent.[6] By leaving his nationality unnamed N'Kwala can stand in for all Indi-genous peoples, softening rather than contradicting the erasure of Indigenous peoples in the film's fantasy landscape. The role of "wise Indian guide" is stereotypical, but less overtly racist than most Indigenous characters in classic Western films. He is not here to be the "savage" against which the white men prove their superiority, but instead represents another key Canadian myth: that Canada was less racist towards Indigenous peoples than the United States and Indigenous peoples are a welcome piece of the Canadian multicultural mosaic.

The Myth of Canadian Multiculturalism

The Canadian nation-state has long struggled with the lack of a defining origin story; unlike the United States with its War of Independence against its former colonial rulers, Canada is still a constitutional monarchy subject to the British Crown, which makes it harder to point to a moment when "Canada" became "Canada." Historian Gillian Roberts argues that since the 1970s, "multiculturalism" and "the act of welcoming the stranger" have become central components of Canada's national imaginary. This discourse asserts that a Canadian "mosaic" exists and welcomes differences, and is morally superior to the American "melting pot" where everyone is expected to assimilate.[7] Historian Daniel Francis adds that the myth of the mosaic insists that

> Canadian society is characterized by a tolerance for ethnic and cultural diversity quite unlike other countries, and especially unlike the United States. The mosaic conjures up an image of a society in which different groups live amicably side by side, each appreciating the characteristics and contributions of all the others.[8]

By contrast, sociologist Himani Bannerji cautions that while this discourse has served as a powerful "ideology of unification and legitimation" within Canada, it cannot hide the fact that "Canadians" are still, by default, European-descent white settlers.[9] The myth of the mosaic may contend that all are welcome in Canada and none will be forced to assimilate, but this belief has more to do with discursive posturing than lived reality.

The residents of Barclay's Brush and its hinterlands are the ideal microcosm of this myth of the Canadian multicultural mosaic: there are a lot of white people from a range of European backgrounds, playing out particular scripts from Canadian history, and the small number of racial minorities are well-treated. For example, the two shopkeepers, Carl Parker (Shawn Campbell) and Claude Payette (Paul Coeur), are from England and Quebec, respectively. They represent the long-standing Canadian myth that England and France were the "two founding nations" of Canada, and in Barclay's Brush the two solitudes share a general store with an invisible line drawn down the middle to separate the two halves.[10] Each side of the store sells different items and invokes different stereotypes. The French-Canadian merchant Payette seems more relaxed and fun-loving because he sells alcohol on his side, while his partner/rival Parker sells tea, bullets, and dry goods, and has a portrait of Queen Victoria prominently displayed behind his half of the counter.

Only three other white men in the film have clearly identified backgrounds: one is from Peterborough, Ontario; the second from Moncton, New Brunswick; and the third is from Uppsala, Sweden. In the late nineteenth century white, English-speaking Central and Eastern Canadians were dominant groups among the tiny number of settlers who migrated to southern Alberta, and Scandinavians were one of the European groups that the Canadian federal government courted to come settle the Canadian West.[11] Similarly, as historian Carl Betke notes, Canadian officials assumed that white settlers like the British and Scandinavians were coming with enough capital and previous farming experience to become economic assets quickly, and "they shared acceptable cultural values, emphasizing cleanliness and neatness, following similar Protestant religious traditions (for the most part) and, in striving for the comfortable life, accepting the virtue of self-sufficiency."[12] With the exception of the female lead character Jane Taylor (Sienna Guillory), whose accent marks her as a British newcomer, the rest of the white characters are not demarcated with any kind of ethnic origin.

Strikingly absent, except as the Others in the film, are white Americans who made up a significant proportion of western settlers in the 1870s and 1880s and who were also deliberately courted by the Canadian government. Canadian officials wanted Americans because they assumed that they were usually white farmers with some capital and experience, and because any such recruitment efforts would play into emerging nationalist narratives about Canada's superiority over the United States.[13] Showing white Americans as peaceful settlers would disrupt both a key facet of Canadian myth-making and a key piece of the film's plot; as I will discuss at more length below, *Gunless* needs the American men to signify everything that the Canada is not.

Evidently, the Canadian mosaic, at least as far as the range of white people is concerned, is alive and well in Barclay's Brush. Besides N'Kwala, the only other people of color in the film are Chinese. Comprised of about 10 or 12 people, mostly young men but also one three-generation family, the little Chinese community is also there to serve key narrative, nationalist purposes. In the late 1870s and early 1880s Canada recruited more than 17,000 young Chinese men to build its first transcontinental railroad, the Canadian Pacific Railway, just north of the border with the United States. Chinese men were desirable laborers for this dangerous, deadly work because they could be paid far less than white men and were perceived as so unimportant that officials would not be held accountable for the high death toll during construction. However, Canada took steps to bar Chinese women from entering the country and passed restrictive anti-Chinese immigration legislation in 1885 as soon as the railway was completed.[14] Barclay's Brush has an ahistorical abundance of both white and Chinese women. Most of the white men have white wives, and the young Chinese girl, Adell Kwon (Melody B. Choi), who serves as the Montana Kid's local guide when he first arrives, seems to have both a mother and grandmother present in her life. In reality, the North American West in the late nineteenth century was characterized by a distinct lack of non-Indigenous women. The census data for southern Alberta in the early 1880s includes very few white women and no Chinese women. The former did not begin to settle the southwest corner of the Canadian prairies until after the railroad was completed, and the Canadian federal government was using its immigration legislation to keep the latter out of the country altogether.[15]

Somewhat improbably, therefore, the first person the Montana Kid meets when he arrives in town is young Adell Kwon. Adell later explains to him that the Chinese men living in the tents on the outskirts of town are "railroad work-ers," and her grandparents let them rest here in between building the lines. Racist recruitment practices and immigration policies means that there is no way this multi-generational Chinese community could actually have existed anywhere in the Canadian West in the late nineteenth century. But that is not the point; the film needs these racialized Others so that the white Canadian characters can be portrayed as less racist than the white American characters. The Chinese community is appropriately placed at the margins of town life: they own and operate a laundry and the immediate family seem to live in the building, while the young male railroad workers live in tents on the outskirts of town. Further-more, Adell is never shown playing with the white children, but sits apart from them reading a book, none of the Chinese can be seen at the community dance at the NWMP fort, and Adell's grandfather (Tseng Chang) sits at the back of the schoolroom during the adult-education evening class, trying to learn English while the whites in the room debate the philosophy of violence. Like N'Kwala, the Chinese are seen adding their uniqueness to the Canadian mosaic, and their presence allows the white community to demonstrate their ability to welcome "strangers." Unlike N'Kwala, the presence of Chinese women, a child, and a seat in the schoolhouse suggest that they have a future in the Canadian mosaic that the lone Indigenous man does not.

The Gunslinger and the Mountie

It's no accident that these racialized communities and ethnicities are also explicitly gendered – the Western film genre is nothing if not centrally concerned with the masculinities of white men and their Others, and *Gunless* is no exception. As lit-erary scholar Lee Clark Mitchell argues, the one element that brings together the wide range of possible ingredients and makes a film "a Western" is "the problem of what it means to be a man ...." Westerns are about men – their bodies, con-flicts, honor, transformation, and redemption – and the "freedom to achieve some truer state of humanity."[16] What matters are masculinities, and here *Gunless* excels at portraying the range of acceptable and unacceptable masculinities in the Canadian West. The white men in Barclay's Brush own rifles for hunting, but not handguns because they see them as only good for killing people. When the Montana Kid "calls out" Jack, the blacksmith (Tyler Mane), and sees him as less masculine because he does not have a pistol, the situation is meant to be funny because the blacksmith is eight inches taller and more heavily muscled than the Kid; the blacksmith does not need a gun to be a physically dominant male. The audience learns during the shoot-out at the end of the film that Jack is also a really good shot, as he is able to shoot the American bounty hunter's gun out of his hand from a hundred feet away. On the other end of the manliness spectrum is Adell's grandfather Mr. Kwon, who is placed in the feminized role that many Chinese men were accorded in the North American West in the late nineteenth century. Not only does Kwon run a laundry, he is the victim who has to be rescued during the climactic shoot-out.

In *Gunless* the central male character, the one most in need of redemption, is the American gunslinger who finds his humanity in Barclay's Brush. The first time we see him his masculinity is already in some doubt – where the classic Western fetishizes the image of a man sitting tall on his horse, the Montana Kid is riding backwards, with a noose around his neck and dragging a tree branch. A key step in his transformation and redemption occurs with another classic Western ingredient – the man in the bath. Mitchell notes that "No other genre has men bathe as often as Westerns, where they repeatedly strip down to nothing more than an occasional hat, cigar, and bubbles to soak the dust away."[17] This isn't just about the physical act of cleaning his body, getting rid of the dirt and smells that he has dragged into town with him and which all the residents comment on; it is a key moment in his transformation into something cleaner, more civilized, and in this case also more Canadian. *Gunless* uses that scene to tie back to its argument about multiculturalism. The Montana Kid takes his first bath in the Chinese laundry, and then has to dress in a Chinese-style silk tunic and loose pants because his own clothes were so filthy that the women had taken them away to be cleaned and repaired.

Throughout much of the film the Montana Kid's behavior is meant to be a stark contrast to that of the other white men in town, and none more so than the young, squeaky-clean, North West Mounted Police officer Corporal Jonathan Kent (Dustin Milligan). *Gunless* both embraces and subtly undermines Mountie stereotypes. As discussed above, the Canadian nation has had to fabricate its national mythologies without the benefit of a clear foundational myth, and since at least the early twentieth century, the Mounties have been a key feature of that fabric.[18] Canada is perhaps one of the only nations in the world that has chosen "a police force as their proudest national symbol." They represent "the importance of law and the subservience of the individual to the community," and capture how many "Canadians like to see themselves: honest, brave, modest, law-abiding, polite."[19] It would be difficult to exaggerate the central role that the Mounties play in Canadian culture and identity. When the Disney Corporation bought the rights to license the "Mountie image" in 1995 there was national outrage, "a mixture of disbelief and horror" that this "iconic Canadian symbol" was now owned by an iconic American company.[20] However, the Mounties are a "national" symbol with a very specific Western history. Their origin story focuses on the role they played in "facilitating the 'peaceful occupation' of the North-West Territories" and forging supposedly great working relationships with Western Indigenous peoples. Canada did not have any Indian Wars, the story goes, because the NWMP brought law, order, and mutual respect to the western settler frontier.[21] As a result, the specific kind of white masculinity the NWMP supposedly created in the West is equated with settler Canadian masculinity.

FIGURE 5.1 Before. Filthy Montana Kid at the beginning, still very American. Photo courtesy of Alamy.

In *Gunless*, Corporal Kent, is, for the most part, everything a Canadian audience expects a Mountie to be: white, handsome, unassuming, patient, impartial, self-disciplined, sober, and incorruptible. He is a stickler for rules, procedures, and justice, and seems to have a close working relationship with N'Kwala. Kent is the bulwark of order in this dusty borderlands region, but what could have been a stereotypically faultless Mountie character is prevented from being too perfect. He is a bit clumsy, unsophisticated, and unobservant, from getting his coat caught on a loose nail and accidentally whacking people with the sword he carries on his hip, to not noticing when his horse has wandered off or that the young schoolteacher is clearly interested in him. He also plays a key role at the start of the Montana Kid's transformation into a Canadian local: his first appearance in the film is when he shows up to check on the Montana Kid and gets him to sign in. We learn that the Montana Kid's real name is "Sean Lafferty," and thereafter most of the town's residents begin to call him by that name.

FIGURE 5.2 After. Clean Sean Lafferty at the end, about to save the town and become a "good" Canadian. Photo courtesy of Alamy.

Given how central this image of the "good" Mounties is to Canadian myths about its settler colonial expansion, the presence of some badly behaved Mounties in *Gunless* is striking. Kent commands a group of men who are older than he is and less committed to fairness and the law. Halfway through the film there is a scene where the local white community has been invited to a dance at the NWMP post, and Lafferty is attending with Jane Taylor. Several Mounties confront him outside and tell him it is against the law for a "foreign national" to carry a gun inside one of "her Majesty's military posts."[22] They try to scare him by asking him if he knows what they do to "murderers who ride up into our country." Lafferty is not actually carrying his gun and denies ever murdering anyone, but the men start beating him up anyway and he makes no effort to defend himself. Just before Kent arrives to stop the beating, Lafferty can be heard saying "I thought you Canadians were supposed to be polite?" Kent stops the fight, berates the other men, and apologizes to Lafferty. It is another key step in Lafferty's transformation: he knows enough about "Canadians" to know how they should act, and he shares this knowledge when he is a victim of violence at the hands of Mounties.

Being Not-American

That scene both reinforces and challenges the final, distinguishing, feature which marks *Gunless* as not just a Canadian Western but a Canadian, settler colonial, borderlands fantasy: the pervasive anti-American narrative. As discussed above, white

Canadians have struggled since the late nineteenth century to define what makes their identity unique, and being "not American" quickly emerged as a key component. As sociologist Ian Angus has written, the United States "is not just any axis of comparison in English Canada; it is the axis that has been historically essential" to white Canadians' "claims of distinctiveness." Over the course of the twentieth century it became commonplace for many settler Canadians to believe that they "*just are* more peaceable, less greedy, more concerned with justice, and so on – simply and naturally better than Americans."[23]

North of the 49th parallel, a deep belief in the "contrast between Canadian order and American violence" has become "one of those self-congratulatory myths which bind a nation together," and the Mounties are at the heart of that belief.[24] The NWMP were created in reaction to the June 1873 Cypress Hills Massacre, or at least the way the Canadian press at the time reported on the Massacre. A group of white men, "at least half and perhaps two-thirds" of whom were Canadian, attacked a group of Assiniboines camped in the Cypress Hills, just north of the border in what is now southwest Saskatchewan, and killed at least twenty people. Canadian media coverage at the time insisted that the killers were American "wolfers" and whiskey traders, because a "story about Canadians killing Canadian Indians would not make very good Canadian propaganda."[25] The massacre raised the specter that the violence of the American "Indian Wars" could easily move north, and was the last push the Canadian government needed to create a paramilitary organization charged with making sure that neither violence, nor any other forms of American expansionism, crossed the 49th parallel.[26] The more familiar version of the NWMP's creation story is that the federal government created them to "protect" western Indigenous peoples from "American" whiskey traders, utterly ignoring the fact that alcohol had been a time-honored trade good for the Hudson's Bay Company long before there were any "American" traders to worry about. Either way, the NWMP kept a very close eye on Americans, because they "were convinced that all Americans were the potential bearers of anarchy, disorder, and violence."[27]

The anti-American narratives are performing crucial nationalist labor in a film set in the borderlands. This need to be not-American means that the border between the two countries has a lot of work to do when it comes to defining differences. In *Gunless*, the line itself is marked by nothing more than a small Red Ensign flag (Canada's flag from 1867–1965) on a little stick, flapping in the wind as the four American bounty hunters ride past. Exactly half-way through the film the line has been crossed, but how is the border-crossing moment itself to be understood? On the one hand, that little flag and little stick seem laughably small, and they certainly don't do anything to stop the riders or even slow them down. Yet on the other hand they are doing an admirable job at marking a space of difference – halfway through the film the people living north of the line have demonstrated values that mark them as different from the people who live south of the line. Everything is better north of the border: the people are nicer to each other and outsiders, the racism is less racist, and violence is never the answer, no matter what the provocation. As much as the film gently pokes fun at Canadian stereotypes – Kent is earnest but awkward, and the gang of Mounties who attack Lafferty are not being polite – it draws a clear line between desirable and undesirable characteristics by associating the latter with the five American men in the film, Lafferty himself and the four bounty hunters chasing him. At first everything about Lafferty's masculinity sets him apart from the locals, particularly the other white men in town. The film slowly introduces the ways in which he is also different from the American bounty hunters.

The "Canadians are less racist than Americans" narrative is rarely explicit in the film but is a key narrative thread. As noted above, a major component of the myth of the NWMP's role in colonizing Western Canada is that they had a mutually respectful working relationship with the Indigenous nations they had been sent west to pacify; it is a common stereotype in Canada that on the American side of the border all the US Army did was lie to and massacre Native Americans. In this myth, Canada's moral superiority and the superiority of British justice are literally embodied by the Mounted Police.[28] Similarly, the first thing the American bounty hunters do after crossing the line into Canada is terrorize the Chinese community, including killing a young boy's dog and threatening to murder Adell Kwon's mother, to get information about Lafferty's whereabouts. Until that scene they were just four men, riding as fast as they could across a dusty landscape towards the town, and perhaps their cause was just. But their first real introduction comes in a scene of racist violence, waving their guns at and mocking the accents of the Chinese. Shooting the dog is particularly shocking, but it reminds viewers of a story Lafferty had told earlier about his past, where he shot a man who had killed a dog. When Lafferty tells that story, over dinner with a few of the white married couples in town, it is part of a narrative about his violent past; its echoes in this scene are a clue that Lafferty is morally superior to the bounty hunters, and firmly establishes the Americans as bad men.[29] Oddly enough, the NWMP are nowhere to be seen in Barclay's Brush once the American bounty hunters arrive and start threatening to kill people; the Mounties do not reappear until after the final shootout is over, when the bad guys have been defeated (but not killed) and Kent can escort them out of the country.

Conclusion

Gunless isn't just a "Canadian" Western, although it does a beautiful job of borrowing and subverting the classic themes and tropes established by the American genre. It is at heart a borderlands fantasy – the invisible line that the bounty hunters gallop across, marked only by a tiny flag, marks the separation between the cleaner, kinder, Canadian West and the racism, violence, and filth of the American West. The Montana Kid always had the potential to be less American and more Canadian, as evidenced by his story of shooting a man who killed a dog, and by the end of the film his

"Canadianization" is complete. He refuses to shoot the blacksmith when he finally has the chance, and uses his gunfighting skills to free Adell Kwon's grandfather and help the town defend themselves against the bounty hunters. In the end, Sean Lafferty leaves his alias behind and chooses to stay in Barclay's Brush because he now appreciates not just the charms of Jane Taylor, but the community's superior social values.

In the late nineteenth century, the Canadian state and its settlers saw what they wanted to see when they looked at the Alberta-Montana borderlands. The Indigenous peoples already living there were rendered invisible, and their place names erased from the maps. This empty space could then be re-filled with a suitable mix of white settlers, protected by the benevolent justice of the North West Mounted Police and from the violence and racism which was assumed to flourish south of the line. *Gunless* plays that nineteenth-century fantasy back to the present day, creating the kind of foundational myth that Canadians want to believe in, on the blank nameless spaces of the borderlands.

Notes

1 Although the film was actually shot in British Columbia, the dry, dusty plains, foothills, and distant mountains, to say nothing of a protagonist named the Montana Kid, would suggest a southern Alberta setting to most Canadian viewers. IMDB says the film is set in 1878, but the presence of the Chinese railroad workers' camp indicates that it must be set between 1881, when construction on the CPR started, and 1885, when the line was completed.
2 Many Canadian viewers will appreciate the in-joke of having Gross play an American outlaw in Canada because one of his best-known roles is as RCMP Constable Benton Fraser on the TV show Due South (1994–1999), which was set in Chicago.
3 I am profoundly grateful to Blackfoot Elder Mike Bruised Head for sharing with me his insights about colonial naming practices, the elimination of Indigenous place-names, and the creation of settler colonial landscapes in the West.
4 Paul Carter, *The Road to Botany Bay: An Exploration of Landscape and History* (Minneapolis, MN: University of Minnesota Press, 1987), 3; Daniel Francis, *The Imaginary Indian: The Image of the Indian in Canadian Culture* (Vancouver: Arsenal Pulp Press, 1995), 59. See also Elizabeth A. Povinelli, *Economies of Abandonment: Social Belonging and Endurance in Late Liberalism* (Durham: Duke University Press, 2011); Povinelli, "Citizens of the Earth," in *Varieties of Sovereignty and Citizenship*, eds. Sigal R. Ben-Porath and Rogers M. Smith (Philadelphia: University of Pennsylvania Press, 2013); Jill Milroy and Grant Revell, "Aboriginal Story Systems: Re-mapping the West, Knowing Country, Sharing Space," *Occasion: Interdisciplinary Studies in the Humanities* 5 (March 2013), 1–24.
5 Patrick Wolfe, "Settler Colonialism and the Elimination of the Native," *Journal of Genocide Research* 8, no. 4 (2006), 389.
6 See, for example, Rebecca Weaver-Hightower, *Frontier Fictions: Settler Sagas and Postcolonial Guilt* (London, UK: Palgrave MacMillan, 2018).
7 Gillian Roberts, *Discrepant Parallels: Cultural Implications of the Canada-US Border* (Montreal, QC, and Kingston, ON: McGill-Queen's University Press, 2015), 14; Himani Bannerji, *The Dark Side of the Nation: Essays on Multiculturalism, Nationalism, and Gender* (Toronto, ON: Canadian Scholars' Press, 2000), 8.
8 Daniel Francis, *National Dreams: Myth, Memory, and Canadian History* (Vancouver: Arsenal Pulp Press, 1997), 80.
9 Bannerji, *Dark Side of the Nation*, 97, 64–65.

10 The title of Hugh MacLennan's 1945 novel, *Two Solitudes* (Toronto, ON: MacMillan, 1945), quickly became a convenient shorthand in Canadian political commentary for capturing the centuries of miscommunication between English-speaking and French-speaking settler Canadians.

11 Sheila McManus, *The Line Which Separates: Race, Gender, and the Making of the Alberta-Montana Borderlands* (Lincoln, NB and London, UK: University of Nebraska Press, 2005), 140.

12 Carl Betke, "Pioneers and Police on the Canadian Prairies, 1885–1914," in *The Mounted Police and Prairie Society, 1873–1919*, ed. William M. Baker (Regina, SK: Canadian Plains Research Centre and University of Regina, 1998), 214.

13 McManus, *The Line Which Separates*, 126.

14 For more on Canada's history of Chinese Exclusion see Patricia E. Roy, *A White Man's Province: British Columbia Politicians and Chinese and Japanese Immigrants, 1858–1914* (Vancouver, BC: University of British Columbia Press, 1989); Lisa Rose Mar, "Beyond Being Others: Chinese Canadians as National History," BC Studies 156/157 (Winter 2007): 13–34; Kornel Chang, *Pacific Connections: The Making of the U.S.-Canadian Borderlands* (Berkeley, CA: University of California Press, 2012).

15 McManus, *The Line Which Separates*, 143–144.

16 Lee Clark Mitchell, *Westerns: Making the Man in Fiction and Film* (Chicago, IL and London, UK: University of Chicago Press, 1996), 3, 5.

17 Mitchell, *Westerns: Making the Man in Fiction and Film*, 151.

18 Beth LaDow, *The Medicine Line: Life and Death on a North American Borderland* (New York, NY: Routledge 2001), 19; Francis, *National Dreams*, 31.

19 Francis, *National Dreams*, 29–30, 50.

20 Roberts, *Discrepant Parallels*, 64.

21 Amanda Nettelbeck and Robert Foster, "On the Trail of the March West: The NWMP in Western Canadian Historical Memory," in *Place and Replace: Essays on Western Canada*, eds. Adele Perry et al. (Winnipeg: University of Manitoba Press, 2013), 76; Francis, *Imaginary Indian*, 80–81.

22 The NWMP did indeed spend a lot of their time trying to regulate firearms in the Canadian West in the late nineteenth century, precisely because they associated too many guns with the "Wild West" south of the 49th parallel.

23 Ian Angus, *A Border Within: National Identity, Cultural Plurality, and Wilderness* (Montreal, QC, and Kingston, ON: McGill-Queen's University Press, 1997), 105, 113, 116, 119.

24 Desmond Morton, "Cavalry or Police: Keeping the Peace on Two Adjacent Frontiers, 1870–1900," in *The Mounted Police and Prairie Society, 1873–1919*, 3.

25 LaDow, *The Medicine Line*, 31. To this day, the official Parks Canada webpage about the massacre still says that the white men who attacked the camp were Americans. http s://www.pc.gc.ca/apps/dfhd/page_nhs_eng.aspx?id=1633 (accessed 5 January 2020).

26 Morton, "Cavalry or Police," 5–6.

27 R. C. Macleod, "The NWMP and Minority Groups," in *The Mounted Police and Prairie Society, 1873–1919*: 129. See also LaDow, *The Medicine Line*, 123.

28 Francis, *National Dreams*, 34.

29 LaDow, *The Medicine Line*, 32.

6

THE UNBEARABLE SETTLER WEST IN *THE BALLAD OF BUSTER SCRUGGS*

Janne Lahti

The Ballad of Buster Scruggs (2018), from Joel and Ethan Coen, frames the nineteenth-century American West through six short stories. They offer narratives in very typical Western scenarios. We have cowboys, gun fighters, bank robbers, prospectors, showmen, farmers, and even a vulnerable pioneer lady in need of rescue. We also get wagon trains, frontier towns, Indian attacks, and stagecoach rides – the usual Western tokenisms applied to characterize frontier and pioneer life and the advance of white civilization. It seems that only the US Cavalry and the railroads are missing from the prototypical Western imagery.[1] However, while *The Ballad of Buster Scruggs* operates in classic settler colonial narrative settings, it does not offer typical settler colonial narrative solutions.

Many commenters have interpreted the movie as a dark-humored blitz on Western tropes. One observant critic notes that the film advances "giddy Western revisionism" laughing at the expense of old Western legends, those "titanic heroes" still eagerly consumed by American politics and society as historical truths.[2] The film does more than "giddy," however. This essay will argue that it destabilizes the traditional narrative storyline of the Western and thus subverts the settler experience on the silver screen, recalibrating the settler West as emotionally twisted, as a sad, violent, and purposeless space. In the film, the settler lives random lives, wanders aimlessly, and dies abruptly, never overcoming nature, taming the land, or pacifying the violent frontier town; there is no "settling down" or starting a heterosexual nuclear family. The settler finds no righteousness, no justice, and no opening to enter his "house justified," to borrow the famous quote from director Sam Peckinpah's *Ride the High Country* (1962). In Peckinpah's classic depiction of Western masculinity, a former gunfighter Steve Judd (Joel McCrea), out of time and out of luck, wants to do the right thing and find redemption in life through honest work. He seeks no earthly riches, peer admiration, or power, but states that "All I want is to enter my House justified." There is no such prospect in *The Ballad of Buster Scruggs*. Its settler West is too unbearable for that.

That the emotional community in *The Ballad of Buster Scruggs* conveys a twisted settler West can be interpreted as undermining the legitimacy of archetypical historical narratives of America's western expansion, as subjecting settler penetration and the taking of the land to criticism while stripping the white settlers of their aura of virtue and respectability. Yet, the movie never goes as far as to question the US settler colonial project in the West. There is no narrative of individual settlers turning back, and there is no giving back of the land. Importantly, the settler West remains unbearably white, as if the settler colonial experience would only concern white people. When hiding the ethnic diversity of the historic West, this film reaffirms the prevailing public perceptions of settler colonial West as a white space, although now an emotionally twisted one. In the end, we still have a depiction of the white settler experience, no matter how ugly, told from the white settler perspective and through white settler emotions.

This essay contributes to an ongoing conversation about the ways in which the Western normalizes whiteness, and justifies and questions domination[3] by arguing that the settler West of *The Ballad of Buster Scruggs* constitutes an emotional community defined by purposelessness, randomness, and futility. As its analytical framework, this article employs the idea of "emotional communities" from historian Barbara H. Rosenwein.[4] While she uses the notion to refer to the systems of feeling that historical social communities express and share in real life, here "emotional community" refers to the kind of narrative strands of feeling that constitute the settler West on screen. *The Ballad of Buster Scruggs* represents the West as a specific type of twisted and unbearable emotional community marked by fear and sadness, the coldness and the randomness of settler existence.

The first part of this essay briefly discusses the Western as a prototypical settler colonial narrative and situates *The Ballad of Buster Scruggs* in the genre. The next section highlights how the first three episodes in *The Ballad of Buster Scruggs* represent the settler West as an emotional community through narrative solutions that destabilize our expectations. The last section zooms into the ways the familiar themes of land and the settler get similarly undermined in the final three episodes, while discussing what it indicates that whiteness continues to define the settler West.

The Western as Settler Colonial Formula

The American film genre commonly called "the Western" has been extensively studied and debated for decades already and by scholars in multiple disciplines. As literary scholar Scott Simmon notes "There are a number of ways to write about the relationship between the Western film and the [historic] West, each full of compromises." He goes on to state that it has been widespread among scholars to complain about Hollywood's distortions over what actually happened in the West, or to make a clear-cut difference between the real and reel West.[5] Yet, at the same time it has been very common for scholars to argue that the Western is intimately American, and thus integral to US national identity and history, giving meaning and signifying what makes the US exceptional, what defines the national experience. The lure of the West has been its settler colonial narrative of advancement, mobility, and dynamism, which links individual triumph with community morals and prosperity. The Western settler narrative at its core has promoted an ideal of overcoming struggles, demonstrating one's true moral respectability and physical mettle, coming together (often as a nuclear family), and building a brighter future. Like literary scholar Jane Tompkins argues, the West and the Western function as a "symbol for freedom, and of the opportunity for conquest," as a place for "self-transformation."[6] This sounds awfully settler colonial.

Offering the kind of settler colonial narrative that Americans could accept, the Western can also be understood as a prototype for a global settler colonial narrative. While most scholars who have discussed the Western have shied away from making the connection between the genre and settler colonialism, those scholars working on settler colonial cinemas, including more than a few in this book, seem to consider the Western as the formula and the standard to which to compare other settler colonial narratives in places around the world. Classic elements of the Western have proven highly portable – whether seemingly unstoppable white settler conquest, mobility as triumphant struggle through epic landscapes, the setting up of communities on "free land," and depictions about settler masculinity, individualism, and community. Its iconography includes tropes familiar to settler narratives worldwide. There are the Natives, frequently cast as (noble or ignoble) savages whose "role is to be the obstacle over which the whites must ride," as film historian Edward Buscombe notes.[7] There are traders, prospectors, cowboys, and gunfighters, epitomes of the violent edge of settler incursion. While they may hail from different class or national backgrounds, the settlers are nearly always white. The kind who build towns, schools, and churches are defined as the "common people," the universal ideal. It is they who are engaged in far-settlement, "discovering" the land, making it blossom, and claiming it as theirs and for their offspring to come. *How the West Was Won* (1962, dir. John Ford, Henry Hathaway, and George Sherman) is the classic film anthology showcasing this fantasy in its most epic dimensions and unapologetic tone. The film provides a multigenerational saga of settler colonialism that sweeps the continent, reinvents the land, and gives meaning to its peoples. This kind of archetypal Western settler colonial narrative is grounded on notions of advance forward and on a didactic of destruction, substitution, and rebirth: the Natives must step aside and/or disappear, by force if needed; the settlers must arrive to a particular destination, claim, occupy, and "settle" it; and while the settlers transplant their values, norms, and societies with them, they and the land itself, are also remade and regenerated as result of the settler colonial process.[8]

The Ballad of Buster Scruggs skirts all of this. Although it operates in a character-istically settler colonial setting, it challenges the exemplary settler colonial outcomes. While the landscapes stand as epic and the central archetypes are present, the story-lines show no overcoming of natural obstacles, no taming of the land, no subjugation of Natives, no building of civilization, no personal success stories, or no triumph of good against evil by the settlers. Films like Arthur Penn's *Little Big Man* (1970) or Sam Peckinpah's *The Wild Bunch* (1969) mounted a furious attack on triumphant settler narratives, epitomized in films such as *They Died with Their Boots On* (dir. Raoul Walsh, 1941) or John Ford's "cavalry trilogy," *Fort Apache* (1948), *She Wore a Yellow Ribbon* (1949), and *Rio Grande* (1950), by depicting a racist and bloody settler world built on exploitation and genocidal violence. Yet, *The Ballad of Buster Scruggs* goes beyond this more traditional criticism of the settler West as racist and violent when depicting the settler West as an emotional dead end, as dreary, pointless, and short on purpose or meaning.

The Settler, Interrupted

The Ballad of Buster Scruggs' opening scene depicts a lone white rider in Monument Valley. By commencing in this epic western location made famous by numerous John Ford films, including *The Searchers* (1956), as well as by Sergio Leone's revisionist epic *Once Upon a Time in the West* (1968), *The Ballad of Buster Scruggs* immediately situates itself in the heart of the settler colonial narrative canon. It appears to grasp for authenticity and emotional continuity by locating itself in the most iconic of reel West places. It is here that settler farming communities are bound to the earth and families are tormented by violent Comanche attacks and the killing and kidnapping of innocent white children – as in *The Searchers*. It is here that the honorable and brave US Cavalry punish the wily and savage Apaches, making the land safe for pioneer settlers – as in *Fort Apache* and *Rio Grande*. It is here that the settler wagon trains reach the promised land, as in *Wagon Master* (dir. John Ford, 1950) And it is here that the railroads, with all their corruption, greed, and violence, bring settler civilization to tame the land – as in *Once Upon a Time in the West*. For filmic settler narratives, Monument Valley embodies the greatest settler myths of white triumph.

Yet, we soon discover that this is not your usual settler story as the narrational archive this film mobilizes toys with and destabilizes our expectations of what Western settler narratives should contain. Our lone rider in the Monument Valley is Buster Scruggs (Timothy Blake Nelson), a singing cowboy and a narcissistic dandy dressed in white. He does not look or sound very masculine. In short, he is no John Wayne, Randolph Scott, Joel McCrea, Clint Eastwood, or even Kevin Costner. Unlike the silent, sturdy, Western hero and antihero, Buster waffles a lot and sings aloud of his longing for cool water and green grass, both of which are in scarce supply during his day journey. Singing of water in a desert is another way the film undercuts the settler narrative and makes fun of it. Of course, desert sand did little to prevent previous generations of filmmakers setting up settler farming utopias in Monument Valley. Perhaps they took their cues from the famous nineteenth-century settler myth that "rain follows the plough." Well it didn't, not in real life anyway, as the Dust Bowl in the 1920s aptly demonstrated. Here also the song about "the big green tree, where water is running free and it is waiting there for you and me" stands in stark contrast to the natural surroundings of parched rocks and dust under the scorching sun. There is no water, no stand of green trees, or in fact anything green in sight. Neither does Buster encounter any settler families or farms, only a forlorn tavern filled with dirty and desperate mischiefs prone to violence, and soon dead from Buster's pistols. Parodying and subverting Western settler clichés, but also adhering to them with the gunfight in the tavern and by setting itself in Monument Valley in the first place, these opening moments show that this settler story is not going to end up the way one thinks.

As the film progresses, it becomes evident that, while Buster seems very frail and likeable, jolly and talkative, he is actually a psychotic killer, as deadly a man as there is, likely made that way by the wickedness of the settler West he occupies. Showing no remorse, or justification, Buster kills men around him until he himself is gunned down in the middle of the street by another gunfighter, dressed in black, and also singing. We witness Buster's ghost ascending to heavens, singing about the end of a cowboy's life, and in hopes of going to a better, kinder, and more honest place. There men can leave behind "all the meanness in the used-to-be," referring to all the violence that consumes the settler society.

This kind of random and violent emotional community also permeates the second story "Near Algodones." Here the protagonist, simply dubbed as "Cowboy" (James

FIGURE 6.1 Buster Scruggs, the singing settler dreaming of water and green grass while making his way in Monument Valley. Photo courtesy of Alamy.

Franco), is desperate and out of luck as tragedy and violence consumes his life and throws him from one calamitous situation to the next in arbitrary manner. First he engages in a futile robbery attempt of an isolated bank in the middle of the open prairie, only to have the teller (Stephen Root) shoot at him and chase him out in hail of bullets, eventually knocking him out cold with the end of his rifle. The Cowboy wakes with a rope around his neck, facing a white settler posse eager to distribute some peer justice after what they claim had been "a fair trial" under the open sky while the Cowboy was unconscious. This form of arbitrary and merciless "justice," one of the white settlers remarks, is "like we do here in New Mexico." Yet, the Cowboy is saved by a random, unexplained, Indian attack, where the other whites are slayed. It is not that the Indians are there to rescue the Cowboy, but that he just happens to be the only white man they don't kill, and for no apparent reason. It is just another indicator of the randomness of this settler West. It is also difficult to say why the Indians are there. They are angry, probably. It is as if they stem from a landscape of violence, where people appear to be naturally mean and malevolent towards each other. This emotional community seems to have little room for logic in its saturated violence.

Saved by random violence, the Cowboy is then rescued from the end of the rope (where he was put by the posse and left hanging by the Indians) by another cowboy (Jesse Luken) passing by. This brief glimpse of hope and comradery soon gives way to despair as this second cowboy turns out to be a rustler. While he escapes, our Cowboy gets caught by a posse and loses his life when hanged in a public courtyard of a settler community. So, in this second story the protagonist also lives a life of violence and dies a random death. The narrative style offers no explanations for why he was robbing the bank in the first place, why the Indians attacked, who the rustler was, or of the events – arrest, jailing, and trial – that led to the gallows. Everything seems random and lives pointless, as if being called by a roll of some cosmic dice where the protagonist has little to say. What is clear by now is that this settler West is not grounded on justice, heroism, or hope. It seems to offer no window for prosperous futures or chance of settling down. The most merciless example, however, of the meaninglessness and soullessness of this rotten settler world is the third story, "Meal Ticket."

This narrative follows a touring duo traversing wintry mountains and performing in small settler villages, "a freak show" consisting of an "Impresario" (Liam Neeson) and the "Artist," a handicapped – quadriplegic – boy (Harry Melling). The Artist is devoid of all of his limbs, and thus totally reliant on the Impresario for this daily survival. This is no friendship, or even an odd couple, just two sad and lonely men begging for their livelihood by performing outdoors to small crowds (consisting of as few as three people on one occasion). They hardly talk to each other or to anyone else, except on stage where the boy recites, in a monotonous fashion – and thus seemingly bored out of his senses – the same repertoire that includes lines from, for example, Shakespeare, the Bible, and the Gettysburg Address. There is no display of any kind of affection between the men, or between them and their audiences. While present in the settler villages, they remain perennial outsiders and have very little actual interaction with other people outside the show. Their life seems endlessly repetitive, dull, and dreary. The only solace is when they visit a brothel together. While the Impresario enjoys some intimacy, he denies this to the Artist and makes the boy sit on the floor facing the wall while he has sex with a prostitute. And again, it all ends abruptly, the Impresario dumping the Artist into a freezing and snowy river gorge to die, without any explanation. There is no preceding dispute, or clash between the men. It is a heartless act in a heartless settler world.

The Land, So White

So far, the principal cast of all the vignettes discussed have been white men, and this changes only slightly in the last three episodes, "All Gold Canyon," "The Gal Who Got Rattled," and "The Mortal Remains." The first three episodes pay hardly any attention to the land, although in numerous classic Westerns – *Shane* (dir. George Stevens, 1953), *The Big Country* (dir. William Wyler, 1958), and *El Dorado* (dir. Howard Hawks, 1967) among them – land use, ownership, and disputes form the central theme, while in others dealing with indigenous elimination, land is also typically forming the framework for the plot. After all, settler colonialism is fundamentally about the land and who gets it. "All Gold Canyon," as the title suggests, does shift focus to the land, a lush pristine valley teeming with wildlife and full of magnificent trees, but here the land clearly offers a canvas for one settler's (Tom Waits) obsession. This lonely old prospector, who appears to be alone in the valley, futilely digs a hole after hole on this green soil, coming up empty handed. Delirious, he mumbles to the gold he presumes lies hidden underground that "I'm gonna get you." When he finally makes a major strike, he instantly gets shot in the back by some random stranger. Another arbitrary, sad end? Not this time, as the prospector shoots back, kills his assailant, and then leaves the valley. As he departs, however, we realize he is still fixating over gold. Consumed by his personal creed, he intends to return soon, probably with more supplies. This settler remains driven by his mania to benefit from the land although this almost cost him his life and for the sake of which he killed a man. There is no remorse or reflection, no personal growth or redemption. As a viewer, at this point of the film you expect nothing less from this cutthroat settler realm.

The twisted emotive tensions of sadness, arbitrariness, and the cutthroat get another spin in what at first looks like a predictable Western settler colonial narrative strand, the journey to promised land in "The Gal Who Got Rattled." Much like in classic Western narratives, evidenced in such films as *Wagon Master* and *Westward the Women* (dir. William A. Wellman, 1951), the wagon train party here is composed of moral common people, white heterosexual homesteaders who face ordeals to overcome, obstacles to beat, and struggles that build character. This story typically would show the settlers' sweat and blood spilled to reach the promised land make them belong as if indigenous to the place. Settlers would be righteous, their cause just, and they would prevail.[9] Not so here. The main protagonist is a frail, shy, helpless, and hapless Alice (Zoe Kazan), a female character that makes a mockery even of the stereotype of a fragile Victorian lady by being even more so. She loses her overbearing brother along the way, has problems with her aide, is scared of pretty much everything, gets interested in a man, meets attacking Indians, and dies by her own hand, maybe accidentally but probably shooting herself because of being so utterly petrified. Apparently, the movie's message here seems to be that this callous settler West has no room for middle-class, decent, women. Interestingly, there being no women indicates – as already suggested by the random violence and the sad heartlessness of human relationships – that this settler West might not last: no women, no offspring, no settler futures. But does it have any kind of future?

Once again the Indians have attacked without much reason or logic – as they often do in traditional Western narratives. And that is all they do in many Western films, including *The Ballad of Buster Scruggs*. When viewing *The Ballad of Buster Scruggs* as a critique of settler colonialism, its pervasive whiteness represents its principal fault. Certainly, the film takes the canonical settings and uses them often for undermining the common narrative. Here the frontier does not make for better humans, adversity is not overcome, and challenges don't bring out the best in settlers, let alone create a sense of mission, community, or destiny. The settler present is bleak, and so is the future, although nobody seems to give much thought to it, or to have much of one.

However, exogenous and indigenous alterities have disappeared and only settlers remain – they are normal, although they may not have a future. We could think that this settler society may be in crisis, but then again there is little indication that it is: crazy may be its normal. The settler would seem illegitimate here, of not belonging. But there is nobody else. The film is fundamentally settler-oriented, settler-directed, and settler-centered. There are not even any settler-indigenous exchanges, except two episodes of random violence where the Indians attack, kill, and disappear – all without any explanation or voice (yelling does not count as a voice here). Of course, this is a very characteristic indigenous role in Westerns.[10]

Also predictable is that no other non-whites are seen on screen, and therefore have no voice. Reinforcing antiquated perceptions of racial and gender homo-geneity, the film hides the ethnic diversity of the historic West, suppressing an important part of its history and thus reflecting today's discussion of American identity, borders, and inclusion.[11] Westerns have traditionally reinforced stories of a "white West" rather than exposing the historical diversity of races and ethnicities in the West. For instance, by watching Westerns one would never know that the Chinese were the biggest ethnic group in the California Gold Rush and that some Native Americans such as the Comanches were active expansionists and empire-builders. One is also at odds to find Hispanic or African American cowboys in the numerous cowboy films, including *Red River* (dir. Howard Hawks, 1948), *Cowboy* (dir. Delmer Daves, 1958), or *Wild Rovers* (dir. Blake Edwards, 1971).

While whiteness comes out as deformed, ugly, and sad, it is still all there is in this settler West of *The Ballad of Buster Scruggs*. As a result, the West as an emotional community comes across as both unbearable and unbearably white. By skirting the discussion, by keeping silent instead of exposing and questioning the Western's settler colonial mechanisms of elimination and erasure, the film in fact hides the settler colonial tendency to displace – anthropologist Patrick Wolfe's elimination of Natives – and the tendency of settlers to indigenize themselves in order to legitimize their rule.[12]

Conclusion

By the time the last episode of *The Ballad of Buster Scruggs*, "The Mortal Remains," begins, we have come a long way from Monument Valley. This episode shows a stagecoach ride from nowhere to nowhere, there are no dangers or Indian threats to overcome, or unite the passengers – as in the classic *Stagecoach* (dir. John Ford, 1939). This time the bickering passengers – a trapper, a gambler, two bounty hunters, and a middle-class lady, just keep annoying and arguing with each other over life's meanings. These people seem to share nothing in common and reach no harmony. Suitably, their journey does not end in a thriving settler community. Instead, the end comes suddenly, at a doomed-looking, forlorn hotel, isolated and uninviting in a dark, lonely night. That the bounty hunters have hauled a dead corpse they have killed in cargo, and end up carrying it to their hotel room for the night, brings little solace and, if anything, makes the settler condition look bleaker. This final episode seems to reaffirm the movie's message of settler colonialism as a callous enterprise, a failure, where the settler experience is consumed by loneliness and purposelessness. It is a hallowed and haunted world the settler has built. But this episode also shares the film's major shortcoming, the stagecoach cast is, once more, all white.

Surely, the settler experience in *The Ballad of Buster Scruggs* is far from an archetypal settler colonial fantasy. Rather it has the feel of an anti-fantasy, a grim, heartless, and violent panorama tainted by the greed and selfishness of the settlers. This is a settler space that appears emotionally bankrupt, degenerate, and desperate. It is an aimless emotional community filled with dread, sadness, fear, and violence. It is also a haunted space of failure, seemingly short on any prosperous settler futures. Yet, it is an unbearable settler experience that remains unbearably white in its cast and its perspectives, reiterating the settler colonial West as a white space. What this means is that while *The Ballad of Buster Scruggs* undercuts the Western canon by telling twisted accounts in typically settler colonial scenarios, it never goes as far as to counter the racial blueprints of the canonic narrative. The settler wagons apparently cannot be turned around, and this is the tragedy of it all. The settler is condemned to live in the legacies of his sins, enduring the futility and arbitrariness of violence in a West that has lost its moral and communal bearings.

Notes

1 On the Western imagery, see Michael Coyne, *The Crowded Prairie: American National Identity and the Hollywood Western* (London: Tauris, 1997); Jennifer L. McMahon and B. Steve Csaki, eds., *The Philosophy of the Western* (Lexington: University Press of Kentucky, 2010); Jane Tompkins, *West of Everything: The Inner Life of Westerns* (Oxford: Oxford University Press, 1993).

2 Richard Brody, "Review: The Coen Brothers' 'The Ballad of Buster Scruggs' is Six Giddy, Cruel Twists on the Western," *The New Yorker*, November 14, 2018, https://www.newyorker.com/culture/the-front-row/review-the-coen-brothers-the-ballad-of-buster-scruggs-is-six-giddy-cruel-twists-on-the-western (accessed January 28, 2020).

3 Robert B. Pippin, *Hollywood Westerns and American Myth: The Importance of Howard Hawks and John Ford for Political Philosophy* (New Haven: Yale University Press, 2010); Jonna Eagle, *Imperial Affects: Sensational Melodrama and the Attractions of American Cinema* (London: Rutgers University Press, 2017); Julia Leyda, "Black-Audience Westerns: Race, Nation, and Mobility in the 1930s," in Julia Leyda, *American Mobilities: Geographies of Class, Race, and Gender in US Culture* (Bielefeld: transcript Verlag).

4 Barbara H. Rosenwein, "Worrying about Emotions in History," *American Historical Review* 107, no. 3 (2002), esp. 842–843. See also Barbara H Rosenwein and Riccardo Cristiani, *What is the History of Emotions?* (Cambridge: Polity, 2018), 26–62.

5 Scott Simmon, *The Invention of the Western Film: A Cultural History of the Genre's First Half-Century* (Cambridge: Cambridge University Press, 2003), xiii.

6 Tompkins, *West of Everything*, 4. On the Western and American identity, see also Mary Lea Bandy and Kevin Stoehr, *Ride, Boldly Ride: The Evolution of the American Western* (Berkeley: University of California Press, 2012); John E. O'Connor and Peter C. Rollins, "Introduction: The West, Westerns, and American Character," in *Hollywood's West: The American Frontier in Film, Television, and History*, eds. Rollins and O'Connor (Lexington: University Press of Kentucky, 2005), 1–34; Patrick McGee, *From Shane to Kill Bill: Rethinking the Western* (Oxford: Blackwell, 2007); Lee Clark Mitchell, *Westerns: Making the Man in Fiction and Film* (Chicago: University of Chicago Press, 1996).

7 Edward Buscombe, *'Injuns!': Native Americans in the Movies* (London: Reaktion Books, 2006), 81.

8 Janne Lahti, "Settler Passages: Mobility and Settler Colonial Narratives in Westerns," *Journal of the West* 56, no. 4 (2017), 67–77.

9 On settler wagon train narratives in Westerns, see Lahti, "Settler Passages."

10 On depictions of Native Americans in Westerns, see Angela Aleiss, *Making the White Man's Indian: Native Americans and Hollywood Movies* (Westport, Conn.: Praeger, 2005); Jacquelyn Kilpatrick, *Celluloid Indians: Native Americans and Film* (Lincoln: University of Nebraska Press, 1999); José Armando Prats, *Invisible Natives: Myth and Identity in the American Western* (New York: Cornell University Press, 2002); Janne Lahti, "Silver Screen Savages: Images of Apaches in Motion Pictures," *Journal of Arizona History* 54, no. 1 (2013), 51–84.

11 For new research on the racial diversity of the historic American West, see, among many others, Erika Lee, *The Making of Asian America: A History* (New York: Simon & Schuster, 2016); Kelly Lytle Hernández, *City of Inmates: Conquest, Rebellion, and the Rise of Human Caging in Los Angeles, 1771–1965* (Chapel Hill: University of North Carolina Press, 2017); Manu Karuka, *Empire's Tracks: Indigenous Nations, Chinese Workers, and the Transcontinental Railroad* (Berkeley: University of California Press, 2019).

12 Patrick Wolfe, "Land, Labor, and Difference: Elementary Structures of Race." *American Historical Review* 106, no. 3 (2001), 866–905.

7

UNSER HAUS IN KAMERUN: THE RESTORATION OF SETTLER COLONIAL MEMORY IN GERMAN POST-WORLD WAR II CINEMA

Wolfgang Fuhrmann

The interior of an African farmhouse: the living room is furnished in a German style mixed with African trophies. On the walls are souvenirs and illustrations with African motifs.

   Doris, who has recently arrived from Germany, and Christine, sitting in a wheelchair, are at the dining table. A record player in the background is playing the German military march "Old Comrades."

DORIS: "Tell me Christine, can I be helpful here…, cooking for example, I am very good at it."

CHRISTINE: "Good heavens! That's Bismarck's task; if you mess with him, hm… he is very sensitive about that."

Obviously bugged by the music, Christine turns to the record player.

CHRISTINE: "I've had enough!"She takes the disc and smashes it on the floor.

DORIS: "What are you doing?"

CHRISTINE: "Well in a burst of carelessness father once remarked to Bismarck that he likes to listen to the song and now Bismarck plays it at least twenty times a day."

Bismarck, a tall white-haired African, enters the living room.

CHRISTINE: "Oh Bismarck, I…I just wanted to turn the disc and then it dropped."

BISMARCK: "Ohh."

Aunt Edith enters the room.

AUNT EDITH: "Good morning kids."
DORIS, CHRISTINE: "Good morning."
AUNT EDITH: "What happened?,"
BISMARCK: "Old Comrades, kaput."
AUNT EDITH: "How wonderful!"

This scene from Alfred Vohrer's *Unser Haus in Kamerun* (Our House in Cameroon) from 1961 tells of how, after World War II, German history was dominated by the *Vergangenheitsbewältigung*, the coming to terms with the past, meaning with Nazi Germany and the Holocaust. In the process, Germany's colonial past shifted to the background. In fact, Germany's colonial past almost disappeared from the discussion and from German cultural productions. *Unser Haus in Kamerun* forms an interesting and important exception to this general trend. First, it is probably the only German feature film in the post-World War II period that was actually shot in a former German African colony, in this case East Africa (then already Tanganyika), not Cameroon like the title would suggest. Second, the film has a number of references to the colonial past and German settlement efforts in Africa that are, however, never properly contextualized. Indeed, *Unser Haus in Kamerun* is set in a timeless present. It never mentions the German colonial loss after World War I, but instead does its upmost to reaffirm and update the notion of Germany as a benevolent colonizer during a time when the actual decolonization of Africa was already in full swing. When the film was released in December 1961, Cameroon had been independent for two years and Tanganyika was just severing its ties with the United Kingdom. The outcome is not only a representation of a timeless, generic, German colonialism but an awkward, outdated, view of German presence in Africa. At the time of the film's release German television was just about to initiate a critical debate about Germany's colonial past with the documentary *Heia Safari* (dir. Ralph Giordano 1966/67).

Historian Frederik Schulze has recently pointed out the relevance of non-textual primary sources for German colonial historiography.[1] His analysis of films like *Land und Leute in Südamerika* (Country and People in South America, 1929) or *Deutsche Ansiedler in Südbrasilien* (German Settlers in Southern Brazil, 1933) shows how the idea of German settler colonialism was still playing a crucial role for German nationalism after Germany's colonial loss. According to Schulze, these films demonstrate "German self-perception as a settler nation."[2] Contributing to this scholarship, this article discusses how the image of a German colonial settler family was revitalized in German popular cinema of the 1960s through *Unser Haus in Kamerun*. The first part of the essay discusses the film within the confines and conventions of the *Heimatfilm* (homeland film) genre, the most popular film genre in Germany at that time. Then, by focusing on three film motifs in the film – the faithful servant, the benevolent settler colonizer, and colonial sexual economy – this article argues that elements of German colonial ideology were still present in popular German cinema, and, as such, could be seen to construct a questionable historical continuity of German colonialism. However, in contrast to reviews that criticized the film for its colonial nostalgia, this article argues for a more detailed critique. The film's treatment of colonial settling should be understood in the context of West Germany's new self-perception after World War II: a recovered nation that wanted to be perceived as a new political and economic power in the world, and also on the African continent.

Unser Haus in Kamerun tells the story of a German settler family, the Ambrocks. The head of the family is the widower Willem Ambrock (Hans Söhnker), who, together with his two sons Georg (Götz George) and Rolf (Uwe Friedrichsen), his walking-impaired daughter Christine (Katrin Schaake), and his sister-in-law Edith (Berta Drews) run a second-generation coffee plantation in East Africa. The family's house servant is an African native called "Bismarck" (Kenneth Spencer). Then there is Manuela (Helga Sommerfeld), the neighbor's daughter, who loves Georg. Willem decides to send Georg to Hamburg in Germany for a year, where his old friend, Counsel Steensand, runs a shipping company. There Georg is expected to get some commercial practice in Steensand's company so as to be a successful settler in Africa upon his return. He is also to sort out whether he really loves Manuela.

While in Hamburg, Georg meets Steensand's dubious son, Klaas (Horst Frank), who is officially engaged to a rich young lady from Hamburg high society but who also has an affair with Doris (Johanna von Koczian), an accountant in a hotel. When Georg falls in love with Doris, she follows him to Africa after Georg learns about his brother's death. With her commercial talent, Doris manages to modernize the Ambrock plantation. But when Klaas shows up in Africa, he blackmails Doris to leave with him or risk having the Ambrocks learn about Doris' illegitimate daughter. On their way from the plantation, Klaas dies in a car accident and Doris survives. Together with Georg, who has already learned about her past, she starts a new life in Africa. So, while Germany no longer has any colonies in Africa, it does not mean that there could not be German settler futures there, as Doris and George attest.

Unser Haus in Kamerun was produced by Rialto-Film, a popular Danish–German production company that was known for its adaptions of the crime stories of British novelist Edgar Wallace. From the late fifties until the early seventies, Wallace films drew millions of German viewers into the movies and became a trademark for popular German cinema.[3] In the early sixties, the German Rialto started a second franchise with adaptions of westerns from German adventure author Karl May. The first May western, *Der Schatz im Silbersee* (The Treasure of Silver Lake), was released in December 1962, exactly a year after *Unser Haus in Kamerun*.

The production details of *Unser Haus in Kamerun* share important features with both Rialto series: Alfred Vohrer was as the director of many Edgar Wallace films and he strongly influenced the series' look when directing some of the Karly May adaptations. Furthermore, Vohrer's regular film composer Martin Böttcher worked for both series. His score for *Der Schatz im Silbersee* remains one of the most iconic in German film history. For *Unser Haus in Kamerun*, Böttcher used a very similar musical theme for soundtracking the

Africa steppe, which makes the film almost a musical blueprint for the May films that were produced in the following years. Götz George, the main protagonist in *Unser Haus in Kamerun*, was also cast for *Der Schatz im Silbersee*. Last but not least, like many of the Karl May films, *Unser Haus in Kamerun* was addressing an international market and audience. The film was released in Denmark, France, the Netherlands, Italy, Portugal, and elsewhere.

A Colonial *Heimatfilm*

Unser Haus in Kamerun focuses on family relations and constellations that are characteristic for the most popular genre of post-World War II German cinema, the *Heimatfilm* (homeland film). The genre is typically identified by films with exceedingly simple storylines that are shot in prototypical, and "mythic," German sceneries, such as the Black Forest or the Alps. The African and colonial setting, however, makes the film an "exterritorialized Heimatfilm."[4] For decades, Heimatfilms were considered to provide the German audience with a "holiday from history," an obfuscated reality that, after World War II, aligned the audience "with the reactionary ideology of the decade."[5] Recent scholarship has, however, produced a new understanding of the Heimatfilm genre. Heimatfilms, as film scholar Sabine Hake notes, showed "an acute awareness of contemporary problems in their preoccupation with incomplete, dysfunctional, or unconventional families."[6]

Unser Haus in Kamerun corresponds in many ways to Hake's notions of the dysfunctional family and the integration of traditional structures into processes of social, technological, and spatial modernization that should form the basis on which a brand new and modern West Germany identity needed to be built.[7] Yet, this process of intersecting the old and the new is riddled with tensions. Willem Ambrock is a widower and the family's patriarch who stands for traditional beliefs and values, while Aunt Edith represents the lost mother, and balances Willem's conservatism. She supports the younger generation in their rebellion against old traditions. Edith is also presented as progressive in that she drinks whiskey and defies table manners. The losses suffered by the Ambrocks provide a specific moral lesson: an unstable or risky life will result in misery. Georg loses his brother Rolf through the latter's foolhardy affection for flying airplanes without paying attention to technical standards; risky adventurers have short futures.

Dysfunctionality also characterizes Manuela and Doris' family situation. Manuela, the neighbors' daughter, seems to be raising herself. She talks about her parents but they are never shown in the film. In turn, Doris, being a single mother, has to work hard to finance her daughter's boarding school. Due to her profession, willingness to work, and skills as an accountant, she takes over the management of the plantation and produces a small German *Wirtschaftswunder* in Africa. Doris is both modern and moral, and thus deserves happiness and prosperity as a German settler in Africa.

With its exotic setting, *Unser Haus in Kamerun* overlaps with another popular genre of the 1950s and 1960s, the travel film. Relocating film stories to exotic places, mainly southern European neighboring states, the West German film industry reacted to the boom in German tourism that was caused by the German economic miracle after World War II, the *Wirtschaftswunder*. German film companies produced a number of films with stories about benevolent and friendly Germans abroad, either in the Americas, the South Seas, or in Africa.

The story of a German colonial settler family abroad, more specifically in a former German colony was perfectly suited to transfigure the image of German colonialism in the 1960s, a period of time that saw the beginnings of efforts for a more benevolent German commitment on the Africa continent through job creation and humanitarian aid, as shown in the film. The movie sought to restore the self-perception of Germany as a settler nation, a nation that should be recognized for its positive contributions in the world.

Unser Haus in Kamerun was not the first West German film production that was filmed on the African continent. One such film series was the trilogy *Liane, das Mädchen aus dem Urwald* [Liane, Jungle Goddess] (Eduard von Borsody, FRG 1956), *Liane, die weiße Sklavin* [Nature Girl and the Slaver] (Hermann Leitner, FRG 1957), and *Liane, Tochter des Dschungels* [Liane, Daughter of the Jungle] (Hermann Leitner, FRG 1961). This was the reworking of the popular colonial adventure theme of a white jungle girl who lives with an African tribe and who gets discovered by white expeditioners.[8]

Unser Haus in Kamerun was neither shot, nor does its story play in Cameroon. Production took place in what was then the British colony Tanganyika, and what used to be German East Africa. Apparently the decision not to shoot in Cameroon was for purely technical reasons. The press, however, speculated that renaming the film in "Unser Haus in Tanganjika" (Our House in Tanganyika) would be less "attractive" than using the still valid name of a former German colony.[9] The film never explicitly makes a reference to German colonial history in the dialogue, but the possessive pronoun in the film's title leaves no doubt that there still was a German "house" in Africa forty years after Germany's colonial loss, and that in this house there were still German settlers keeping German entrepreneurship alive.

The Ambrocks are a settler family and their plantation and estate, once referred to as Willemsland, has been theirs for two generations. It is their land and their home. They view themselves as indigenous to the place, belonging to Africa with a legitimate claim to the land. While never clearly stated, it seems apparent that Willem Ambrock must have come to the colony before World War I. There is a photograph of General von Lettow-Vorbeck on the wall of Willem's office, indicating his admiration for this past colonial soldier, hero, and German expansionist. The movie also suggests that either he or his father once fought in the colonial *Schutztruppe* in German East Africa, and thus were actively involved in the initial violent capture of the land from the Africans. Willem's nostalgia for the song "Old Comrades," one of the most popular German military marching song celebrating the solidarity among soldiers in the company and battle, speaks of his possible regret that times are changing and that, with the loss of the colony in World War I, the German settler dream is not what it once was.

Bismarck, the Faithful Askari

The film does not pay any attention to the relations between the Ambrocks and their African workers, though obviously, the plantation would not exist without a sufficient labor force. From the very first scene onward, the film shows the African workers as a diligent, jolly, and singing anonymous mass. The only African in the film who is characterized in any detail is Bismarck, the family's servant. His name goes back to German Reich Chancellor, Otto von Bismarck (1815–1898), under whose government Germany became a colonial power. Similar to the real von Bismarck, who was also known as the "Iron Chancellor" of the German Reich, the name of the Ambrock's servant is not mockery, rather it underlines his social status as the custodian of the house. His appearance as tall and dignified, his grey hair, and a set of teeth that he gets back after Georg's visit to town, connote him as an elderly man, maybe the same age as Willem, and his intimacy with each family member suggests that he has been the Ambrocks' servant for decades. His grief for the broken disc "Old Comrades" emphasizes his profound affection for Willem, whereas the claim of playing the song every minute of the day indicates that Bismarck himself is an "Old Comrade." Curiously, Bismarck's clothing never changes in the film. A red fez and a white kurta with a red sash cast him as a stereotype of an African servant. His faithful service to the family and his fixed image correspond to the image of the "faithful Askari" that turned into a colonial myth after the Versailles treaty of 1919.

After the loss of its colonies in World War I, the notion of Germany as a somehow benevolent colonizing nation was heavily attacked by the victorious

FIGURE 7.1 Bismarck – the faithful servant. Screenshot from *Unser Haus in Kamerun* by the author.

allied powers. It was argued that Germany was never able to administrate its colonies in a civilized way and had therefore lost the right to have colonies. On the German side the discussion became known as the colonial guilt lie (*koloniale Schuldlüge*), and colonial revisionists demanded the return of the lost colonies to German administration. One of their main arguments was that German colonial rule could not have been so terrible because many African mercenaries, the Askari, were willing to support it and had followed General von Lettow-Vorbeck in defending German East Africa during World War I.

How persistent the image of Germany as a benevolent colonizer and the myth of the faithful Askari were in German collective memory in the 1960s is aptly demonstrated by the two-part television documentary broadcast in October 1966, five years after *Unser Haus in Kamerun*. [10] Written and directed by the young German journalist Ralph Giordano, *Heia Safari. Die Legende von der deutschen Kolonialidylle in Afrika* (Heia Safari. The Legend of the German Colonial Idyll in Africa) was based on research in Tanzania and Cameroon as well as official German documents. The documentary clearly attacked the myth of successful German colonialism in Africa. For Giordano, *Heia Safari* was intended to work as a provocation against German colonial myths and the admiration of General Lettow-Vorbeck, who had passed away two years before, but who was still honored in Germany despite his racist and anti-democratic viewpoints.

In his opening speech in the first part of his documentary, Giordano stated that the time had come to realize that there was no reconciliation between colonial reality and colonial legend. Already, the documentary's title indicates that Giordano was ready to provoke. *Heia Safari* was a popular marching song that was written during World War I in German East Africa. In its first verse the song remembers the collaboration of the Askari in the *Schutztruppe*: "How often have we marched on a narrow negro path (*Negerpfad*), through the wide steppe, when early morning comes. How did we listen to the sound, the old familiar song of bearer and Askari: Heia, heia, Safari."

The first part of the documentary depicted the various armed conflicts between Germans and the African population living in the colonies, while the second part focused on the manifestation of colonial rule through forced labor, expropriation, expulsion, and corporal punishment. Giordano exclusively interviewed Africans and focused on their suffering in the hands of the Germans. To avoid any apologetic or glorifying moments of German colonialism, Giordano abstained from any interviews with German contemporary witnesses. [11]

Heia Safari evoked an unexpectedly violent storm of protest, especially from older generations. On February 9, 1967, the WDR broadcasted a panel discussion of historians, museum directors, a representative of the Afrika-Verein (a lobby group of the German economy supporting the cooperation between Africa and Germany), Ralph Giordano, the editor in charge, and invited viewers. The most outrageous reactions came from representatives of the older generation, who still had vivid memories of the colonial era and who were not prepared to accept criticism of German colonial rule. The TV discussion did not result in a transformation of their opinion about Germany's colonial past. Public opinion was that the older generation soured the debate. The discussion "failed primarily because of the obstinacy (*Unbelehrbarkeit*) of the invited guests, who still regarded the colonial era as fundamentally positive and whose interventions had a one-sidedly accusing aggressive character."[12]

In his analysis of the television panel, historian Eckard Michels points out that the main argument among the protests against Giordano's take on German colonial history was "that German colonial rule could not have been as bad as claimed in *Heia Safari* because of the Africans' loyalty, either as bearers or Askari, to Lettow-Vorbeck in the First World War."[13] As one viewer wrote:

> How do such malicious agitators want to explain that in the First World War not only our Askari but also the simple bearer…thousands of them remained faithful to the last day in distress and death when often only a leap into the bush would have given them freedom and return to their homeland?[14]

The discussion about Germany's benevolent role in Africa that characterized the public discussion about *Heia Safari* is also visible in *Unser Haus in Kamerun*. The representation of Africans as grateful workers and Bismarck's devotion to the family shares this line of thinking from the critics of *Heia Safari*. Still, in the 1960s many viewers' understanding of German colonial rule in Africa boiled down to this: German colonialism had been, above all, an economic benefit and a blessing for the local population.

Benevolent German Settlers

The benevolent character of the Ambrock family is epitomized in Aunt Edith's commitment to improving local lives. Photographs of colonialized Africans that are lining up in front of a colonial doctor's desk to get medical treatment are legion in colonial photography and they usually illustrate the good intentions of Europeans devoted to civilizing and helping the locals. It is exactly the same motif that reappears in *Unser Haus in Kamerun*: Edith is a medical doctor, who cures African women in the Ambrock's garden.

Furthermore, the viewer learns that Willem has donated the regional hospital to the people, where Edith also works. When Doris arrives at the Ambrock plantation Edith gets an emergency call from the hospital about an impending birth, and she invites Doris to join her. At the hospital, Edith asks Doris to hold the newborn, and when she takes it up, an African doctor comments: "You are holding the baby very skillfully – like a mother." These words remind Doris of her own child and her neglect as a mother. However, the scene puts Edith and Doris in a particular role in regard to German medical support in Africa: Doris and Edith deliver and take care of the newborn. Doris does not just behave like a mother, she is "Mother Africa," the symbolic ancestor and origin of the human race.

The film brings forth another important colonial trope that is represented through a female protagonist, even though, in this case, it comes with an interesting twist. In his lucid analysis of racial representation in the Weimar cinema, film scholar Tobias

FIGURE 7.2 Dr. Edith Ambrock. Screenshot from *Unser Haus in Kamerun* by the author.

Nagl writes that in colonial revisionist films such as *Allein im Urwald. Die Rache der Afrikanerin* [Alone in the Jungle. Revenge of the African Woman] (dir. Ernst Wendt, 1922), or *Ich hatt' einen Kameraden* [I Once Had a Comrade-in-Arms] (dir. Conrad Wiene, 1926), the African female protagonists are never perceived as sexual partners. In both films, an African woman loves a white protagonist but they have to accept that their love goes unfulfilled. These women are either relegated to deviant sexual relations and/or they are doomed to death.[15]

The exclusion and/or the invisibility of the black desiring woman can be seen in another Heimatfilm that was shot three years before *Unser Haus in Kamerun*. *Noch einmal die Heimat seh'n* [See the Heimat Once Again] (dir. Otto Meyer, 1958) tells the story of a rivalry between young forest wardens, Michael and Bertl, who both love the same woman, Gerda. To get rid of Michael, Bertl accuses Michael of having shot a man. Michael escapes to his old wartime comrade Robert, who lives in Africa. Homesickness drives Michael and Robert back to the Alps, where Michael's innocence finally is proved.

Most instructive are the first images of Michael's new life in Africa. It starts with a shot of little Koko, a small African child that sneaks into Michael's tent, where she takes a chocolate bar out of Michael's first aid kit, while her mother, Amada, is preparing food at a campfire for Michael and Robert. Amada is soon in love with Michael, especially after he saves her life from an attacking leopard. Amada is portrayed through the most simplistic racial stereotypes of an African woman. She wears a grass skirt and a necklace with a predator's teeth, and is mostly shown topless. This stereotypical racial representation did not go unnoticed in the reviews. The *Filmdienst* wondered why "a pretty Negro woman (*Negerfrau*), who, despite civilized manners, is the only one who has constantly to walk around uncivilized, that is to say undressed."[16] Michael, however, is immune to her physical attraction, her caring, and her devotion. He never responds to Amada's affection and she finally has to accept her unfulfilled love when Michael and Robert return to Germany.

Unser Haus in Kamerun did not cast a black female actor, yet this does not mean that similar denied sexual relations and tensions do not exist in the film. The Italian film poster of Unser Haus in Kamerun, released as Mal d' Africa, mal d'amore (Sick of Africa, Sick of Love), shows a female body, neither black nor white, wearing a black slip with some glittering fringes, huge earrings, and arm rings, who ecstatically dances at night at a campfire in front of white men and women. The illustration has no reference to the film as no such scene exists in Unser Haus in Kamerun. However, if there is any resemblance to a female protagonist in the film, it is Manuela, the neighbors' daughter, who is the only female that corresponds in her physiognomy to the graphic body.[17]

In contrast to Doris, who is presented as a reserved, slightly conservative woman, Manuela is characterized as an athletic, impulsive young woman who is ready to explore her sexuality. She is never shown in a domestic context like Doris, but appears exclusively on her horse and in the wilderness. All her attributes connote Manuela as a girl who lives outside the social norms; she is wild and unsuited to becoming a respectable settler wife. She has perhaps "gone native," being Africanized by her environment. At her first meeting with Georg, Manuela is depicted as a modern Amazon. She is riding a black horse and stops Georg and his African workers on their way back to the plantation. She tells Georg about her vacation in Switzerland, where she has learned to kiss. Georg remarks that her breasts have grown since they met the last time, and Manuela shows Georg how good she has become at kissing and tells him that she loves him.

With her attitude of a sexually curious young woman, Manuela corresponds to the image of the young pubescent women (Backfisch), who appears in a number of films to challenge the conservative sexual morals of the 1950s and early 1960s. One can also read her role as a substitute for the black desiring woman who has to accept her rejection in favor of the educated, professional, motherly Doris. Nagl notes that Weimar cinema often used German black-face actors to avoid controversial debates about the role of black female actors in a white patriarchal sexual economy: the more attractive a character was supposed to be, the more white she had to be.[18] Having said this, Unser Haus in Kamerun offers colonialism's ultima ratio in racial purity. Manuela is a white black woman who can only attract Georg's attention in the jungle as long as he has not met a real white woman in civilization.

Conclusion

The presentation of German colonial history after World War II went hand in hand with a significant change in the media landscape. Cinema was going to lose its position in shaping public opinion in favor of television. Whereas the German cinema audiences halved between 1956 and 1962, television was able to increase its spectator numbers almost tenfold during this period. In his analysis of *Heia Safari*, Michels shows that the controversy about the documentary could not have been possible without television's growing significance in public debates and its ability to polarize opinion. The "TV scandal" was above all a generational conflict in which only the younger viewers were prepared to deal with the colonial past alongside, and in addition to, the more recent past of Nazi rule and the Holocaust. This does not mean that the older generation was pro-colonial as such, but rather that many television viewers did not want to be deprived of yet another illusion pertaining to their country's already checkered history in the twentieth century.[19]

Unser Haus in Kamerun was promoted as a "grand family film of international standard." It was Rialto's first color film and, together with Martin Böttcher's intriguing soundtrack, the film offered its audience an entertaining visual and acoustic experience. Reviews, however, almost unanimously criticized the colonial context of the film and the stereotypical representation of Africa and Africans, especially Bismarck's role. The *Deutsche Zeitung und Wirtschaftszeitung* criticized the film for ignoring Africa's "hot political reality" that does not any longer allow for a "house and garden film about a planter's good and bad times."[20] The *Deutsche Volkszeitung* wondered what Alfred Vohrer and his scriptwriter wanted to say with the film: "Do you want to go back to those times when we were still proud colonial masters?"[21]

The film invites a reading of colonial nostalgia, but considering the historical context of the film's release, it demands a more complex answer. In contrast to the 1920s, in which films about the German colonies supported a colonial revisionist discourse, *Unser Haus in Kamerun* could not ignore that the times had changed. In a short but significant scene when Georg returns to Africa we see a group of Africans singing and dancing at the airport. One expects that they are waiting for Georg but their welcome is for an African leader who is on the same plane as Georg (and Doris). At that moment, the film shows the new political context of an independent Africa. Thus, seeing the film solely as through colonial nostalgia turns out to be too short-sighted. Instead, the film posits that Germany, even without colonial territories, was still a significant economic and stabilizing political power on the African continent.

Film scholar Tim Bergfelder notes that anecdotes, legends, and myths abound as to why the Rialto film company embarked on the adaption of Karl May novels.[22] Whatever the answer is, if Rialto planned to continue with productions in an African-colonial settler setting, *Unser Haus in Kamerun* proved to be the wrong formula. Karl May's imagined Wild West turned out to be a much safer place than Germany's colonial past. The attempt to make colonial settler ideology part of Germany's new international profile in the world was a failed one. *Unser Haus in Kamerun* was not only an ideological minefield but colonial history, in general, was not a subject that German cinema was ready to critically deal with, not in the 1960s and not today.

Notes

1 Fredrik Schulze, "German Settler Colonialism in Southern Brazil in German Documentary Films of the 1930s." In *Archiving Settler Colonialism: Culture, Space and Race*, eds. Yu-ting Huang, Rebecca Weaver-Hightower (London/New York: Routledge 2019), 84–99.
2 Schulze, "German Settler," 86.
3 Tim Bergfelder, *International Adventures: German Popular Cinema and European Co-Productions in the 1960s* (New York: Berghahn, 2004), 138–171.
4 Johannes von Moltke, *No Place Like Home: Locations of Heimat in German Cinema* (Berkeley: University of California Press, 2005), 235.
5 Johannes von Moltke, "Evergreens: The Heimat Genre." In *The German Cinema Book*, eds. Tim Bergfelder, Erica Carter and Deniz Göktürk (London: British Film Institute, 2002), 18.
6 Sabine Hake, *German National Cinema*, 2nd edition (New York: Routledge, 2008), 118.
7 Wolfgang Fuhrmann, "Fortschritt, Modernität und Lebensentwürfe. Brasilienbilder im westdeutschen Kino der 1950 Jahre." In *Kulturdialog Brasilien – Deutschland: Design, Film, Literatur, Medien*, eds. Geane Alzamora, Renira Rampazzo Gambarato, and Simone Malaguti (Berlin: edition tranvía, 2008), 321–334.
8 Michael Flitner, "Das Mädchen aus dem Urwald. Über Geschlecht und Nation in einem Filmhit der 1950 Jahre," *Geographische Revue* 7 (2005), 7–24.
9 N.N.: Fahr'n Sie nicht nach Kamerun…, *Film Revue* 26 (1961), 9–11.
10 Eckard Michels, "Geschichtspolitik im Fernsehen, Die WDR-Dokumentation 'Heia Safari' von 1966/67 über Deutschlands Kolonialvergangenheit," *Vierteljahreshefte für Zeitgeschichte* 56, no. 3 (2008), 467–492.
11 Michels, "Geschichtspolitik," 478.
12 Michels, "Geschichtspolitik," 488.
13 Michels, "Geschichtspolitik," 483.
14 Michels, "Geschichtspolitik," 484.
15 Tobias Nagl, *Die unheimliche Maschine: Rasse und Repräsentation im Weimarer Kino* (München: edition text und kritik, 2009), 438.
16 *Filmdienst*, 20.11.1958. Supplement to *Noch einmal die Heimat seh'n*. DVD, Kinowelt 2006.
17 https://rateyourmusic.com/images/all?type=F&assoc_id=170847 (accessed 12 November 2019).
18 Nagl, *Die unheimliche Maschine*, 494.
19 Michels, "Geschichtspolitik," 482.
20 Günter Seuren, "Nur die Hyäne kläfft nicht deutsch," *Deutsch Zeitung und Wirtschaftszeitung*, January 30, 1962.
21 Pk, "Alte Kameraden, " *Deutsche Volkszeitung*, February 9, 1962.
22 Bergfelder, *International Adventures*, 181.

8

NEGOTIATING BETWEEN HOMELANDS: SETTLER COLONIAL SITUATION AND SETTLER AMBIVALENCE IN TAIWAN CINEMA

Lin-chin Tsai

Taiwan's settler colonial past, and its continued colonization in the present, involves multiple colonialisms and serial waves of Han Chinese immigrants. The Dutch occupied the territories of southwestern Taiwan and began to recruit Han Chinese settlers to facilitate colonial rule as early as in 1624. This was followed by the first Han Chinese-style regime of the Zheng family (1661–1683) and the Qing Empire (1683–1894), during which Han settlers outnumbered Indigenous populations and became the demographic majority. Thus, Taiwan can be considered a settler colony.

The triangular relations among colonizers, settlers, and Indigenous peoples in Taiwan intensified during the Japanese colonial period (1895–1945). After the end of World War II, a new wave of Han settlers (mainlanders) migrated to Taiwan with the Nationalist government due to their failure in the Chinese Civil War (1945–1949). The Nationalist government promulgated the Martial Law (1949–1987), governed Taiwan through what came to be referred to as the White Terror, and imposed a hegemonic Han Chinese national and cultural ideology upon all inhabitants: the earlier waves of Han settlers, mainlanders, and Indigenous peoples. It wanted to consolidate authoritarian rule and claim itself as the only legitimate and authentic Chinese polity, the Republic of China (ROC), rather than the People's Republic of China (PRC) the Chinese Communist Party founded in 1949.[1] Mandarin Chinese was promoted as the national language, whereas the use of Indigenous languages, Japanese, and other local languages (including Hoklo and Hakka, which Han settlers used) was restricted.[2] The Nationalist authoritarian rule during the Martial Law resulted in mounting tensions between the two waves of Han settlers, and have constituted at least two different modes of Han settler consciousness.[3] In brief, Taiwan's Han settler colonial consciousness is a consequence of the shifting triangular relationships that different colonizers, Han settlers, and Indigenous communities established throughout its layered and successive colonial history, as well as the continued tensions between the old and new Han settlers that coexist in contemporary Taiwan.

In addition to Taiwan's history of multiple colonialisms, the Cold War structure, as well as Taiwan's ambiguous international status and uncertain geopolitical position, also played central roles in shaping Taiwan's settler colonialism. At the inception of Nationalist rule, the ROC was an American ally in implementing the anti-communist containment policy in Asia. The Sino-American Mutual Defense Treaty in 1954 served as a legal ground to maintain diplomatic relations between the two settler polities. America's military, economic, and technological assistance allowed the Nationalists to represent the ROC as "Free China," and sustain its claim to the territorial integrity between China, Taiwan, and other surrounding islands. In historian Rwei-Ren Wu's words, it was "the American Empire of the Cold War that created a geopolitical space" for the Nationalist settler state to reign under American neocolonialism since the 1950s.[4] However, a series of international setbacks since the 1970s, including the United Nations' recognition of the PRC as the representative of China in 1971, and the US's shift in diplomatic relations from the ROC to the PRC in 1978, together with the abrogation of the Mutual Defense Treaty, not only transformed the triangular relationship between Taiwan, the US, and China, but also affected the formation of Han settler consciousness.

To investigate the Han settler colonial consciousness in the aforementioned context, this chapter studies two settler films from Taiwan, *Home Sweet Home* (*Jia zai Taibei*, dir. Bai Jingrui, 1970) and *The Land of the Brave* (*Long de chuanren*, dir. Lee Hsing, 1981), both produced by the state-run studio Central Motion Picture Corporation (CMPC). By analyzing these two films' distinct settler narratives and the way they reveal a specific mentality of settler ambivalence and anxiety during the period, this essay argues that Taiwan's Han settler colonial consciousness has been shaped by, and should be understood through, multiple "homelands" (China, Taiwan, and the US), and the ever-changing international relations among them in the global context. This specific form of settler colonialism constructed by a triangular structure due to the Cold War has yet to be fully addressed by scholarship.

Weary Birds Must Fly Back to Their Nests: *Home Sweet Home*

Home Sweet Home is based on Taiwanese writer Meng Yao's novel, *Flight of the Swallow* (*Feiyan qulai*). Beginning with the first shot that projects its title both in English and Mandarin Chinese ("Home is in Taipei," literally), the film attempts to capture the viewers' full attention by presenting a sensory cultural feast with miscellaneous fragments of Chinese civilization in split-screen shots. These include festive dragon and lion dances, Peking opera masks for various roles, traditional elements of Chinese performance and theatre, and temple fairs' parades, synchronized with its jubilant theme song employed repetitively throughout the film. A scene of a China Airlines passenger aircraft heading to the Taipei Songshan Airport follows this opening sequence, in which the main characters—returnees from America flying back to their homeland, and their family members and friends in Taipei—are introduced to the audience.

The story is then divided into three independent, but interconnected plotlines after a reunion scene at the airport. The first part centers on Xia Zhiyun (Wu Chia-chi), a US-trained doctor specializing in zootechnics, who returns to his parents' ranch with his wife. While they decide to stay in Taiwan after experiencing a bucolic and tranquil time with the family, Zhiyun's younger sister Zhixia (Chang Hsiao-yen) is intoxicated with her naïve fantasy of America. When Zhixia meets He Fan (Chiang Ming), a frivolous and boastful dandy who represents the materialistic, consumerist, and decadent facets of the US, she falls in love with him because he is the one who can fulfill her American dream. The second part relates an extramarital affair between Leng Lu (Lee Hsiang) and a young artist Wang Pu (Feng Hai). Leng, a woman who married and lived in the US for years, distinguishes herself when she is first introduced to the audience by her delicate Western-style dress, fancy accessories, and fashionable hairstyle. In contrast, Leng's lover Wang appears to be trapped in Leng's luxurious apartment full of expressionist oil paintings, Warholian postmodern collages, and plastic art. It is not until the scene in which Wang draws a sketch of a young girl (the daughter of Leng's friend who runs an orphanage), in front of the palatial Zhongshan Hall (see Figure 8.1),[5] that he is able to be himself. Thereafter, Wang breaks up with Leng as he feels that she "did not learn anything good, but picked up everything bad while living abroad." After the breakup with Wang, Leng

FIGURE 8.1 *Home Sweet Home* (dir. Bai Jingrui, 1970). Courtesy of CMPC.

changes into a plain Chinese-style cheongsam, and ultimately finds her sense of belongingness in Taipei at the orphanage that her friend manages.

The film reaches its climax in the final melodrama that deals with the moral dilemma of Wu Daren (Ko Chun-hsiung), an engineer who returns to Taipei primarily to seek a divorce so he can marry his new lover in America. Wu's dedicated wife, Shuyuan (Kuei Ya-lei), peddles homemade pickled vegetables to support the family, and she has raised their son while Wu was studying abroad. Wu's intention to divorce her causes a severe dispute within the family. However, after Wu witnesses the rocketing progress of science and technology in Taiwan, particularly in the textile factory, and the magnitude of Zengwen Dam in Chiayi (a county in southwestern Taiwan), he decides to resume his responsibility for both his family and homeland, and contribute to the construction projects for water conservation. The film ends with the scene at Songshan Airport that we saw at the beginning, in which all of the characters reunite again, and decide not to return to America (except the newlyweds He Fan and Zhixia), but instead to stay in their "sweet home"—Taipei.

The film depicts a typical settler colonial narrative that historian Lorenzo Veracini formulates: unlike the "circular form" of classic colonial narratives, settler colonialism evinces a "linear narrative structure" in which settlers arrive at, and occupy new territories with the intention to stay permanently.[6] The airplane plays a pivotal role in driving this mode of settler narrative and articulates the linear route of settler colonialism: the returnees (who are all Han settlers) arrive on the island by air, realize that Taipei is their eternal homeland, and decide to stay. Toward the end of the film, viewers do not see the airplane's departure, but instead, a truck marked with three eye-catching Chinese characters "Taibei shi" (Taipei City) on the back, loaded with miscellaneous articles of furniture, carrying all of Wu's family members to their new apartment—their permanent, lovely, sweet home in Taipei. This scene is synchronized with the theme song that once again accentuates its refrain, the film's core message: "Taipei! Taipei!" The airport, as film scholar James Wicks points out, "serves as a transitory portal; it is *Home Sweet Home* where peoples are expected, indeed mandated, to stay."[7] I argue that the airport is not so much a space of transportation or movement that is open, penetrable, and connected to other locales or places, but more a spatial rhetorical device of the settler narrative—it signifies Han characters' permanent settlement and residency in the new settler colony, which is referred to as "Taipei."

The film exhibits Taiwan's landscape, cultural landmarks, and national infrastructure to bolster its settler colonial narrative. It is at Zhongshan Hall, a building that encapsulates the aesthetics of Chinese architecture and the imperial garden, as well as the values of Chinese civilization, that Wang is able to revitalize his artistic soul and rediscover his identity as an artist. Similarly, Wu realizes fully how modernized his homeland is only when he sees Zengwen Dam and decides to take part in the project of nation-building. The idyllic ambience of the Xia family's ranch and the visit to the glorious tourist spot, Sun Moon Lake in central

Taiwan, also are crucial factors in the young couple's decision to remain with their family. Zengwen Dam and the Xia family's ranch not only demonstrate Taiwan's technological and agricultural development in the process of settler nation-building, but also express the psyche of settlers' attachment to land. This settler colonial psyche is premised on a set of dichotomies between Taipei as the settlers' permanent home and America as an exogenous other.

Although the film articulates the Han settler consciousness by telling a story of Taipei, its actual spatial manifestation has already extended beyond its geographical boundary. In addition to Zengwen Dam and Sun Moon Lake, the scenes of the Xia family ranch were in fact shot in Kenting National Park (the southernmost national park established in postwar Taiwan) and Qingjing Farm (a tourist attraction in Nantou). These sites serve as testimonies of settlers' usurpation of Indigenous land and the environmental injustice in Taiwan, because most national parks are areas carved from Indigenous traditional territories. Indigenous traditional economic and cultural activities, such as hunting, fishing, gathering, and trapping, are either restricted or criminalized in national parks.[8] The film's spatial construction of Taipei as a homeland is thus based on Han settlers' disavowal and elimination of Indigenous peoples.

The discrepancy between the film's original title (*Home is in Taipei*) and its spatial construction beyond Taipei's actual geographical border warrants further investigation. Although the film does not confine its spatialization to Taipei, it remains reluctant to address "Taiwan" verbally while articulating it as a sweet home for Han settlers. Instead, the cinematic spatial construction of Taiwan is used to overtly formulate a structure of feeling of Chineseness as a strategy to evoke the settler viewers' national and cultural identity. As film scholar Shiao-ying Shen observes,

> Viewers might see *Home Sweet Home* as showing us more of Taiwan than Taipei, but this is exactly what Taipei is meant to be. In 1970, Taipei represents the nation, a home for Chinese families. *Home Sweet Home* formulates a Taipei that embodies the ideals of a nation.[9]

This attempt on the film's part resonates with Nationalist propaganda to establish Taiwan as "a model province" during the Cold War era. Taiwan, as a geopolitical entity, was treated as a province of the ROC, rather than a sovereign nation-state, as the Nationalist government still clung to its insistence on reclaiming the mainland. Thus, "Taiwan" in the film's settler narrative only can present itself by its absence, demonstrating its visibility in the form of invisibility. I argue that this discrepancy, or more specifically, the ambivalent attitude toward Taiwan (as a factual new colony for Han settlers) and China (as Han settlers' ancestral origin in a symbolic, cultural sense) should be understood as what Veracini has referred to as the "inherent ambiguity" embedded in the settler colonial consciousness.[10] The film seems to identify the new colony (Taiwan) as a permanent homeland by foregrounding its landscape and settlers' attachment to the land, but insists simultaneously on its political and cultural legitimacy to represent the old metropole (China), as the settler projects of nation-building in the new colony (Zengwen Dam) and the cultural reproduction of the old home (Zhongshan Hall) can coexist at once in the film. "Taipei," in this ambivalent settler narrative, becomes a metonym, or a synecdoche, for "Taiwan" as a new settler homeland that cannot be articulated directly.

This settler ambivalence also rests in the film's traditional morality and the excessive, yet inconsistent use of its stylistic and flamboyant cinematic language. Wicks notes the discrepancy between the film's narrative simplicity in its projection of the Nationalist ideology and complexity in the formal elements such as editing and artistic design. This phenomenon can be sensed not only in the discrepancy between the somewhat conservative moral teachings in the film's content and visual style; it can also be clearly observed in the film's inconsistent use of such formalist elements and visual style (the highly stylistic split-screen shots in the opening sequence and varicolored setting of Leng's over-decorated apartment, for instance). Emilie Yueh-yu Yeh and Darrel William Davis note that, compared to the first two stories, Bai loses his "faith, or interest, in visual experiments when depicting such egregiously unfilial behavior" as in the last story of *Home Sweet Home*. [11] I contend that this stylistic discontinuity is another revelation of Han settler ambivalence toward Taiwan's exogenous other in the film—the US.

Although the film ostensibly criticizes Han settlers' American dream (particularly via the characterizations of He Fan and Zhixia), it still bears obvious traces of American influence that can be observed via its cinematic language and aesthetics. The Cold War structure has resulted not simply in the domination of American culture in Taiwan. Instead, America has become a central mediator through which the Taiwanese people access Western culture. It was American neocolonialism that strengthened and enabled the ROC to represent itself as the only legitimate Chinese polity during the Cold War era. In this vein, the US has become another "psychological home country" for Taiwan with respect to its cultural, economic, and military influences on the island,[12] which complicates the ambivalent Han settler mentality further than Veracini theorized. In other words, the film's inconsistency and discontinuity in its cinematic language and aesthetics expose another layer of Han settler ambivalence that negotiates between multiple "homelands" (rather than the old-and-new dialectics between China as an ancestral origin and Taiwan as a new settler colony). In Michael Berry's words, the conceptualization of "home" and the complex dynamics among these homelands in the film are always "contingent" upon one another.[13]

"Descendants of the Dragon": *The Land of the Brave*

In mid-December, 1978, President Jimmy Carter's announcement of America's recognition of the PRC as the sole legal government of China and the annulment of diplomatic relations with the ROC not only challenged the Nationalist government's political legitimacy but also provoked social upheaval in Taiwan. Taiwanese musician Hou Dejian composed a song, "Descendants of the Dragon," to express his personal grievance and galvanize a collective consciousness of patriotism and nationalism among the Taiwanese. The mythological imagery of the dragon is a symbol of imperial power and a cultural totem for the Han Chinese people. This song soon became extremely famous during the "campus folk song movement," a grassroots music movement that emerged from Taiwan's colleges during the late 1970s and became rapidly popular in the 1980s. In 1981, Taiwanese director Lee Hsing completed a film, *The Land of the Brave*, in which he appropriated Hou's song as the original title and the theme song. With a star-studded lineup, including Chin Han, Joan Lin (Lin Feng-jiao), Kenny Bee (Chung Chun-to), and Sihung Lung (Lang Hsiung), Hsing attracted the audience and aroused Han settlers' patriotic sentiment and national identity in the face of Taiwan's international setbacks.

If *Home Sweet Home* articulates its settler colonial narrative in part through its satirical critique of the Taiwanese people's American dream, then *The Land of the Brave* expresses a more explicit collective resentment against the US from its opening. The film begins with a pseudo-newsreel sequence of President Carter's diplomatic recognition of the PRC and the Taiwanese people's reaction to this shocking news. This sequence effectively sets the tone for the film by foregrounding the Taiwanese people's vexation, anxiety, and indignation, together with the protests against the US government, synchronized with the stirring melody of "Descendants of the Dragon" performed by a symphony orchestra. The story revolves around two families' (Fan and Zhang) members and other related characters. Fan Jintao (Kenny Bee), a young college student majoring in music, relinquishes his dream to study abroad in Italy after the termination of Taiwan-US diplomatic relations, and organizes a choral group with other cohorts. The group then embarks on a tour of Taiwan's countryside to perform "campus folk songs." Lin Chaoxing (Chin Han), a US-trained doctor specializing in agronomy, returns to Taiwan, where he works at a governmental agricultural research institute and serves as an adjunct professor at a university. He becomes acquainted with the department's teaching assistant, Jintao's older sister Fan Jinwen (Joan Lin), and falls in love with her. The narrative threads then focus on the romances between the main characters, the generational conflicts among the family members, and the ways these conflicts are resolved through a transcendent, collective level of settler national reconstruction. The film ends with a scene of the numerous attendees of a flag-raising ceremony—all of the main characters participate, standing in front of the Presidential Office Building on National Day in 1981 in celebration of the ROC's seventieth anniversary, and waving the national flags, accompanied by the song "Descendants of the Dragon" in chorus.

The campus folk songs play a pivotal part in stimulating viewers' senses of nationalism and patriotism, crucial components of Han settler consciousness in the film. The emergence and development of the "campus folk song movement" was attributable to US neocolonialism, particularly the American economic and cultural influence on Taiwan during the Cold War era. Scholars have generally treated Taiwanese musician Lee Shuang-tzu's calls for the Taiwanese people to "sing our own songs" during a Western folk concert at Tamkang University in 1976 as a key trigger of the subsequent "campus folk song movement."[14] Hence, this anti-neocolonial gesture on the part of the "campus folk song movement" is used to undergird the Han settlers' resentment against the US in the film, and the songs are employed to enhance the film's nativist characteristics and praise the simplicity and the beauty of Taiwan's countryside. One famous song "Catching Pond Loaches," for instance, is used in the scene in which Jintao is eating noodles with his girlfriend at a local food stand after he refused to have Western cuisine with his family members at a sumptuous restaurant. The rustic atmosphere the song conveys, coupled with a radio program in Hoklo and the characters' pre-ference for local food, explicitly reveals the film's embrace of the local lifestyle and its nativist orientation.

This nativist quality is fully manifested in the sequence of the choral group's tour to the countryside via the song "Let's Go See the Clouds." The film presents a pastoral view of paddy fields, in which all members are sitting on the moving farm wagons and singing the song together. The members then perform this song in various rural locales, and passionately interact with the villagers. Meanwhile, Chaoxing leads an agricultural investigation team to the countryside to under-stand the agrarian development in Taiwan's rural areas better. This sequence concludes with an ensemble in front of a traditional temple, with a slogan attached to the pillars on the two sides that read: "Culture should benefit society; art must embrace people" (see Figure 8.2). All chorus members dress in uniform, and the villagers and other viewers actively engage in the performance by singing or clapping along with them. The two male protagonists encounter each other in this scene, and establish a deeper friendship based on their mutual appreciation. Moreover, the film invites the audience to join this ensemble by cutting back and forth between the viewers and the performers in this sequence, and by having Hou Dejian, Li Jianfu (the first singer who recorded "Descendants of the

FIGURE 8.2 *The Land of the Brave* (dir. Lee Hsing, 1981). Courtesy of CMPC.

Dragon"), and other campus folk singers play roles in the performance. In this sense, the film deftly stitches the actual spectators into the cinematic space in the ensemble scene, followed by the two main characters' reunion. In Yeh's words, the film successfully presents a picture of revisionist nationalism in which the distinction between the urban and rural, elites and peasants, and the nation and the local, are all blurred and welded into harmony through its nativist cinematic practice with the idyllic and exhilarating campus folk song.[15]

The chorus tour and the investigation team not only demonstrate the film's celebration of Taiwan's rural landscape and local practice; the teams the two male protagonists lead should also be construed as a cinematic mode of settler colonial expedition, revealing both the settlers' attachment to, and craving for, land. Jintao's choral group sets off on its tour to the countryside and unites people of different classes, ages, and backgrounds, occupying Taiwan's rural landscape through its audio presentation of the campus folk song. Chaoxing's investigation team, in turn, performs an act of settler territorial governance through its systematic surveying of agricultural land. The sequence portrays a timeless, highly romanticized and idealized vision of Taiwan's countryside—an ethnographic fascination in the eyes of the two vigorous and virile settler protagonists. The expeditions also exhibit the Han settler projects of nation-building in two respective dimensions, the spiritual (reinvigorating the collective national and patriotic consciousness through music) and the physical (controlling land by scientific surveys). Therefore, the two protagonists' reunion symbolizes the integration of the two settler projects into a more elevated prospect of nation-building.

The song "Descendants of the Dragon" further fortifies such settler nationalism and patriotism during the final scene of the flag-raising ceremony. Through a similar technique of editing as that previously seen in the ensemble scene, we as spectators seem to be positioned among the crowd in front of the Presidential Office Building, watching the national flag as it waves in the twilight and waiting for the sunrise. All of the conflicts between the two families and the generation gaps among the characters are reconciled, as these people are all "descendants of the dragon," standing together unflinchingly on "the land of the brave" and moving toward a hopeful future for the nation. If the film's original title invokes a temporal sense of settler national identity by accentuating the Han people's ancestral and cultural roots, then the English title articulates the intention to settle permanently in even more overtly spatial terms by conjoining territorial occupation and settler nationalism.

Nevertheless, while the film unravels the settlers' self-fashioning of localization through its audiovisual intersection of the campus folk songs and Taiwan's rural scenery, quite ironically, the lyrics of the theme song (and some other songs used in the film) bear almost no traces of Taiwan's actual geographical markers. Instead, they highlight the landmarks and cultural referents of China. This is most evident in the theme song:

The far East has a river. Its name is called the Long River.

The far East has a river. Its name is called the Yellow River.

Although I haven't seen the beauty of the Long River, I have always dreamed I traveled on it.

Although I haven't heard the glory of the Yellow River, its strong currents are in my dream.

The ancient East has a dragon. Its name is called China.

The ancient East has a group of people. They are all descendants of the dragon.

Growing up under the feet of the giant dragon, I became the descendant of the dragon.

Black eyes, black hair, and yellow skin, forever and ever I am the descendant of the dragon.

Here, the Long River (the Yangzi River, the longest in Asia) and the Yellow River (usually considered the birthplace of Chinese civilization) are employed to emphasize the splendor of Chinese history and geography, and the imagery of the dragon crystalizes the everlasting strength and persistence of China and its people, the Han settlers. The last section of the song further alludes to the imperialist invasion and humiliation the Qing Empire faced since the First Opium War during the mid-nineteenth century to indicate the ROC's international setbacks and the crisis of its political legitimacy in the 1970s. The lyrics thus epitomize this ambivalent Han settler consciousness of the film—while the Han settlers stand unyielding on the land of Taiwan, they turn simultaneously to the imagined geography and history of China, the Han settlers' origin that exists only in dreams.

What is more ironic is that "Descendants of the Dragon," a patriotic song that fits the Nationalist ideology perfectly, was once censored by the government after the composer left for China in 1983. This song that was written originally to justify the ROC's legitimacy later became popular in China, as it was rendered by the Chinese people as a work that trumpets the unification of the two polities. Thus, the song's ambivalent settler consciousness was unexpectedly appropriated to support the PRC's pro-unification discourse that undermined the Nationalist government's legitimacy as a settler regime. On the other hand, 1983 was also a decisive moment in Taiwan's Indigenous peoples' rights movements. It saw the publication of the Indigenous magazine, *High Mountain Green* (*Gaoshan qing*), followed by the founding of the first Indigenous non-governmental organization, the Alliance of Taiwan Aborigines in 1984. All of the above, together with the whirlwind of the more radical social and democratic movements in the 1980s, led the island to its next page of settler colonial history.

Conclusion

The Han settler colonial consciousness in contemporary Taiwan has always been haunted, and thereby shaped, by multiple phantoms, including the PRC's threat during the Cold War era and its recent rise as an economic superpower, America's ongoing neocolonial dominance and its shifting national interests in the global economic and political arena since the 1950s, and Taiwan's own ambiguous status in the international community. As literary scholars Yu-ting Huang and Rebecca Weaver-Hightower point out, "While settler colonialism desires completion and comfortable 'settled-ness,' it is always imagined amidst anxiety, guilt, self-doubt, and the immanent possibility of moral or actual collapse."[16] *Home Sweet Home* and *The Land of the Brave* manifest a specific ambivalent mentality of Han settlers' wavering multiple "homelands," and reflect this settler anxiety in response to the ROC's ambiguous international status and uncertain geopolitical position from the 1970s to the early 1980s. Furthermore, the two films demonstrate that Taiwan's settler colonial situation should be understood only through the transnational triangular context between the old colonial metropole (China), settler colony (Taiwan), and Indigenous population. It also should be conceptualized through another triangular relationship, that between the exogenous neocolonial power (US), the Han settlers, and Indigenous peoples, a consequence attributable to the Cold War structure.[17]

Most importantly, these two films' Han settler narratives, with respect to "home" and "land" via their cinematic constructions, are premised on the elimination of an Indigenous population and the usurpation of land. With respect to both the visual and audio senses on the silver screen, Taiwan is the "sweet home" and "land of the brave" exclusively for the Han settlers, with no Indigenous peoples. President Tsai Ing-wen's belated apology to Indigenous peoples in 2016 has not put an end to Taiwan's settler colonialism. On February 23, 2017, many Indigenous activists set up a campsite in front of the Presidential Office Building (the place that we see in the final scene of *The Land of the Brave*) to protest the controversial regulations by which Indigenous traditional territories are demarcated. This place now is called Ketagalan Boulevard, as it was renamed in 1996 to acknowledge the Ketagalan Indigenous people in Taipei. Unfortunately, the police evicted the Indigenous activists and demolished their campsite ruthlessly. Taiwan's settler colonialism is still exercised "in the metropole's very core,"[18] as land dispossession, ethnic/racial discrimination, and other forms of exploitation and suppression, are not yet finished.

Notes

1 I would like to express my gratitude to Michael Berry and Yu-ting Huang for reading earlier drafts of the chapter and their insightful comments. My thanks also go to Janne Lahti and Rebecca Weaver-Hightower for inviting me to participate in the volume, as well as to Shu-mei Shih, for her mentorship and encouragement.

Wan-yao Chou, *A New Illustrated History of Taiwan*, trans. Carole Plackitt and Tim Casey (Taipei: SMC Publishing, 2015); Katsuya Hirano, Lorenzo Veracini, and Toulouse-

Antonin Roy, "Vanishing Natives and Taiwan's Settler-Colonial Unconsciousness," *Critical Asian Studies* 50, no. 2 (2018), 196–218; Shu-mei Shih, "The Concept of the Sinophone," *PMLA* 126, no. 3 (2011), 709–718.

2   This does not mean that these languages were forbidden entirely during the Martial Law era. The Nationalist government had also adopted Hoklo (the language that the majority of the early Han settlers used) as a tool to propagandize the state ideology and historiography. See, for example, Bai Ke, *Descendants of the Yellow Emperor* [Huangdi zisun], (1955). See also Guo-juin Hong, *Taiwan Cinema: A Contested Nation on Screen* (New York: Palgrave Macmillan, 2011), see chap. 2; Lin-chin Tsai, "Mapping Formosa: Settler Colonial Cartography in Taiwan Cinema in the 1950s," *Concentric: Literary and Cultural Studies* 44, no. 2 (2018), 19–50.

3   The Nationalist violent crackdown on the uprising by old Han settlers on February 28, 1947 caused the conflicting tension between the earlier wave of Han settlers (or the so-called *benshengren*, Taiwanese locals) and mainlanders (or *waishengren*), and intensified the two modes of settler consciousness and national identity (Taiwan-oriented consciousness versus China-centered identity). Yet the distinction between the two modes of settler consciousness has never been stable and rigid between the old and new settler communities. The revival of Taiwanese consciousness due to a series of social movements since the late 1970s caused more and more second-generation mainlanders to form a national and cultural identity differing from their parents' generation. Meanwhile, the ongoing economic interaction between Taiwan and China after the lifting of the Martial Law in 1987 has continued to influence the formation of national and cultural identity among the Taiwanese people. The two tendencies of Han settler consciousness continue to coexist in Taiwan.

4   Rwei-Ren Wu, "Fragment of/f Empires: The Peripheral Formation of Taiwanese Nationalism," *Social Science Japan* 30 (December 2004), 18.

5   The Zhongshan Hall is a building in traditional Chinese architecture located on Yangmingshan National Park established in 1966 to commemorate the centennial birthday of Sun Yat-sen. It was used as a meeting venue for the National Assembly until the suspension of the Assembly in 2005.

6   Lorenzo Veracini, *Settler Colonialism: A Theoretical Overview* (New York: Palgrave Macmillan, 2010), 96–100.

7   James Wicks, "Projecting a State That Does Not Exist: Bai Jingrui's *Jia zai Taibei/Home Sweet Home*," *Journal of Chinese Cinemas* 4, no. 1 (2010), 20.

8   Scott Simon, "Of Boars and Men: Indigenous Knowledge and Co-Management in Taiwan," *Human Organization* 72, no. 3 (2013), 220–229; Chun-Chieh Chi, "Capitalist Expansion and Indigenous Land Rights: Emerging Environmental Justice in Taiwan," *Asia Pacific Journal of Anthropology* 2, no. 2 (2001), 135–153.

9   Shiao-ying Shen, "Stylistic Innovations and the Emergence of the Urban in Taiwan Cinema: A Study of Bai Jingrui's Early Films," *Tamkang Review* 37, no. 4 (2007), 41.

10 Lorenzo Veracini, *Settler Colonialism*, 21.

11 Emilie Yueh-yu Yeh and Darrel William Davis, *Taiwan Film Directors: A Treasure Island* (New York: Columbia University Press), 41.

12 Shu-mei Shih, "Theory in a Relational World," *Comparative Literature Studies* 53, no. 4 (2016), 737.

13 Michael Berry, "Immigrant, Nationalism, and Suicide: Pai Hsien-yung and Pai Ching-jui's Chinese Obsessions and American Dreams," *Bulletin of Taiwanese Literature* 14 (2009), 74.

14 At the concert, Lee brought a bottle of Coca-Cola to protest the domination of Western music in the 1970s (especially American popular songs) and advocated composing and singing "songs of our own." On the "campus folk song movement" as a consequence of, and anti-neocolonial resistance to, America's cultural domination in Taiwan, see Chao-wei Chang, *Shui zai nabian chang ziji de ge: Taiwan xiandai minge*

yundong shi [Who Is There Singing Our Own Songs: A History of Modern Taiwan Folk Songs] (Taipei: Rock Publications, 2003).

15 Yueh-yu Yeh, "Yingxiang wai de xushi celue: Xiaoyuan minge yu jiankang xieshi zhengxuan dianying [Beyond Visual Narration: College Folk Songs and Policy Films]," in Yueh-yu Yeh, *Gesheng meiying: gequ xushi yu Zhongwen dianying* [Phantom of the Music: Song Narration and Chinese-Language Cinema] (Taipei: Yuanliu, 2000), 88–89.

16 Yu-ting Huang and Rebecca Weaver-Hightower, "Introduction: Settler Colonialism and Its Cultural Archives—Ways of Reading," in *Archiving Settler Colonialism: Culture, Space and Race*, eds. Yu-ting Huang and Rebecca Weaver-Hightower (New York: Routledge), 6.

17 Shu-mei Shih, "Theory in a Relational World," *Comparative Literature Studies* 53, no. 4 (2016), 737.

18 Lorenzo Veracini, *The Settler Colonial Present* (New York: Palgrave Macmillan, 2015), 59.

PART III

Natives

9

HERO OR DUPE: JAY SWAN AND THE AMBIVALENCES OF ABORIGINAL MASCULINITY IN THE FILMS OF IVAN SEN

Barry Judd

This chapter explores the representation of Aboriginal masculinity developed through the central protagonist of the Ivan Sen films *Mystery Road* (2013) and *Goldstone* (2016). As one of few Australian-based filmmakers who addresses settler and native relations in contemporary contexts, Sen, a *Kamilaroi* man, utilises the character of Detective Jay Swan, played by *Arrernte* man Aaron Pederson, to explore the position that Aboriginal men occupy in twenty-first-century Australia. Scholars, including Julia Martínez and Claire Lowrie,[1] and Bernard Whimpress,[2] have analysed Australian Aboriginal masculinities, confirming that settler colonial society represents them in overtly negative terms and therefore as inferior to white men and masculinities associated with whiteness. This essay challenges those assessments by showing how the representation of Aboriginal masculinities in Sen's films provides a rare example in which dominant discourses about Aboriginal men and their relationship to the settler colonial state are unsettled. Sen achieves this outcome by constructing Jay Swan as a character defined by ambivalence. Swan remains a mystery as Sen purposely leaves audiences wondering who he is and where his place is within contemporary Australian society. Significantly, Sen asks the audience to consider the limits of possibilities faced by Aboriginal men in contemporary Australia given the weight of settler colonial history that rests upon their shoulders.

As a scholar who claims an Aboriginal heritage, I view the character of Jay Swan as an intriguing portrait of contemporary Aboriginal masculinity. When casting Swan as a detective, a position that requires intelligence and commands respect within settler colonial society, Sen disrupts the discursive contours that shape race relations between Aboriginal peoples and Anglo-Australia. Whereas Peter Kirkpatrick[3] and Greg Dolgopolov[4] analyse Sen's films for their import of the American genres of the Western and film noir to address settler colonialism in

Australia, I build on work by Anne Rutherford[5] in arguing that the characterisation of Swan as a highly ambivalent figure located in the "in-between" is an important development in the history of Australian cinema. I do so by first providing a brief overview of the how Anglo-Australian discourses about Aboriginal people have functioned to stereotype Aboriginal men and (mis)present them in powerful ways. I then show how such discourses have functioned to not only authorise and confirm binary hierarchies of race and culture, but also to exclude Aboriginal men from ideas of Australian national belonging. Discourses about Aboriginal peoples that originate in the stories told by former colonists, I argue, have become embedded in the psychology of the settler-Australian state and operate as powerful determinants of the life opportunities available to Aboriginal men, placing serious question marks over the relevancy Indigenous masculinities might have in twenty-first century Australian society. I show how Australian cinema and films of the "New Wave" were complicit in reaffirming the stories of former colonists, and therefore stereotypes misrepresenting Aboriginal masculinities, before turning my attention to an analysis of Sen's Jay Swan. In doing so, I argue that the ambivalent position Swan occupies draws on past representational tropes of Aboriginal men in order to unsettle and disrupt the present. In the absence of Indigenous studies scholarship directly addressing the issue of contemporary Aboriginal masculinity in Australia, I draw upon the work of Aotearoa scholar Brendan Hokowhitu to demonstrate the contradictory position that Indigenous men and masculinities occupy in contemporary settler colonial contexts and the ethical challenges that they face as they strive to be heroes at the risk of being duped.

Aboriginalism: Eliminating the Aborigine from Australian National Identity

Historian Bain Attwood and Australian studies scholar John Arnold coined the term "Aboriginalism" to describe the various discursive modes that settler colonialists have used to construct the Aborigine as Other as a rationale central to the process of settler colonialism in Australia.[6] The essential characteristics of the Aborigine as Other were confirmed through the colonial desires of government and settler alike. While considered both "objective" and "universal," the science of Anthropology was applied to represent the Aborigines as "creatures, often crude and quaint, that have elsewhere passed away and give place to higher forms." Confined to the past, the Aborigine became stereotyped as "traditional," "authentic," "pristine," and "full-blood"– a figure anomalous to the civility of settler colonial Australia. According to anthropologists like Baldwin Spencer and Frank Gillen, the Aborigine was a "dying race," his inferior and less-evolved culture and intelligence were said to be unable to compete with the white man.[7]

Aboriginal men have often been specifically targeted and impacted by the representational "truths" that settler colonialism has constructed about them. In the time of the frontier wars it was Aboriginal people who were killed; in the age of pastoral expansion it was Aboriginal men who were murdered in retaliation for the killing of stock or in competition over sexual access to Aboriginal women. It was Aboriginal men who were stripped of their power and authority to make decisions and assume leadership in matters concerning their peoples' religion, economics, law, and governance as they became subject to highly restrictive legislation and bureau-cratic controls that made every decision on their behalf. It was Aboriginal men who provided Anthropology with the raw material to make truth claims about the Aborigine. More recently, when the Australian state imposed the Northern Territory Intervention – legislation that denied Aboriginal people citizenship rights by removing protections due them under the Racial Discrimination Act [1975][8] – it referenced popular tropes that (mis)represented Aboriginal men as universally lazy, incompetent, corrupt, criminal, and sexual predators of children.[9] An enduring impact of the (mis)representation of Aboriginal men has been their characterisation as physical men, driven by emotion and instinct rather than intellect and reason.

Portrayals of Aboriginal Men in Australian Cinema

As an influential component of settler colonial (mainstream) popular culture, Aus-tralian cinematic output is in a powerful position to sway national audiences through the stories that filmmakers choose to tell. Historically Australian filmmakers have used cinematic media to retell the stories of former colonists. Films such as *Jedda* (dir. Charles Chauvel, 1955) and *The Chant of Jimmie Blacksmith* (dir. Fred Schepisi, 1978) reaffirmed negative images of Aboriginal men as savages. They were portrayed as threats to settler colonial Australia. *The Chant of Jimmie Blacksmith* draws attention to the threat that Aboriginal men represent in settler imaginaries. The film dramatizes the life of Jimmie Governor, who embarked on a killing spree across central western New South Wales.[10] He successfully utilized skills learned as an Aboriginal man to evade capture for a number of months during 1900. In retelling this story, the filmmaker Fred Schepisi focuses on the terror Governor instilled in settlers, pointing to the fragility of national aspirations of the time and the internal security threat posed by weaponised Aboriginal men.

Not only has cinema operated to confirm the discursive "truths" of Aboriginalism, but filmmakers have also used their media to reassert ideas of national belonging that confirm the exclusion of Aboriginal masculinities from narratives of citizenship. They have done so through the retelling of national histories in which Aboriginal peoples either are completely absent from the field of view, or exist at the very margins of the stories told. The new wave that commenced in the 1970s produced a number of period films that reinforced the national type of the bushman/soldier as emblematic of national values and characteristics so prevalent in settler colonial lit-erature. *Sunday Too Far Away* (dir. Ken Hannam, 1975), *Picnic at Hanging Rock* (dir. Peter Weir, 1975), and *Gallipoli* (dir. Peter Weir, 1981) told stories about the process of nation building in which Aboriginal people were largely absent or represented in terms that confirmed the truth claims of Aboriginalism.

More recently, Australian cinema has adopted a more inclusive stance. Films such as *Rabbit Proof Fence* (dir. Phillip Noyce, 2002), *The Tracker* (dir. Rolf de Heer, 2002), *Australia* (dir. Baz Luhrmann, 2008), and *Ten Canoes* (dir. Rolf de Heer, 2006), all made by non-Indigenous filmmakers, are indicative of the tendency to address issues arising from settler colonialism in the context of historical melodramas, allowing Australian audiences distance from personal guilt.

Directors who claim an Indigenous identity on the other hand "have tended to deal with historical memory through contemporary stories – stories which complicate the moral polarities that representations of frontier conflict seem to invite."[11] One such filmmaker is *Kamilaroi* man Ivan Sen whose projects include *Mystery Road* (2013) and *Goldstone* (2016). Both films were promoted as Australian Westerns and featured an Aboriginal detective-cowboy as leading protagonist. However, reflective of Sen's own complex identity, both films are not easily categorised into standard film genres.

While Jay Swan is costumed as a cowboy, with a white Stetson hat, Cuban heeled boots, and jeans, the character and storyline developed around him are firmly grounded in Australia and the complex history of race relations between settlers and natives, their disparate understandings of country, and the consequences these have for contemporary Australian society. Although fictious, the events portrayed in *Mystery Road* are directly influenced by Sen's background and experiences growing up in small-town, northern New South Wales. The plot of *Mystery Road*, for example, is established in the opening scene where the body of a young Aboriginal woman, Julie Mason, is found in a culvert by a passing truck driver on the outskirts of an unnamed country town. The body is in a state of semi-decay; "wild dogs" have been eating the corpse. It is presumed the victim had been prostituting herself to passing truck drivers to pay for her drug habit. The murder of young Aboriginal women in country towns isn't considered a newsworthy story in Australia. Sen utilises his filmmaking skills in an effort to make it a national conversation. Speaking in the *Australian* newspaper prior to the film's release, Sen provided insight into what an Aboriginal identity means in contemporary Australian life when he revealed that "three women in his extended family have been murdered or gone missing, presumed dead, within the last decade."[12] The personal dimensions of Sen's filmmaking were further elaborated in the Press Kit that accompanied the release of *Mystery Road*. In the Directors Statement, Sen writes:

> A few years ago, a distant cousin of my mother was found dead under a roadway in northern NSW. She had been stripped and brutally murdered. The police have seemingly done very little to bring her killer to justice and this has brought resentment from the local Indigenous community.[13]

Just as the plot of *Mystery Road* (and its sequel *Goldstone*) is grounded in the substantive experience of Aboriginal people throughout Australia, the position that Jay Swan occupies as the key protagonist is similarly one that Sen constructs from his knowledge of settler colonial history. Positioned as both an Aboriginal man and member of the settler-state police force, Sen builds the character of Jay Swan as both emblematic of (post)colonial identity and as a metaphor for the problems of contemporary race relations and the position that Aboriginal men occupy within their own communities and the broader Australian populace. Positioning Swan as both Aboriginal man and detective, Sen prompts his audience to critically assess whether his protagonist is a hero whose position of relative power can be harnessed to help his community, or a dupe used to further the aims of settler colonial logic to eliminate the Aborigine.

Hero and Dupe: Aboriginal Masculinities in Contemporary Settler Colonial Society

Working in Aotearoa, Indigenous masculinities scholar Brendan Hokowhitu has noted how settler colonial society operates through imperial British sporting cultures to construct discourses of Māori masculinity in ways that emphasise their physical capabilities while at the same time dismissing their intellectual abilities. According to anthropologist Gina Hawkes, one of the most striking outcomes of the discursive representations that Hokowhitu points out

> is the purposeful and structured ways Māori were pushed away from intellectual pursuits by British colonialists, and into physical ones ... natural New Zealand Māori athleticism was a myth created by British colonialism aimed to enslave Māori in manual pursuits rather than intellectual ones.[14]

According to Hokowhitu, this is the reason why Māori men dominate the British imperial game of Rugby Union in New Zealand today. Significantly, he argues that restrictive settler colonial articulations of Indigenous hypermasculinity and machoism have functioned to supress Māori understandings of masculinity. These understandings differed from the binary understanding of gender that the British imposed throughout their Empire; with Māori regarding gender differences as more subtle, complex, and involving categories that intersected both masculine and feminine. According to Hokowhitu, the Māori athlete, is both "hero and dupe."[15] Hawkes explains that he is

> caught up in a paradox – the Indigenous man or man of colour is both glorified and demonised. The Pasifika rugby league player often represents this type of glorified hypermasculinity – with his war dances, large stature, tattoos etc. he is often admired for the very same qualities he is demonised for – these are physical not intellectual qualities, he can have these things, but he cannot move outside of them. He is limited by them.[16]

This insight can be applied to the (mis)representation of Aboriginal masculinities in Australia. Here Aboriginal men were also defined by their physicality, with

Indigenous men restricted to employment in jobs and sporting pursuits that required brawn, not brains. Aboriginal men achieved widespread acclaim in athletics, boxing, rugby league, Australian (rules) football, and cricket. The first Aboriginal men to graduate from university only did so in the 1960s. Aboriginal men who work in intellectual professions as medical doctors, lawyers, accountants, teachers, and academics continue to be underrepresented and unacknowledged by settler colonial society.

Jay Swan, a police detective who also happens to be an Aboriginal man, serves to both confirm and disrupt settler colonial understandings of contemporary Indigenous masculinity that are contained within the discourse of Aboriginalism. Swan is not cast as a low-ranked constable. As a detective, he has relative freedom to make his own decisions about how he works. Swan is able to determine, to some degree at least, what matters and what does not. In *Mystery Road* Swan determines that it is the lives of young Aboriginal women that matter. In the film's sequel, *Goldstone*, Swan similarly determines that it is the lives of young Chinese women that matter as he seeks to shut down a human trafficking operation. In both films it is the determination of Swan to save vulnerable women positioned as the disposable playthings of white, patriarchal power structures that makes him heroic. Swan becomes an advocate for both Aboriginal peoples and other groups marginal to the settler colonial mainstream. The heroics of Swan are underlined by the tensions that exist between the Aboriginal detective and his white police colleagues and the often hostile members of the settler populace he encounters as a result of his investigative work. These tensions stem from how Swan disrupts settler colonial power relations. Aboriginal men are not supposed to occupy positions of power and authority. Nor are they supposed to acquire such status through the application of their intellect. In *Mystery Road*, the audience discovers that Swan, like many Aboriginal men, is an alcoholic, that his relationship with his wife has broken down, and that he struggles with the role of being father and role model to his teenage daughter. Yet, despite these difficulties, Swan is an Aboriginal man made good. He has a job that demands the respect of the non-Indigenous community, a job that is based not on his physicality, but on his intellectual ability to solve complex crimes.

The opening credits of *Goldstone* are telling as a series of black and white photographs recall the colonial frontier of the nineteenth century. Images of dispossessed Aboriginal peoples, Chinese gold miners, and British settler-pastoralists and shop keepers appear across the screen in quick succession. These images set the context for a film that is set in the arid, desolate outback mining outpost of Goldstone. Sen uses these powerful images to insert a circular reading of time and space, one that may be read as drawn from Aboriginal philosophies contained in *Tjukurpa* (Dreaming) – a sense that there is no separation between the past, the present, and the future. The presence of such narrative devices not only positions Sen as an Aboriginal filmmaker, but as one whose works may be justifiably categorised as cinematic post-colonial critique. It is important to recognise that the highly ambivalent position Swan occupies as both hero and dupe draws upon a deep well of Aboriginal collective memory of the settler colonial past and the destruction it brought Indigenous societies.

Sen's location of Swan as both Aboriginal man and police detective, situates him as a contemporary version of Aboriginal men who became functionaries of the settler colonial state through employment in "native-police" forces. In Victoria, native policemen, recruited from the *Wurrung*-speaking confederation of peoples known as *Kulin*, were utilised by the colonial government to enforce the controversial miner's tax on the goldfields. As a result, settler colonists who sought a living through gold mining came to despise the "black police."[17] These *Kulin* policemen were also used to subdue and disperse Aboriginal peoples' hostile to settler colonial intrusions including the *Gunditjimara* peoples of western Victoria.[18] In Queensland, the native police force was used extensively to dispossess Aboriginal peoples of their country. Their cruel efficiency created a notoriety among Aboriginal peoples that persists to the present day.[19] Among Aboriginal peoples, there remains little regard or sympathy for black men who chose to do the dirty work of settler colonialism.

The history of native police forces contextualises the character of Swan as one defined by deep ambivalence. Swan becomes the subject of not only settler colonial doubts that concern his intellectual abilities to do the job, but also of questions of a moral and ethical nature as settler characters wonder whose side he really is on. While Aboriginal characters in Sen's works do not question Swan's intellectual capacity to perform the tasks necessary to be an effective detective (because they know the racist hierarchies of settler colonialism are myth), they do ask whether his loyalties are to his own people or to the interests of the settler colonial state. Swan seems to be inspired not only by the stereotypes present within the discourse of Aboriginalism, but also specific stories that are drawn from the past, both recent and ancient.

In *Mystery Road*, the ambivalence of Swan as Aboriginal man and policeman is directly confronted in two key scenes. In the first scene, Swan, seeking new leads for his inquiry, approaches a group of young Aboriginal boys playing on the street. The dialogue directly references the deep level of distrust that Aboriginal people feel towards the police:

SWAN: How you going, my little brothers?
ABORIGINAL BOY: Good. You a copper, brah?
SWAN: Yeah.
ABORIGINAL BOY: We hate coppers, brah. We kill coppers, brah.

While both Swan and the boys with whom he converses (aged only five or six) acknowledge their shared identity as Aboriginal males, expressed colloquially in spoken Aboriginal English as "Brah" meaning brother, one boy draws direct attention to the significant history of bad blood between natives and settler colonial police forces. The boy tells Swan "We hate coppers, brah. We kill coppers, brah." This statement indicates that those perceived to work in the oppression of Aboriginal people are considered enemies. The statement by the young boy reminds Swan that despite their common identity, his direct collaboration with the settler colonial state as a police detective positions him an immediate target for Aboriginal hatred.

In the second scene, Swan acknowledges the ambivalent position he occupies in conversation with a local Sergeant (Tony Barry). Sitting in a bar with his white colleague "Sarge," Swan is advised to stop his investigation of the murder of Aboriginal women. As Swan's inquiries lead him to suspect the involvement of the local police, Sarge warns him about being caught in-between his allegiance to the Aboriginal community and the police force:

SWAN: What do you know about Johnno before he joined the cops?
SARGE: What do you mean?
SWAN: Well, I saw him out on the highway last night with Robbo. He was acting a bit strange.
SARGE: Probably thought the same thing about you.
SARGE: He's from up north.
SARGE: He got in a bit of trouble with the police up there.
SARGE: Had to cop a transfer.
SWAN: What kind of trouble?
SARGE: I don't know the details, to be honest.
SARGE: What do you reckon he was doing out there?
SWAN: Not too sure.
SARGE: Now, come on, Jay. Don't get all paranoid on me. Sometimes Johnno's gotta go for a while without a wash. That red dust can be hard to get off.
SWAN: What if that red dust don't come off no matter how hard you try?
SARGE: Ah, come on, Jay. Your hands are gonna get a bit grubby from time to time. You'll get used to it. Johnno's doing a good job. He's got some big busts coming up. Make sure you don't get caught in the middle.
SWAN: That's OK. Been there all my life. What, caught in the middle?
SARGE: Yeah, I guess you have, you poor bugger.

Together these scenes are pivotal to Sen's development of Jay Swan in *Mystery Road* and *Goldstone* as a character who is defined by an ambivalence of being in-between or as the films dialogue puts it "caught in the middle." Although deeply distrustful of the police, the Aboriginal community view Swan as their potential hero. They hope Swan digs deep enough in his investigations to find and deliver justice to whoever is murdering young Aboriginal women. On the other hand, the police hope that Jay Swan remains their Indigenous dupe by investigating crimes to benefit the settler colonial state and, more importantly, in ways that protect his colleagues.

In thinking about the ambivalence of Swan as both hero and dupe, the story of the real-life *Bunuba* resistance fighter *Jandamarra* (c. 1873–1 April 1897) comes to mind. *Jandamarra* lived at a time when the Kimberley region of Western Australia experienced widespread frontier violence. Initiated into *Bunuba* law, *Jandamarra* had worked on cattle stations since around the age of ten. An intelligent individual, he gained a sophisticated knowledge and understanding of both settler and *Bunuba* society. His work with cattle made him an expert stockman and his initiation into *Bunuba* society enabled him to become expert as a tracker, providing him with skills to live off the land. Trusted by his white overseers and peers, he also became skilled with rifles and renowned for his shooting. He developed an inseparable friendship with the Englishman Bill Richardson while working the cattle, and when his friend joined the police force in the 1890s, *Jandamarra* joined as a black tracker. Unusual for the period, the white policeman and the black tracker became a widely celebrated partnership, with many regarding *Jandamarra* as the key to Richardson's success. When *Bunuba* people commenced a guerrilla campaign against settlers in their country by spearing cattle, Richardson and *Jandamarra* were ordered to track them down. Having taken a group of his people prisoner at Lillimooloora Station, *Jandamarra* was forced by his uncle and senior law man *Ellemarra* to decide whether his loyalties to Richardson and the police should outweigh his moral responsibilities to his own people. In response he shot Richardson and became a fugitive, leading his people in a war of armed resistance against the colony of Western Australia for three years. The skilfulness demonstrated by *Jandamarra* in evading police made him a mythical figure who *Bunuba* and other Aboriginal peoples throughout Kimberley believed possessed magical powers. When he was shot and killed in April 1897, it was by the black tracker known as Micki, a man also thought to possess magical powers.[20]

The story of *Jandamarra* serves a template for Sen's Jay Swan. *Jandamarra* is regarded as a heroic freedom fighter by *Bunuba* today, and his mythical exploits have gained him widespread admiration amongst Aboriginal peoples throughout Australia. Swan has not yet been called upon by his Elders to decide his loyalties, yet the moral dilemmas faced by Aboriginal men who find themselves in jobs paid for by the settler colonial state remain the same as they were for *Jandamarra*.

If the *Jandamarra* story provides a recent colonial-era inspiration for the paradoxical position that Sen's Swan character occupies as both hero and dupe, ancient stories from the *Tjukurpa* (Dreaming) provide another clue to the inherent ambivalence of this character. In *Mystery Road*, the narrative makes reference to wild dogs on numerous occasions. Indeed, the theme of "wild dogs," a euphemistic term for the dingo, is introduced from the opening scene as the medical examiner charged with documenting the circumstances of Julie Mason's death informs Swan that the body has dog bites. Jay Swan, as both Aboriginal man and detective, parallels the dingo as a figure both native to Australia and not native at the same time. When Swan speaks to a local farmer whose property faces the highway where the body of Julie Mason is found, the hostile old white man named Bailey (David Field) draws together the ambivalence that defines the historical stories of the native police and of the dingo with more general discursive (mis)representations of Aboriginal men. In doing so he directly questions Jay Swan's ability to do his job and where his loyalties lie.

SWAN: Do you remember seeing anything strange out here lately?
BAILEY: Well …
BAILEY: We got these wild dogs running around everywhere.
BAILEY: Killed two of me young calves last week.
BAILEY: Only other strange thing is …
BAILEY: These young hoodlums come out from town, tryin' to steal everything I own.
BAILEY: Yeah I got signs and guard dogs and bloody car alarms.
BAILEY: Don't stop there little black hands getting' on somethin'.
BAILEY: Are you a real copper or are you …
BAILEY: One of them black trackers who turns on his own type?
BAILEY: No disrespect intended.
SWAN: How much land you got here Mr. Bailey?
BAILEY: Far as you can see.
SWAN: That's a lot of dirt.
BAILEY: Yeah I guess.
SWAN: Well, your children will have a pretty good future, then, won't they, eh?
SWAN: You're a lucky man.
BAILEY: You know your way back to town, don't you?

As a species that came to Australia long after the continent was first occupied by humans, the dingo stands outside of the laws set down during the creative period when humans, animals, and plants first emerged from the void that preceded them. According to Aboriginal *Tjukurpa* (Dreaming), the dingo known for its cunning intelligence is therefore widely characterised as a transgressor of law. In northern Australia, the *Yarralin* people hold that the dingo is what men would be if they were not human.[21] Amongst many Aboriginal peoples the dingo is associated with shape shifting and the belief that it can transform itself between dog and human forms. While many *Tjukurpa* stories position the dingo as a malevolent force, others position the dog as critical to life, with many water sources in inland Australia associated with the dingo and commonly known as dingo soaks. In such stories, the dingo is represented as guardian of water – protector of life. The dingo was also a prized companion animal for Aboriginal peoples. It was a vital hunting aid, its meat was a critical food source, its milk nourished human babies, and its fur was a blanket against the bitter cold. The dogs themselves were considered diviners of ground water.[22]

In *Goldstone*, Sen continues to reference *Tjukurpa* stories of the dingo as Swan's white police colleague, Josh (Alex Russell), uses the wild dog as a metaphor for the native police. In doing so, Sen's script references settler fears of miscegenation that view the "half-caste" Aborigine as akin to the dingo – able to thrive in hostile Australian environments as the natives do, but with the superior cunning intelligence that can only be attributed to the input of the white race.

SWAN: What's the old Winchester for?
JOSH: Mostly wild dogs.
JOSH: And whatever else comes out of the desert.
JOSH: Ferals around here have been mixing with the dingos.
JOSH: Making some crazy half breed. Wilder than the purebreds.
JOSH: Twice as cunning.

Conclusion

The character of Jay Swan that Ivan Sen develops in *Mystery Road* and its sequel *Goldstone* represents an important development in the history of Australian filmmaking. Sen refuses to reconfirm the constructs of Aboriginal masculinities that are inherent in discourses of Aboriginalism. He also refuses to protect Australian audiences from the continuing consequences of settler colonialism by setting his films in the past. Instead, Sen uses the character of Swan to ask a series of questions about what it means to be a relevant Indigenous man in contemporary Australian society. Sen asks his audience to consider the complexity of contemporary Aboriginal masculinities and how the weight of history and cultural meaning, black and white, continues to weigh heavily on the life experiences of Aboriginal men in twenty-first century Australia. Swan, to apply Hokowhitu's terminology, is both a hero and a dupe. The position he occupies, somewhere in-between Aboriginal and settler colonial Australia, is complex and characterised by an ambivalence that both speaks to the colonial history of the native police and the ancient storytelling tradition of Aboriginal peoples that gives cultural meaning to the dingo. In my mind, Sen's Jay Swan might represent a modern day *Jandamarra*.

As a scholar who himself claims an Aboriginal identity, Sen's films and the positioning of Swan in the paradoxical position of *both* Aboriginal man and police detective, force me to ask where my loyalties really lie. To the institutions who pay me a salary to be a professional academic, or to the Aboriginal peoples who I claim to represent through my scholarly writings? There is, perhaps, no black or white answer to such questions. The value of Sen's intervention in Australian cinema, and his complex representation of Aboriginal masculinities defined by a deep ambivalence, is that he accurately portrays a reality that few others have had the insight to grasp. Because of this, for me, at least, Sen's Jay Swan is more hero than dupe.

Notes

1 Julia Martínez and Claire Lowrie, "Colonial Constructions of Masculinity: Transforming Aboriginal Australian Men into 'Houseboys'," *Gender & History* 21, no. 2 (2009): 305–323.
2 Bernard Whimpress, *Passport to Nowhere: Aborigines in Australian Cricket 1850–1939* (Sydney: Walla Walla Press, 1999).
3 Peter Kirkpatrick, "From Massacre Creek to Slaughter Hill: The Tracks of *Mystery Road*," *Studies in Australasian Cinema* 10, no. 1 (2016): 143–155.
4 Greg Dolgopolov, "Balancing Acts: Ivan Sen's 'Goldstone' and 'Outback Noir'," *Metro Magazine: Media & Education Magazine*, No. 190 (2016): 8–13.
5 Anne Rutherford, "Walking the Edge: Performance, the Cinematic Body and the Cultural Mediator in Ivan Sen's *Mystery Road*," *Studies in Australasian Cinema* 9, no. 3 (2015): 312–326.
6 Bain Attwood and John Arnold, *Power, Knowledge and Aborigines* (Bundoora, Victoria: LaTrobe University, 1992), i-xvi.
7 Baldwin Spencer and Frank Gillen, *The Arunta: A Study of a Stone Age People* (London: Macmillan, 1927).
8 Barry Judd, "Sporting Intervention: The Northern Territory National Emergency Response and Papunya Football," in *'And there'll be NO dancing': Perspectives on Policies Impacting Indigenous Australia Since 2007*, eds. Elizabeth Baehr and Barbara Schmidt-Haberkamp (Cambridge: Cambridge Scholars Publishing, 2017), 110–127.
9 Alissa Macoun, "Aboriginality and the Northern Territory Intervention," *Australian Journal of Political Science*, 46, no.3 (2011): 519–534.
10 Laurie Moore and Stephen Williams, *The True Story of Jimmy Governor* (Crows Nest, NSW: Allen & Unwin, 2001).
11 Kirkpatrick, "From Massacre Creek," 143–155.
12 Sharon Verghis, "Outsider Knowledge in Ivan Sen's Mystery Road," *The Australian*, September 21, 2013.
13 Press Kit: *Mystery Road: A Film by Ivan Sen* (Sydney: Mystery Road Films 2013).
14 Gina Hawkes, "Diasporic Belonging, Masculine Identity and Sports: How Rugby League Affects the Perceptions and Practices of Pasifika Peoples in Australia" (PhD thesis, RMIT University, 2019).
15 Brendan Hokowhitu, foreword to *Native Games: Indigenous Peoples and Sports in the Post-Colonial World*, eds. Chris Hallinan and Barry Judd (London: Emerald Group Publishing, 2013).
16 Hawkes, "Disaporic Belonging," 144.
17 Fred Cahir, *Black Gold: Aboriginal People on the Goldfields of Victoria, 1850–1870* (Canberra: ANU Press, 2012).
18 Jan Critchett, *A 'Distant Field of Murder' : Western District Frontiers, 1834–1848* (Carlton, Victoria: Melbourne University Press, 1990).
19 Jonathan Richards, *The Secret War* (St Lucia, Queensland: University of Queensland Press, 2008).
20 Howard Pedersen and Banjo Woorunmurra, *Jandamarra and the Bunuba Resistance*, new ed. (Broome, Western Australia: Magabala Books, 2011).
21 Deborah Bird Rose, *Dingo Makes Us Human: Life and Land in an Aboriginal Australian Culture* (Melbourne: Cambridge University Press, 1992).
22 Justine Philip, "The Cultural History of the Dingo," *Australian Geographic*, https://www.australiangeographic.com.au/topics/wildlife/2017/08/cultural-history-of-the-dingo/ (accessed 10 September 2019).

10

IN THE LAND OF THE HEAD HUNTERS: KWAKWAKA'WAKW ARCHIVES AND THE SETTLER COLONIAL LENS

Natale A. Zappia

When the film *In the Land of the Head Hunters* premiered to a packed crowd in Seattle in 1914, it hit all of the settler colonial flavors readily consumed by its intended audience.[1] As the "traditional" Kwakwaka'wakw epic unfolded on screen, the crowd laughed, gasped, and perhaps cried in unison. The spectacle of the elaborate costumes, dances, rituals, and, of course, head hunting that enthralled the non-Native audience—when viewed from the twenty-first century—confirms many of the precepts of settler colonial ideologies. As anthropologist Patrick Wolfe stated, settler colonialism is more of a "structure, not an event," alluding to the ongoing process of colonial dismantling of Indigenous culture while simultaneously romanticizing and lamenting the "vanishing race"—a phrase frequently employed by the director of the film, Edward Curtis.[2]

A century later it is obvious that the "race" did not vanish. In fact, when a faithfully restored version appeared on screen to another packed room at the Chan Centre for the Performing Arts at the University of British Columbia in 2008 (it also premiered at the Getty Center in Los Angeles and the Moore Theatre in Seattle that same year), a very different audience—among them First Nations Kwakwaka'wakws whose relatives starred in the film—similarly cheered, laughed, and cried at the genius of their forebearers who spoke to them across time. This early piece of cinema—at quick glance, filled with timeless, exotic tropes manifest in all its settler colonial representations, and critiqued as such (like much of Curtis' work) for acting as a "structure"—more accurately and directly served an Indigenous community and their existential needs than non-Native viewers from 1914 realized. *In the Land of the Head Hunters* was actually a true collaboration between Curtis and the Kwakwaka'wakw people, who in 1914 perhaps anticipated a moment in the future when their descendants could access and celebrate their culture preserved forever on film.

This chapter explores these ways that Native communities spoke to each other through settler colonial structures in *In the Land of the Head Hunters* in order to preserve, protect, and convey cultural autonomy, preserving an Indigenous archive of knowledge. These efforts reflect the awareness and foresight of Native communities who understood the designs of settler colonial fantasies, but who also recognized the power of such venues to speak to their own people across space and time. Curtis' efforts, no doubt fueled the settler colonial master narrative. In a time when it was illegal to hold Native ceremonies and express Indigenous spiritual practices, the all-Native performances of potlatches and other rituals in the film were remarkable and a decision made along Indigenous lines. But Curtis, too, was a more complex man then he was at first perceived in that his efforts contained a critique against settler colonial violence and dispossession. His projects (and especially his films) relied on his relationships with Indigenous collaborators, as well as the expertise, vision, input, and acceptance of Native cultural authorities.[3] This chapter closely examines this relationship between Curtis and his Indigenous collaborators before, during, and after the filming of *In the Land of the Head Hunters*.

The Cinematic Gaze of Edward Curtis

Edward Curtis' film is part of a larger multi-decade effort that etched his photography in popular culture for a century. During a period when anthropology, history, and other social sciences were becoming professionalized, the unschooled Curtis utilized his professional networks in Seattle (where he owned a professional portrait studio) to gain access to wealthy patrons like Theodore Roosevelt and John Piedmont Morgan. Largely eschewed by professional academics, Curtis' photography popularized the image of the "noble savage" that permeated the zeitgeist of mainstream white America. He embarked on the film project to help support his other more ambitious effort, the twenty-volume *North American Indian* (NAI) encyclopedic survey of indigenous cultures. Undertaken over two decades and by any measure a monumental effort, the *NAI* featured thousands of Indigenous portraits of material culture, environments, and other "pre" modern accoutrements viewed by the white settler culture as rapidly in decline and on their way towards extinction.[4] This sentiment was particularly in vogue when Curtis began his effort to visit dozens of Native nations in the U.S. and Canada. The intended audience for these prohibitively expensive volumes were arguably the very architects of Indigenous destruction: infrastructure barons (like J.P. Morgan, who bankrolled Curtis), as well as private and government institutions (including the Smithsonian). At the time of production, each volume cost anywhere between $3000 to $4200. Thus, Curtis' targeted audience invariably revolved around the titans of industry, politics, and culture.[5]

In the Land of the Head Hunters, in contrast, hoped to popularize Curtis' more exclusive venues and bring the *NAI* to a larger, mainstream audience. As in the twenty-first century, the film served to bring ideas to the masses. Although quickly forgotten after its initial release and costing Curtis thousands of dollars out of his own pocket, *In the Land of the Head Hunters* has taken its place in film studies scholarship as a pioneering work of cinema.[6] It is not accidental that the western dominated cinema for decades.[7] No matter the sympathies or attempts to get at "accurate" Native histories, the story arc was usually the same: Indigenous life crumbled in the face of settler colonialism and modernity. Curtis' film focused on the "pre" historical period before colonization, but this setting made his film even more evocative of the "before/after" equation essential to the staying power of settler colonial ideology.[8] This desire, of course, continues to pervade the big screen today in films like *The Revenant* (2015) and *Hostiles* (2017).[9]

Framed within a melodramatic arc including a love triangle, spectacular coastal scenery, dramatic ritual performances, and even a whale hunt (not part of Kwakwaka'wakw culture), Curtis' film follows the hero Motana, whose journey includes a vision quest and battle with a sorcerer who covets Motana's maiden Naida. The culminating moments in the film include a dramatic chase scene by canoe between the protagonist Motana and his nemesis, the sorcerer. Both rivals square off with their accompanying war parties. The dramatic scenes include elaborate Pacific Northwest Coast costumes, masks, totem poles, canoes, and homes. Throughout the film, Curtis includes drums, chants, and other "tribal" songs that match the dramatic visuals. Throughout the 65 minutes of reel time, Curtis never indicates what time period the film touches on or indeed gives any sense of historicity. The 80 title cards interspersed between and during the scenes never provide specific cultural references or places. Not one mentions the Kwakwaka'wakw, but rather generically refers to the "primitive life on the shores of the North Pacific."

Harnessing the power of new media technology, Curtis' film and photos evoked (and continue to evoke) the settler colonial gaze through which non-Native (and largely Euro-American) audiences viewed, interpreted, and mythologized the "winning" of the American West. But as scholars have recently pointed out, and in contrast to Wolfe's formulation, perhaps settler colonialism is more of a "process" rather than a "structure" and thus less totalizing than it appears.[10] As with many parts of the cultural kaleidoscope of Native America, there were in fact many "gazes" in all forms of media: white to non-white, white to white, Native to non-Native, and Native to Native. These exchanges complicate the theoretical underpinnings of cinematic settler colonialism, revealing both its explanatory strength but also weaknesses. In over a century of settler colonial films, Indigenous actors have, in fact, shaped these messages in both subtle and more dramatic ways. If what Wolfe and others have argued about settler colonialism rings true, then the uneven yet significant Indigenous answer to this totalizing force is important to locate, understand, and decode.[11] This is particularly clear in *In the Land of the Head Hunters*, which evoked such stunning and powerful imagery for audiences experiencing cinema for the first time. The lush, misty coastal mountains stirred the desire to observe "untouched nature" while the scenes of the elaborate potlach ceremony further tugged at the romanticized sentiments about "traditional" prehistoric cultures. A century removed from this novelty, it is easy to overlook or underestimate the resonance and "magic" of this experience, or to see it is simply as another tool in the settler colonial arsenal. But just as the steady Indigenous gaze into the camera has revealed hidden messages to scholars and empowered contemporary Native communities, so too do the movies unveil other structures *and* events both a century ago and today.[12]

New scholarship has ably described the commercial project undertaken by Curtis and its grounding in the settler colonial paradigm, and this chapter briefly summarizes this.[13] But rather than start with this perspective, it might make better sense to situate ourselves in the villages and cultural geography of the Kwakwa-ka'wakw nation of 1914. What was the Indigenous context? Why did Curtis seek out this Indigenous nation at this time and for this film? What does it tell us about Native cultural landscapes?

The Cinematic Gaze of Kwakwaka'wakws

For at least two decades before Curtis arrived at the Pacific Northwest Coast in the early 1900s, other professional anthropologists, commercial photographers, and amateurs traveled to document and exploit the "untouched" cultures of the region for academic and personal gain.[14] Curtis was a latecomer to this relatively inaccessible but deeply rutted ethnographic destination. These earlier anthropological forays themselves arrived at least a century after the Indigenous Pacific Northwest plugged into the world economy, primarily through the fur trade. In fact, the accumulation of material wealth, expansion of totem pole art, rise of slavery, and increase in Native oceangoing exploration all correlated with the larger and more active participation of Indigenous people in the fur trading networks across the Pacific.[15]

In addition to hunting and manufacturing furs, Native Pacific Northwesterners even sailed to Hawaii, Canton, and Alta California.[16] Prominent Indigenous leaders (like the famed fur trader at the strategic Indigenous port of Yukot in the Nootka Sound, Maquinna) proved to be formidable trading adversaries and partners with British, Spanish, French, Russian, New England, and Chinese merchants.[17] These nuanced interactions complicate the notion of "untouched" communities shrinking in the face of modernity. While new technology, diseases, and their accompanying political repression had infiltrated the Kwakwaka'wakws long before Curtis arrived on their shores, they imported and employed technology (including weaponry, metal tools, etc.) and global material culture on their own terms.[18]

Thus, a deep awareness and knowledge of globalization informed the Kwak-waka'wakws and allowed them to embrace or resist colonial technology. Some of the most iconic illustrations of Indigenous northwest culture—the potlatch and totem poles—incorporated this new global status.[19] During the potlatch of 1792, for example, Maquinna (who was not Kwakwaka'wakw but from the neighboring Mowachaht/Muchalaht nation) hosted the explorer George Vancouver with an elaborate spectacle of pelts but also silver plates, and other non-Native items.[20]

Several recent studies have begun to carefully locate this "intentional design" in the rhythms of global trade that began to stitch Native America with the world during this period, reexamining the role of Indigenous consumption in shaping things like the firearm trade, to take one example.[21] Indigenous demand determined much of the continental (and by extension global) trading relationships.[22] Highlighting these Indigenous contours complicates and even challenges the totalizing nature of settler colonial theory by locating Indigenous producers, consumers, infrastructure, land use practices, and energy with European-dominated exchange networks. When examining these interactions from within an Indigenous archive, the complex, interregional, and deeply layered history is evident.

Indeed, thinking about Indigenous archives not only unveils these histories in *In the Land of the Head Hunters*—for example by decoding the potlatch ceremony, expert Kwakwaka'wakw sea canoe paddling, and traditional Gwa'wina dancing positions—but challenges historians and other scholars to rethink the "archive." Over the past two decades, the steady but uneven emergence of the "Indigenous archives" has invigorated debates and uncovered previously overlooked perspectives about Native American cultures, regions, and timelines. For historians, in particular, Indigenous sources have challenged the very heart of the discipline's methodological assumptions: that history only happens in written primary texts. The first waves of Native-centered scholarship effectively extracted Indigenous texts from colonial documents, whether they were by or about Native communities. More recently, "non-traditional" sources have been recognized as vital entry points into understanding Native history. Such sources include oral history, dance, material culture, language, visual art, music, and traditional ecological knowledge (TEK).[23]

As their twenty-first-century descendants from U'Mista Cultural Centre have argued, the Kwakwaka'wakw actors no doubt viewed their effort as an act of archival preservation.[24] For example, in a pivotal scene from the movie, the Kwakwaka'wakw actors perform the Galsgamila, a sacred ceremony. This dance required permission (and thus acted as an intentional form of archival preservation) since Kwakwaka'wakw communities viewed ceremonies as the personal property of particular families. As William Wasden Jr. (Waxawidi), founder and director of the Gwa'wina Dancers who comprise many tribes of the Kwakwaka'wakw community, pointed out during the 2008 screening of *In the Land of the Head Hunters* (the Gwa'wina Dancers performed alongside the screenings), "A song cannot be used without permission, and the same is true of dances." Wasden further elaborated on the precision of these performances in the film and how they informed contemporary practices:

> the Kwakwaka'wakw and their culture are alive and thriving…we own our culture…no one else. We are a proud and strong people with teachings that could help all people. We are not reviving or reinventing our culture. Our elders hung on…and [we] are in control of what the creator gave us.[25]

By the late nineteenth century, though, sustained (if not direct) contact with outsiders portended dramatic changes for the Kwakwaka'wakws that Curtis encountered. Foreign diseases decimated Indigenous populations. The new provincial Canadian government outlawed the same potlatch ceremonies witnessed by European traders just decades earlier. Simultaneously, the government denied legitimacy to Native expressions of religion and culture while anthropologists deliberated over what constituted "primitive" traditional culture. These efforts documented traditional culture but very rarely intervened to protect or celebrate it on Indigenous terms.

Under pressure to assimilate but also perform in turn-of-the-century shows like the Chicago Columbian Exposition of 1893, Native communities straddled a delicate line that continues to shape their efforts to maintain, strengthen, and expand cultural and political sovereignty today.[26] This was thus both a familiar path and an unprecedented crossroads for Native communities inundated by settler colonialism: how to best protect and also innovate Indigenous culture, ideas, and kin while also adopting colonial technologies to document and preserve language and history? How to best speak to their Indigenous neighbors of the present and future? In the language of film, the Kwakwaka'wakws had their vehicle to preserve politically illegal acts like the potlatch dance. Films, like musical recordings, could act as effective Indigenous archives. *In the Land of the Head Hunters,* then, was a vital opportunity, both in 1914 and today.

Refocusing the Cinematic Gaze: Sifting through Myth and History

Much has been written about the settler colonial stereotypes perpetrated in thousands of films depicting colonialism in the Americas, Africa, and Asia. Within the North American context, nearly every American origin myth—from Jamestown to Plymouth Rock to New Amsterdam to the Gold Rush—has made its way to the silver screen, and this proved especially true during the earliest period of cinema. And in each of these early films, the stereotypical Indian makes its appearance. In the recent documentary, *Reel Injun,* native director Chris Eyres documents more than 100 films portraying this. The vast majority, he argues, have non-native actors portraying Native characters. Most famous one being the Italian-American Espera Oscar de Corti (aka Iron Eyes Cody). Appearing in over 200 films (mostly westerns), Cody dubiously claimed Cherokee heritage and appeared as the "crying Indian" in the public service announcement (PSA) "Keep America Beautiful" announcements of the 1970s.[27] Both Native and settler colonial communities watched and internalized these "cowboy and Indian" myths. In this way, "settler cinema," as this volume argues, proved an especially effective weapon for attacking Native cultures. In the period of Curtis' screening, dozens of films depicting the "frontier" permeated cinema.[28] This makes *In the Land of the Head Hunters* all the more extraordinary in its narrative, cinematography, Native actors, and Kwakwaka'wakw vision. At least 12 ceremonial dances were preserved in the film—all of which are practiced by a growing number of Kwakwaka'wakw performers today.

While the Kwakwaka'wakw film portrayed authentic Indigenous perspectives, its director was undoubtedly part of the settler colonial regime, serving as part of the settler colonial gaze. Curtis, as much as any other documentarian of his or any period, epitomized this. His efforts to dress Native people, insist that they act stoic, and utilize "Indian props" have been explored endlessly by scholars.[29] His work continues to make its way into coffee table books, gallery premieres, museum exhibits, and romanticized hagiographies. As the Kwakwaka'wakw photographer David Neel points out:

> [a]lthough the images are impressive from an artistic perspective, the ideas they represent, and the misconceptions they perpetuate, will remain problematic for contemporary viewers and for the descendants of Curtis's subjects....Curtis's images taught me a lot about photography, including how not to photograph Native American people.[30]

Curtis was the most famous but not the only producer of these types of works, which included others like the photographer Joseph Dixon who coined the phrase "vanishing race" in his 1913 book by the same name.[31] By any measure, though, the *NAI* was unique in its depth, breadth, and Indigenous participation. Indeed, Curtis' reputation spread across Indian country long before he arrived. While his "gaze" was no doubt of the settler colonial variety, he recognized the local needs, politics, and dignity of his collaborators. He thus spent much more time than other outsiders cultivating relationships, gaining trust, and becoming "Indigenized." This method, in fact, stands in stark contrast to many "parachute anthropologists" derided by Native communities today.[32] In Curtis, Native communities knew what they were getting and manipulated his intentions, exploited his expertise, and extracted as much as they possibly could from his budget. Almost all of these Indigenous nations, like the Kwakwaka'wakws, engaged in this give and take for at least a century. Yes, the film reified the non-Native gaze, but also allowed—through *In the Land of the Head Hunters*—the Kwakwaka'wakws to proudly look at each other across time.[33]

By the time the film project idea percolated amongst the Kwakwaka'wakws, Curtis had already invested perhaps more time in the region than any of his other trips. He dedicated a whole *NAI* volume (volume 10), in fact, to the Kwakwaka'wakws. Curtis visited and collaborated extensively with Kwakwaka'wakws thanks to the cooperation of Tlingit interpreter George Hunt. For decades before Curtis, Hunt worked extensively with the anthropologist Franz Boas, and his negotiating, translating, and co-directing proved essential to the completion of the film, as revealed in Hunt's primary position holding the megaphone in Figure 10.1. [34] And unlike the second life for Curtis's photography (with some noted exceptions), the film's audience today is viewed for its preservation of culture, rather than simply settler colonial fantasy.

Not unlike his photographic volumes, though, the efforts by Hunt, Curtis, and the Kwakwaka'wakws failed to capture the imagination of the public. As quickly as the film was released, it disappeared, not to be rediscovered until decades later thanks to the painstaking decade of restoration work by Bill Holm and George

FIGURE 10.1 Filming of *In the Land of the Head Hunters*. Tlingit collaborator George Hunt is holding the megaphone. Picture in public domain.
Source: Bill Holm and George Quimby, Edward S. Curtis in the Land of the War Canoes: A Pioneer Cinematographer in the Pacific North West (Seattle: University of Washington Press, 1980).

Quimby.[35] In between the fizzle after the release and its rediscovery, Kwakwaka'wakws continued to practice many of the very same dances, songs, potlatches, and ceremonies (although many others were lost until the film's rediscovery) that they performed in *In the Land of the Head Hunters*. These include the Yawitłalał (welcome dance), Hamat'sa (cannibal dance), and the Kwan'wala (thunderbird dance), among several others. Many of the dances, outlawed by the Canadian government in their forced assimilation policy that remained on the books until 1951, never lost their accuracy, meaning, and cultural nuances that evaded the government authorities.[36] Hence when the film appeared again in 1973, and then again in 2008, the Kwakwaka'wakws were there to interpret, celebrate, and share their culture through the film. As William T. Canmer, Chair of the U'mista Cultural Society reminds us

> We continue to learn by watching the dance movements and the expert paddling in the film. The young people who participated in the live performance…are descendants of the people you see in the film. Because they have all been initiated and named in our ceremonies, they bring a true spiritual connection with them in their singing and dancing. The Kwakwaka'wakw people helped make Curtis's film in 1914 and then helped again in 1974 when it was remade. We are proud to have been involved in the current project, as this film is part of our history.[37]

Conclusion

There is no doubt that Edward Curtis was engaged in a "cinematic settler" project that stoked public romanticism lamenting the "noble savage." This sentiment, like other aspects of settler colonialism, continued unabated during Curtis' time and yet again decades later, in the 1970s through to today. When we expand to include the other forms of media (Curtis' prolific collection of photography and audio recordings), an even larger cascade of settler colonial ideology (particularly in the "second wave") created indelible (for non-Natives) and insidious misperceptions. Without a doubt, film has served as an agent of this ideology. And yet, William Cranmer's comments above serve as a reminder and invitation to think about Indigenous actors as producers and consumers of modern culture, both within and in spite of settler colonialism. As scholars become more attuned to these Native maneuvers, new forms of archival knowledge will surely follow, and enrich and expand the field of settler colonial studies.

Notes

1 In 1973, scholars Bill Holm and George Quimby restored and renamed Curtis' film *In the Land of the War Canoes*. The more recent re-release in 2008 returned to the original title of the film, *In the Land of the Head Hunters*. See Brad Evans and Aaron Glass, eds., *Return to the Land of the Head Hunters: Edward Curtis, the Kwakwaka'wakw, and the Making of Modern Cinema* (Seattle: University of Washington Press, 2014), 27–28.

2 See Patrick Wolfe, *Settler Colonialism and the Transformation of Anthropology: The Politics and Poetics of an Ethnographic Event* (London and New York: Cassell Press, 1999), 2. For a recent reassessment of Curtis' employment of the term "vanishing race," see Shannon Eagan, "'Yet in a Primitive Condition': Edward S. Curtis's North American Indian," *American Art* 20, no. 3 (2006), 58–83.

3 For an overview of the Canadian government's attack on the potlatch, see Douglas Cole and Ira Chaikin, *An Iron Hand Upon The People: The Law Against the Potlatch on the Northwest Coast* (Seattle: University of Washington Press, 1990).

4 The scholarship on Edward Curtis is even more vast and wide-ranging than the NAI project. For just a few of the most recent works, see Shamoon Zamir, *The Gift of the Face: Portraiture and Time in Edward Curtis's The North American Indian* (Chapel Hill: University of North Carolina Press, 2014); Mic Gidley, ed., *Edward S. Curtis and the North American Indian Project in the Field* (Lincoln: University of Nebraska Press, 2010).

5 See http://curtis.library.northwestern.edu/description.html for a detailed explanation of the subscription strategy and even a sales brochure from Curtis' marketing production. In 2012, a complete set sold for $1.4 million. See "Edward S. Curtis' 'The North American Indian' sells for $1.44 Million at Auction," *Indian Country Today* 10 October 2012: https://newsmaven.io/indiancountrytoday/archive/edward-s-curtis-the-north-american-indian-sells-for-1-44-million-at-auction-59z9sRnoYUO4pe8ulEu8sg/.

6 See Pauline Wakeham, "Celluloid Salvage: Edward S. Curtis's Experiments with Photography and Film," in *Taxidermic Signs: Reconstructing Aboriginality* (Minneapolis: University of Minnesota Press, 2008), 87–128; Catherine Russell, "Playing Primitive: 'In the Land of the Head Hunters' and/or 'War Canoes'," *Visual Anthropology* 8, no. 1 (1996), 55–77; George I. Quimby, "Curtis and the Whale," *Pacific Northwest Quarterly* 78, no. 4 (1987), 141–144.

7 For the intersection of the American West and settler colonialism, see Janne Lahti, "Introduction: What is Settler Colonialism and What It Has to Do with the American West?" *Journal of the West* 55, no. 4 (2017), 8–12. For the western, see Scott Simmon,

The Invention of the Western Film: A Cultural History of the Genre's First Half-Century (Cambridge: Cambridge University Press, 2003).

8 For a recent critique of "pre" history, see Juliana Barr, "'There's No Such Thing as "Prehistory"': What the Longue Durée of Caddo and Pueblo History Tells Us about Colonial America," *The William and Mary Quarterly* 74, no. 2 (2017), 203–240.

9 For recent analyses of Indigeneity and cinema, see Marubbio, M. Elise and Eric L. Buffalohead, eds., *Native Americans on Film: Conversations, Teaching, and Theory* (Lexington: University Press of Kentucky, 2013); and Jeremy Stoddard, Alan Marcus, and David Hicks, "The Burden of Historical Representation: The Case Of/for Indigenous Film," *The History Teacher* 48, no. 1 (2014), 9–36.

10 For an excellent discussion of this tension between "structure" and "process," see the most recent forum on settler colonialism and early American history, Jeff Ostler and Nancy Shoemaker, "Settler Colonialism in Early American History: Introduction," *The William and Mary Quarterly* 76, no .3 (2019), 361–368.

11 Ashley Glassburn, "Settler Standpoints," *The William and Mary Quarterly* 76, no. 3 (2019), 399–406.

12 For the "gaze" into Curtis' camera, see Gerald Vizenor, ed., *Survivance: Narratives of Native Presence* (Lincoln: University of Nebraska Press, 2008).

13 Mic Gidley's *Edward S. Curtis and the North American Indian, Incorporated* (Cambridge: Cambridge University Press, 2000) explores the commercial nature of the *NAI*.

14 For a global perspective on the "ethnographic boom" of early cinema, see Wolfgang Fuhrmann, "Early Ethnographic Film and the Museum," in *Early Cinema and the "National"*, eds. Abel Richard, Bertellini Giorgio, and King Rob (Bloomington: Indiana University Press, 2016), 285–292.

15 David Igler, "Hardly Pacific: Violence and Death in the Great Ocean," *Pacific Historical Review* 84, no. 1 (2015), 1–18; Anya Zilberstein, "Objects of Distant Exchange: The Northwest Coast, Early America, and the Global Imagination," *The William and Mary Quarterly* 64, no. 3 (2007), 591–620; Robin Fisher, "George Vancouver and the Native Peoples of the Northwest Coast," in *Enlightenment and Exploration in the North Pacific, 1741–1805*, eds. Stephen Haycox, James K. Barnett, and Caedmon A. Liburd (Seattle: University of Washington Press, 1997).

16 Paige Raibmon, "'Handicapped by Distance and Transportation': Indigenous Relocation, Modernity and Time-Space Expansion," *American Studies* 46, no. 3/4 (2005), 363–90.

17 The new scholarship on an Indigenous global Pacific Basin is burgeoning. Recent notable works include Joshua Reid, *The Sea Is My Country: The Maritime World of the Makahs* (New Haven: Yale University Press, 2015); Ryan Tucker Jones, "Running into Whales: The History of the North Pacific from below the Waves," *American Historical Review* 118, no. 2 (2013), 349–377; and David Igler, *The Great Ocean: Pacific Worlds from Captain Cook to the Gold Rush* (Oxford: Oxford University Press, 2013).

18 Josh Reid's *The Sea is My Country* brilliantly navigates the early modern Indigenous waters of the Northwest coast. See chapter 1.

19 See Gail Ringel, "The Kawkiutl Potlatch: History, Economics, and Symbols," *Ethnohistory* 26, no. 4 (1979), 347–362.

20 See Valerie Sherer Mathes, "Wickaninnish, a Clayoquot Chief, as Recorded by Early Travelers," *The Pacific Northwest Quarterly* 70, no. 3 (1979), 110–20; and Charlotte Coté, *Spirits of our Whaling Ancestors: Revitalizing Makah and Nuu-chah-nulth Traditions* (Seattle: University of Washington Press, 2017), esp. chap. 1. At another potlatch, Maquinna also gave away firearms and gunpowder seized from British ships in 1803, as reported by British captive John Jewitt. See Richard Alsop, ed., *The Captive of Nootka or the Adventures of John R. Jewett (1841)* (Kessinger Publishing, 2010).

21 For the Indigenous continental firearms trade, see David Silverman, *Thundersticks: Firearms and the Violent Transformation of Native America* (Cambridge: Harvard University Press, 2016).

22 For a discussion of Indigenous empires, see Pekka Hämäläinen, *The Comanche Empire* (New Haven: Yale University Press, 2008) (esp. introduction). Also see Andrew Isenberg, *The Destruction of the Bison: An Environmental History* (Cambridge: Cambridge University Press, 2000).

23 For a recent overview of the expansion and inclusion of Indigenous archives, see Alyssa Mt. Pleasant, Caroline Wigginton and Kelly Wisecup, "Materials and Methods in Native American and Indigenous Studies: Completing the Turn," *The William and Mary Quarterly* 75, no. 2 (2018), 207–236.

24 For speculation into this rationale, see the "U'Mista Statement of Participation": https://www.curtisfilm.rutgers.edu/project/umista-cultural-centre-mainmenu-30.

25 Evans and Glass, *Return to the Land of the Head Hunters*, 304–306.

26 For primitivism, see David Murray, *Matter, Magic, and Spirit: Representing Indian and African American Belief* (Philadelphia: University of Pennsylvania Press, 2007), esp. chap. 3, "Primitivism, Modernism, and Magic," 71–101. For Indigenous portrayals at the Columbian Exposition, see David R.M. Beck, "Fair Representation? American Indians and the 1893 Chicago World's Columbian Exposition," World History Connected, October 2016 <https://worldhistoryconnected.press.uillinois.edu/13.3/forum_01_beck.html> (accessed 7 Jan. 2020).

27 Ludmilla Marttanovschi, "Mediating the Native Gaze: The American Indian Youth's Cinematic Presence in Chris Eyre's Films," in *Mediating Indianness*, ed. Cathy Covell Wadgner (East Lansing: Michigan State University Press, 2015), 145–162; Jennifer K. Ladino, "'A Tear for the Fate of America': The (Crying) Indian as Spokesperson for a Vanishing Natural World," in *Reclaiming Nostalgia: Longing for Nature in American Literature* (Charlottesville: University of Virginia Press, 2012), 119–126.

28 Dominique Brégent-Heald, *Borderland Films: American Cinema, Mexico, and Canada during the Progressive Era* (Lincoln: University of Nebraska Press, 2015).

29 Gidley, ed., *Edward S. Curtis and the North American Indian Project in the Field*.

30 Evans and Glass, *Return to the Land of the Head Hunters,* 247.

31 Richard Lindstrom, "'Not from the Land Side, but from the Flag Side': Native American Responses to the Wanamaker Expedition of 1913," *Journal of Social History* 30, no. 1 (1996), 209–227.

32 For a discussion and critique of past ethnographic practices, see Henk Driessen and Willy Jansen, "The Hard Work of Small Talk in Ethnographic Fieldwork," *Journal of Anthropological Research* 69, no. 2 (2013), 249–263.

33 The scholarship on early twentieth-century Native American music, art, and labor is immense. Notable works include see Philip J. Deloria, *Indians in Unexpected Places* (Norman, OK: University of Oklahoma Press, 2004), 183–223.

34 Evans and Glass, *Return to the Land of the Head Hunters*, 169. For a recent reevaluation of Hunt's work and legacy, see Judith Berman, Judith, "George Hunt and the Kwak'wala Texts," *Anthropological Linguistics* 36, no. 4 (1994), 482–514. For other Indigenous collators with Curtis, see Shamoon Zamir, "Native Agency and the Making of "The North American Indian": Alexander B. Upshaw and Edward S. Curtis," *American Indian Quarterly* 31, no. 4 (2007), 613–653.

35 Bill Holm and George Irving Quimby, *Edward S. Curtis in the Land of the War Canoes: A Pioneer Cinematographer in the Pacific Northwest* (Seattle: University of Washington Press, 1980).

36 Cole and Chaikin, *An Iron Hand Upon The People.*

37 Evans and Glass, *Return to the Land ochaikinf the Head Hunters*, xi. The 2008 film screening (which toured several spots around the country) included a live performance by Kwakwaka'wakw dancers.

11

DISRUPTING SETTLER INNOCENCE IN LATIN AMERICAN FILMS

M. Bianet Castellanos

> The Indians of South America are still engaged in a struggle to defend their land
> and their culture. Many of the priests who, inspired by faith and love, continue to
> support the rights of the Indians for justice, do so with their lives.

These words scroll over the final scene of *The Mission* (dir. Roland Joffé, 1986), in which Guaraní children, in the aftermath of a colonial massacre, board a canoe and escape into the jungle. Taking place along the Paraguay-Argentina-Brazil border in 1758, the film spotlights the transfer of the Jesuit missions from Spanish to Portuguese rule and its violent repercussions for Guaraní peoples, the native inhabitants of this region. It critiques the conquest by telling brutal stories of empire and foregrounding Indigenous resistance. Similarly, the official trailer for *Even the Rain* (*También la Lluvia*, dir. Icíar Bollaín, 2010), another film that critically examines Indigenous conquest through the lives of Spanish priests, concludes with a quote from historian Howard Zinn: "The memory of oppressed people cannot be taken away and for such people revolt is always an inch below the surface." *Even the Rain* examines the 2000 Cochabamba Water War through the eyes of a Spanish and Mexican film crew shooting a film on the conquest while on location in Bolivia.

The Mission and *Even the Rain* frame settler colonial conquest as an allegory for Indigenous oppression under neoliberalism.[1] Both films have been lauded for their critical exposé of the conquest and their evocative efforts to draw parallels between colonialism and modern regimes.[2] However, they diverge in their portrayals of Indigenous peoples. *The Mission* follows in the tradition of conquest films like *Christopher Columbus* (dir. John Glen, 1982) and *1492: Conquest of Paradise* (dir. Ridley Scott, 1992) that oscillate between depicting Indigenous peoples as innocent or savage. However, influenced by the New Latin American cinema that relied on social realism to counter the commercialization permeating

Hollywood films, *Even the Rain* offers a corrective by presenting flawed and complex Indigenous characters. Despite these efforts, *Even the Rain*, like *The Mission*, is a story of redemption that aims to recuperate and absolve white settlers who sacrificed themselves on behalf of Native peoples. Tales of Indigenous survivance form part of the background, not the foreground of these films. As an anthropologist who works with Maya communities in Mexico, it is this contradiction—a gritty, humanistic tale of settler violence that also makes a case for white absolution—that prompted my examination of these two films.

In spite of *The Mission* and *Even the Rain*'s efforts to offer realistic and critical depictions of colonial encounters, both films reproduce a settler colonial gaze redolent with tropes of Indigenous peoples needing to be saved by white settlers. Through a comparison of these two award-winning films, I draw attention to how settler colonial tropes are reproduced in films about Latin America colonialism. Settler colonial theory has been instrumental in tracing the structures and logics that have led to Indigenous dispossession and elimination in the Anglophone world, but it is not widely used as a framework to analyze similar processes in Latin America.[3] I apply a settler colonial lens to films centered on the Latin American conquest to show how settler colonial narratives of discovery and Indigenous elimination dominate cinematic representations of colonialism in Latin America as well. Although there are clear distinctions between colonial and settler colonial projects,[4] these distinctions collapse as tales of the conquest are packaged for a global audience by transnational film productions. I propose that settler colonial narratives of discovery and Indigenous elimination are pivotal in advancing the character development of settler identities as socially progressive, even innocent, while simultaneously reinforcing the trope of the disappearing Indian and noble savage. Settler colonial studies have suggested that similar moves toward innocence in other contexts absolve settlers of white guilt.[5] I show similar processes at work in Latin America by arguing that both films are stories of redemption that deftly gloss over Indigenous narratives of resistance by promoting settler innocence. Indigenous identities may be rendered sympathetic, and at times revolutionary, but their primary purpose is to serve as a foil for white innocence.

Cinematic Legacies

Hollywood film and television have deeply influenced our understanding of colonial encounters in Latin America. As Comanche essayist and curator Paul Chaat Smith reminds us, "everything about being Indian has been shaped by the camera," reducing Indians to a plot device used to work through national anxieties and reenact imperial fantasies of westward expansionism.[6] In Hollywood films, Indians are depicted as simplistic caricatures lacking historical specificity and complex personhood.[7] This maneuver reflects settler colonial narratives of erasure in which "Hollywood Indians" are assembled into the following types: noble savage, bloodthirsty savage, Indian maiden, and dimwitted sidekick.[8] Following

Smith, I use the term "Indian" to refer to an imaginary ideal, not a people. The Indian as ideological trope is embedded, indeed forms part of the structure, of settler cinema. When Indigenous peoples are depicted onscreen as "Indians," they are alienated from the lived reality of Indigenous life and morph into symbols that solidify imperial fantasies of conquest and buttress national myths of Indigenous erasure. To subvert this colonial gaze, Indigenous filmmakers have produced community-based collaborative films that portray Indigenous resistance and cultural practices as rich, complex, and flourishing in the present day.[9] While the relationship between Indians and Hollywood has been robustly examined within the context of the United States, the relationship between Indigenous peoples and film in Latin America also begs an interrogation. The Indian trope is a common fixture in Latin American cinema. If cinematic representations of Indians are "usually about the idea of us, about what people think about that idea," as Smith explains, then what does this trope tell us about the place of Indigenous peoples in Latin American imaginaries and film traditions?[10]

Latin American cinema is not monolithic and has been heavily influenced by a history of revolution, political dictatorships, and a period of government invest-ment.[11] The film traditions that have shaped cinema in Latin America—national cinema, political cinema, and contemporary Latin American cinema—represent Indigenous peoples in distinct ways. In countries where cinema was heavily subsidized by the state, such as Mexico, Brazil, and Argentina, early nationalist dramas of the conquest depicted nostalgic renderings of the noble/ignoble savage as fixed symbols of the tragic aftermath of empire and the glory of nation build-ing.[12] Inspired by the Cuban revolution, political cinema revolved around revo-lutionary ideals and thus created space for Indigenous peoples as agentive.[13] As governments divested from film production because of the economic crises beginning in the 1980s, film production became transnational, making the Hollywood machine and European film companies key players in Latin American cinema. Contemporary Latin American cinema continues to rely on a social rea-list lens, but these infrastructural and economic shifts galvanized a more intimate, reflexive approach to filmmaking that aims to break down Indian stereotypes.[14] *Even the Rain* emerges from this tradition.

Like *The Mission*, *Even the Rain* is a transnational co-production with roots in European cinema. *The Mission* was produced by the UK's Goldcrest Films and distributed by Warner Bros., a venerable Hollywood institution. Written and directed by Brits Robert Bolt and Roland Joffé, respectively, it includes American and British actors. *Even the Rain* was produced by production companies in Spain (Morena Films), Mexico (Alebrije Cine y Video), and France (Mandarin Cinema). Directed by Spaniard Icíar Bollaín, the screenplay was written by Scotsman Paul Laverty. These production histories matter because who is writing, directing, and producing films determines how a story gets told. As transnational co-productions, these film productions must continually negotiate the Hollywood machine and its telescopic view of Latin America.[15]

In light of these structural entanglements, it is not surprising that settler colonial narratives proliferating in Hollywood films are also embedded in Latin American films. Historian Lorenzo Veracini cautions not to conflate colonial and settler colonial societies because they entail distinct, albeit dialectical, ideological projects.[16] Colonialism in Latin America is considered to be rooted in labor extraction and Indigenous incorporation, in contrast to settler colonialism in the United States, which is characterized by land dispossession and Indigenous elimination. Yet the logics of elimination and dispossession were also pivotal to Spanish and Portuguese colonial projects.[17] These logics also animate films on Latin America. For example, in Argentina, as literary critic Cynthia Tompkins suggests, films relegate Indigenous peoples to the past and negate their continued existence in order to promote the mythical idea of Argentina as a nation of European immigrants.[18] A settler colonial reading of films on the Spanish conquest provides an opportunity to critically examine how tactics of erasure and elimination went hand in hand with policies promoting integration and assimilation through *mestizaje* (racial mixing). I propose that a settler colonial reading of films like *The Mission* and *Even the Rain* reveals how integral narratives of Indigenous erasure and elimination are to stories of conquest in Latin America.

Despite their divergent production origins, both films complicate grand narratives of Spanish conquest by providing a corrective to colonial narratives of Indigenous elimination. *The Mission* concludes with Guaraní children, survivors of genocide, getting into a canoe and paddling upstream deeper into the jungle. Retreat was a tactic that ensured Indigenous survival. While we may have witnessed a massacre onscreen, the retreating Guaraní represent a sign of hope against settler violence. In *Even the Rain*, Indigenous people dominate scenes, where they thrive as actors, extras, waiters, street vendors, and protestors in mass social movements where they demand justice.

Yet both films are stories of redemption that recuperate white innocence, a settler colonial tactic. *The Mission* condemns some settlers, but it recoups others, in this case the martyred Jesuit priests who defended Guaraní peoples against enslavement. The storyline follows Father Gabriel (Jeremy Irons) through his first encounter with Guaraní peoples and as he bears witness to their subsequent slaughter by colonial governments. To vindicate the Jesuits, the film perpetuates settler colonial narratives of discovery and Indigenous elimination. The conquest becomes the backdrop for the priests' transformation from settlers into martyrs. In the role of Captain Mendoza, actor Robert de Niro gives us a hero that is flawed—a former slave trader who kills his brother in a jealous rage. As a penance for his sins, Mendoza takes refuge with the Jesuits and works with Father Gabriel and Guaraní converts to erect the mission of San Carlos. After he joins the Jesuit order, he dies trying to save the mission and its Guaraní inhabitants from a colonial massacre. In *The Mission*, Jesuit priests are shown to be the staunch and suffering allies of Guaraní converts. In *Even the Rain*, the Dominican friars Antonio de Montesinos and Bartolomé de Las Casas are hailed as Indigenous allies who condemn the exploitation of Indigenous labor. The film follows a Mexican and Spanish film crew as they make a film about the Dominican friars Montesinos and Las Casas who accompanied Christopher Columbus to the New World. They travel to Bolivia in search of cheap Indigenous extras. The exploitation of Indigenous labor is a recurring theme throughout the film, captured through the relationship between the conquistadors and Taíno slaves, and through the relationship between Daniel (Juan Carlos Aduviri), an actor who plays Taíno chief Atuey, and Costa (Luis Tosar), the Spanish producer. Since Daniel is leading the protest against the privatization of water, the film crew becomes embroiled in the protest. When the protestors occupy the city, the crew is forced to decamp Cochabamba and abandon the Indigenous actors who made their film possible. By highlighting priestly martyrdom on behalf of Indigenous peoples, these films emphasize that not all settlers are villains.

This redemption, however, cannot happen without the presence of Indigenous peoples. Yet the films are not told from an Indigenous perspective, but through the settler point of view. We first encounter Indigenous peoples in these films through *their* encounters with foreigners or missionaries. The onscreen confrontations between conquistadors/foreigners and Indigenous peoples perpetuate settler innocence, rather than convey the complexity of Indigenous lives. I consider how these encounters, through their reliance on the tropes of celluloid Indians and white innocence, make visible the insidious violence of settler colonial narratives.

"Indians" in South America

Cinematic representations of Indigenous peoples in Latin America reproduce the settler gaze. To call attention to a pan-Indigenous experience with colonialism, the postscript in *The Mission* refers to "the Indians of South America." However, by lumping Indigenous peoples together as "Indians," the filmmakers erase the historical and cultural specificities that distinguish Indigenous peoples throughout South America. Guaraní communities cannot be conflated with Quechua communities in Bolivia or Mapuche communities in Argentina, despite their experiences with Spanish colonialism. Moreover, Indigenous peoples in Latin America do not call themselves "Indians/*indio*." The filmmaker's reliance on the term "Indian" throughout the movie removes Guaraní people's experience from its historical specificity and context. We are not told of Guaraní people's long-term struggle to hold onto their territory and avoid slavery, their successful rebellions in 1539 and 1542, their participation in *encomiendas* established by the colonial government, the alliances they forged with Spanish and Paraguayan settlers and traders, their knowledge as horticulturalists, and the significance of agriculture for their survival.[19] In response to the 1750 Treaty of Madrid that redrew the border between the Spanish and Portuguese territories, Guaraní leaders, like Nicolás Ñenguirú, wrote and sent missives to Spanish authorities and coordinated with the Jesuits to protest the transfer of the missions into Portuguese hands.[20] Instead, the film portrays ahistorical Guaraní fixed in time as hunter-gatherers with warlike tendencies. This collapse and generalization are common characteristics of the celluloid Indian, who stands in for all Native Americans regardless of historical, geographic, cultural, and linguistic differences. We learn very little about Guaraní traditions and worldviews. While the protagonists are given names—Captain Rodrigo Mendoza and Father Gabriel—Guaraní remain nameless throughout the movie. During the hearing to discuss the closing of the missions, Cardinal Altamirano (Ray McAnally) and the local governing elite refer to Guaraní as children, as animals, as creatures, as noble souls, and as slaves. They do not merit names in the credits, where Guaraní actors are identified as "witch doctor," "Indian," "Indian chief," "Indian boy," and "boy singer." By reducing Guaraní to nameless Indians, they are robbed of the complex personhood granted to characters like Captain Mendoza whose narrative arch entails a religious conversion and martyrdom.

The Mission mimics the discovery narrative, thus reinforcing indigeneity as a fundamental difference that precludes incorporation into a national imaginary. The audience becomes the voyeur as we observe Father Gabriel and Captain Mendoza "discover" Guaraní peoples as they journey from the town of Asunción to the mission of San Carlos, located in Guaraní territory. We feel their struggle to climb the steep falls and the wonder and fear evoked the first time they encounter aggressive Guaraní. The Indigenous people presented in *The Mission* are trapped between the polarized stereotypes of noble/dangerous heathen. Cardinal Altamirano has been sent by the Spanish crown to deliberate over this very question: Are Guaraní worth saving? Do they have a "noble soul" as Father Gabriel attests, or are they savage "animals" as Paraguayan governor don Cabeza (Chuck Low) asserts? Guaraní are presented through a mediated settler gaze that is fixed on an imaginary Indian envisaged and reduced to a singular type.

This is not just a visual but also an auditory experience. The haunting beauty of Guaraní children singing hymns is part of the film score. Yet when Guaraní speak, their words are not translated. The audience is reliant on translations provided by Father Gabriel and Captain Mendoza. We hear the anger and aggression in the words Guaraní hurl at the Jesuits, but their actual intentions are conveyed to us through Father Gabriel and Captain Mendoza's response to their actions. We are shown glimpses of Guaraní life through settler eyes: their devotion to Christianity, their love of music, their fighting skills, and the humor with which they greet the everyday. Regardless of these scenes, the film does not grant Guaraní peoples a voice. Nor do we learn about the alliances forged between Guaraní and Spaniards through trade and marriage.[21]

Even the Rain also relies on the Indian as a key trope to understand colonialism, even as it complicates this image. The film within the film presents Indigenous peoples as noble savages abused by Spanish settlers. The main plot is centered on an Indigenous protagonist, Daniel, and his efforts to prevent the privatization of water. Due to his aggressive and outspoken persona, Daniel is recruited to play the role of Atuey, a Taíno chief who rebelled against the Spanish conquistadors.

The film offers a corrective to traditional Hollywood blockbusters by granting significant screen time to Indigenous protestors and by including charismatic Indigenous protagonists like Daniel and his daughter Belén (Milena Soliz). But these attempts are undermined by the lack of historical references to Indigenous cultures in Bolivia. Indigenous peoples in the film within the film are identified as Taíno, and Indigenous peoples in Bolivia are identified solely as Quechua. For a country with 36 recognized Indigenous peoples, where Quechua and Aymara are spoken as frequently as Spanish, and with a population of whom 41% identify as Indigenous, this oversight speaks of settler tactics of erasure. In making Taíno people's experience of colonization a central narrative, the film neglects narrating the history and struggles of Indigenous peoples in Bolivia.

Even the Rain intentionally draws parallels between colonialism and contemporary neoliberalism in Bolivia to show that settler violence is ongoing. As anthropologist Patrick Wolfe reminds us, settler colonialism is a structure, not as event.[22] The push to privatize local water is a clear example of structural violence and its impact on Indigenous communities. Water becomes an allegory for Indigenous subjugation. This critique of colonialism omits the fact that the Cochabamba Water War was a protest that was led by the urban proletariat in conjunction with Indigenous organizations, engineers, small farmers, neighborhood water associations, water cooperatives, and labor unions.[23] The movement included Indigenous participants, but the protest was not hailed as an Indigenous movement. *Even the Rain*, however, presents the protest as an Indigenous movement, rather than a populist movement, with Daniel at its helm. In so doing, the film grants Indigenous people's a voice to critique neoliberalism, but this voice is singular and must resort to violence to be heard. History and memory, along with documentary footage of the protests, become blurred, a pastiche meant to evoke a gritty, realistic portrait of a contemporary Bolivia that remains trapped by the past.[24]

The film becomes a site of violence when it lumps Indigenous peoples together. In the opening scene, we confront this violence as Costa forces Sebastián (Gael García Bernal) to select extras from a line of hundreds of people. For Costa, all natives look the same, regardless of location, be it Bolivia, Peru, or the Dominican Republic. While driving to the filming location, he reminds Sebastián why they are filming in Bolivia. Speaking of himself in the third person, he argues "Costa knows this place is full of starving natives and that means extras, thousands of extras." Sebastián quibbles by pointing out, "Have you seen their faces. Please, they are Quechua. They are Indigenous to the Andes. Why is Columbus meeting with Indigenous peoples from the Andes?" Sebastián identifies the local people as Quechua, demanding a specificity that Costa refuses to acknowledge. Yet at the same time, by lumping all the extras as Quechua, Sebastián ignores Bolivia's multi-ethnic history. Costa responds, "From the Andes or from wherever. They are Indigenous. That's what you wanted…They are all the same." Costa rehashes colonial narrations of sameness and abjection that were used to justify Indigenous elimination. The film falls into this trap as well. Indians abound in *Even the Rain*. Not only because the extras were most likely cheap, but because we are not granted any insight into what it means to be Quechua in contemporary Bolivia and how Indigenous rights are being forfeited with the privatization of Bolivia's resources. The protestors involved in the rebellion speak ardently about the need for water but none of these discussions were directly linked to Indigenous practices or demands for Indigenous autonomy and rights.

Like *The Mission*, when Indigenous people speak in their native language, the film does not provide subtitles. Instead, intermediaries like Daniel become cultural and linguistic translators. In a harrowing scene at the river where the conquistadors are chasing escaped Indigenous slaves, Sebastián directs the female actors to go through the motions of drowning their children. The women, speaking in their native language, stand still and speak back to Sebastián. Daniel, who intercedes on Sebastián's behalf, listens quietly as the women explain why they refuse to act out the drowning scene. Daniel does not stop them as they walk away from the film crew. When Sebastián demands to know what's going on, Daniel explains, "They can't even imagine the idea of doing it." Sebastián calls forth history to back up the scene, "I'm not making this up. It's what happened." When Daniel states, "some things are more important than your film," he reminds Sebastián that reenacting this traumatic moment is another form of settler violence (see Figure 11.1).

Settler Innocence

The Mission and *Even the Rain* pivot around Indigenous dispossession, but this dispossession ends up becoming an allegory for settler innocence. In *The Mission*, Mendoza's character development captures this move toward innocence as he transforms from a nefarious slave trader into a Jesuit martyr. *The Mission* pays careful attention to Indigenous enslavement and servitude, a practice that took

FIGURE 11.1 Daniel explains to Sebastián that some things are more important than a film. Screenshot from *Even the Rain* by the author.

place throughout the Americas, but has not received much attention.[25] What this enslavement meant for Indigenous families is not revealed. In contrast, Mendoza's guilt—for the death of his brother (not slave trading)—is revealed in his acts of repentance, from the bundle of armor he drags up the Iguazu Falls to refusing to participate in a boar hunt. The childlike wonder he displays as he lives and plays with Guaraní women and children and his willingness to fight and die to protect the mission complete this transformation. Not all settlers were evil, the film reminds us. Some settlers not only helped Indigenous peoples but tried to stop the carnage.

A similar narrative of martyrdom runs through *Even the Rain*, except in this case Dominican priests and a foreign film crew play this role. The film within the film focuses on the quandary experienced by Montesinos and Las Casas as they develop a social conscious over the treatment of Indigenous peoples. Montesinos' famous Christmas Eve Sermon of 1511, during which he demands, "Tell me, by what right or justice do you hold these Indians in such cruel and horrible slavery?" becomes a testament to his righteousness and foresight in rejecting Indigenous slavery. Although the friars were complicit in the Indigenous slave trade and servitude (for example many, like Las Casas, held *encomiendas*) and relied on Indigenous labor to build the missions, their martyrdom and ideological conversion absolves them of settler violence.

In *Even the Rain*, the film crew play a similar role. Made up of Mexican and Spaniards, the film crew are sympathetic characters. They are empathetic to the plight of the water protestors; it is the local government that is painted as oppressive. Despite their ties to Spain, the film crew remains oblivious to their own complicity with colonial and neoliberal projects. They see themselves as disconnected from the past, while the extras and actors from Bolivia are perceived as rooted in the past via their poverty, language, and culture. When Costa receives a phone call from a foreign investor, he takes the call in English. Assuming Daniel who is standing beside him cannot speak English, he crows over the cheap labor. "Two fucking dollars a day and they feel like angels. Now you can throw in some water palms and give them some old trucks when you are all done and *listo*…200 fucking extras." As Costa speaks, the camera keeps the focus on Daniel—the stillness of his body and the scrunching of his forehead as he hears the import of Costa's words, followed by the sarcastic smile he dons as he confronts Costa's callous disregard (see Figure 11.2). Daniel, however, refuses to fit into Costa's vision of the Indian. "Two fucking dollars, right," Daniel castigates Costa in English. "And they're happy. I've worked in construction for two years in the United States. I know this story." Daniel challenges Costa to acknowledge his complicity in a neocolonial and settler colonial system of dispossession and labor extraction.

When the Bolivian government declares a state of emergency in response to the occupation, the film crew is frightened. As they debate whether to abandon the film and Bolivia, Antón (Karra Elejalde) who plays Christopher Columbus in the film within the film calls the crew "cowards." He demands, "What would Bartolomé do? Yeah, lots of *yaku*, lots of 'poor Indians,' and now what? Fuck

FIGURE 11.2 Daniel confronts Costa about being paid 2 dollars a day. *Even the Rain.* Screenshot from *Even the Rain* by the author.

them!" Antón deliberately draws parallels between the friars' conundrum to support or oppose slavery and the current situation in Bolivia. This argument convinces the crew to remain in Bolivia, albeit in a secure location. When Teresa, Daniel's wife, seeks Costa's help to locate Belén who was injured while participating in the protests, Costa hesitates to head into the fray. Fearing for Costa's life, Sebastián pleads with him to stay with the crew, but Teresa begs and calls upon their friendship. Costa feels obligated to help, especially after disparaging Daniel and the extras. "If anything happens to the child, I will never forgive myself," he explains to Sebastián. Costa and Antón become the crew's moral compass and refuse to abandon Daniel and Bolivia. Costa's rescue of an injured Belén absolves him from colonialism's taint. By the end of the film, he is reborn as a modern-day crusader demanding justice for Indigenous peoples.

Conclusion

Encounters between settlers and Indigenous peoples in Latin American cinema mediates how we understand Indigenous lives. These encounters imagine Indians as vulnerable or dangerous and settlers as innocent. These types of encounters cannot account for the complexity of Indigenous lives under colonialism and neoliberalism. What we need is a cinema that is not just anti-colonial and realist, but one that unpacks settler colonial narratives and represents Indigenous peoples as more than just types. The recent debate over Yalitza Aparicio's role as Cleo in *Roma* (dir. by Alfonso Cuarón, 2018) highlights how insidious these narratives can be, especially in transnational productions from the Hollywood machine. Although Cleo reflected the daunting experience of being a maid in 1970s Mexico, her experience as an Indigenous woman took a backseat to her complicated relationship with her *patrona* (employer). In the end, this story, like all colonial narratives, is not about Indigenous peoples, but about white settler innocence and redemption.

Notes

1 Fabrizio Cilento, "*Even the Rain*: A Confluence of Cinematic and Historical Temporalities," *Arizona Journal of Hispanic Cultural Studies* 16 (2012), 245–257; Paul A. Schroeder Rodríguez, *Latin American Cinema: A Comparative History* (Berkeley: University of California Press, 2016).
2 Stephen Holden, "Discovering Columbus's Exploitation," *New York Times*, February 17, 2011, https://www.nytimes.com/2011/02/18/movies/18even.html; Roger Ebert, "The Mission," November 14, 1986, https://www.rogerebert.com/reviews/the-mission-1986
3 M. Bianet Castellanos, "Introduction: Settler Colonialism in Latin America," *American Quarterly* 69, no. 4 (2017), 777–781.
4 Lorenzo Veracini, "Introducing *Settler Colonial Studies*," *Settler Colonial Studies* 1, no .1 (2011), 1–12.
5 Eve Tuck and K. Wayne Yang, "Decolonization is Not a Metaphor," *Decolonization: Indigeneity, Education & Society* 1.1 (2012), 1–40. For a discussion of settler guilt, see Rebecca Weaver-Hightower, *Frontier Fictions: Settler Sagas and Postcolonial Guilt* (New York: Palgrave MacMillan, 2018).
6 Paul Chaat Smith, *Everything You Know About Indians is Wrong* (Minneapolis: University of Minnesota Press, 2009), 4.
7 See Jacquelyn Kilpatrick, *Celluloid Indians: Native Americans and Film* (Lincoln: University of Nebraska Press, 1999); M. Elise Marubbio, *Killing the Indian Maiden: Images of Native American Women in Film* (Lexington: University of Kentucky Press, 2006). For a discussion of imperialist nostalgia, see Renato Rosaldo, *Culture & Truth: The Remaking of Social Analysis* (Boston: Beacon Press, 1993).
8 See Kilpatrick, *Celluloid Indians*; Marubbio, *Killing the Indian Maiden*.
9 See Jeff D. Himpele, *Circuits of Culture: Media, Politics, and Indigenous Identity in the Andes* (Minneapolis: University of Minnesota, 2008); Michelle H. Raheja, *Reservation Reelism: Redfacing, Visual Sovereignty, and Representations of Native Americans in Film* (Lincoln: University of Nebraska, 2010); Beverly R. Singer, *Wiping the War Paint Off the Lens: Native American Film and Video* (Minneapolis: University of Minnesota, 2001); Freya Schiwy, *Indianizing Film: Decolonization, the Andes & the Question of Technology* (New Brunswick: Rutgers University Press, 2009); Freya Schiwy and Byrt Wammack Weber, eds. *Adjusting the Lens: Community and Collaborative Video in Mexico* (Pittsburgh: University of Pittsburgh Press, 2017).
10 Smith, *Everything You Know*, 39.
11 See Ignacio M. Sánchez Prado, *Screening Neoliberalism: Transforming Mexican Cinema 1988–2010* (Nashville: Vanderbilt University, 2014); Rodríguez, *Latin American Cinema*.
12 See Cilento, *Even the Rain*; Adela Pineda Franco, *The Mexican Revolution on the World Stage: Intellectuals and Film in the Twentieth Century* (Albany: State University of Albany Press, 2019).
13 Prado, *Screening Neoliberalism*.
14 Rodríguez, *Latin American Cinema*.
15 See Luisela Alvaray, "National, Regional, and Global: New Waves of Latin American Cinema," *Cinema Journal* 47, no. 3 (2008), 48–65; Rodríguez, *Latin American Cinema*.
16 Veracini, "Introducing *Settler Colonial Studies*."
17 Castellanos, "Introduction."
18 Cynthia Margarita Tompkins, *Affectual Erasure: Representations of Indigenous Peoples in Argentine Cinema* (Albany: State University of New York Press, 2018).
19 James S. Saeger, "The Mission and Historical Missions," *The Americas* 51, no. 3 (1995), 393–415.
20 Tamar Herzog, "Guaranis and Jesuits: Bordering the Spanish and Portuguese Empires," *ReVista: Harvard Review of Latin America* (Spring 2015), https://revista.drclas.harvard.edu/book/guaranis-and-jesuits

21 Saeger, "The Mission and Historical Missions," 394–397.
22 Patrick Wolfe, *Settler Colonialism and the Transformation of Anthropology* (London: Cassell, 1999).
23 William Finnegan, "Leasing the Rain," *The New Yorker*, March 31, 2002; Willem Assies, "David Versus Goliath in Cochabamba," *Latin American Perspectives* 30, no. 3 (2003), 14–36.
24 Cilento, *Even the Rain*.
25 Linford D. Fischer, "'Why Shall Wee Have Peace to Bee Made Slaves': Indian Surrenders During and After King Philip's War," *Ethnohistory* 64, no. 1 (2017), 91–114.

12

THE "KNACK" OF THE WILDERPEOPLE: POST-SETTLEMENT CINEMA IN AOTEAROA NEW ZEALAND

Misha Kavka and Stephen Turner

It is not uncommon to assume that we're all post-colonial now, as colonial governance recedes into a murky past and the brave new world of self-determination within globalization looms large. This view is nonetheless challenged by contemporary calls for decolonization[1] – of institutions, methodologies, practices, behaviors, and mindsets. In most settler countries the line between a colonial and a post-colonial phase has never been clearly demarcated. In Aotearoa New Zealand,[2] the promise of post-settlement seems to hover as both a settler ideal and a tribal reality, since the Waitangi Tribunal, an inquiry commission established by parliamentary act in 1975, has enabled the settlement of numerous Indigenous land and resource claims by Māori iwi (tribes) in recent decades.

If New Zealand has entered a post-settlement phase, hence Aotearoa New Zealand, which imagines that colonialism has been ended by the settlement of claims to historical injustice, then the enduring coloniality of New Zealand society can nonetheless be grasped in its contemporary cinema. Films made in or about Aotearoa New Zealand rehash the beautiful tourist imagery of a still-colonial country[3] or, more interestingly, allude to anxieties about colonial settlement as a general condition of the country's filmmaking practices. While Peter Jackson's *Lord of the Rings* (*LOTR*) trilogy (2001–2003) notably illustrates the former, the works of Taika Waititi offer an interesting example of the latter. The economics of Jackson's filmmaking show how national cinema has "gone Hollywood," a development that makes New Zealand cinema at once an arm of national branding (as "Middle Earth") and a franchise of Hollywood (since the trilogy is produced by New Line Cinema).[4] Like an earlier generation of successful directors (e.g. Geoff Murphy and Lee Tamahori in the 1980s and 1990s, respectively), Waititi, too, has worked in Hollywood, but more locally his films appeal to, and reconstruct, a national audience with striking success and deserved critical acclaim. They achieve this in part by providing the audience with a thicket of popular cultural references, often to other media works, which triggers a sense of community through shared knowledge. Yet, at the same time, they allude to an equally shared sense of violent colonial history, albeit differently conceived by Indigenous Māori and non-Māori settlers (called Pākehā, referring to settlers of European descent, or Tauiwi, referring more broadly to foreigners and strangers[5]). Such allusions in Waititi's local films trouble the popular; indeed, they show New Zealand popular culture itself to be troubled by enduring coloniality. Here we pay particular attention to his film *Hunt for the Wilderpeople* (2016) in order to argue that post-settlement cinema operates according to a double structure, offering audiences the pleasure of communal nostalgia while indicating the wounds of a colonial trauma, but without showing who might be responsible. Although Jackson may have blazed the trail, Taika Waititi, as we will see, has the "knack."

Settler Colonial Jouissance

Stretching back to his Oscar-nominated short film *Two Cars, One Night* (2004), Waititi's films share a tendency to expose the still-colonial situation of settlement, but his most recent New Zealand-themed film, *Hunt for the Wilderpeople* (hereafter *Wilderpeople*), is noteworthy as the top-grossing New Zealand film to date ($12.2 million NZD). The local popularity of this film helps us to understand the conditions of successful filmmaking in the New Zealand context and, in particular, to understand its audience, of which Waititi is avowedly a master, given that the previous box office record was also set by him with the hugely successful *Boy* (2010). Waititi's astute understanding of the mixed local audience, consisting of both minority Māori and majority Pākehā as well as other Tauiwi, enables him to field the difficult consequences of colonial history in the broader context of its disavowal. Indeed, Waititi is well aware of what happens when the colonial legacy is addressed head-on, as seen by local anger when he openly called New Zealand "a racist place" in an interview with the US-based magazine *Dazed*. [6] The art of his films, unlike his straight talking in the *Dazed* interview, offers a reversed lens in which the anxieties of majority non-Māori can be simultaneously exposed and assuaged through the pleasure of humorous (self)-recognition. This double structure, which we will call "settler colonial jouissance," can be found in all of Waititi's local filmwork (and even, arguably, in *Thor: Ragnarok* [2017]), but is most palpably present in *Wilderpeople*.

The term "settler colonial jouissance" draws on Jacques Lacan's notion of *jouissance* as exquisitely painful pleasure in order to describe the paradoxical pleasure to be gained from the open wound of settler colonialism. For majority Pākehā/Tauiwi, this paradox amounts to a knowing unknowing - an uncomfortable and often disavowed knowledge that colonialism happened "because of and yet somehow despite me." The injurious consequences of colonialism, as writer and filmmaker Barry

Barclay says, are "not a hurt that local [Māori] people can be talked out of"[7]; they persist in the form of greatly reduced resources (through stolen lands), inequity in health and education, highly disproportionate prison numbers, social discrimination, and diminished life chances. The consequences of colonizing history are not avoidable for non-Māori either, yet through popular media Pākehā/Tauiwi also take pleasure as much as pain in a shared culture of a sort. The experience of the colonized is very much present in Waititi's films, but it tends to be fielded, or enfolded, in a way that a non-Māori audience must recognize but need not feel directly responsible for. What emerges in these films is the "typical" society of a still-colonial place as refracted through an outsider figure, such as the protagonists of *Wilderpeople*.

Ricky, the pre-teen delivered into foster care at the start of the film, instantiates the social deprivation and institutional violence of typical settler colonial society, ramped up toward the end of *Wilderpeople* in a bewildering array of agencies, both governmental and military, organized to hunt the odd wildercouple. The show of state power echoes the paramilitary "terror" raids on Tūhoe people of October, 2007,[8] and, much earlier, the government-ordered round-up of the rightful occupants and allies of Takaparawha (Bastion Point) in May, 1978 (the subject of *Bastion Point: Day 507* [dir. Merata Mita, 1980]). Through his shared trials with the socially isolated and, it turns out, illiterate Hec, the typicality of still-colonial society is exposed as national orthodoxy, a congealed norm that works to occlude the institutional and social pathologies of New Zealand society. In the outsider figure, so crucial to settler colonial jouissance, we note how marginalized characters in New Zealand cinema[9] both acknowledge and assuage the pleasure/pain of film audiences in a settler colonial country.

Wounded History

Our use of "post-settlement cinema" challenges and transforms what Barclay dubbed the "national orthodoxy" at work in New Zealand film – that is, the typical purview and hegemonic attitudes of majoritarian Pākehā/Tauiwi.[10] "Settlement" in the New Zealand context usually refers to the invasion of Māori territories by Pākehā/Tauiwi in the nineteenth century, initially as a trickle of missionaries and then, by the second half of the century, as a demographic tsunami of land-clearing and -grabbing farmers, supported by an imposed and self-serving legislative body of settlers and militias. The word can also refer, however, to the numerous "settlements" of historical injustice claims under the Treaty of Waitangi (te Tiriti), which was signed in 1840 by a representative of the British crown, Lieutenant Governor Hobson, and numerous rangatira (chiefs) from a great number of – but not all – iwi. The Waitangi Tribunal was set up in 1975 as a state instrument seeking juridical settlement as a means of redress for the violence of settlement. The reparation process continues to this day, but it is a mistake to think that it will or can dispose of the long history of Aotearoa. As much as the "settling" of claims suggests that the country can move beyond a colonial phase, the Tribunal itself exposes the divisions in a putatively consensual national orthodoxy and challenges its constitutional basis.[11] To speak of post-settle-ment, then, does not suggest that settlement is over in either meaning of the term; rather, it draws attention to the fracture of history introduced by colonial settlement, which may be appeased but in no way reconstituted by piecemeal juridical settle-ments. The ever-evolving "nation" is a work-in-progress that both straddles and seeks to suture the fractured line of a broken history, or, more simply, the vexed relation between first (Indigenous) and second (settler) peoples.

How does the post-settlement nation instill a sense of community, or commonality, given the colonial legacy? There are signs of hope on the Māori side, as witnessed by the success since 2004 of Māori TV, which operates as de facto public television,[12] as well as signs of a will to interweave past and present on the Pākehā/Tauiwi side. The defining affect of this will is nostalgia, not for early settler colonial days, but rather in terms of taking pleasure in media representations of a common New Zealand past that a more direct or detailed examination of violent history might otherwise make impossible. Evident in the etymology of the word "nostalgia," which in Greek refers both to both pain and the past,[13] this affect helps to suture the wound of broken his-tory for a majority audience. At the same time, the nostalgia of post-settlement national cinema suggests a "double structure" of wound and history.

Aotearoa New Zealand is a place where earth and flesh have been pulled apart – the tangata whenua (the people of the land, or people-land) torn asunder as local peoples were invaded and displaced by invasive settlement. National cinema – which at regular intervals has retold the story of the violent colonial period (e.g., *Utu* [dir. Geoff Murphy, 1983], *River Queen* [dir. Vincent Ward, 2003]), *The Piano* [dir. Jane Campion, 1993]) and the legacies of colonial violence (*Once Were Warriors* [dir. Lee Tamahori, 1994]) – is by now deeply infused with an awareness of "what happened here." Short of constitutional transformation[14] and wholesale reformation of the education system to reorient it around local Indigenous histories, however, it seems at this time that the consequences of colonial history can only be equally acknowledged and disavowed, embraced and elided. It seems, in other words, that such acknowledgement works in the pop-ular domain by making the wound of history apparent only to the extent that no one is held responsible for it; one can wince at the pain of colonial history yet take pleasure in a common cinematic culture that is the product of media itself. It is this mediatized history, as the shareable content of popular culture, that fills out the common sensibility, while at the same time it reminds a majority audience of what has happened without overtly inflaming its conflicted memory.

Unease to Ease

New Zealand film – taken to mean films by and about New Zealand(ers) – has been historicized in a number of stages, usually beginning with the nation-making stage from the 1920s to the 1970s, consisting of the production of newsreels, documentaries, and promotional films by the National Film Unit (founded in 1936), as well as a handful of feature-length films by pioneering directors such as Rudall Hayward (director of *Rewi's Last Stand*, 1925, remade 1940) and John O'Shea (director of *Broken Barrier*, 1952). A second stage, from the late 1970s to the 1990s, is marked by the establishment of the New Zealand Film Commission, a government agency tasked with funding and promoting New Zealand films, and the nearly simultaneous release of *Sleeping Dogs* (dir. Roger Donaldson, 1977), which according to *NZ on Screen* "heralded a new wave of Kiwi cinema."[15] The landmark films of this second stage – from *Smash Palace* (dir. Roger Donaldson, 1981), *The Scarecrow* (dir: Sam Pillsbury, 1982), and *Vigil* (dir: Vincent Ward, 1984) to *The Piano* (dir: Jane Campion, 1993), *Once Were Warriors* (dir: Lee Tamahori, 1994), and *Heavenly Creatures* (dir: Peter Jackson, 1994) – have been broadly categorized as "The Cinema of Unease," which is the title of Sam Neill's 1995 documentary reflecting on the bleakness that is redolent in films of this period. More recently, since the mid-2000s, another phase has arguably appeared, which could be called post-settlement cinema. These phases are not by any means discontinuous, as evidenced by the fact that the National Film Unit ended up in the hands of Peter Jackson renamed as Park Road Post, while Sam Neill himself, who played the central runaway character in the seminal *Sleeping Dogs*, does a star turn as Uncle Hec in *Wilderpeople*. Continuity, however historically haphazard, is itself indicative of nostalgia, since it holds open a door to the past. The nostalgia of the recent post-settlement phase of New Zealand film takes various forms, from a shared sense of local and global media culture, which includes the repurposing of previous New Zealand media, to the revamping of the New Zealand landscape for global consumption.

Through the operations of post-settlement nostalgia, unease has given way to ease, a more cheerful, albeit never celebratory, tone of a post-colonial nation that has seemingly acknowledged its settler history without yet delving into the trauma of colonial legacy and its unequal distribution amongst Māori and settler-migrant legatees. This move to ease has been helped in no small part by the global recognition of Kiwi comedy, beginning in the early 2000s with the slow-burn international success of the duo Flight of the Conchords (Brett MacKenzie and Jemaine Clement), but also including a number of comedic films and TV shows about Pacific migrant communities, such as *No. 2* (dir. Toa Fraser, 2006) and *bro'Town* (created by Elizabeth Mitchell and the Naked Samoans, TV3, 2004–2009).

In this vein, recent New Zealand filmmaking has been dominated by Taika Waititi's comic genius and that of the actors he has worked with. For instance, *What We Do in the Shadows* (2014), a mockumentary horror comedy about house-sharing vampires, recasts Wellington as a noir-esque cityscape hosting banally homespun vampires and werewolves. Co-directed by Jemaine Clement and Waititi, this film shares the deadpan, self-effacing comedy familiar from Flight of the Conchords, juxtaposing the bleak situation of misfits in an out-of-sorts world with a naïve irony that makes it not only bearable but enjoyable. A similar tonality appears in the character of Korg, played by Waititi himself, in *Thor: Ragnarok*. With his local accent and self-deprecating naivety, Waititi-as-Korg brings to Hollywood the distinctive humor of his earlier film *Boy*, which uses comedy to rupture the bleakness of life in a poverty-stricken, rural Māori community bereft of jobs, its men and a future. As part of its feel-good overlay, *Boy* is full of popular cultural references that construct a shared sense of time and place, however remote the setting might be for the majority of New Zealand audiences. Michael Jackson, whose music and iconography seeped into small-town childhoods of the 1980s, features heavily, and the film culminates in a brilliantly choreographed, all-cast "Thriller" tribute set to the tune of the local breakthrough hit "Poi-E" by the Patea Maori Club. In this mash-up style of popular humor, the Māori comedian Billy T. James/Te Wehi Taitoko (1946–1991) is a significant antecedent as someone whose self-caricaturing performance invited audiences to laugh with him but ultimately at themselves. Similarly, the difficult questions mooted in *Boy* about rural displacement and Māori imprisonment are both veiled and fielded through the homespun humor that "we" can all recognize and enjoy.

First to Fourth Cinema

Instead of going to Hollywood, as many New Zealand directors had done, Peter Jackson invited Hollywood to New Zealand, and in the process of making *Lord of the Rings* converted New Zealand into a place available for signifying imprints of various kinds, most notably as Middle Earth. Despite not being about Aotearoa New Zealand (narratively) or funded by a state body (unless we count the taxation deal struck by Jackson with the government[16]), the *Lord of the Rings* trilogy put New Zealand itself, along with New Zealand filmmaking, on the global map. Even locally, it retains a mythic power to overwrite the place as it is with a better version of itself, if ongoing tourist campaigns are anything to go by. As a result, post-settlement film has become connected to a more recent commercial nationalism, whereby the government has come to understand that branding is its business and, indeed, a major part of its modus operandi.[17] This use of the film industry for branding purposes has played a role in making available the landscape and its related elements for investment by outsiders, such as the government's willingness to sell large estates to wealthy foreigners looking for a bolt-hole.[18] Peter Jackson's work since 2000 is central to the commercial nationalism of the post-settlement phase, and the choice of Tolkien's pre-modern fantasy to project onto the New Zealand landscape (in both *LOTR* and *The Hobbit* trilogies) reveals the significance of nostalgia for images which occlude the historical conditions of their production.[19] For New Zealand audiences, Middle Earth on screen operates as a shared collective reference; the manipulation of the landscape is what New Zealanders already know from the historical archive of filmic images of New Zealand, images which themselves retell the colonial past without directly addressing the roots – or the consequences – of colonial violence. Whereas "The Cinema of Unease" phase danced around the contemporary consequences of such violence by engaging with allegories of the colonial past, from troubled coming-of-age narratives to conflict epics, commercial nationalism offers up an emptied-out landscape to be enjoyed as a form of nostalgia for what never was.

There is, however, one strand of New Zealand film which has slipped the knot of "The Cinema of Unease," namely films made by Māori directors, or what Barry Barclay dubbed Fourth Cinema.[20] Beginning with Barclay's first feature-length film, *Ngati* (1987), Merata Mita's *Mauri* (1988), and formative documentary work (*Bastion Point: Day 507* [1980] and *Patu!* [1983]) and extending, arguably, through *Once Were Warriors*, such films are deeply entrenched in an understanding of the impact of colonial violence and postcolonial administration, particularly on Māori communities. That such filmmaking by Māori directors continues to this day (e.g., *Taua – War Party* [dir. Tearepa Kahi, 2007]; *Mahana* [dir. Lee Tamahori, 2016]; *Waru* [dir. Briar Grace-Smith, 2017]) suggests a decolonizing drive and critical viewpoint embedded in long Indigenous Māori history that is perceptible, even though less overt, in some forms of post-settlement cinema. In his book *In Our Image*, Barclay decries the burden placed on Māori filmmakers by funders to "be Māori" for non-Māori, and seems to anticipate the irreverence of Waititi's work, and, in particular, *Boy*.[21] As Māori-attuned post-settlement cinema, Taika Waititi's films both field an inner Māori story of long history *and* reference other New Zealand cinema, television and media, humorously drawing on an established bank of collective reference and exposing the basis for the nostalgia of settler colonial jouissance. If the violent colonial past that we have in common cannot be shared, because Māori and Pākehā/Tauiwi cannot occupy the same position in relation to a wounded history, then what "we" do have in common is a sense of collective reference. It is only in this collective reference that something called "New Zealand" seems to reside.

The Bush in Popular Culture

The bush similarly provides material for the inscriptions of popular culture - a veritable thicket of media reference - to create a collective or shared mediascape for the local audience, even if the majority of this audience is more likely to recognize Hec and Ricky's "going bush" as a trope rather than an actual experience. Like *Boy*, *Wilderpeople* provides nostalgic pleasure through pop cultural references, connecting both the global and the local in the bushscape; for instance, helicopter shots over mountainous bush (such as the opening shots of the film) evoke *Lord of the Rings* cinematography; Ricky knowingly references the first appearance of the charging Ring-wraiths in *The Fellowship of the Ring* as he and Hec hide from police under an overhanging bank; and crazed child welfare officer Paula, confronting Ricky in the bush, tells him, "I'm relentless. I'm like the Terminator." More popular references include the startling appearance of locally iconic newsman John Campbell, best known for his current affairs show *Campbell Live* (TV3, 2005–2015), who appears as an over-excited investigative journalist (complete with his catchword "maaah-velous") reporting on the hunted duo. Campbell is himself an institution of televisual nostalgia, who reminds us of a bygone era when New Zealanders largely watched films and TV shows with which everyone was familiar. The shared recognition forms a web of national experience, at once tapped into and sustained by the popularity of *Wilderpeople*.

That the bush is also a site of Māori remembering – which, unlike post-settlement nostalgia, is a process of willed return and rebirth – is foregrounded by foster-mom Bella's imagined return to the land of her people on her death. Popular knowledge of the generic "bush" is significantly interrupted by her reference to Makutekahu, a lake "so high up that it wets the cloak of the sky. It's the first place our spirits go on their way to Reinga."[22] Before Ricky and Hec scatter her ashes (when Hec's dog Zac is killed by a wild pig), Hec washes his hands and sprinkles his head in a ritually appropriate way with water. The iconic bush, a filmic non-place of popular cultural reference, becomes the basis of family through the link provided by tangata whenua; thus familiarized, the bush becomes a familial image. "We Māoris," says Kahu, whose family, encountered by Ricky, embraces both Ricky and Hec at the film's end, "should stick together." Going bush may be the white, male settler's version of the pain of nostalgia – the nihilism for settlers of there being no whenua (land) to return to – but in the film it is also the basis for a particular post-settlement family of the displaced and deracinated: Hec tells Ricky that "Bella didn't know where she was from … She was just making it up." Ricky protests, but Hec is adamant: "Look, Bella didn't have any family. Like you. Like me. That's why she wanted to look after you, and took pity on me."

Hec's cantankerous bushman persona and rural surroundings present him as an obvious homage to Barry Crump, the self-mythologizing and wildly popular author of *Wild Pork and Watercress* (1986), whose story forms the basis of the film. In a round-about reference to Crump's mythology, Paula asks about Hec, "Who's that Crocodile Dundee character over there?" Crump also played a Kiwi bloke in the 1964 New Zealand film *Runaway* (dir. John O'Shea), uniting the man-on-the-run with the outsider motif,[23] a characterization which he continued to develop through his writing and his work in television advertising. As an early example of cross-media celebrity in the New Zealand context, Crump's legacy looms large as a (nearly) unspoken but omnipresent cultural reference in *Wilderpeople*.

We say "nearly" because Crump is actually referenced in the name, appearance, and all-terrain performance of the red pick-up truck that Ricky and Hec drive in the film's ultimate chase scene. The truck is called "Crumpy" by its owner, Psycho Sam, in allusion to a memorable, long-running 1980s advertising campaign for Toyota featuring the self-confident country bloke Crump and his wimpy townie sidekick, Scotty. What the local audience enjoys in the chase sequence that replays the 1980s' Toyota ads is a nostalgia for something they all know, experienced through filmic recognition rather than as a place that they might actually drive through (the chase scene may start in the Waitakere Ranges, but it improbably ends on the Central Plateau, some 300 kms to the south).

The Knack

In the film narrative, the name "Wilderpeople" springs from a book about wildebeests that Ricky discovers in a hut they come upon in the bush. The association between "wilder" people and the hunted who successfully fight back is made by Ricky because

FIGURE 12.1 Barry Crump (on left) carrying a boar (photo: Graeme Brown, Vision Media; retrieved from Radio New Zealand, Afternoons with Jesse Mulligan, Galleries: Barry Crump)

FIGURE 12.2 Sam Neill as Hec (on right), screenshot from *Hunt for the Wilderpeople*.

of his admiration for Hec's bush skills and the allure of his bushman gravitas. Hec has "the knack," which he describes as "a way of figuring things out without having to think too hard or … or talk, more importantly" (although he then admits that the knack means staying calm and following water to higher ground). For our purposes, having the knack means not only surviving in the bush interior, but also capitalizing on (for filmmakers) and gaining pleasure from (for majority town-dwelling Pākehā/ Tauiwi audiences) the very conditions of post-settlement cinema.

Given the film's wide-ranging popularity, the knack suggests the ability to balance long and short history, to straddle the border between violent colonial invasion and willful settler forgetting, in order to accede to a post-settlement present which has, at least on a surface level, more fully acknowledged this past. The non-place of the bush is the scene of this pedagogy; it is an imaginary space in which we, too, can develop the knack through a mutual self-recognition of place in terms of the present–past, or the consequences of the past in and for the present. Of course, the actual bush is never a non-place; it always has its own past and present/presence, even though it continues to operate as a trope for the majority of New Zealanders, who live in towns and cities. The detachment from the interior adds to the mystique of the bush and helps to explain the over-determined role of dense bush both in (cinematic) images of the country and in the imagination of its mostly urbanized inhabitants. For lack of knowledge otherwise, stories such as *Hunt for the Wilderpeople* can be imagined to take place there. And, from the cinematic experience of this imagined place, viewers are returned to their city/townscapes with greater accommodation of the past and some inkling of, or at least a feel for, the legacies of colonialism. The characters' healing by the end of the film is thus not just their own. It is also, in some larger sense, that of the local audience.

Given the film's trove of cultural references, which in the first instance confirms nothing so much as our familiarity with them, the film makes us feel as though "the knack" is something we all have. Self-deprecating humor is as much a cultural touchstone as images of the "good, keen man" (the title of an earlier novel by Crump [1960]) in the bush. To understand the humor, to embrace the yarn, connects one via cultural similarity to other people who also understand it. The "knack," then, is not just the skill set needed to survive in the bush; it is the knack that Taika Waititi has to make films that enable a range of audiences to feel local with one another.

The dominant affect of nostalgia in post-settlement cinema, as we have discussed it in terms of a vexed colonial history which is both exposed and elided by settler colonial jouissance, is no better evidenced than by Ricky and Hec's encounter with the extinct huia bird. The moment has a "did they really see it?" quality, which also encompasses the pathos of "if only." Extinction cuts deep in Aotearoa, a brutally colonized place which has suffered world-leading degradation of land- and water-bodies and loss of biodiversity in a short period.[24] The wound of loss is sutured by the "if only" feeling, however slim the possibility of seeing a huia. More importantly, it is also sutured by the fact that this is a moment of deep bonding for Ricky and Hec, as the only witnesses to the still-living bird, which Ricky brings up when he and Hec reunite at the film's end:

RICKY: Reckon you can find that bird?
HEC: Yeah. I think I know where it is. Seem to remember it was a pretty beautiful place, was it?

RICKY: Yeah. Majestical.
HEC: Come on. Let's go.

Their unity, hope, and wonder are made available for everyone who has watched the film, albeit against a backdrop of very deep loss. For the New Zealand audience, settler colonial jouissance is the self-knowing nostalgia of wishful thinking.

Notes

1 Eve Tuck and K. Wayne Yang, "Decolonization Is Not a Metaphor," *Decolonization: Indigeneity, Education & Society* 1, no. 1 (September 2012), 1–40.
2 Aotearoa is the Māori name for New Zealand. Originally used for the North island, it has since come to refer to the whole country, translated as (land of) the "long white cloud." Throughout our discussion, it should be taken that "New Zealand," as a product of short settler history, is at the same time suspended in view of Aotearoa and its long Indigenous Māori history.
3 Ian Conrich notes the prevalence of such imagery in his short review of little-discussed action films from the 1980s, "Global Pressure and the Political State: New Zealand's Cinema of Crisis," *Post Script* 24 (2–3).
4 See Misha Kavka and Stephen Turner, "'This is Not New Zealand': An Exercise in the Political Economy of Identity," in *Studying the Event Film*: The Lord of the Rings, eds. Harriet Margolis, Sean Cubitt, Barry King, Thierry Jutel (Manchester: Manchester University Press, 2008), 230–238.
5 'Māori Dictionary, https://maoridictionary.co.nz/search?idiom=&phrase=&proverb=&loan=&histLoanWords=&keywords=tauiwi'
6 *Dazed*, April 5, 2018, https://www.dazeddigital.com/music/article/39590/1/unknown-mortal-orchestra-ruban-nielson-taika-waititi-interview (accessed 10 May, 2018).
7 Barry Barclay, *Mana Tūturu: Māori Treasures and Intellectual Property Rights* (Auckland: Auckland University Press, 2005), 165.
8 This link is explored by Pounamu Jade William Emery Aikman in "Trouble on the Frontier: *Hunt for the Wilderpeople*, Sovereignty and State Violence," *Sites: New Series* 14, no. 1 (2017), with particular reference to the on-going violence of the settler state that seeks to separate Māori children from their whanau and heritage. A longer article would explore the real "terror" of the bush for Pākahā/Tauiwi, given its self-sovereign bond with *tangata whenua*, long articulated by Tūhoe. To alleviate the threat, the unredeemable wild pig, who is the third protagonist, along with Ricky and Hec, in film posters for *Wilderpeople*, must be shot and removed as an actor.
9 Such characters include Weirdo in Taika Waititi's *Boy;* Arthur, the self-proclaimed second son of God, in *Insatiable Moon* (dir. Rosemary Riddell, 2010); Niki (played by Waihoroi Shortland, who also plays Weirdo), the schizophrenic son of an elderly Māori woman in *Rain of the Children* (dir. Vincent Ward, 2008), whose mother Puhi had been the subject of Ward's earlier documentary *In Spring One Plants Alone* (1980); and Genesis, the Māori chess master struggling with bipolar disorder in the fact-based film *The Dark Horse* (dir. James Napier Robertson, 2016). See also Taika Waititi's TED talk in Doha on creativity (2017), which evokes the outsider in the figure of his own artist father and the influential "naïve" artist Henri Rousseau (1844–1910).
10 Barry Barclay, "Reflections on Fourth Cinema," *Illusions* 35 (2003), 7–11.
11 See He Whakaaro Here Whakaumu mō Aotearoa/Report of Matike Mai Aotearoa – The Independent Working Group on Constitutional Transformation, https://nwo.org.nz/resources/report-of-matike-mai-aotearoa-the-independent-working-group-on-constitutional-transformation/ (accessed 14 December, 2019).

12 See Jo Smith, *Māori Television: The First Ten Years* (Auckland: Auckland University Press, 2017).

13 "From Greek *algos* 'pain, grief, distress' (see -algia) + *nostos* 'homecoming,' from *neomai* 'to reach some place, escape, return, get home'." https://www.etymonline.com/search?q=nostalgia

14 See He Whakaaro Here Whakaumu mō Aotearoa/Report of Matike Mai Aotearoa – The Independent Working Group on Constitutional Transformation, https://nwo.org.nz/resources/report-of-matike-mai-aotearoa-the-independent-working-group-on-constitutional-transformation/ (accessed 14 December, 2019).

15 https://www.nzonscreen.com/title/sleeping-dogs-1977

16 See John Braddock, "Behind the Making of *The Lord of the Rings*," World Socialist Web Site, March 21, 2002, https://www.wsws.org/en/articles/2002/03/lor2-m21.html (accessed 14 December 2019).

17 Alfio Leotta, *Touring the Screen: Tourism and New Zealand Film Geographies* (Bristol, UK/Chicago: Intellect, 2011).

18 See Mark O'Connell, "Why Silicon Valley Billionaires Are Preparing for the Apocalypse in New Zealand," *The Guardian*, February 15, 2018, https://www.theguardian.com/news/2018/feb/15/why-silicon-valley-billionaires-are-prepping-for-the-apocalypse-in-new-zealand (accessed February 16, 2018).

19 For the white fantasy structure at work in the threatened hobbits of LOTR, see Alice Te Punga Somerville, "'Asking that Mountain': An Indigenous Reading of *The Lord of the Rings*," in *Studying the Event Film: The Lord of the Rings*, eds. Harriet Margolis, Sean Cubitt, Barry King, Thierry Jutel (Manchester: Manchester University Press, 2008), 249–258.

20 Barclay, "Celebrating Fourth Cinema," *Illusions* (July 2003), 7–11.

21 Barclay dreams of a Māori kung fu movie: "How good it would be if kids could go down to the video parlour and get out a film called the *The Taiaha Kid* instead of kung fu film from Hong Kong" (Barry Barclay, *Our Own Image: A Story of a Māori Filmmaker* [Minneapolis: University of Minnesota Press, 2015; orig. 1990], 21).

22 Cap Rēinga/Te Rerenga Wairua, the northern-most tip of the North Island, is the "jumping-off point" for departed spirits in Māori cosmology.

23 The man-on-the-run myth was given seminal form in John Mulgan's 1939 novel, *Man Alone*, about an English ex-soldier and would-be Kiwi farmer who ends up on the run in the Kaimanawa Ranges, reiterated in the cinema of unease by Sam Neill (*Sleeping Dogs*), Bruno Lawrence (*Smash Palace*), and Harvey Keitel (*The Piano*).

24 Eleanor Ainge Roy, "'Decades of Denial': Major Report Finds New Zealand's Environment Is in Serious Trouble," *The Guardian*, April 18, 2019, https://www.theguardian.com/world/2019/apr/18/decades-of-denial-major-report-finds-new-zealands-environment-is-in-serious-trouble (accessed April 18, 2019).

PART IV
Space

13

LANDSCAPES, WILDLIFE, AND GREY OWL: SETTLER COLONIAL IMAGINARIES AND TOURIST SPACES IN WILLIAM J. OLIVER'S PARKS BRANCH FILMS, 1920S-1930S

Dominique Brégent-Heald

During the interwar period, the Calgary-based filmmaker, William (Bill) J. Oliver, filmed the majority of motion pictures for Canada's Parks Branch (now known as Parks Canada). These were silent, black-and-white films lasting between ten and twenty minutes, and typically marketed as educational films, wildlife films, scenics, travel films, or travelogues. The Parks Branch circulated these short subjects throughout the United States, Canada, and overseas in theatres. Yet these were primarily distributed through non-theatrical circuits to community clubs, chambers of commerce, hunting and fishing organizations, boards of trade, public schools, and post-secondary extension programs, typically accompanied by a lecturer, with the purpose of drumming up tourism, especially from the United States. Despite their wide distribution and effectiveness as advertising media, these motion pictures (and travel films in general) have been disparaged by such contemporaneous documentarians as John Grierson, the first commissioner of Canada's National Film Board, who argued that Canada should *not* represent itself solely as a place to engage in "fishing, golf and the observation of wild animals."[1] Rife with clichéd tropes of the travelogue genre, Oliver's films nonetheless are significant in that they formulated cultural representations of the settler colonial state that the parks in turn used to sell themselves to another settler state, the American tourist market. In the process, Oliver visually communicated the complex and ongoing legacy of Indigenous elimination and land appropriation consistent with settler colonial spaces.

Settler colonialism, as anthropologist Patrick Wolfe states, is an enduring societal structure, not a singular or set of historical events, which requires continual shoring up through discursive means.[2] Taking a cue from Wolfe's insights, one might similarly position tourism as drawing from and perpetuating this settler colonial logic and connected practices relating to space, including the treatment of nonhuman animals and people within it. The Dominion's establishment of the national parks in the late nineteenth century involved the removal and exclusion of the First Nations that had resided upon those lands – actions justified under the pretext of development and conservation.[3] As Indigenous peoples were forcibly removed from their homelands, "Indians," such as Grey Owl, were subsequently restored as spectacles or guides for settler colonial consumers.[4] The settler state thus covered its tracks by making the trauma that characterizes the processes of settler colonial displacement and substitution invisible.[5] Film is complicit in these practices of erasing and creating spaces in the ways that it deletes, appropriates, and reinscribes Indigenous cultures to promote a particular destination brand rooted in these settler colonial power relations. This discussion of Oliver's Parks Branch travelogues demonstrates the ways in which film and tourism's synergistic relationship has played a crucial role in the need for modern settler colonial societies to bolster constructed myths of nationhood through claims of legitimacy and development, and through practices of erasure and appropriation. This essay begins with a brief discussion of William J. Oliver and the National Parks Branch's investment in film production, followed by a discussion of its motion pictures that emphasized vehicle-friendly landscapes and recreational opportunities. Next, the essay explores Oliver's Parks Branch films that promoted the abundance of undomesticated nonhuman animals. Finally, Oliver's "beaver films," which featured ersatz Indigeneity in the persona of Grey Owl who, in reality, was the English-born writer and conservationist Archibald Belaney, are examined.[6]

William J. Oliver, the Parks Branch, and Landscapes

Born in England in 1887, William J. Oliver immigrated to southern Alberta as a young man in 1910 where his interest in photography quickly developed into a career at the *Calgary Herald*. In 1912, he opened his own studio and soon began experimenting with moving images. By the early 1920s, Oliver had become a sought-after cameraman specializing in outdoor filming. For example, he shot scenes for *The Last Frontier* (dir. George B. Seitz, 1926), a Western partially filmed in National Buffalo Park near Wainwright, Alberta; worked for the Canadian edition of the Fox Film Corporation's expanding newsreel service; and, provided on-location filming for Universal Studio's *The Calgary Stampede*, starring Hoot Gibson (dir. Herbert Blaché, 1925). Meanwhile, Oliver contributed moving pictures to the Parks Branch's growing film library, and by the late 1920s would devote his energies to the National Parks full time.[7]

The Parks Branch had begun investing in film production since the late 1910s, convinced that this new technology provided a leading-edge advertising medium to attract tourists. Its first commissioner, former journalist James B. Harkin, established a separate publicity division under J. C. Campbell in 1921.[8] That same year William J. Oliver filmed *Jasper of the Lakes* (dir. William J. Oliver, 1921), his first contribution to the Parks Branch, featuring bears, squirrels, and beavers, as well as mountain scenery. Largely due to the expansion of car culture in the United States, the postwar period proved an opportune time for the national parks to expand its brand presence south of the border through the distribution of travel films. Automobile ownership by the early 1920s had become one of the most powerful symbols of the advent of a more modern secular culture, marked by pleasure, leisure, and consumption. While this emergent category of recreational motorists was far from inclusive, the rise of an ostensibly more democratic motor age contrasted motion pictures of elite train travel through the parks sponsored by the Canadian Pacific Railroad since the turn of the twentieth century.[9]

With the completion of the Banff-Windermere Highway (1923) and the Kicking Horse Trail (1927), Harkin and Campbell rebranded the parks as a destination for this new class of auto tourists brought about by the growth of road-based travel and the rise of paid vacations for an increasing number of workers. Oliver produced a series of films in step with this vision of the national parks that combined a reverence for the seemingly undeveloped and unsettled landscapes of the Canadian Rockies, based on the false concept of *terra nullius* (nobody's land), and the modern automobile infrastructure that enabled more visitors to enter these spaces.[10] Evincing settler colonial narratives, these films constructed a landscape aesthetic that effaced Indigenous ontologies and claims to territory, transforming their ancestral lands into "wild" yet accessible tourist playgrounds. For example, *Motoring through the Canadian Rockies* (dir. William J. Oliver, 192?) privileges the "the grandeur of scenery" along the Banff-Windermere Highway as a fleet of Studebaker passenger trucks departs Banff and travels through the Yoho Valley. Beyond functioning as a form of "armchair tourism," the scenic functions "as an advertisement of Alberta's great scenic highway" to incentivize travel among spectators.[11]

Other films by Oliver also framed the parklands as attractive areas for American motoring vacationists who owned personal vehicles. *Sunshine Trails* (dir. William J. Oliver, 1929) and *Holidaying Among the Peaks* (dir. William J. Oliver, 1930) each begins with young tourists from Great Falls, Montana, who drive across the border into Alberta where they take in the natural beauty of the region via their automobiles and enjoy the outdoor recreational activities (golfing, hiking, swimming, boating, fishing, and tennis) available in the Waterton Lakes Park area. Similarly, *Through Mountain Gateways* (dir. William J. Oliver, 1930) focuses on a wealthy couple from Spokane, Washington, who plan a trip to the Kootenay National Park and Banff. The travelogue cuts to a road map with an animated superimposed car that situates the viewer and reinforces the geographies of mobility (see Figure 13.1). Rather than picturing an isolated wilderness, these films emphasize movement, flexibility, and accessibility, depicting Alberta as an easy drive from the United States, and a place where visitors could experience a short restorative vacation away from the duress of urban life while still having the benefit of contemporary amenities.

These films conceptualize the parks as leisure spaces for the temporary and transitory enjoyment of settler colonial tourists. More than a form of transportation that takes visitors from point A to point B, the automobile in *Motoring through the Canadian Rockies, Sunshine Trails, Holidaying Among the Peaks*, and *Through Mountain Getaways* is steeped in cultural significance, signifying tourism, technology, mobility,

FIGURE 13.1 Screenshot from *Through Mountain Gateways* (dir. William J. Oliver, 1930), https://youtu.be/xjlPmeCROFY (accessed 24 October 2019).

freedom, and independence for the white middle class as it moves through these sites of dispossession. At the same time, they signal settler access to the land, possession and mastery of it, and the settler gaze that gives meaning to these places while seeking to convey settler belonging. Oliver thus uses the filmic medium to reconcile the machine with the natural world, and the settler with the land that used to be Indigenous. "For fifty miles we travel," states an intertitle from *Through Mountain Gateways*, "by still lakes, through green aisles of silence, and around breathless hair-pin curves." Motor vehicles thus function as a convenient means of accessing nature while the destructive impact of this new technology (noise, pollution, speeding, spatial reorganization) is erased from the diegesis. Moreover, the absence of Indigenous peoples from these filmic landscapes reveals the ongoing processes of settler colonial place-making, that is, the discursive and structural ways that the settler state has expunged First Nations from national parks to turn these protected areas into symbols of Canadian nationhood and to serve the burgeoning tourist economy.

Wildlife

In addition to promoting colonial-nationalist landscapes, Oliver specialized in wildlife films. The erasure of Indigenous communities and the concomitant preservation of native nonhuman animals in their natural habitat has been central to the Canadian park imaginary since its founding. Harkin implemented increased protection for fur-bearing animals, established sanctuaries for fowl and migratory birds, and put other conservation measures in place to provide visitors with opportunities to engage with wildlife. From "the recreational point of view," the widespread presence of mountain sheep and goats, bears, moose, elk, beavers, grouse, ptarmigans, ducks, and geese, according to the commissioner, "constitutes one of the most important features of the parks. It is of no less consequence than the scenery itself, in fact it is almost said to be a part of the scenery."[12] Poet and scholar Billy-Ray Belcourt (Driftpile Cree Nation) argues that settler colonial epistemologies surrounding interactions between human and nonhuman animals were made possible because of the obliteration of Indigenous bodies and their forced evacuation from their lands to enable western expansion and the establishment of "protected areas," such as national parks.[13]

Dismissing Indigenous knowledges of human and other-than-human relations defined by interconnectedness, kinship, and reciprocal relationships, the regulatory environment of the Parks Branch drew sharp distinctions between domesticated (privately owned) and wild (unowned or common property resources), and operated as another form of settler power by constructing nonhuman animals as colonial subjects (or more appropriately as objects). It is the Dominion that has the authority to act as a steward over the (formerly Indigenous) natural resources it has conquered, including the land, water, as well as the flora and fauna contained within. In the paradigm of settler colonialism, Indigenous lifeways – fishing and hunting undomesticated mammals and birds for subsistence – are deemed "barbaric" in contrast to the "civilized" harvesting of nonhuman animals within the state's management wildlife resources designed to ensure preservation of species.[14]

During the early twentieth century, Canadian-themed wildlife films focused on the settler practice of sport hunting and fishing with the goal of appealing to a middle-to-upper-class, urban, white, and masculine tourist sensibility. Yet Oliver's Parks Branch films of the interwar period promoted shooting nonhuman "wild" animals with cameras, not guns, as part of an ostensibly more humane form of settler colonial tourism. *Sanctuary* (dir. William J. Oliver, 1930), for example, provides views of wildlife in an area protected from hunters. Oliver filmed *Hunting Without a Gun* (dir. William J. Oliver, 1930) while on a trail trip in Jasper National Park with the noted guide and outfitter, Jack Brewster. The film is noteworthy for Oliver's close-up views of a grizzly bear. Similarly, Oliver filmed Brewster and Dan Byck, an American businessman, in *Stalking Big Game* (dir. William J. Oliver, 1934). Armed with only cameras, Oliver filmed them photographing caribou, black bears, and Rocky Mountain sheep and goats.[15] Camera hunting appears as a nonintrusive and respectful mode of consumption, while the moving images Oliver captures for the screen appear ahistorical and unchanging – disassociated from the moment of their creation. The seeming spontaneity and authenticity masks the artifice of technological representation (setting up cameras, staging scenes, editing, etc.), the park's conception of idealized encounters with wildlife, and the underlying settler colonial processes that enabled this practice; "wild" animals can only exist in the fictional *terra nullius*.

Oliver's wildlife productions fostered human–nonhuman animal relationships based on an appreciation for the authentic creatures within the protected boundaries of the nation. Researchers would later refer to such settler colonial interactions with nonhuman animals, "wherein the focal organism is not purposefully removed or permanently affected by the engagement," as "non-consumptive wildlife-oriented recreation."[16] These films encouraged the emergent category of "wildlife tourism," which emphasized experience over product, and also positioned nonhuman animal subjects in such a way to elicit an emotional response, thereby potentially resulting in the cultural conditioning of attitudes towards nonhuman animals.[17] This emphasis on benign observation as mediated through both the lens of the photographer and the film screen nevertheless conceals colonial hierarchies of power. *Sanctuary, Hunting Without a Gun*, and *Stalking Big Game* demonstrate how humans *should* relate to nature and close off possibilities for alternative ways-of-seeing and knowing, namely, Indigenous perspectives and approaches.

The "Beaver Films" and Grey Owl

Throughout the 1920s and 1930s, Oliver's wildlife films for the Parks Branch positioned bears, elk, buffalo, caribou, mountain goats, birds, and other denizens of the forests and mountains as "screen stars" – a trademark to draw visitors to the national parks.[18] Above all, Oliver's films that centered on the interactions between beavers and Grey Owl, the imagined identity of Archibald Belaney, epitomized the Parks Branch's pledge to wildlife protection and the humane treatment of nonhuman animals, as well as aroused interest in Canada's scenic playgrounds. Perhaps more than any other species, the beaver (*Castor canadensis*) evinces the complicated legacy of settler colonialism. This is achieved through its association with the fur trade, the exchange of beaver fur and other pelts for goods between Indigenous and Métis trappers and French or English traders, as well as imperial struggles between Britain and France and their respective Indigenous allies over territory.[19]

Before the arrival of Europeans, millions of these large bucktoothed rodents not only inhabited almost all of present-day Canada wherever fresh water and wood were plentiful, but also shaped "the physical and ecological landscapes of North America."[20] First Nations peoples consumed beaver meat, used hides to make or adorn garments, fashioned the teeth into tools, and used the castor glands for medicinal purposes. Indigenous peoples also maintained a deeply spiritual cross-species bond with these semi-aquatic mammals.[21] Through to the mid-nineteenth century, the European and North American penchant for men's felted hats, as well as perfume, transformed beavers into commodities (pelts and Castoreum, or, glandular secretions). As sociologist Margot Francis argues, the beaver "served as a symbolic medium through which European explorers produced themselves as civilized, respectable, and enterprising, in contrast to Indigenous peoples."[22] As beaver populations dwindled in the east due to over-trapping and the destruction of natural habitats, the search for more of its distinctive water-repellent, reddish-brown fur pushed colonial expansion and settlement further north and west. Hunted to near-extinction by the mid-1800s, the switch to silk hats likely prevented the complete demise of this mammal that had become a collective symbol of nationhood predating Confederation in 1867.[23] By the 1930s, the Hudson's Bay Company, the Parks Branch, and provincial governments undertook more concerted initiatives to reinvigorate the decimated beaver population.[24]

At this time, Grey Owl, the alias of the English-born Archibald Belaney, became the public figure of beaver conservation in Canada. This was fostered through a series of Parks Branch motion pictures filmed by Oliver that centered on Grey Owl's interactions with his "pet" beavers in spaces of settler colonial dispossession. Belaney had immigrated to Canada as an adolescent where he adopted a new identity: Grey Owl (Wa-sha-quon-asin), the son of a Scots frontiersman and an Apache mother. As historian Philip Deloria and others demonstrate, settlers erase Indigenous bodies and cosmologies and then emulate "Indianness." In the settler colonial imagination, Grey Owl appears as a liminal figure, existing somewhere between human and nonhuman animal. By tapping into notions of Indigenous spiritualities and the interconnected relationship between First Nations and nature (including nonhuman animals), Grey Owl seemingly spoke from a position of authority and authenticity. Attired in buckskins and moccasins, his hair braided and adorned with feathers, Belaney displayed the settler colonial signifiers of the "noble savage" or the "ecological Indian" by presenting himself as a trapper turned conservationist.[25]

Grey Owl centered his broad naturalist message on the beaver – an imperial and national signifier – whose population had declined across northern Canada due to over-hunting. According to Anahareo (Gertrude Bernard), Belaney's Mohawk/Algonquin common-law wife, she rescued a pair of beaver kits after one of their traps killed their mother and the couple raised them as pets.[26] In the fall of 1928, the foursome moved to rural Québec to start a beaver colony. The following year Belaney published an article in the British periodical *Country Life*, and, in 1930, in *Forest and Outdoors*, issued by the Canadian Forestry Association, in which he championed the beaver as intelligent, industrious, possessive of a distinct language, and capable of human-like emotions.[27] Sometime between 1928 and 1930, Oliver filmed Grey Owl, Anahareo, and their domesticated beavers (likely Jelly Roll and Rawhide). The silent *The Beaver People* (dir. William J. Oliver, 19?) displayed the assiduousness of the beaver and the nonhuman animal–"Indian" bond, and bemoaned the "ruthless greed and slaughter" of the historic fur trade. The beaver, however, is apparently a forgiving creature. As one of the intertitles explains, the former trapper "and his young wife have become conservationists" who have befriended "the Beaver so that they will come at call, sharing food, friendship and even play."[28] Grey Owl and Anahareo embody a teleological narrative of Canada's evolution from resource-based economy to a more enlightened and conservation-minded nation and belies Indigenous erasure within the settler colonial "wilderness" spaces.

In 1931, on the verge of publishing the first of his four books, *The Men of His Last Frontier*, Grey Owl gave a lecture accompanied by a screening of *The Beaver People* to the annual Canadian Forestry Association meeting. The enthusiastic response convinced Harkin and Campbell that Grey Owl and his beavers would draw tourists and project the Parks Branch's conservationist ideals.[29] Grey Owl thus began work as the caretaker of park animals in Riding Mountain National Park, Manitoba, where Oliver filmed *The Beaver Family* (dir. William J. Oliver, 1931).[30] Oliver then shot *Strange Doings in Beaverland* (dir. William J. Oliver, 1932) after Grey Owl and his tame beavers moved to Prince Albert National Park, Saskatchewan, which had opened in 1928 and largely catered to automobile tourists.[31] These short films offered numerous close-ups of his beavers eating, grooming, and building a dam. Moreover, scenes focus on Grey Owl communicating with his beavers, emphasizing interspecies kinship, and indirectly importuning audiences to heed his missive of wildlife protection. Oliver later filmed *Grey Owl's Neighbours* (dir. William J. Oliver, 1933?), featuring Grey Owl "and his furred and feathered neighbors," and *Pilgrims of the Wild* (dir. William J. Oliver, 1935), a similar production that shares the same title with what would become Grey Owl's most widely-read written work.[32]

By the mid-1930s, Grey Owl had become one of the most famous Canadians, and credited for singlehandedly saving the beaver from extinction. According to Harkin, Oliver's films provided a means to publicize "the results of the Government's policy of wild life protection" while directing "the attention of recreation seekers throughout the world to the great advantages of a holiday spent in Canada's national playgrounds."[33] Prefiguring the anthropomorphized nonhuman animals in the Walt Disney Corporation's *True-Life Adventures*, a series of short and full-length nature films between 1948 and 1960, the Grey Owl–beaver films were lighthearted, privileged feeling over fact, and encouraged audiences to emotionally invest in the survival of the species. T. D. A. Cockerell, an American professor of zoology, referred to the films as "a major factor in determining the Canadian policy with reference to the beaver" because of their "appeal both to the intellect and the emotions." He explained that "thanks to the courtesy of the Canadian Park Service," his wife screened the films in the 1930s "to many thousands in Colorado, California, and Wyoming, always meeting with enthusiastic appreciation and requests to have them repeated." He argued that such public showings created "lively interest and sympathy" that had the potential to bring about "the democratization of conservation."[34] In other words, Cockerell articulates the unique ability of motion pictures to engage spectators and foster a connection between humans and marginalized nonhuman animals resulting in not only potential tourists but also concrete policy initiatives rooted in broader settler colonial practices.

FIGURE 13.2 Screenshot of Grey Owl and one of his pet beavers in *The Beaver Family* (dir. William J. Oliver, 1931), in public domain, https://www.nfb.ca/film/beaver_family/ (accessed 28 June 2019).

In Oliver's films the beaver functioned as the axis for both a declentionist narrative (a story of loss and degradation) and a more progressive paradigm – that pseudo-Indigenous knowledge and government-led management could stop or even reverse that decline. In practice, however, the Grey Owl–beaver films provided the parks with public exposure that facilitated tourism promotion under the aegis of delivering a conservationist message. "There is not the slightest doubt," Harkin stated, "that we have secured for our Parks ... countless thousands of dollars' worth of publicity through Grey Owl, his beaver, his books, his magazine articles and the motion pictures which we have secured of him and his beaver."[35] Likewise, J. C. Campbell averred that the Grey Owl films drew large crowds during his 1935 lecture tour of such American cities as Dayton, Cleveland, Spokane, and Seattle. The publicity director predicted that the result would be an uptick in American tourist traffic to Prince Albert National Park: "If we are to judge the enthusiasm with which our programs depicting Canada's National Parks on the screen were received as any criterion of the interest of prospective tourists we may look for a splendid year in the parks."[36] By the end of the year, Campbell claimed that the Parks Branch were shipping upwards of 15,000 films to the United States, "which means quite a lot of publicity in that country."[37]

Conclusion

Recognizing the tourism industry as an economic generator, during the interwar period the Parks Branch expanded its publicity activities to promote auto tourism, wildlife conservation, and imagined Indians through filmmaker William J. Oliver. Though largely forgotten today, as nature writer W. H. Corkill (pen name Harper Cory) wrote of Oliver's career, "few men have so effectively made Canada known the world over."[38] Harkin and Campbell wagered on film's unique ability to appeal to the senses, stimulate emotion, and nurture the appropriate mental imagery to actuate travel. That is, the repetition of images and themes (pristine scenery, accessibility, recreation, amenities, and wild animals) would foster positive associations in viewers towards the various parks. Ideally, these abstract feelings would morph into a concrete decision to visit these protected areas.

Within this film-induced tourism framework, Oliver's Parks Branch films were also predicated on the myth of *terra nullius* and the legacy of Indigenous expulsion. Appearing as uncultivated spaces, these motion pictures obfuscate the violent processes used to dispossess and/or assimilate First Nations. Moreover, undomesticated nonhuman animals within these "wilderness" spaces were interpolated into this settler colonial imaginary. While most of Oliver's motion pictures expunged Indigenous peoples and perspectives, as part of a broader process of reframing First Nations lands as accessible tourist spaces, the Grey Owl–beaver films demonstrate that appropriation is equally central to transnational settler colonial tourist narratives and the construction of settler colonial space. This essay is not meant to defame Oliver as non-Indigenous filmmaker who purported a settler colonial perspective in his filmic oeuvre, but rather its goal is to reveal larger patterns of settler colonial power at work in the promotion of Canadian tourism and Canadian spaces through film.

Notes

1 *The Citizen* (Ottawa), 3 June 1938; 4 June 1938; 10 June 1938, 19 January 1940, RG20-C-2-g, R202–28–3-E, Canadian Government Motion Picture Bureau, Library and Archives Canada (LAC), Ottawa, Canada.

2 Patrick Wolfe, "Settler Colonialism and the Elimination of the Native," *Journal of Genocide Research* 8, no. 4 (2006), 387–409.

3 The method of setting aside so-called empty lands as protected areas, regulating resources, excluding Indigenous communities, and encouraging visitors, was not unique to Canada. Settler colonial governments in the United States, New Zealand, and Australia engineered similar processes. See Bernhard Gissibl, Sabine Hohler, and Patrick Kupper, "Introduction - Towards a Global History of National Parks," in *Civilizing Nature: National Parks in a Global Perspective*, ed. Bernhard Gissibl (New York: Berghahn Books, 2015), 1–28.

4 I use the term "Indian" to evoke a settler colonial conception of the original inhabitants of Canada (Turtle Island) or where historical context dictates its usage. While I recognize the imprecise nature of these labels, I use the terms Indigenous or First Nations to refer collectively to the descendants of the first inhabitants of Turtle Island.

5 Lorenzo Veracini argues that settler colonialism "covers its tracks and operates towards its self-supersession in his "Introducing," *Settler Colonial Studies*, 1, no. 1 (2011), 3.

6 It was only after his death in 1938 that the truth about his racial impersonation became public. For an account of Belaney's life see, for example, Donald B. Smith, *From the Land of Shadows: The Making of Grey Owl* (Vancouver: Greystone Books, 2000).

7 For more background on Oliver, see Sheilagh S. Jameson, *W. J. Oliver: Life Through a Master's Lens* (Calgary: Glenbow Museum, 1984).

8 In addition to motion pictures, the Parks Branch produced and distributed printed matter, colored slides, and still photography. E.J. Hart, *J. B. Harki: Father of Canada's National Parks* (Edmonton: University of Alberta Press, 2010), 231–32.

9 On the promotion of automobile tourism in this period see John Sandlos, "Nature's Playgrounds: The Parks Branch and Tourism Promotion in the National Parks, 1911–1929," in *A Century of Parks Canada, 1911–2011*, ed. Claire Elizabeth Campbell (Calgary: University of Calgary Press, 2011), 53–78.

10 Although Oliver filmed *The Highlands of Cape Breton* (1937) to advertise Cape Breton Highlands National Park in Nova Scotia (established in 1936), and two Atlantic sea fishing adventures, *Warriors of the Deep* (1936) and *Battling the Tuna* (1937), the bulk of his films for the Parks Branch were shot in western Canada.

11 "Will Interest Tourists," n.d., Scrapbook of Clippings, 1918–1947, file 173, William J. Oliver Fonds, R7658-0-4-E Volume 1 (MG30-D402), (LAC). The exact release of the film is unknown.

12 Canada, "Report of the Commissioner of Dominion Parks," 1918, http://parkscanadahistory.com/publications/NPBr_annual_reports_1912-21.pdf (accessed 25 January 2018).

13 Billy-Ray Belcourt, "Animal Bodies, Colonial Subjects: (Re)Locating Animality in Decolonial Thought," *Societies* 5 (2015), 1–11.

14 For a discussion of the distinction between "domesticated" and "wild" nonhuman animals in Euro-Canadian thinking see Michael Asch, "Wildlife: Defining the Animals the Dene Hunt and the Settlement of Aboriginal Rights Claims," *Canadian Public Policy* 15.2 (1989), 205–219. On the evolution of wildlife management in the parks see Tina Loo, *States of Nature: Conserving Canada's Wildlife in the Twentieth Century* (Vancouver: UBC Press, 2006).

15 On filming nonhuman animals see Derek Bousé, *Wildlife Films* (Philadelphia: University of Pennsylvania Press, 2000); Gregg Mitman, *Reel Nature: America's Romance with Wildlife on Films* (Cambridge: Harvard University Press, 1999).

16 David A. Duffus and Philip Dearden, "Non-Consumptive Wildlife-Oriented Recreation: A Conceptual Framework," *Biological Conservation* 53, no. 3 (1990), 215.

17 See David Newsome, Ross Dowling, and Susan Moore, *Wildlife Tourism* (Clevedon: Channel View Publications, 2005).

18 *The Lethbridge Herald*, 2 February 1933, 11, https://newspaperarchive.com/lethbridge-herald-feb-02-1933-p-11/ (accessed 28 June 2019).

19 The history of the fur trade is too complex to do justice to it here. For Indigenous and settler perspectives on the subject see Carolyn Podruchny and Laura Peers, eds., *Gathering Places: Aboriginal and Fur Trade Histories* (Vancouver: UBC Press, 2014).

20 Glynnis Hood, *The Beaver Manifesto* (Victoria: RMB, 2011), 6.

21 Harriet V. Kuhnlein and Murray M. Humphries, "Beaver," http://traditionalanimalfoods.org/mammals/furbearers/page.aspx?id=6142 (accessed 25 June 2018).

22 Margot Francis, *Creative Subversions: Whiteness, Indigeneity, and the National Imaginary* (Vancouver: UBC Press, 2014), 30. See also Frances Backhouse, *Once They Were Hats: In Search of the Mighty Beaver* (Toronto: ECW Press, 2015).

23 In 1975, an Act of Parliament established the beaver as the official emblematic animal of Canada. On the association of Canada with beavers (or more specifically dead beavers), see Jody Berland, "The Work of the Beaver," in *Material Cultures in Canada*, eds. Jennifer Blair and Thomas M. Allen (Waterloo: Wilfrid Laurier University Press, 2015), 25–49.

24 Loo, *States of Nature*, 96–117.
25 Philip Deloria, *Playing Indian* (New Haven: Yale University Press, 2007). See also David Chapin, "Gender and Indian Masquerade in the Life of Grey Owl," *American Indian Quarterly* 24, no. 1 (2000), 91–109; Fenn Stewart, "Grey Owl in the White Settler Wilderness: 'Imaginary Indians' in Canadian Culture and Law," *Law, Culture and the Humanities* 14, no. 1 (2018), 161–81.
26 Grey Owl had been married three times prior to Anahareo. She left him in 1936 and he went on to remarry for a fifth time. Anahareo and Sophie McCall, *Devil in Deerskins: My Life with Grey Owl* (Winnipeg: University of Manitoba Press, 2014).
27 See Albert Braz, "Beaver Voices: Grey Owl and Interspecies Communication," in *Experiencing Animal Minds An Anthology of Animal-Human Encounters*, eds. Julie A. Smith and Robert W. Mitchell (New York: Columbia University Press, 2013), 51–64.
28 *The Beaver People* (1928), https://www.nfb.ca/film/beaver_people/ (accessed 28 June 2019).
29 W. H. Corkill, "The Romance of Grey Owl," *Canada's Weekly*, 10 January 1947, 415, Vol. 1770 PA272 pt 1 Prince Albert National Park – Grey Owl (Archie Belaney) – Clippings and Correspondence 1931–1938 (Reel T 14389), LAC; Smith, *From the Land of Shadows*, 90–91.
30 The National Film Board states that *Beaver Family* is from 1929, however, Grey Owl was not at the Park until 1931, https://www.nfb.ca/film/beaver_family/ (accessed 14 May 2019).
31 Grey Owl argued that the water conditions in Riding Mountain National Park were detrimental to the beavers. "Memorandum by H. Howett, Deputy Minister of the Interior," n.d., Vol. 1768 PA174–18 pt 1 Prince Albert National Park – Grey Owl (Archie Belaney) 1931–1937 (Reel T 14388), LAC.
32 "Catalogue of Motion Picture Films Distributed by the National Parks Bureau of Canada," RG 84 A-2-a Vol. 163 U113–60 pt 1 Universal – Catalogue of motion picture films 1937–1946 (reel T 12919), LAC. Associated Screen News (ASN), the Montreal-based commercial producer and distributor of films, re-edited *The Beaver People* and *The Beaver Family* together, which it theatrically released as *Grey Owl's Little Brother* (1932). The film was nominated for an Academy Award. ASN also released *Grey Owl's Strange Guest* (1934), a sound version of *Strange Doings in Beaverland*. Gordon Sparling, head of ASN's commercial production unit, supervised these theatrical sound shorts released under his *Canadian Cameo* series (1932–1954).
33 "Report of the Commissioner, Year Ended 31 March 1931, 11, Department of the Interior, National Parks Canada, http://parkscanadahistory.com/publications/commissioner_report-1931.pdf (accessed 28 June 2019).
34 T.D.A. Cockerell, "Zoology and the Moving Pictures," *Science* 82, no. 2129 (October 1935): 369–70, https://science.sciencemag.org/content/82/2129/369 (accessed 28 June 2019).
35 "Memorandum," 25 April 1936, Vol. 1768 PA174–18 pt 1 Prince Albert National Park – Grey Owl (Archie Belaney) 1931–1937 (Reel T 14388), LAC.
36 *The Lethbridge Herald*, 18 March 1935, 7, https://lethbridgeherald.newspaperarchive.com/lethbridge-herald/1935-03-18/page-7/ (accessed 29 June 2019).
37 "Letter from J.C. Campbell to M. B. Williams," 2 December 1935, M. B. Williams Fonds, R12219-1-5-E Volume 1, LAC. M. B. (Mabel) Williams served as a *de facto* publicist for the Parks Branch between 1911 and 1930, when she was laid off during a series of depression era budget cuts.
38 W. H. Corkill, "As the Crane Flies," *Canada Weekly*, 29 March 1946, 716, M-8119–292, Miscellaneous News Clippings, 1922–1982, Sheilagh S. Jameson Fonds, Glenbow Museum Archives, Calgary.

14

FROM COLONIAL CASBAH TO CASBAH-*BANLIEUE*: SETTLEMENT AND SPACE IN *PÉPÉ LE MOKO* (1937) AND *LA HAINE* (1996)

Maria Flood

The national past, argues cultural historian Patrick Wright, "is capable of finding splendor in old styles of political domination and of making an alluring romance out of atrocious colonial domination."[1] Supporting Wright's declaration, a 1954 BBC short film made in colonial Algiers depicts the Orientalist fantasies of the era.[2] The film represents Algiers as a heterogonous, multi-faceted, modern city, albeit one in which two distinct populations exist. To sprightly flute music, the clip depicts the lifestyle of settlers in Algiers as one of rotating pleasures: eating and drinking on terraces and skimpy sunbathing on the beach. However, the tone switches abruptly when the film turns to the Casbah, and the curling strains of the North African instrument, the mizwad, emerge on the soundtrack. The Casbah is a site of excitement, desire, adventure, and excess for the settler colonial population, for as the voiceover breathily declares, "Algiers is wild and wicked, gay and naughty. The European there always saw something exotic about the Southern shore of the Mediterranean." This documentary fragment highlights some of the prevailing fantasies about Algiers, and particularly the Casbah, in the mid-twentieth-century European imagination. Built on the site of Roman and later Berber ruins, most of the houses in the contemporary Casbah of Algiers date from the Ottoman period of the late eighteenth century. However, *Kasbah* also means citadel, fortress or keep, and the Casbah of Algiers has been associated with bilateral conflict, resistance and thwarted incursion, most notably in Gillo Pontecorvo's iconic Casbah-set *The Battle of Algiers* (1966).

This chapter examines the Casbah as a symbolic barometer of the shifting narratives of space, settlement, and identity in two French films from the mid- and late twentieth century: Julien Divivier's *Pépé le Moko* (1937) and Mathieu Kassowitz's *La Haine* (1996). These works focus on the relationship between the French settler and state authorities and outsiders through the geographic and symbolic space of the

"Casbah." I use the Casbah as a figure that designates the physical space of Ottoman Medina of Algiers, which encompasses the non-settler section of the settler colonial city in *Pépé le Moko*. Secondly, I draw on the idea of the Algerian Casbah to refer to a "Casbah-*banlieue*" in *La Haine*, defined as a zone that shares many of the colonial Casbah's characteristics (maze-like structures, lawlessness and heavy-handed policing, and heterogenous populations), while also being a non-white settler space located in *banlieues* ("suburbs" or "ghettos") of metropolitan France. If the Algerian Casbah in the 1930s was a site of French fantasies about the colony, the Casbah-*banlieue* of the 1990s offers similar projections, even if, as in *La Haine*, these projections are tempered with sympathy for the characters' plight.

As I have argued elsewhere in relation to Xavier Beauvois's *Of Gods and Men* (2010), settler colonial fantasies about racial, ethic, and religious others and the spaces they inhabit still inform French cinematic narratives about the history of colonialism.[3] This chapter takes up this theme, and it is structured into three sections. Firstly, I briefly outline the symbolic connections between the settler colonial Casbah and the Casbah-*banlieue*. Secondly, I consider how these urban spaces of otherness are represented in the two films. Thirdly, I show how structures of policing and the representation of diverse characters in *La Haine* echo the settler colonial narratives about heterogeneity and the forces of order found in *Pépé le Moko*. Ultimately, I argue against critics like geographer Amy Siciliano, who views *La Haine* as a progressive film that serves to "challenge hegemonic representations of "Frenchness," and instead suggest that the evocation of settler colonial tropes in Kassovitz's movie functions as an othering mechanism that serves to further distance the inhabitants of the *banlieues* from the literal and figurative center of France, represented by central Paris.[4]

Urban Space: Linking the Casbah and the Casbah-*Banlieue*

Postcolonial and psychoanalytic theorist Frantz Fanon's description of the colonial city maps onto visual representations of the distinction between the European and "Moslem" quarter of Algiers, the Casbah, in the mid-twentieth century. Fanon writes that "the colonial world is a world cut in two [...] the settler's town is a strongly built town, all made of stone and steel. It is a brightly lit town [...] a town of white people, of foreigners." By contrast, the area of the city occupied by the colonized is "a place of ill-fame, peopled by men of evil repute [...] it is a town of niggers and dirty arabs [sic]."[5] Fanon lived in Algeria from 1953 to 1957 and he likely drew inspiration for this evocation of the colonial urban space from Algiers and the contrast between the Casbah and the Baroque and neoclassical architecture of the European quarter. However, Fanon's words can equally be applied to the distinction between French metropolitan city centers and the *zones urbaines sensibles* (sensitive urban zones) that surround them, notably in Paris. France is home to the largest African and Muslim populations in Europe, mostly descendants of France's former colonial subjects and many of whom live in *banlieues* on the outskirts of large urban areas. If, as visual studies critic Bülent Diken suggests, "urban reality is always structured through symbolic mechanisms,"[6] the infrastructural girdle of the *Boulevard Périphérique*, a multi-lane highway that circles the 20 *arrondissments* (boroughs) of Paris, works to decenter and cut off those who live outside this boundary.

In the films examined here, the Casbah and the Casbah-*banlieue* are mapped spatially in relation to an urban center, figured as central Paris, enlarged to encompass the values and norms of France generally. According to Francophone Studies scholar Laila Amine, Paris is "appropriated to stage [France] as a modern, ordered, clean, and bourgeois nation."[7] A similar metonymic shift also takes place in relation to the Casbah and the Casbah-*banlieue*. They figure, in Fanon's dichotomous scheme, as the opposite: primitive, chaotic, dirty, and heterogeneous in class and racial terms, standing in for the non-settler sections of a settler colony, or the post-colony, as a symbol of otherness. Indeed, scholars have already connected the space of the colonial Casbah to the urban *banlieue*. Amine tracks the representation of postwar Muslim populations in French news media, noting that journalists characterized the *bidonvilles* (shantytowns) outside French cities as "small casbahs." She also argues that in contemporary France, the urban space operates according to "a racialized 'imaginative geography'" of segregation, recalling Fanon's distinction between the racial and ethnic groups who live in the opposing quarters of the city.[8] Similarly, French Studies scholar Adrian Fielder has argued that the shantytowns of the 1960s, located on the sites of what would later become the high-rise *banlieues*, "came to be perceived in the French media and political discourse as mini-casbahs inscribed on French soil."[9]

Urban Space: *Pépé le Moko* and *La Haine*

Made in the wake of the 1931 "Exposition coloniale" in Paris, *Pépé le Moko* (1937) prefigures the dualistic segregation of settler colonial space outlined by Fanon. The film focuses on the trials of the loveable French rogue Pépé (Jean Gabin), a gangster lothario who is eventually brought down by his love for the Parisian tourist and social climber Gaby (Mireille Balin). Pépé, a jewel thief, continues to evade the grasp of the colonial authorities by never leaving the Casbah. From the outset, the Casbah in *Pépé le Moko* is figured as an exotic space, atmospherically contrasted with the civility and order of the scenes shot in the settler European quarter. The Casbah is not an orderly settler space, but rather a world of spiraling staircases, steep diagonal and almost vertical lines, narrow passageways, and tight doorways, and the cinematography reflects this sense of confinement and containment (Figure 14.1).

In the scenes shot in the Casbah, each frame is filled with faces, background décor, or objects – very little sky peeks through. Moreover, low angle shots predominate, which give the impression both of menace and fear, while in some cases canted low-angle close-up shots, particularly of women, are designed to convey the grotesque otherness of this space. By contrast, the scenes in the

They intersect, overlap, twist in and out,

FIGURE 14.1 The narrow spaces of the Casbah. Screenshot from *Pépé le Moko* (1937) by the author.

European quarter, such as the policemen's barracks, eschew the low and canted close-ups of the Casbah in favor of long and medium still shots.

The twisting spirals on the columns in the Casbah and the Arabesque murals that appear in the background of many shots reflect Pepe's endless circling of this space – leaving the Casbah means freedom but also death. Historian Janne Lahti argues that settler colonial narratives in the American Western are focused on "settler mobility," "advancing," and a forward-facing storyline that "cannot be turned back."[10] By contrast, Pépé, perhaps in an implicit condemnation of the fact he has "gone native" by living in the Casbah and romancing the women there, is trapped in endless loops, and he is denied the forward-facing narrative of the proper settler. Unlike the Western settler colonial film, which charts characters as they move forward in space and time, Pépé's Casbah entraps and ensnares its residents, because it is a non-settler space in a settler city, the Other within the settler realm. Space in the Casbah is figured as circular, epitomized in the looping waltz Pépé shares with Gaby as they turn in circles around the spiral columns of a bar. However, the narrative itself is linear; there is a clear trajectory for Pépé, even if this is one that ends in tragedy. He has two choices: stay in the Casbah and live as a "native," or leave the Casbah and die. Both may be intolerable, but they are clearly mapped from the outset of the film.

Moreover, Pépé has a defined end goal: to return to Paris. Gaby represents all that Pépé has lost in leaving Paris, and their seduction scene demonstrates the ways in which dreaming of Paris creates affection between the characters. Filmed in soft focus, with Gaby's white pearls, skin, eyes, and satin dress glimmering in the low light, Pépé and Gaby engage in a game of mutual seduction by taking it in turns to name streets and places in Paris. The final name they cite together, La Place Blanche, a site of the 1871 Paris Commune and location of the Moulin Rouge, connects them through its association with rebellion, class, and romance, but it also summons Algiers. The city itself has been called "Algiers La Blanche" [Algiers the White] because of the white stucco walls of the Casbah, visible from the sea. Thus, their love can only exist in a fantasy of Paris or the strictures of Casbah.

Made almost sixty years later, *La Haine* (1996) is set in the *banlieue* of Chanteloup-les-Vignes, a series of tower blocks constructed in 1966, which was designed with no direct access to the neighboring village of La Noë and was initially surrounded by a sea of empty fields.[11] The film tracks a day in the life of three young men from the *banlieue*: Saïd (Saïd Taghmaoui), Hubert (Hubert Koundé), and Vinz (Vincent Cassal), as they navigate police violence and rioting in their own neighborhood, and police and street violence as they journey into the city-center of Paris. This "black, blanc, beur" (Black, White, Arab) trio are second-generation children of colonial or violent histories. Vinz, the only white member, is of Eastern European Jewish ancestry, while Hubert and Saïd are of Sub-Saharan and North African origin, although the precise location is not made explicit. The trio represents the demography of the urban *banlieue*: while the majority of the inhabitants are first, second, and third generation immigrants from former French colonies, there are a minority of working class and poor whites who live there as well. In contrast to *Pépé le Moko*, where space loops in endless constricted spirals in the Casbah, in the Casbah-*banlieue* many spaces are wide and open. But paradoxically, the film manages to use large spaces to convey a similar sense of containment and restriction. In an early scene, Saïd stands at the center of the horseshoe shaped ring of tower blocks, shouting up to Vinz's sister in their apartment. Filmed in a low angle shot from Saïd's perspective, a man in a neighboring building opens his window to tell Saïd to stop shouting. The effect generated is one of the panopticon, described by philosopher Michel Foucault as an institutional architectural model designed to permit the surveillance and control of large and diverse groups of people.[12] The panopticon has been linked to colonial apparatuses of surveillance and control, and this sense of being surveyed is further reinforced throughout *La Haine* through the helicopters that hum in the background and the journalist who swoops into the *banlieue* with a large camera.[13]

The camera in *La Haine* is dizzyingly observant: it guides and directs the viewer's attention, a rapid zoom in onto Vinz's ring or the swift swooping tilt to allow the viewer to look at the box in which he keeps his marijuana. This cinematography and documentary-like attention to detail conveys the sense that this space can be seen and understood. This accessibility contrasts with the reality that these urban zones are, in fact, poorly understood by the majority of the French population. As author François Maspero writes, "many Parisians saw [the *banlieue*] …as a shapeless muddle, a desert containing ten million inhabitants…a circular purgatory, with Paris as paradise in the middle."[14] Yet the *banlieue* as filmed by Kassovitz is anything but shapeless: instead, the camera picks out sharp vertical and horizontal planes, the flat spaces of empty parking lots and the burned out gym. The camera also tracks the central characters' movements through the area in wide circular motions, as they journey up and down stairs and onto rooftops, run through narrow corridors to escape the police, and greet acquaintances. In most instances, walls and buildings frame the characters, but often glimmers of sky peek through the two abutting walls. The camera even allows the viewer an overview of this space, in the scene in which the DJ plays a mix of Edith Piaf's "Non, je ne regrette rien" and DJ Cut Killer's "Nique la police" (Fuck the police), a floating, swaying aerial shot of the city follows the path of the music as it winds its way through the suburb.

If the containment of the Casbah is conveyed in *Pépé le Moko* through the restricted spaces of closed, cramped interiors, and steep walls and narrow stairwells, in *La Haine* it is the temporality of the young men's existences that most clearly captures the postcolonial Casbah's restrictions. Time in *La Haine* is both linear and circular; the digital clock interface that marks moments in time throughout the day captures the mundane and the extraordinary, surfacing at moments to remind us of the lack of direction in the characters' lives. The clock also heightens tension; in the final sequence the dial moves from 6:00 to 6:01, after Vinz has been shot and Hubert and the policeman face each other with their guns pointed. The inevitability and circularity of this outcome is suggested by the fact the film opens and closes on the same shot of Saïd's anguished face, as well as Hubert's prophetic iteration that "what counts is not the fall, but the landing." In a society that excludes and marginalizes portions of its population, the film suggests that such violence and mutual destruction is the predictable result. Yet the film also carefully builds in enough moments of randomness – the old man's story in the toilet, the final gunfight – to suggest that this outcome may be logical, that is, linear, but it is not inevitable.

While *Pépé le Moko* operates in a dialogical mode where the Casbah is confinement and Paris is freedom, *La Haine* points towards the fact that space is a relative construct, dependent of the social and structural systems, which bind the characters that move through it. Indeed, unlike Pépé, who cannot leave the Casbah for fear of capture and arrest, the boys can and do leave, making the train journey into central Paris. But on arrival they are ill-equipped to cope with the social mores they encounter (most notably, in the scene in the art gallery). Thus, while the boys have the concrete spaces of the playgrounds, car parks, and burned out buildings to wander through, too much space can also equate with being ignored, excluded, and marginalized, just as having too much time can lead to ennui and destructiveness. The uneasy coexistence of circularity and linearity, confinement and open space in *La Haine* may reflect its status, and those of its characters, as neither colonial nor postcolonial, neither fully French nor entirely other.

The social border between the "Casbah," where the characters live, and central Paris (France) – the settler colonial metropole and a site of true belonging to the settler state – is figured as unbridgeable in both films: just as Pépé stares at the port and the boats that leave for France, so too do the characters in *La Haine* stare at the glimmering Eiffel Tower in the distance. However, in *Pépé le Moko* the settler colony is not a land of physical pain, trial and tribulation, but a site of emotional pain and longing. The film expresses a nostalgia not for France in general but Paris in particular as a site of fulfilment and hope, a return that would be possible if it were not for Pépé's individual, personal failures – his desire for women, his thirst for adventure, and his resultant inability to pursue the settler ideal of being married with a family. In *La Haine*, there is no idealized space (like Pépé's Paris) to which the characters long to return. It is the dead end of the post-settler colonial world. Although Paris is a source of hope and fantasy for Pépé, Amine argues that postcolonial subjects quickly found themselves disabused by the reality of Paris: "idealization" is followed by "deep disillusionment." She cites Algerian author Driss Chraïbi who describes Paris as "the mirage of Europe" and as a "tapeworm" which devours "poor dumb Arabs," highlighting that the space of Paris for decolonized subjects is one of disappointed fantasies and consuming monstrosity.[15] For the characters of *La Haine*, ostensibly denizens of the city, Paris cannot be imagined as a source of hope or salvation.

Population and Policing in the Casbah and Casbah-*Banlieue*

In spite of the negative qualities (danger, exclusion, violence), the sites of the Casbah and the Casbah-*banlieue* are figured as radically heterogeneous, non-settler places, containing diverse bodies, customs, and lives. They become spaces of belonging for those pushed to the margins of the settler colonial realm. As film scholar Will Higbee notes, the *banlieue* "remained the only real space of community."[16] In *Pépé le Moko*, the Casbah incarnates the mix of languages, classes, and cultures that merged in early-twentieth-century colonial Algiers: French working class gangsters mix with Spanish, Maltese, and Italian immigrants, as well as Jewish Algerians, North African policemen and spies, Sub-Saharan African traders, prostitutes, gypsies, and opium addicts. The film's raucous soundtrack, which mixes French chansons with Arabic traditional music, seems to celebrate this diversity. Similarly, *La Haine* defiantly foregrounds its "black, blanc, beur" trio and as each character is introduced, racial and ethnic markers are foregrounded. Kassovitz seems to delight in stereotyping and labelling his characters; within the first 10 minutes, Saïd calls Vinz a Jew, and Vinz's grandmother berates him for not going to the synagogue as a menorah stands in the background. Saïd also threatens to slit the throat of Vinz's sister, a practice stereotypically associated with North Africans in France due to the practice of making halal meat and the actions of Algerian FLN members in the War of Independence.[17] Additionally, Hubert is introduced as a muscular and adept boxer, awkwardly evoking the ways in which sport, and particularly boxing, was used as a way to "'civilize' indigenous subjects," according to anthropologist Paul A. Silverstein and French studies scholar Philip Dine.[18] We later see Hubert listening to Barry White in his bedroom, with posters of Tommy Smith and John Carlos, as well as Mohammed Ali in the background, linking him to a transcultural African American lineage of sporting prowess and political activism.

Upon first inspection, such recognition and celebration of diversity is laudable, but difference can quickly become threatening within the settler colonial and postcolonial imaginaries of *Pépe le Moko* and *La Haine*, respectively. Pépé's Casbah swings between danger and excitement, and Pépé's longing for Paris might be read as a longing for French values. By the end of the film, Pépé appears to no longer tolerate the cultural diversity of the Casbah – he violently breaks up a group of Algerian "natives" fighting outside, wincing at the sounds of their speech and music. In a similar sense, Silverstein has shown how diversity in France can be strategically publicized and celebrated, and simultaneously vilified, using the example of the French national football team.[19] Racial and ethnic difference, expressed through music, language, customs, and religion, can be perceived as threatening to the deeply held French value of universalism. Universalism is the belief in a shared public existence with a common set of immutable and non-relativist values. Opposed to expression of difference in the public sphere, universalism, writes historian Naomi Schor, "was grounded in the belief that…rational human nature was universal, impervious to cultural and historical differences."[20] Schor explains that universalism was a key component in France's colonial mission, and in the present day, universalism is bound up in an assimilationist approach to immigration, the inverse of a cultural relativism that foregrounds differences, as found in the discourses of multiculturalism in the UK and the US. Universal citizens in France, anthropologist and French studies scholar Susan Terrio writes, "are entitled, even required, to come together as equals to enact secular rituals and to reinforce the shared values of the social order."[21]

In these films, the inhabitants of the Casbah and the Casbah-*banlieue* exist outside of ritual, law, and the social order, and one of the prime ways they do this is by mixing with diverse racial, ethnic, linguistic, and religious groups. Yet while there may be unity and coexistence in the Casbah or Casbah-*banlieue*, there is hierarchy and exclusion. Indeed, one of the major critiques of universalism by feminists such as Joan W. Scott and race theorists like Fanon is that it assumes the position of the white, male, and often property-owning subject as the norm, and espouses this perspective as an impartial and logical. Pépé, the white French man, is called the "caïd" (leader, "big shot") in this space, and it is one in which women are called angels, mice, and children, whose place is "in the home."

Perhaps most troubling is *Pépé le Moko*'s exclusion of Arabs from the litany of populations and "types" listed in its opening section. This omission summons what settler colonial studies scholars Anna Johnston and Alan Lawson call "the suppression or effacement of the native" in settler colonial narratives.[22] However, there are two Arab characters in *Pépé le Moko,* Ayrab (Marcel Dalio) and Slimane

(Lucas Gridoux), the former a minor character who betrays Pépé, and the latter the Algerian policeman who finally catches the hero. Slimane is depicted as a sly double-dealer, a man who treats Pépé with solicitude to his face but plots his downfall behind closed doors. Slimane is the perfect "mimic man" as elaborated by postcolonial theorist Homi K. Bhabha – he has integrated so successfully into the French police that he is more efficient than them, becoming "a subject of a difference that is almost the same but not quite."[23]

The film places the duty and final success of apprehending Pépé on an Algerian policeman. This may be a nod to the inefficiencies of the settler colonial police force, but is most likely a way for the audience to remain without divided loyalties – Pépé is a criminal, but he is also a very likeable character played by Jean Gabin, often viewed in France as "the proletarian hero *par excellence.*"[24] Therefore, the fact that an Algerian policeman catches him means that the viewer does not have to choose between upholding the values of French law and order and a symbolic "everyman." Slimane's success in catching Pépé further points to the "successful" assimilation and the usefulness of such figures to the French colonial project – approximately 150,000 *harkis* (Algerian Muslim auxiliaries) fought on the side of the French during the Algerian War of Independence. The "native" is not effaced, but rather integrated into a shared system of values – the ultimate aim of universalism.

As Fanon notes in relation to the colonial city, "the frontiers are shown by barracks and police stations [...] the policeman and the soldier are the official, instituted go-betweens."[25] The opening scenes of both films also demonstrate a colonial and postcolonial obsession with mapping and spatial control through the forces of law and order: one of the first shots in *Pépé le Moko* is of a map of Algiers, with the Casbah at its center, as the policemen explain to a colleague from Paris that Pépé is impossible to catch because of the topographical specificity of the space itself. As one of them notes, "in Pigalle, he would have been behind bars long ago," a statement that speaks to settler colonial fears around loss of spatial control. Slimane is the only policeman who enters the Casbah – the space may be a prison or a cage for the central character, but it is also a space of refuge and the police are figured as inefficient, befuddled by its structural complexity.

The idea of the Casbah as impenetrable has also been imported into contemporary France in the figure of the Casbah-*banlieue*. As Silverstein notes, recent right-wing media reports about the *banlieue* as a place where "police supposedly refuse to set foot merely echo long-standing domestic fears of sectarianism (*communautarisme*) and the development of American-style ethno-racial 'ghettos' as 'areas outside the law'." However, Silverstein suggests that this figuration of the *banlieue* as a no-go area, a lawless zone run by criminal gangs (like the Casbah of *Pépé le Moko*), is radically at odds with the lived experience of its residents who argue that "the law is overly enforced and their lives are overly policed."[26] The opening scenes of *La Haine* demonstrate the violent police penetration of the *banlieue*, and in contrast to *Pépé le Moko*, where the audience is first introduced to Pépé from the policeman's perspective, from the outset of *La Haine* we are aligned with the inhabitants of the *banlieue*.

The viewer sees documentary footage of a solitary man wearing a tracksuit, his back facing the camera as he stands in the left side of the frame. Train tracks traverse the center of the image, and in the background, a line of innumerable police in uniforms stand erect. As a spectator we are certainly invited to position ourselves beside – if not quite in alignment with – this man as he shouts "You can shoot. We only have stones" (Figure 14.2). Thus, from its opening image, *La Haine* underscores the unequal power relations that exist between the *banlieue* inhabitants and the police. This theme is continued as the opening documentary segment progresses, with the film dedicated to all those who died during its production. If *Pépé le Moko* individualizes Pépé's ultimate downfall (he is a criminal, and in the end he kills himself), *La Haine* is careful to underscore the structural and systemic failings that produce the final tragedy.

Yet by portraying the *banlieue* as a site of perpetual conflict, films like *La Haine* may help re-enshrine these neighborhoods as radically Other: Casbah-*banlieues*, spaces as distant and different as the non-settler spaces in the colonies were in the 1930s.[27] By representing the Casbah-*banlieue* as a space of racial, ethnic, and religious heterogeneity, *La Haine* inscribes its troubling difference from French normative values and ideals, specifically universalism. Indeed, by figuring the *banlieue* as a site of racial and ethnic heterogeneity, Amine argues that the postcolonial urban suburbs are viewed by the mainstream media as an "extension of the colony [...] in its general exclusion of non-whites."[28] Drawing on settler colonial imaginaries of the Casbah, the Casbah-*banlieue* becomes a site of confinement, violent excess, racial and ethnic heterogeneity, and male aggression and dominance, structurally and symbolically tied to the colony, and its associations with the "outside," the foreign, and the exotic.

FIGURE 14.2 A scene of escalating violence. Screenshot from *La Haine* (1996) by the author.

Conclusion

If the Casbah in the settler colony became a kind of fantasy, this comparative discussion demonstrates that similar phantasmatic projections are at work in the figuration of the Casbah-*banlieue* in *La Haine* in the 1990s. While both films assign humanity to marginalized protagonists, they serve to reinscribe the margins between inside and outside, subject and object (of state power, police surveillance, normative values), and proper settler space and non-settler realm, of true France versus its outer rims and others. Central Paris remains the key reference point from which normative identities are categorized. If the Casbah keeps Pépé safe even if he can never leave it, at least he can dream of a return to Paris. The prognosis for the characters in *La Haine* is grim: for the second- and third-generation children of immigrants, there is no alternate homeland to which they dream to return. They appear lost and unwanted in the margins of the former settler colonial empire.

Notes

1 Patrick Wright, *On Living in an Old Country* (London: Verso, 1985), 254.
2 "Algier 1954" (dir. Anon., 1954). Public Domain Algerian War documentary. National Archives and Records Administration. https://commons.wikimedia.org/wiki/File: Algier1954.ogv (accessed 19 June 2019).
3 See Maria Flood, *France, Algeria and the Moving Image: Screening Histories of Violence* (Oxford: Legenda, 2017), 104–132.
4 Amy Siciliano, "*La Haine*: Framing the Urban Outcasts," *ACME* 6, no. 2 (2007), 211–230, 214.
5 Frantz Fanon, *The Wretched of the Earth* (1961; reprint, London: Penguin Modern Classics, 2001), 30.
6 Bülent Diken, "*City of God*," *City* 9, no. 3 (2005), 307–320, 313.
7 Laila Amine, *Postcolonial Paris: Fictions of Intimacy in the City of Light* (Madison WI: University of Wisconsin Press, 2018), 23.
8 Amine, *Postcolonial Paris*, 5, 8.
9 Adrian Fielder, "Poaching on Public Space: Urban Autonomous Zones in French *Banlieue* Films," in *Cinema and the City: Film and Urban Societies in a Global Context*, eds. Tony Fitzmaurice and Mark Sheil (Oxford: Blackwell, 2001), 270–281, 271.
10 Janne Lahti, "Settler Passages: Mobility and Settler Colonial Narratives in Westerns," *Journal of the West*, 56, no. 4 (2017), 67–76, 67 & 68.
11 Hervé Viellard-Baron, "Chanteloup-les-Vignes: le risqué du ghetto," *Esprit* 132 (1987), 9–23.
12 Michel Foucault, *Discipline and Punish: The Birth of the Prison* (London: Penguin Social Sciences, 1991).
13 Martha Kaplan, "Panopticon in Poona: An Essay on Foucault and Colonialism," *Cultural Anthropology* 10, no. 1 (1995), 85–98.
14 François Maspero, *Roissy-Express: A Journey through the Paris Suburbs* (New York: Verso, 1994), 16.
15 Amine, *Postcolonial Paris*, 27.
16 Will Higbee, "Re-Presenting the Urban Periphery: Maghrebi-French Filmmaking and the *Banlieue* Film," *Cineaste* 33, no. 1 (2007), 38–43, 38.
17 Flood, *Screening Histories of Violence*, 21.

18 Paul A. Silverstein, *Postcolonial France: Race, Islam, and the Future of the Republic*, (London: Pluto Press, 2018), 125; Philip Dine, *Sport and Identity in France: Practices, Locations, Representations* (Oxford: Peter Lang, 2012).

19 Silverstein, *Postcolonial France*, 98–114.

20 Naomi Schor, "The Crisis of French Universalism," *Yale French Studies* 100 (2001), 43–64, 46.

21 Susan Terrio, "Crucible of the Millenium? The Clovis Affair in Contemporary France," *Comparative Studies in Society and History*, 41, no. 3 (1999), 438–457, 441.

22 Anna Johnston and Alan Lawson, "Settler Colonies," in *A Companion to Postcolonial Studies*, eds. Henry Swarz and Sangeeta Ray (Malden: Wiley-Blackwell, 2000), 369.

23 Homi K. Bhabha, *The Location of Culture* (New York: Routledge Classics, 2004), 122. Italics in the original.

24 Ginette Vincendeau, "Community, Nostalgia and the Spectacle of Masculinity," *Screen*, 26, no. 6 (November-December 1985), 18–39, 18.

25 Fanon, *The Wretched of the Earth*, 29.

26 Silverstein, *Postcolonial France*, 25.

27 Silverstein, *Postcolonial France*, 116.

28 Amine, *Postcolonial Paris*, 5.

15

BETWEEN SHERWOOD FOREST AND THE RED SEA: SETTLER COLONIAL SOUTH AFRICA IN EARLY HOLLYWOOD

Ian-Malcolm Rijsdijk

A Place on a Map

At a conference on early cinema some years ago, film historian Brian Jacobson presented a paper on film studio architecture in early Hollywood. It included a map (reproduced below), purportedly a Paramount Studio location map depicting the outline of the state of California, with regions of the state allied to regions of the world (Figure 15.1). The Sacramento River doubles for the Mississippi, while the area around Monterey represents the Nile. The northern Sierra Nevada, in turn, makes a handy French Alps and the Channel Islands off Los Angeles supplies scenery for the South Sea Islands. Down towards the border with Mexico – north of the Salton Sea – one can see Sherwood Forest and the Red Sea. Hemmed in between them is South Africa. It is distinct from Africa, which is located in a broad area between Monterey and Santa Barbara.

The provenance of the map is interesting. It can be found in the book *The American Film Industry* as part of a prospectus produced in 1927 by Halsey, Stuart, & Co., titled "The Motion Picture Industry as a Basis for Bond Financing."[1] In a scanned copy of the original Halsey, Stuart, & Co. document from the Museum of Modern Art Library, however, the map is not present. In fact, while the text of the two documents is the same, most of the images are different.[2]

The map shows the extent to which studios combined the efficiencies of the soundstage with the landscapes of the back lot to produce a more cosmopolitan *mise-en-scène*.[3] At the same time that Hollywood reached out to the world to sell countries versions of themselves on screen, it centralized the production process by producing a world in one country or, in this case, one state. Cultural geographer Chris Lukinbeal writes that,

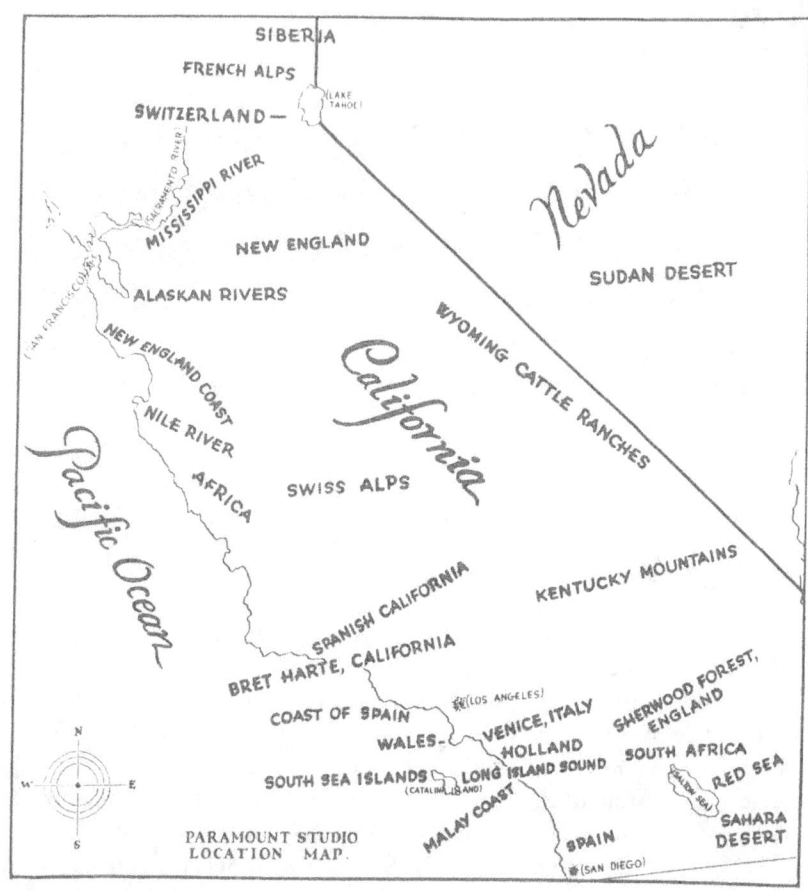

FIGURE 15.1 Paramount Studio location map, 1927.

"Doubling" of landscapes allowed a location's meaning to be flexible and mal-
leable, which in turn saved money through lowering travel costs…Los Angeles
provided a stable economic base for production while surrounding areas provided the geographic realism needed to ground a diverse array of narratives.[4]

From a South African perspective, the map immediately prompts the question:
what made South Africa so distinct to Hollywood filmmakers in the late silent era
that the country received a space separate from "Africa" on the "global" map of
California? What kinds of films were made, and what does it mean to say that a
film "takes place" in a particular location if place – a term connoting rootedness –
is so ambiguous?[5] Filmmaker Peter Davis answers the first question, arguing that,
"South Africa's appeal came from the raw material of fable that it had to offer –
its wealth of gold and diamonds, intrepid pioneer history, and savage Zulus."[6]

The British Empire's cinematic interest in South Africa formed part of a colonial image economy that promoted British interests through its global domain by circulating fictional stories, newsreels and advertising. But what was the origin of this fascination with diamonds and Zulus? And were there other political and cultural factors – South Africa's colonial history as a settler society, for example – that influenced South Africa's complementarity with early Hollywood narratives and aesthetics as well?

This chapter looks at South Africa as imagined by Hollywood in the silent era. Many of the films under consideration no longer exist, though recurring narrative and aesthetic motifs can be seen in productions stills, reviews, and histories of the time. I will examine one surviving film, William Nigh's *Desert Nights* (1929), which includes many of the elements of Hollywood's South African fantasy: remote communities, harsh environments, and colonial adventurers. I will show that these settler narratives represent the circulatory relationship between Britain, South Africa, and the United States at a time when global hegemony was shifting from Britain's vast territorial empire in the nineteenth century to American economic and cultural imperialism after World War I. Caught between these two powerful forces, South Africa held its own conflicts. It was a power within the British Empire that contained nascent Afrikaner nationalism and the capitalist enterprise of mining that forced the subjugation of the majority of the country's indigenous peoples by the European settler minority.

An examination of specific proto-cinematic forms (such as live tableaux) and early films will show that South Africa offered a compelling combination of anthropological fetishism and exotic colonial fantasies of adventure that complemented America's own settler ideologies and entertainments. The new form of cinema proved crucial in recording, displaying, and disseminating representations of Western superiority through apparently benign colonial adventures, reinforcing the structures of colonialism through its industrialized form. This chapter will argue that Hollywood's cinematic South Africa was, in fact, an indefinite place, a strange fabrication of topicality and mythology.

While several histories of South African cinema have examined films made in South Africa that established the country's colonial and later Afrikaner nationalist identity on screen, there has been comparatively little attention paid to films made outside the country that represented South Africa to audiences abroad.[7]

Circuits of Power: Hollywood and the Colony Film

Films about British colonies were popular in the early decades of Hollywood, whether fiction, like *The Four Feathers* (filmed for Metro Pictures in 1915 and Paramount in 1929) and many adaptations of novels by H. Rider Haggard, or non-fiction, like the safari films by Martin and Osa Johnson, most notably *Simba: King of the Beasts* (1928).[8] The entanglement of British settler colonialism (shaken in South Africa by the South African War [ending in 1902] and partially rehabilitated by the declaration of the Union of South Africa in 1910) with American imperialism (represented by the many Americans working in South Africa's booming mining and agricultural industries) underpinned Hollywood's interest in South African narratives of empire that reflected that most American of film genres, the Western. The frontier – the driving mythology of America's nineteenth-century expansion – could be reconceived in South Africa's veld and deserts with similar settler colonial archetypes: heroic, individualist adventurers; opportunistic villains; strange Indigenous peoples (loyal or terrifying); and white women (good or bad) trapped by circumstance and in need of rescue.

Hollywood's fascination with the British colonies exploited exotic locations for a growing American audience. But settler narratives provided more than just exotic settings and adventure yarns: colonial settings perpetuated the fears of a "civilized" white, minority group battling their encirclement by unrelenting, warlike Others. At the same time, by showing American films in the colonies, Hollywood had become the "silent salesman" of American interests abroad and a global ambassador for American values. This lead Will Hays, chairman of the Motion Picture Producers and Distributors of America (MPPDA), to boast, "every foot of American film sells $1.00 worth of manufactured goods."[9]

There were genuine concerns in London about the effect of Americanization on film audiences in Britain, and the depletion of British profit and power in the colonies. In a House of Commons debate, Col R. V. K. Applin quoted from the *Daily Express*,

> The plain truth about the film situation is that the bulk of our picture-goers are Americanized to an extent that makes them regard a British film as a foreign film…We have several million people, mostly women, who, to all intent and purpose, are temporary American citizens.[10]

Worse still, Hollywood companies had exploited the precarious postwar conditions in Europe and Britain by selling their film in blocks, dumping films at affordable prices for exhibitors, who then offered less space for local films on the screen.[11]

Concern about British identity on screen was amplified in the colonial context to a "moral panic." As anthropologist Brian Larkin writes, the alarm "centered on fears that the circulation of American cinema, with its images of crime, violence, and sexuality, were providing negative images of white culture to native audiences and eroding the prestige of the white man and woman upon which colonial authority rested."[12] Hollywood was not only bad for the youth and the working classes, but bad for "natives" too. America's new media imperialism influenced whole societies "informally" through the related spread of American goods and American values in the form of mass media (including cinema).[13] Cinema represented a new "circulatory system of American power," which moved more swiftly than the nineteenth-century communication systems that defined the British Empire.[14]

The American empire of the interwar years was one of influence as well as possession, supra-territorial in the sense that its dominance moved beyond its territorial claims abroad. American imperialism was also characterized by its own interior contradictions: cultural anthropologist Engseng Ho succinctly describes America as an "invisible" empire, one that "allows the republic to sustain its anti-colonialist self-regard."[15]

Ironically, Britain's concerns over America's cinematic influence were matched to some extent by Hollywood's interest in British colonial stories. Art and film scholar Julie Codell observes:

> In the 1930s, Hollywood made so many films about the British Empire that British directors and producers making empire films complained that Americans were taking all the good subjects. What are now called empire films, films focusing on and heroizing the British Empire…were very popular on both sides of the Atlantic.[16]

Film scholar Peter Limbrick argues that these empire films

> show some of the ways that Hollywood responded to the ambivalence of settler coloniality, producing imperial-themed films that dramatized adventures drawn from a British legacy and offering westerns that narrated a relationship to landscape and space that is crucial to settler negotiations.[17]

As Hollywood began to represent the world on its own terms it promoted a new cultural imperialism, confirming America's ascendency as a world economic and military power while British imperial influence waned.

In South Africa, one finds a unique complex of these "settler negotiations" as American business models (particularly in the film industry) engaged with British colonial authority. The emergence of bioscope culture in South Africa in the first decade of the 1900s represented something new and liberating and, for a period, it destabilized colonial views on the social interactions of gender and race. Behind this new entertainment lay economic and cultural exchanges that bridge the era of proto-cinematic shows and the early decades of cinema.

Circuits of Consumption: "Showbiz Imperialism" in Britain, South Africa, and the United States[18]

Between 1869 and 1871, diamonds were discovered in the dry northern areas of the Cape in South Africa. Tens of thousands of prospectors descended upon the site, transforming the small hills into the vast open pit mine now known as The Big Hole. This led to the establishment of both the town of Kimberley and the global mineral empire of De Beers. A decade later, news spread of gold discoveries in the Witwatersrand area of what is now the Gauteng province. By

1886, the South African gold rush was underway and soon the dusty agglomeration of prospectors' tents known as Ferreira's Camp had become Johannesburg – *eGoli*, the City of Gold. The discovery of these mineral riches played a major role in fomenting conflict between Afrikaners and the British colonial authorities, represented by two wars (1880–1881 and 1898–1902).

As South Africa's settler powers battled for the nation's sovereignty, America and Americans played a substantial role in the formation of what would become modern South Africa. In the mid-1890s, more than half of the mines on the Rand were managed by Americans.[19] Along with American industrial entrepreneurs and products came American cultural productions. Blackface minstrel performers, like the Orpheus Myron McAdoo group, plied their trade through the English-speaking colonies, and most South African towns had a booming minstrel scene.[20] Another great influence from America that integrated the live show and the new medium of cinema was Buffalo Bill's Wild West. Indeed, the combination of breathless action, spectacle, and narrative was almost cinematic in its conception, and one of the scenes shown in Johannesburg using Thomas Edison's Kinetoscope in April 1895 was "Buffalo Bill giving a quick-firing exhibition."[21] Over three decades, William "Buffalo Bill" Cody's extravaganza was seen by an estimated fifty million people around the world, and it paved the way for similar shows like Frank Fillis's "Savage South Africa," which debuted at the Greater Britain Exhibition in London in 1899.[22]

While American culture was becoming established in early twentieth-century South Africa, it is interesting to see how South Africa was perceived in America at that time. One of the most significant and certainly the most historically complex examples is found in the figure of the Zulu, and white audiences' fascination with Zulu performers.

The Zulus entered American popular consciousness during the Anglo-Zulu War of 1879, when the American press featured the feats of King Cetshwayo's regiments in their victory over the British at the battle of Isandhlwana.[23] While the victory helped to elevate the image of Zulus as fearless warriors in the Anglophone world, the Zulu people had been an object of ethnological fascination for several decades before that. Already in 1834, the Zulus had been chosen by the American Board of Missions "as a people worthy of conversion, [being] one of the most well-known, physically perfect and highly organized of South African tribes."[24]

Fetishism of Zulu people and culture reveals something of the relationship between Britain and America's imperialist expansions in the twentieth century. As the dominant imperialist force of the nineteenth century, Britain exercised its imperialism by its colonization of territories around the world, while America's imperialism was increasingly economic and cultural. Along with strange creatures, plants, and landscapes, South Africa's peoples – particularly the Zulu – became part of what historian Glenn Reynolds calls "the scramble for images" as European and American cameras moved through the African continent.[25]

The popularity of Zulus in shows held two fascinations in tension:

> [One] celebrated and normalized white supremacy by starkly contrasting conquering "civilized" whites with subjugated "uncivilized" blacks while another – particularly among African Americans – appreciated the Zulu warrior's ferocity in battle, the strenuous determination of his anticolonial independence, and the premodern virtues of authentic experience, founding beliefs in the myth of American exceptionalism.[26]

By the early twentieth century, Zulu mythology had become embedded in American culture in diverse ways, including the New Orleans Mardi Gras Zulu Social Aid and Leisure Club (the Krewe of Zulu).[27] The mythologization of Zulu military might and physical purity resulted in many African peoples being "diminished to the exotic taxonomy of the Zulus…who served to signify the horrors that needed to be conquered and domesticated if the aims of empire were to be achieved."[28]

The result of this collapsing of ethnic identities was the transmission from show to screen of an archetypal Zulu ethnicity evidenced in several early American films, for example, D. W. Griffith's 1908 film *The Zulu's Heart* (where blacks are played by blacked-up white actors), and *Roosevelt in Africa* (1910, dir. Cherry Kearton). The latter – notable in the context of this chapter – misnamed its East African indigenous characters as Zulus.

Cinematic exhibition in South Africa closely followed the first screenings in Europe and America in 1895, and by the turn of the century cinema had begun to establish itself in South Africa. The country was well served by cinema entrepreneurs importing a steady supply of films. The Second Boer War (now the South African War), fought between the British and the Afrikaner nationalists, also became the first war covered by movie cameras. At the same time, Frank Fillis capitalized on the topicality of his Savage South Africa show, filming its climax, *The Last Stand of Major Wilson*, in 1899 – signaling the broader shift from live amusements to cinema.[29] If Zulus had been popular after the Battle of Islandhlwana, the Boers now captured the interest of British and American audiences. Thus, in 1904, Fillis staged a Boer War exhibit – complete with South African native villages and battle re-enactments featuring veterans of the conflict – at the 1904 Louisiana Purchase Exhibition (St Louis's World Fair). Promising "the greatest, most realistic military spectacle known in the history of the world," Fillis did not disappoint and the show was a huge popular success at the Fair.[30] Historian Neil Parsons also notes that in 1900, the films *Scenes from the British Boer War* and *Actual Scenes of Life of the Transvaal War* were showing in San Francisco. Indeed, demand was such that opportunistic producers staged sham Boer War films in "Lancashire…North London, and as far afield as Paris and New England."[31]

The ethnographic shows, Wild West exhibitions, and scientific expeditions perpetuated nineteenth-century settler fictions into early twentieth-century cinema. Indeed, as film scholar Wolfgang Fuhrman argues, "it is impossible to imagine cinema's emergence without imperial colonialism's modern infrastructure that gave the first film operators access to formerly remote and unknown places."[32]

There is no doubt that British colonial infrastructure in South Africa enabled the growth of American films. Industrialized and increasingly urban, South Africa also had the transportation infrastructure at the time to take films further afield into the continent through Rhodesia, present-day Zimbabwe and Zambia. Isidore W. Schlesinger, the American entrepreneur whose cinema empire dominated southern Africa through to the 1940s, courted British audiences with tales from the colony. His African Film Productions (AFP) movies – many shot by American directors Lorimer Johnston, B. F. Clinton and, most notably, Harold Shaw – comprised dramas emphasizing the reconciliation among whites after Union in 1910 (*De Voortrekkers*, 1916, *The Symbol of Sacrifice*, 1918), colonial adventure narratives (*King Solomon's Mines*, 1918, and *Allan Quartermain*, 1919), and films that featured but also patronized black South Africans (*A Zulu Drama*, 1916, and *The Piccanin's Christmas*, 1917). Schlesinger also set up a company in New York that "exported hundreds of films to Africa" while allowing AFP to send some of its bigger films the other way.[33]

While South Africa's identity as a British colony circulated through the cinemas of the empire, it also found audiences in America. As in the colonial literary tradition, South Africa was "the perfect setting for trials of strength."[34] It offered the visual otherness of an imagined Africa (complete with big game and indigenous people) within the familiar settler romances of the Western (love triangles involving surly frontiersmen and devious criminals). Two American movie entrepreneurs – Sigmund Lubin and William Selig – established the stereotype for settler narratives in Africa that merged colonial stereotypes of safari adventures with American film genres like the Western and the slapstick comedy.

South Africa: An Indefinite Place

Siegmund Lubin was the first producer in America to explore African themes in a sustained fashion. Moving his company of actors seasonally from Atlantic City down to Jacksonville in Florida between 1912 and 1914, director Arthur Hotaling made several Zulu-themed comedy films for Lubin: *Rastus Among the Zulus* (1910), *The Zulu King* (1913), and *Zeb, Zack and the Zulus* (1913).[35] Though these films were shot in Florida, they happily merged stereotypes of cannibal tribes with Zulu iconography and remote "African" locations.

William Selig's company Selig Polyscope produced many of the early films with South African settings. Having set himself up in Los Angeles in 1909, Selig is often credited with establishing the first permanent studio in what would become Hollywood. He brought with him animals he had acquired after his faked African safari documentary about Roosevelt (*Hunting Big Game in Africa*, 1909), and with his growing menagerie produced a consistent line of animal-themed Africa films. Initially these were centered around stars like Kathlyn Williams and Tom Santschi (and wild animals).

What is evident is the emphasis on "British South Africa" seen, for example, in the posters and reviews for *Alone in the Jungle* (1913), and in the letters and telegrams, written in Dutch, that punctuate the narratives of *Alone in the Jungle* and *Back to the Primitive* (1911). At the beginning of *Alone in the Jungle* a letter is sent from "Kamp van Karoo," which is curious, seeing as the Karoo is a vast, arid area in the dry west and center of South Africa, not "jungly" at all. Afrikaans farmers from the Transvaal (site of the Witwatersrand gold mines) are the central characters in *Lost in the Jungle* (1911), *Kings of the Forest* (1912), and *The Tyrant of the Veldt* (1915). In Selig's *A Wild Ride* (1913), the action starts in Johannesburg but decamps to a remote ostrich farm in the country where heroine, Florence McGraw's (Bessie Eyton) wagon is attacked by Zulus before she is saved by the English soldier with whom she has fallen in love. The film collapses settler archetypes – remote locations, encirclement by indigenous foes – with South African particularities as when MacGraw rides her favorite ostrich, Sandy, across the veld.

Otis Turner, who had directed several of these films for Selig (*Rescued by Her Lions*, 1911; *Alone in the Jungle*) then moved to Universal and under the 101-Bison name, continued to make films loosely set in South Africa (*Prowlers of the Wild*, 1914; *Dangers of the Veldt*, 1914). Turner's 1914 film, *Won in the Clouds*, has diamonds, elephants, and stunts courtesy of a dirigible, but moves the action north to a remote unspecified location.[36]

From the mid-1910s on, several films with South African settings were made by Famous Players-Lasky and distributed by Paramount. *The Years of the Locust* (1916), *Thou Art the Man* (1920), and *The Sins of Rosanne* (1920) all involved diamond theft. Two other films aimed for more serious dramatic scenarios, *Under the Lash* (1921) and *The Woman Who Walked Alone* (1922). In *Under the Lash*, Gloria Swanson plays a woman whose unhappy marriage to an "intolerant and bigoted farmer" is interrupted by the arrival of a young Englishman, educated and kind.[37] The love triangle culminates in murder. The film was the first starring Swanson to fail at the box office with one critic grumping: "[Swanson] isn't exactly the type to be found on a Boer farm and she wears a frock in the last scene that is entirely out of character."[38] This comment reveals the limitations of fusing the frontier drama with foreign cultural tensions between British and Afrikaner, something which might be more easily understood by English audiences.

The final thread of the entanglement of colonial narrative and American production that is significant here involves screen adaptations of novels and short stories by popular women writers Cynthia Stockley, Gertrude Page, and Ethel May Dell. Born in South Africa, Stockley spent the major part of her adult life in Zimbabwe (then Rhodesia). She enjoyed tremendous success and eight of her "veld romances" were adapted by Hollywood between 1917 and 1927.[39] The first three adaptations were driven by their female stars – Norma Talmadge, Clara

Kimball Young, and Marion Davies – and it is noticeable that many of the films with South African settings had their colonial adventures intertwined with melodrama and relatively complex women characters.

"No beauty would come to this desolate hole": *Desert Nights* (1929)

Remoteness plays an important role in many films set in South Africa, which is depicted as a land of open veld or desert, while cities like Cape Town are mentioned only in telegrams as points of entry to the country. Locations introduced as being remote convey a combination of exotic strangeness, danger, and removal from the civilizing authority of the city. Like the settler communities in American westerns, the hero-adventurer is aloof in his mastery of the unforgiving environment and stoic in the absence of heterosexual romance. In nearly all of the films mentioned above, the action is displaced into either wilderness, desert, or farm settings. MGM's 1929 silent drama *Desert Nights* plays out the settler romance as cinematic Western against the backdrop of South Africa, here a remote desert.

Remoteness as a property of colonial adventure films was a product of the close proximity of the ranches to the studios, and the variety of their aesthetic resources. Within the well-known history of studio production in California – from barns to extensive sound stages, backlots, and movie ranches – Jacobson argues that,

> While we tend to think of early western filmmaking in terms of location shoots and natural light, the studio was always close at hand…as a physical site for all phases of production…Thus even when western-bound filmmakers traded studio sets for landscapes bathed in natural light, they continued to apply this idea of studio plasticity to non-studio settings.[40]

It is likely that even if locations such as Salton Sea provided excellent facsimiles for a concocted South Africa, the majority of the films would still be shot partly on one of the ranches close to the studio.

At the beginning of *Desert Nights*, Hugh Rand (John Gilbert) is asked by a colleague at the diamond mine if he is enthusiastic at the prospect of a visit by Lady Diana Stonehill (Mary Nolan), "A lady from home! Haven't seen a white woman in years." Rand retorts sourly, "Don't expect too much. No beauty would come to this desolate hole." The exchange contains many of the elements that make up South Africa as imagined by early Hollywood producers. The colonial adventurer – disciplined and adaptable – comes to master a remote land. Only he can extract value from the "desolate hole" where he finds himself, and where he mentors those less capable, protects the vulnerable white woman, and vanquishes the villain.

When Rand actually meets Lady Diana, he is less cynical: "Three years away from the world – a man almost forgets there are women like you." His remark suggests stamina and fortitude: not only has he survived without a (white) woman for three years – an unimaginable feat for a heterosexual colonial adventurer – he has also mastered the remote wilderness where he is stationed.

Later, a group of diamond thieves split off from the master criminal, Steve (Ernest Torrence), when they realize they can no longer endure the harsh conditions of the desert. How they plan to get to Cape Town is not clear, but off they go, leaving behind the trio of intrepid hero (Rand), villain (Steve), and woman (Lady Diana, over whom they compete). Of course, the intrepid hero is the person best suited to handle the environment because he has toughened up and, as a result, the villainous dandy – eager to return to city life with his spoils – is no match. The desert scenes evoke the dry northwest of the region north of the Kimberley diamond fields where the Kgalagadi Desert stretches into what is now known as Namibia. They are mostly plausible but for the incongruous palm trees that seem to belong to a different understanding of the South African desert (Figure 15.2).

It is clear that by the early sound era, the craze in Hollywood for stories of diamonds, fierce Zulu warriors, dour Afrikaner farmers, and "veldt" romances had faded.[41] One reason appears to be the demand for increasing authenticity. In a scathing *New York Times* review of the 1936 film *White Hunter*, the author not only damned the tedium of safari adventures but also noted the well-worn scenery against which they were set:

FIGURE 15.2 Incongruous palm trees compose a constructed South African desert dawn.

The Continent of Africa is being used so incontinently of late to buttress a number of saggingly secondary films that the hardened reviewer who gets wind of a safari being organized in some newly arrived picture may be excused for assuming that it is probably going out in search of a plot. The one uncovered by Mr. Zanuck's Central Avenue beaters in *White Hunter*, at the New Criterion, is very small game indeed, and the old California veldt it is scared up in could hardly look less genuine if it were covered with filling stations.[42]

Colonial narratives in African settings were still popular, but they had moved northwards. In East Africa, *Trader Horn* (1931) was the first synchronized-sound film shot on location in Africa. In North Africa, at least ten Hollywood films were made about the French Foreign Legion during the 1930s, with four in 1930 alone, including Josef Von Sternberg's famous Gary Cooper-Marlene Dietrich romance, *Morocco*. [43]

Conclusion

The 1927 Paramount map is a conundrum. It indicates a "place" that never was, a possible South Africa that had very little to do with the reality of South Africa's people and places. It, however, does draw together several cinematic-historical trajectories. The map brings to the surface the way films represented the explicit and implicit economic and political relationship between Britain, its increasingly independent colony South Africa, and the increasingly global power of the United States. The diamond mine in *Desert Nights* represents both the remote colonial enterprise and harsh settler outpost, offering an exotic international setting for its narrative of white mastery over environments far removed from the urban centers of the empire. Rather than identifying an ideal replica of South Africa, the map points to the way the American imperium of the twentieth century was bringing the world to America in order to take America to the world.

Notes

1 Tino Balio, ed., *The American Film Industry*, revised edition (Madison: University of Wisconsin Press, 1985), 202.
2 Halsey, Stuart, & Co., "The Motion Picture Industry as a Basis for Bond Financing," The Museum of Modern Art Library, https://archive.org/details/motion00hals/page/n1 (accessed June 1, 2019). In a review of the first edition of Balio's book, Pryluck writes of the Halsey, Stuart prospectus: "A small point; the material is still valuable even with the uncertainty about its provenance." Calvin Pryluck, "Review of *United Artists: The Company Built by the Stars* by Tino Balio, *The American Film Industry* by Tino Balio," *Cinema Journal* 16, no. 2 (1977), 85.
3 Brian R. Jacobson, *Studios Before the System: Architecture, Technology, and the Emergence of Cinematic Space* (New York: Columbia University Press, 2015), 168–200.
4 Chris Lukinbeal, "Teaching Historical Geographies of American Film Production," *Journal of Geography* 101, no. 6 (2002), 252.

5 Jonathan Bignell, "Transatlantic Spaces: Production, Location and Style in 1960s–1970s Action-Adventure TV Series," *Media History* 16, no. 1 (2010), 53.

6 Peter Davis, *In Darkest Hollywood: Exploring the Jungles of Cinema's South Africa* (Johannesburg: Ravan Press, 1996), 4.

7 For early South African cinema, see Thelma Gutsche, *The History and Social Significance of Motion Pictures in South Africa, 1895–1940* (Cape Town: Howard Timmins, 1972); Jacqueline Maingard, *South African National Cinema* (London, New York: Routledge, 2007); Martin Botha, *South African Cinema, 1896–2010* (Bristol: Intellect, 2012). A more detailed examination of early cinema in and of South Africa is Neil Parsons, *Black and White Bioscope: Making Movies in Africa, 1899–1925* (London: Intellect, 2018).

8 *She: A History of Adventure*, written by Haggard and published in 1887, was adapted at least five times during the silent era, including as a one-minute trick shot film – *La Colonne de feu (The Pillar of Fire)* – by Georges Méliès in 1899. *Jess* (published in 1885) was filmed three times between 1910 and 1920.

9 In Brian Larkin, "Circulating Empires: colonial authority and the immoral, subversive problem of American film," in *Globalizing American Studies*, eds. Brian T. Edwards and Dilip Parameshwar Gaonkar (University of Chicago Press, 2010), 160.

10 Larkin, "Circulating Empires," 259.

11 Parsons, *Black and White Bioscope*, 177.

12 Larkin, "Circulating Empires," 156.

13 Historian William Appleman Williams describes America's expansive free-trade policies as an "informal empire" in *The Tragedy of American Diplomacy, 2nd revised and expanded edition* (New York: Dell Publishing, 1959)

14 Larkin, "Circulating Empires," 160.

15 Engseng Ho, "Empire through Diasporic Eyes: A View from the Other Boat," *Comparative Studies in Society and History* 46.2 (2004), 231.

16 Julie Codell, "Blackface, Faciality and Colony Nostalgia in 1930s Empire Films," in Sandra Ponzanesi and Marguerite Waller, eds., *Postcolonial Cinema Studies* (New York: Routledge, 2012), 32.

17 Peter Limbrick, *Making Settler Cinemas: film and colonial encounters in the United States, Australia, and New Zealand* (New York: Palgrave Macmillan, 2010), 31.

18 Ben Shephard, "Showbiz Imperialism: The Case of Peter Lobengula," in *Imperialism and Popular Culture*, ed. John M. Mackenzie (Manchester: Manchester University Press, 1986), 94–112.

19 James T. Campbell, "The Americanization of South Africa," in *Here, There and Everywhere: The Foreign Politics of American Popular Culture*, eds. Reinhold Wagnleitner, Elaine Tyler May (University Press of New England, 2000), 39.

20 Veit Erlmann, "Spectatorial Lust': The African Choir in England 1891–1893," in Bernth Lindfors, ed., *Africans on Stage: Studies in Ethnological Show Business* (Bloomington: Indiana University Press, 1999), 121.

21 Gutsche, *The History and Social Significance of Motion Pictures in South Africa*, 8.

22 On Buffalo Bill's success, see John G. Blair, "First Steps Towards Globalization: Nineteenth-Century Exports of American Entertainment Forms," in *Here, There and Everywhere: The Foreign Politics of American Popular Culture*, eds. Reinhold Wagnleitner and Elaine Tyler May (University Press of New England, 2000), 23; on Fillis's "Savage South Africa," see Shepard, "Showbiz Imperialism."

23 Robert T. Vinson and Robert Edgar, "Zulus Abroad: Cultural Representations and Educational Experiences of Zulus in America, 1880–1945," *Journal of Southern African Studies*, 33, no. 1 (2007), 45

24 Mary G. Dick, "The Establishment of a Mission: Being the Work of the American Board of Commissioners for Foreign Missions Among the Zulus of South Eastern Natal, 1834–1860," (MA dissertation, Columbia University, New York, 1933), 1.

25 Glenn Reynolds, *Colonial Film in Africa: Origins, Images, Audiences* (Jefferson, NC: McFarland & Company, 2015), 39–85.

26 Vinson and Edgar, "Zulus Abroad," 44.

27 Felipe Smith, "'Things you'd imagine Zulu tribes to do': the Zulu parade in New Orleans Carnival," *African Arts* 46, no. 2 (2013), 22–35; John Simeran, "For Zulu leaders, blackface remains 'tradition,' 'cultural expression' even amid national reckoning," *The New Orleans Advocate*, February 19, 2019, (accessed May 28, 2019). https://www.theadvocate.com/new_orleans/news/article_d8b7049a -2f16-11e9-832c-4311bec00c93.html

28 Bhekizizwe Peterson, *Monarchs, Missionaries and African Intellectuals: African Theatre and the Unmaking of Colonial Marginality* (Johannesburg: Witwatersrand University Press, 2000), 114, 133.

29 Parsons, *Black and White Bisocope*, 4–6.

30 Floris J. G. Van der Merwe, *Die boere-sirkus van St. Louis (1904); with English supplement,* "Meet me in St. Louis": South Africa at the World's Fair and the Olympic Games of 1904 (Stellenbosch: FJG Publikasies, 1998), 75.

31 Parsons, *Black and White Bioscope*, 9.

32 Wolfgang Fuhrmann, "Patriotism, Spectacle, and Reverie: Colonialism in Early Cinema," in *German Colonialism, Visual Culture, and Modern Memory*, ed. Volker Langbehn (New York: Routledge, 2010), 148.

33 Parsons, *Black and White Bioscope*, 224.

34 Abena P. A. Busia, "Manipulating Africa: The Buccaneer as 'Liberator' in Contemporary Fiction," in *The Black Presence in English Literature*, ed. David Dabydeen (Manchester: Manchester University Press, 1985), 181.

35 Joseph P. Eckhardt, *The King of the Movies: film pioneer Siegmund Lubin* (Madison: Fairleigh Dickinson University Press, 1998), 138–142.

36 *Won in the Clouds* would be remade in 1928, still with a South African diamond mine, but now with Swahili warriors and an airplane (flown by fabled stunt pilot Al Wilson).

37 *Exhibitors Herald.* New York City: Exhibitors Herald Company, October 29, 1921, 67–68. https://archive.org/details/exhibitorsherald13exhi_0/page/n489 (accessed July 16, 2019).

38 Stephen Michael Shearer, *Gloria Swanson: The Ultimate Star* (Thomas Dunne Books, 2013), 76.

39 *Poppy* (1917), *The Claw* (1918, 1927), *April Folly* (1920), *The Sins of Rosanne* (1920), *Wild Honey* (1922), *Pink Gods* (1922), *Ponjola* (1923), *The Female* (1924).

40 Jacobson, *Studios Before the System*, 170.

41 A few British films were made exploiting these trends, from adventure films like *King Solomon's Mines* (1937) to the biopic *Rhodes of Africa* (1936), both shot by Gaumont British Picture Corporation in British colonial territories.

42 *New York Times*, "At the Criterion," November 26, 1936. https://www.nytimes.com/ 1936/11/26/archives/at-the-criterion.html (accessed July 17, 2019)

43 *Renegades* (1930), *Hell's Island* (1930), *Morocco* (1930), *Women Everywhere* (1930) *Beau Ideal* (1931), *Under Two Flags* (1936), *We're in the Legion Now!* (1936), *The Legion of Missing Men* (1937), *Trouble in Morocco* (1937), *Adventure in the Sahara* (1938), *Beau Geste* (1939).

16

SETTLER EVASIONS IN *INTERSTELLAR* AND *COWBOYS AND ALIENS*: THINKING THE END OF THE WORLD IS STILL EASIER THAN THINKING THE END OF SETTLER COLONIALISM

Lorenzo Veracini

Science fiction and settler colonialism as a mode of domination are intimately interwoven. In terms of narrative structures, settling a "new" world across the water, or the prairies across the mountains, or new worlds across outer space makes little difference. Facing existential crisis, the settler has two options. He could further displace and remain consistent to an original behavioral pattern, or he could refuse further displacement and turn himself into an indigenizing settler.[1] Both options are entirely consistent with settler colonialism as a mode of domination. Facing crisis, settler colonists routinely displace – this is the foundational act that constitutes their volitional polities – and they routinely indigenize – this is the foundational act that asserts the legitimacy of their polities. This essay contributes to an ongoing conversation on the ways in which science fiction legitimizes and normalizes domination.[2]

Two recent movies, *Interstellar* (dir. Christopher Nolan, 2014) and *Cowboys and Aliens* (dir. Jon Favreau, 2011), have explored further displacement and indigenization as possible responses to crisis. The crises that they narrate and the options they explore are related, two sides of the same settler colonial coin, and if one faces the possibility of an intractable nonconformity between the settler collective and its environment, the other asserts the ultimate compatibility between the two. These stories and the sensibilities they rely on are symptomatic of a settler colonial present.[3] These "cinematic settlers" emerge as settlers indeed.

The Displacement Option: *Interstellar*

The highly successful science fiction movie *Interstellar* is a settler colonial movie. The *science* underpinning this well-crafted film has been extensively discussed, even its philosophical underpinnings; not so the narrational archive it mobilizes, its *fiction*.[4] And yet *Interstellar* is a very political text, a veritable manifesto in the face of a global environmental crisis. It is about a collective existential crisis, but not anybody's existential crisis; it is about the crisis of a settler society. The protagonists are not Indigenous to where they are and the land has turned against them. Furthermore, the movie outlines a particularly settler colonial way out – if the land turns against you, appropriate another. Indeed, if the opening crisis is a dramatically changing environment, the proposed solution is not regenerative practices or possible adaptation – emplaced change. The proposed solution is to change environment by changing environments – displaced change. This is a very settler colonial approach. And a recurring one: beyond denial (literally a dead end), thinking the Anthropocene and other disasters is often still a way to argue for renewed settler colonialism somewhere else.[5]

Interstellar begins with interviews with children of the Great Depression of the 1930s (another existential crisis). The Dust Bowl was the epitome of the environmental manifestation of a mode of production's physical limits as the 1910s and 1920s had witnessed more land brought into cultivation in the space of a few years than at any time in the history of the settler colonization of the North American continent.[6] More than 5 million acres of native grassland had been turned into wheat fields. The Dust Bowl marked the end of what historian James Belich has called the global "settler revolution:" the process whereby a series of settler societies were established during the nineteenth century in a variety of continents.[7] The voices that open the movie reach us from the end of settlement. *Interstellar* thus begins in a past that is also our future: environmental collapse. Earth is exhausted and there is nothing that can be done. That is, there is plenty that is being done, and the movie explores these attempts, including a single world government, mandated stewardship, and collectively determined allocation of scarce resources. But there is nothing that can be done *that will be effective*. *Interstellar* has given up on Earth as much *Interstellar*'s Earth has given up (see Figure 16.1).

FIGURE 16.1 Note the derelict farmstead, the empty land, and the beckoning stars. Screenshot from *Interstellar* (dir. Christopher Nolan, 2014).

Interstellar mobilizes and interacts with a stubborn and recurrent settler colonial anxiety: a fear that the land may turn against the settler, against "us," a fear premised on the peculiarly settler colonial understanding that we do not ultimately belong to it.[8] The movie also mobilizes the narrative of decline, the declensionist possibility that "we" have turned against our true selves and have failed to conform to the mandates of our settler colonial roots. The two fears are crucially distinct and yet not mutually exclusive, even though in the movie they are juxtaposed and interdependent and reinforce each other. Thus, a failure of settlement, which may prompt a critique of settlement (it normally would, except that within the constraints of a settler colonial ideology it will not), is understood as a failure to settle, that is, as a collective failure as settlers. According to a counterintuitive logic, the catastrophic failure of settler colonialism is to be addressed with more settler colonialism. In one crucial opening scene, before a narrative crisis sets things in motion, the main character, Cooper (Matthew McConaughey) is having a beer on the porch with a wise elder. About to begin his quest, Cooper remarks: "We have forgotten who we are: Pioneers, Explorers." He then sets out to recover this lost legacy by venturing to seek new lands to colonize in outer space.

However, at the beginning of the film we see how settler colonialism as practice has been outlawed. Travel, the very ability to displace, and thus the freedom to move and potentially resettle somewhere else, is proscribed. Even talking about it, telling the truth about historical travel, is forbidden. The Apollo Missions officially never actually happened, and are alleged as mere propaganda. Thus, the *memory* of settler colonial displacement and the *means* to effect it have now been rendered unlawful. Instead, government policy now mandates "stewardship" – legally enforceable sustainable behavior. It is a policy that ultimately entails severely limiting everyone's mobility and consumption. No animals are seen in the film, and no meat and no wheat – only corn – a suspiciously Indigenous and alien food. People must be farmers if this is their lot, and all avenues for social mobility and uplift through displacement are closed. Good stewardship requires a collective disavowal of all mobility but this policy riles the protagonist, Cooper. Like proscribed travel, enforceable stewardship is crucial in this context. Envisaging everyone's stake in privately managed resources, it restricts everyone's ability to dispose of (that is, to waste) their property. Yet stewardship is a failing policy: Earth is dying anyway, and famine is widespread, unavoidable, and irreversible.

The government in *Interstellar* also bans technology. And war. Technology and war are significant foreclosures in this context. As cultural scholars Leo Marx and Richard Slotkin noted long ago, they are both crucial defining features of "America."[9] With a world government deciding their location, the American settler colonial farmers have now been turned into peasants. They don't own the land because they are tied to it, like serfs, immobilized peasants that could be conceived of as the opposite of free settlers. Contradictions have caught up spatially – if America had once moved away from Europe, if it had successfully "fragmented" away, now the Old World has moved to America.[10] America has forgotten who it "really" is. The movie depicts a claustrophobic, post-settler America where everything is turned upside down. Major League baseball is not major at all, while popcorn has replaced hot dogs. Even the dust that should be below is now above, and the land no longer provides with abundance. Abundance once culturally defined America, but now scarcity defines a dystopian anti-America.[11]

Of course, this is not the end of the story. Like the elite individuals who gather in a secluded location to save the world after a revolutionary takeover led by an interventionist government in Ayn Rand's *Atlas Shrugged*, a 1957 classic of right-wing political science fiction, what remains of NASA has now withdrawn to a secret location.[12] NASA is not any organization, its scientists are the custodians of the memory of the ultimate travel, *space* travel, and the practitioners of now proscribed technologies. Rand had narrated a putative gathering of selected objectors, the "Prime Movers," society's most important creative minds. But if Rand's Prime Movers withdraw from the world (curiously a similar Colorado location to which NASA has withdrawn in *Interstellar*) to eventually return to it after collapse and in order to rebuild, *Interstellar*'s NASA-defunded scientists withdraw from the world to move to another after collapse.[13]

The movie follows Cooper's adventures as he begins settlement anew. He finds a map and travels to the Rockies to NASA's secret site. The scientists are actively seeking potentially habitable planets and are reaching them via "wormholes" – space is collapsed through them. They foresaw the crisis long ago and have been proactive. Twelve exploratory manned missions were sent out earlier, and three have activated their beacons – good news. Cooper is co-opted into the mission – he is already a pilot – and tasked with exploring them. If stewardship cannot ultimately save Earth because environmental deterioration is now irreversible, something else is needed. Collective space travel, collective displacement, is the solution here. It is here represented as the only alternative, but of course there are other possibilities, as several "sci-cli" movies dealing with the climate change emergency, a new subgenre relaunched in the new millennium by *The Day After Tomorrow* (dir. Roland Emmerich, a 2004 blockbuster), have shown. Facing a similar global environmental crisis, *Geostorm* (dir. Dean Devlin, 2017) explored the possibility of a technical fix, an orbiting weather-controlling system that enables a return to the pre-crisis *status quo ante*. So did *Snowpiercer* (dir. Bong Joon Ho, 2013), even though in both instances, the technical fix malfunctions. Conversely, *Beasts of the Southern Wild* (dir. Behn Zeitlin, 2012) investigated the consequences of a decision to stay put.

Together with Cooper, the scientists have also concluded that government cannot ultimately suppress "who we really are," and that it should not. Since staying put is not an option, two plans, both premised on preemptive displacement, are drawn up. "Plan A" involves removing as many people away from immediate danger and seeking refuge in an orbiting space station (even though how to overcome gravity and send the ark into orbit is unknown yet). "Plan B" involves colonizing another planet with selected human material – sending frozen embryos out, terraforming, and repopulating.

Like the anxieties they are meant to assuage, Plan A and Plan B are intimately linked. It sounds like the future but it is very much like the past, and these plans refer to foundational stories about preemptive displacement in the face of crisis the writers know their audience knows. *Interstellar* tells a very ancient story. The "Puritans" in the American colonization narrative had also gotten to New England to find "refuge," but could only sustain their "sacred experiment" through further settlement and the successive ongoing colonization of "empty" spaces.[14] But if Plan B is a prerequisite for Plan A (what is the point of refuge without sovereignty?), Plan A is ideologically necessary for Plan B: it is only thanks to it that a threatening determination to invade can be recoded as a more morally acceptable absolute necessity. This is indeed "who we are": settler colonizers, a collective embodying in its self-representations the paradoxical figure of refugees that dominate.[15]

Astroship Endurance leaves Earth and the narrative can now move forward. Future Cooper communicates with present-day Cooper and gives him clues – a settler from the future sanctions the project of a settler of the present. And forward it moves, literally, like all settler colonial stories, as the protagonists travel back in time towards "who we are," and as they move forward in space to a place they have never been to. It is a space wormhole and its gravitational time dilation that allow the protagonists to simultaneously travel back in time and forward through space like the settler wagons had enabled the settlers on the Oregon trail to move back to a putative "original beginning" as they crossed the plains and the mountains. Later in the movie, we see farmers moving through blackened plains with all their belongings and columns of black smoke – they are reenacting the rural exodus of the 1930s. The writers do not need to make this connection explicit and safely expect their viewers to know what they are referring to. The resilience of the Dust Bowl as trauma in the public imagination should not be surprising – if we dwell in a settler society, settlement's prospected end must be profoundly traumatic. The movie is pivoting back to its opening, but this time there is no California at the end of the grapes of wrath, or better, California this time is up, not forward.

In one of the movie's twists, the gravitational equation is finally resolved, and NASA's space station will now save humanity from immediate danger. The NASA bunker itself is then shot up from its secret location to form not a "city on the hill," but a city in the sky. It will now sustain human life until plan B works out. Meanwhile, a suitable planet is also found. Cooper then returns to the now fully functioning space station after incredible adventures. After his travels, however, Cooper is transformed and he cannot adapt to life in the space station. Like a true explorer and pioneer, an interstellar Daniel Boone, he cannot permanently remain in what is left of the "Old World." This is also a well-rehearsed narrative – the frontier and its freedom call. He needs to keep moving, and decides to return to "who he is," that is, to return to the new planet and contribute to the colonization effort there. That's where his love interest has also gone. It is a tough environment, but a bracing climate makes betters humans; this is what frontiers are supposed to do. The settler, now intent on a reproductive mission, can continue being true to himself. He never forgot "who we are": settlers.

Plan A has worked out, and Plan B will eventually too. Humanity, that is, a settler colonial humanity – Indigenous peoples in this context do not belong to it by definition – has lost Earth, a planet it probably did not really like much anyway, but has found again who it really is. This, we are led to believe, is no small thing, and is fair trade for what used to be an excellent piece of inter-planetary real estate but is now depleted beyond repair. In the process of claiming a future elsewhere, this humanity has already redeemed itself – this is what settlers typically do. A settler humanity has found itself and another planet. It will "improve" it, and build a new land there for itself. Luckily this time there will be no Indigenous peoples to spoil a nice prospect, or to remind the new settlers of everyone's stewardship duties and the advisability of sustainable practices. None of them will come over for the American Thanksgiving holiday because "we" will not need to even temporarily share. There is no more settler colonial story than this one, and no more settler colonial response to environmental degradation. Against global warming, no adaptation – displacement (even though the nature of the crisis is only implied and climate destruction is never mentioned in the movie, we are led to believe it contributed to the crisis). Against Earth's exhaustion, no restorative action – displacement. *Interstellar* is not denying the crisis, it is embra-cing it – bring it on. Who needs wormholes in the soil when you have worm-holes in the sky, thousands of frozen embryos, and a brand-new planet?

The Indigenizing Option: *Cowboys and Aliens*

Cowboys and Aliens (2011) offers another opportunity to explore the intimate relationship linking cinematic science fiction and settler colonialism as a distinct mode of domination. Like *Interstellar, Cowboys and Aliens* faces a settler colonial quandary and proposes a settler colonial solution.

The settler is illegitimate. He has stolen the land. This is another existential crisis. What can assuage this predicament, what can possibly supersede the Indigenous-settler relation and the questionable legitimacy that follows? In other words, as cultural scholar Mahmood Mamdani rhetorically asked, "When does a Settler Become Native"?[16] It's not that easy, and simply waiting long enough will not fix it. As "settler" and "Indigene" are co-constitutive cate-gories in a relational context, there are only two logical ways out of this pre-dicament: either the Indigenous collective disappears, leaving the settler polity as the default new-Indigenous group (hence settler colonialism's propensity for the "logic of elimination"), or the settler collective fully indigenizes, thereby acquiring a type of indigeneity that makes it indistinguishable from the old-

Indigenous group.[17] Either development reconstitutes a unity as it dissolves settler colonialism as a relation.

The first possibility, the forcible disappearance of the Indigenous collective, once widely practiced, has now become unfashionable. However, settler-indigenization, while still fitting, is really hard work and must be done while paying constant attention to the risks of "going native."[18] Appropriation for indigenizing purposes is typically unconvincing, and "repressive authenticity" (the claim that the actual Indigenous person is inauthentically Indigenous) can be used to deny the indigeneity of Indigenous collectives, and it is routinely used to that end, but is an even more destabilizing weapon when directed back at indigenizing settlers.[19] The settler is still illegitimate.

Then again, there is yet a third possibility, indeed a shortcut: a new invasion – the sudden appearance of new settlers bent on invasion – immediately turns the settler into a "native" vis-à-vis the new invaders. If settler invasion establishes the Indigenous-settler relationship in the first place, a new invasion sets up a new indigeneity in relation to a new exogeneity. The possibility of further invasion typically looms large in settler colonial public debate, and settlers are often anxious about this possibility. Recent immigrants are traditionally looked upon with suspicion and settler nativisms typically worry about "Great Replacements" because their polities are the very result of a great replacement.[20] Yet again, fantasies of alien invasions also fulfil a settler craving for immediate indigenization. *Cowboys and Aliens* constitutes an example of this fantasy. Relying on a specifically settler colonial structure of feeling, it is also a political movie. Invasion sets up a structure, the structure is ongoing, and there is no settler-Indigenous relationship without invasion.[21]

The settler's lack of legitimacy remains. But if the fantasy of further invasion unleashes settler nativism, it is because that fantasy sets up another putative relation – a related structure, a lean-to. Worrying about "illegal" or too numerous immigrants makes one feel a settler again because it satisfies a craving for indigeneity. Thus, settlers often entertain fantasies of alien invasion that will fully indigenize them. But it is a double edge sword, and even though there may be some benefits in terms of perceived legitimacy, it will all be in vain if these invasions do not ultimately fail. In other words, the invading aliens must depart at the end, while the indigenization of the settler that their temporary presence brings about must be irreversible. Dread and desire invariably mix: invasions must happen and must fail. *Cowboys and Aliens* provides a candid example of this type of settler wishful thinking and of the narrative structures that sustain it.

Here is the plot: an alien spaceship lands near Absolution, Arizona in 1873 and a newly constituted assemblage comprising local settlers, natives, and a group of outlaws is humanity's only remaining hope. The movie's Arizona setting is significant: a locale that has historically been at the forefront of US debates about unwanted "aliens." It is also set in a "territory," a locale where the political order is by definition still unsettled, even if in the process of becoming established.

Then again, "Absolution" – the name of the movie's main location – is significant. After all, if there is absolution, a sin must have been committed. But this is the point: the history of this alien invasion is also the history of settler absolution (lower case a). Absolution (upper case a) is the movie's proposed solution to the problem of a lack of settler indigenization.

The movie begins as a fantasy of settler self-reproduction involving a beautiful woman, an isolated homestead and surrounding fields. The opening scene is a veritable primal scene, the settler protagonist is … set, but then, the aliens, a very disgusting lot, rupture the fantasy and set the narrative in motion. They brutally kidnap the protagonist, Jake Lonergan (Daniel Craig), and his spouse. She does not survive. The aliens want to take over the planet; they are not ultimately interested in exploiting humans.[22] In order to assess whether their takeover is feasible or advisable, they still need to probe a few human samples. To do this, they are kidnapping the people of Absolution and a few other humans they find in the vicinity. They are also doing some mining and prospecting; they want to take over the land, if it is worth it, and to replace the humans, if it is practicable. In other words, even if they are still considering their options, they are developing a structure, and its dominant feature is replacement, not exploitation. They are settler colonizers and they have arrived to take over the world and to treat humans *like* the Indigenous people of the place (see Figure 16.2).[23]

The denizens of Absolution are the typical settlers of an iconic wild "western" settlement. The Indigenous people of the area have not yet been subdued. But they are eventually "stunned" into an alliance with the settler inhabitants of Absolution. Good alien magic allows this type of "shock and awe." A good and beautiful alien from a planet that was previously conquered and destroyed by the bad and ugly aliens that have recently landed has been dispatched to Earth in order to save it from experiencing the same fate – she is the Pocahontas of

FIGURE 16.2 Note the conventions of the western genre and the coming challenge. Screenshot from Cowboys and Aliens (dir. Jon Favreau, 2011).

another place, but she is still enabling the settlers vis-à-vis the Indians, which is what all Pocahontases typically do in settler fantasies.[24] These Indians, like the Indigenous peoples of all settler stories, are incapable of making rational decisions, so "magic" is essential to prompt them into forming a political alliance with the first settlers against the second ones. In turn, Indian magic allows Jake to finally figure out what is really going on. This is a frequent settler colonial fantasy. Acquiring "secret" Indigenous knowledge, after all, has always been a favorite way to speed up settler indigenization and ensure that the newcomers better belong to their new place. Irrespectively, even if these settler–Indigenous exchanges have been most unequal, indeed exactly because they have been most unequal, the Indian Chieftain and the settler leader begin working together.

When the bandits, who until now had been beyond the limit of the con-solidating political order, also join in, the settler-political regime has finally coa-lesced. For the sake of comparison, it is significant that the bandits don't need magic; their decision is entirely rational – if the aliens take over, they assume, it's over for everybody. Now the only opposition is between Indigenous humans and settler colonial aliens. In the fantasy, and it is a powerful fantasy designed to appease a powerful craving, the settler has become a native.

Alien invasion has united all human agencies. The structuring contradictions separating pastoralists and agriculturalists, newcomers and Indigenous peoples, and law-abiding people and outlaws have all disappeared. Most importantly, Indi-genous and exogenous alterities have now been subsumed within a single political order. Despite the appearance of a coming together and a middle ground, the whole sequence is fundamentally settler-oriented and settler-directed. The story of the coalescence of a political plurality is the real point of the movie's narrative. The answer was inbuilt in the question and in its relational context: the settler becomes a native when the native becomes a settler – settler indigenization through Indigenous subsumption.

What happens next is merely a necessary coda. The film must reach a happy ending. Having performed their role, all aliens – the good one and the bad ones – must disappear. How better to kill two birds with a stone than having them killing each other off? The good alien heroically sacrifices herself to save humanity. Thanks to her, the invasion is defeated, but not its political consequences; nothing goes back to the way it was. The bandits and the Indigenous people also must disappear. Nei-ther collective survives the crisis as autonomous agents. The former depart, and the latter, now incapable of challenging the newly constituted settler colonial order, withdraw away from sight and perform the usual vanishing act that is generally expected of Indians. The settlers thus acquire the land and even the gratitude of the Indigenous people for saving them from mortal danger – another typically settler colonial fantasy, Indigenous gratitude. The exogenous and Indigenous alterities have disappeared and only settlers remain – they are normal. Normalization (upper case n) is down the road from Indigenization (also upper case), not far from Absolution.

Once fiercely independent, the Indians fought valiantly and successfully against the aliens, but their insurgency against the settlers has now been forever quelled. They have now become a domestic dependent nation (emphasis on "dependent"). Why they can't resume their struggle against the invaders and for independence remains unclear, but this is neither alien nor Indian magic; this is settler magic. What is important is that Absolution is absolved, and that the settler has become the default new native – the outcome of an indigenization process prompted by further invasion. Future Arizonians, the movie implies, will keep keeping all aliens at bay, perhaps with the help of a newly built "wall" a decade or so after the movie's release.

Conclusion

Interstellar and *Cowboys and Aliens* retell the history of settler colonialism. It is not merely Hollywood's failure of imagination; stewardship and a genuine negotiation of sovereign capacities with Indigenous collectives remain outside the bounds of a settler colonial ideology and its hegemony. Stephen Hawking, for example, also saw a future replete with Earthlings colonizing space as an insurance against catastrophe and aliens colonizing Earth.[25] He thought that "if aliens visit us, the outcome would be much as when Columbus landed in America, which didn't turn out well for the Native Americans."[26] But there is an outside of this hegemony. Unimaginative science or unimaginative science fiction are not the only possible science or science fiction. Facing crisis, we don't need to imagine the destruction of this world.[27] Imagining decolonization (and its practice), thinking this world's sustainable transformation, may be more rewarding than imagining its end. It wouldn't be the end of the world.

Notes

1 "He" is a deliberate mode of address: settler colonial orders, predicated on the reproduction of a socio-political body in the place of another, are inherently gendered orders.
2 See, for example, Dallas Hunt, "'In Search of Our Better Selves': Totem Transfer Narratives and Indigenous Futurities," *American Indian Culture and Research Journal* 42 (2018), 71–90; Lorenzo Veracini, "District 9 and Avatar: Science Fiction and Settler Colonialism," *Journal of Intercultural Studies* 32, no. 4 (2011), 355–367; Lorenzo Veracini, "On Settler Colonialism and Science Fiction (Again)," *Settler Colonial Studies* 2, no. 1 (2012), 268–272; Phillip Smith, "The American Yeoman in Andy Weir's The Martian," *Science Fiction Studies* 46, no. 2 (2019), 322–341.
3 Lorenzo Veracini, *The Settler Colonial Present* (Houndmills: Palgrave, 2015).
4 See, for examples, Kip Thorne, *The Science of Interstellar* (New York: W. W. Norton & Company, 2014); Oliver James, Eugénie von Tunzelmann, Paul Franklin, Kip S Thorne, "Gravitational Lensing by Spinning Black Holes in Astrophysics, and in the Movie *Interstellar*," *Classical Quantum Gravity* 32, no. 6 (2015) https://iopscience.iop.org/article/10.1088/0264-9381/32/6/065001/meta (accessed: October 10, 2018); Lance Belluomini, "*Interstellar* and Philosophy: The Ethics of Space Colonization," *The*

Blackwell Philosophy and Pop Culture Series, 11/12/14, https://andphilosophy.com/2014/12/11/interstellar-and-philosophy/ (accessed: October 10, 2018).

5 See Bruce Erickson, "Anthropocene Futures: Linking Colonialism and Environmentalism in an Age of Crisis", *Environment and Planning D*, 2018, https://doi.org/10.1177/0263775818806514 (accessed: October 10, 2018); Hannah Holleman, *Dust Bowls of Empire: Imperialism, Environmental Politics, and the Injustice of "Green" Capitalism* (New Haven, CT: Yale University Press, 2018). Yet again, settler colonialism as a mode of domination was traditionally predicated on an ability to endure climate change, to move to another location and successfully adapt to new climates while remaining same.

6 See Donald Worster, *Dust Bowl: The Southern Plains in the 1930s* (New York: Oxford University Press, 2004).

7 James Belich, *Replenishing the Earth: The Settler Revolution and the Rise of the Angloworld* (Oxford: Oxford University Press, 2009).

8 "Us" and "we" are also deliberate mode of address: I live in a settler society dominated by the political descendants of settlers and I am one of them. I benefit from the ongoing dispossession of the indigenous collectives that survived the establishment of an exogenous polity on their lands.

9 Leo Marx, *The Machine in the Garden: Technology and the Pastoral in America* (Oxford: Oxford University Press, 1964); Richard Slotkin, *Regeneration Through Violence: The Mythology of the American Frontier, 1600–1860* (Norman, OK: University of Oklahoma Press, 2000).

10 On "fragment extrication," the process by which new European societies are established outside of Europe, see Louis Hartz, *The Founding of New Societies* (San Diego: Harvest/HBJ, 1964).

11 For a classic statement, see David Potter, *People of Plenty: Economic Abundance and the American Character* (Chicago: University of Chicago Press, 1954).

12 Ayn Rand, *Atlas Shrugged* (New York: Penguin, 1992).

13 For an analysis of Colorado's Rockies role in America's utopian imagination, see Carl Abbott, *Imagined Frontiers: Contemporary America and Beyond* (Norman, OK: University of Oklahoma Press, 2015).

14 See, for example, Sacvan Bercovitch, *The Rites of Assent: Transformations in the Symbolic Construction of America* (New York: Routledge, 1993).

15 In this, *Interstellar* engages with another science fiction classic, Ursula Le Guin's *The Dispossessed*. Le Guin's novel, too, narrated the story of a world set up by settlers who had displaced rather than pursuing their revolutionary fight where they were and face defeat. See Ursula K. Le Guin, *The Dispossessed* (London: Millennium, 1999).

16 See Mahmood Mamdani, "When Does a Settler Become a Native? Reflections of the Colonial Roots of Citizenship in Equatorial and South Africa", Inaugural Lecture as A. C. Jordan Professor of African Studies, University of Cape Town, 13 May 1998, http://www.bard.edu/hrp/resource_pdfs/mamdani.settler.pdf (accessed: October 10, 2018); Raef Zreik, "When Does a Settler Become a Native? (With Apologies to Mamdani)," *Constellations* 23, no. 3 (2016), 351–364.

17 On the "logic of elimination," see Patrick Wolfe, "Settler Colonialism and the Elimination of the Native," *Journal of Genocide Research* 8, no. 4 (2006), 387–409.

18 See, for example, Terry Goldie, *Fear and Temptation: The Image of the Indigene in Canadian, Australian and New Zealand Literatures* (Kingston: McGill-Queens University Press, 1989).

19 On repressive authenticity, see Patrick Wolfe, *Settler Colonialism and the Transformation of Anthropology: The Politics and Poetics of an Ethnographic Event* (London: Cassell, 1999).

20 See, for example, A. Dirk Moses, "'White Genocide' and the Ethics of Public Analysis," *Journal of Genocide Research*, 2019, https://doi.org/10.1080/14623528.2019.1599493 (accessed: October 10, 2018).

21 For the notion that "invasion is a structure not an event", see Wolfe, *Settler Colonialism and the Transformation of Anthropology*, 163.

22 *Captive State* (dir. Rupert Wyatt, 2019) also narrates the aftermath of an alien invasion but focuses on classic colonialism, like the TV series *Colony* (2016–2018) also does. *Captive State* makes references to Paris under occupation during WWII, but the dominating aliens are interested in Earth's resources and the labor of Earthlings. Like *Cowboys and Aliens*, however, *Captive State* also fantasizes about the possibility that a new slavery may supersede the legacies of the old one, and the underground resistance against colonial domination is composed of black and white terrorists, even though the collaborators are all white.

23 Incoming aliens as settler colonizers is not an unprecedented parallel – H. G. Wells' *The War of the Worlds* (1897), a founding text of the science fiction genre, was premised on the same notion, and it is significant that it was written after Wells had read a book about the settler colonial extermination of the Indigenous Tasmanians. H. G. Wells, *The War of the Worlds*, 1897, https://www.fourmilab.ch/etexts/www/warworlds/ (accessed: October 10, 2018).

24 See Rayna Green, "The Pocahontas Perplex: The Image of Indian Women in American Culture," *The Massachusetts Review* 16, no. 4 (1975), 698–714.

25 See Pallab Ghosh, "Hawking urges Moon landing to 'elevate humanity'," *BBC News*, 20/06/17, https://www.bbc.com/news/science-environment-40345048 (accessed: October 10, 2018).

26 Hawking cited in Michael Greshko, "Stephen Hawking's Most Provocative Moments, From Evil Aliens to Black Hole Wagers," *National Geographic*, 02/05/18, https://news.nationalgeographic.com/2018/03/stephen-hawking-controversial-physics-black-holes-bets-science/ (accessed: October 10, 2018).

27 "We" is here a different mode of address from its previous usage in this chapter. It now identifies a putative constituency determined to overcome settler colonialism as a mode of domination.

INDEX

For Product Safety Concerns and Information please contact our EU
representative GPSR@taylorandfrancis.com
Taylor & Francis Verlag GmbH, Kaufingerstraße 24, 80331 München, Germany